Christopher Yohn

JAMES RENNER is the author of two books of nonfiction that detail his adventures in investigative journalism: *Amy: My Search for Her Killer* and *The Serial Killer's Apprentice*. His work has been featured in *The Best American Crime Reporting* and *The Best Creative Nonfiction*. He lives in Ohio.

"A haunting, wickedly clever book. Part Dennis Lehane and part Murakami, the twist of H. P. Lovecraft mixed in gives it a taste like no other. James Renner starts off his fiction career with a bang."
—Jonathan Carroll, author of *The Ghost in Love*

"[Renner] moves from a moving meditation on love, crime, fatherhood, and marriage into more audacious, speculative territory. . . . I gasped in surprise at the juncture between reality and fiction, then exclaimed in delight as the story galloped forth with aplomb. . . . *The Man from Primrose Lane* brims with confidence, the kind that launches a career."
—Sarah Weinman, *Maclean's*

THE MAN FROM PRIMROSE LANE

THE

MAN FROM

PRIMROSE LANE

JAMES RENNER

PICADOR

A SARAH CRICHTON BOOK

FARRAR, STRAUS AND GIROUX   NEW YORK

THE MAN FROM PRIMROSE LANE. Copyright © 2012 by James Renner. All rights reserved. Printed in the United States of America. For information, address Picador, 175 Fifth Avenue, New York, N.Y. 10010.

www.picadorusa.com
www.twitter.com/picadorusa • www.facebook.com/picadorusa
picadorbookroom.tumblr.com

Picador® is a U.S. registered trademark and is used by Farrar, Straus and Giroux under license from Pan Books Limited.

For book club information, please visit www.facebook.com/picadorbookclub or e-mail marketing@picadorusa.com.

Designed by Abby Kagan

The Library of Congress has cataloged the Farrar, Straus and Giroux edition as follows:

Renner, James, 1978–
    The man from Primrose Lane / James Renner. — 1st ed.
        p.   cm.
    ISBN 978-0-374-20095-4
    I. Title.
    PS3618.E5769M36 2012
    813'.6—dc23

                                        2011034948

Picador ISBN 978-1-250-02416-9

First published in the United States by Sarah Crichton Books, an imprint of Farrar, Straus and Giroux

First Picador Edition: March 2013

D 10 9 8 7 6 5 4 3 2

FOR TANNER

"You're going to be roped! And you're going to be caged!
And, as for your dust speck . . . *hah! That* we shall boil
In a steaming kettle of Beezle-Nut oil!"
"*Boil* it? . . ." gasped Horton!
"Oh, that you *can't* do!
It's all full of persons!"

—DR. SEUSS

THE

MAN FROM

PRIMROSE LANE

He was mostly known as the Man from Primrose Lane, though sometimes people called him hermit, recluse, or weirdo when they gossiped about him at neighborhood block parties. To Patrolman Tom Sackett, he had always been the Man with a Thousand Mittens.

Sackett called him the Man with a Thousand Mittens because the old hermit always wore woolen mittens, even in the middle of July. He doubted most people had noticed that the old man wore *different* woolen mittens every time he stepped out of his ramshackle house. Most people who lived in West Akron averted their eyes when they saw him or crossed the street to avoid walking by him. He was odd. And sometimes odd was dangerous. But Sackett, who had grown up just a few houses north of Primrose Lane, had always been intrigued. In a binder somewhere in his basement, alongside boxes of baseball cards and his abandoned coin collection, was a detailed list of each mitten he'd seen the old man wear—black mittens, tan mittens, blue mittens with white piping, white mittens with blue piping, and, once, in the middle of some long-ago May, Christmas mittens with candy canes and reindeer.

On the short drive from the station to the little red house on Primrose Lane, it occurred to Sackett that he had not seen the Man with a Thousand Mittens since the day he had graduated from high school, twelve years ago. He recalled the old man shuffling down Merriman in front of his home, as his mother snapped pictures of his little brother, who had stolen his cap and gown and had stumbled around the lawn buried in maroon and gold rayon. He remembered how excited he had been a few days later, when the strange old man had appeared in a couple of those photos: blurry and distant, but there. As far as he knew, they were the only pictures of the man that existed.

Sackett turned onto Primrose Lane, which was really nothing more than a long driveway, as the Man with a Thousand Mittens was the only person who actually lived on this no-outlet side street. Sitting in the shade of the leaning porch was the young man who had dialed 911. Billy Beachum. He was the only direct contact the old man maintained with the outside world.

Billy Beachum was a delivery boy. Once a week, Billy drove his '99 Cavalier to the house on Primrose Lane, delivered a box of essentials, and took the list for next week from the old man's mitten-covered hands. There was rarely any conversation. It was Billy's job to get everything on the old man's list, no matter how loony the items seemed to be. He was given a credit card on which to charge the items. It was in the name of a business called Telemachus Ltd., a holding company whose true ownership was hidden behind a labyrinth of legal structures and subsidiaries. Bill was given three hundred dollars a month in cash to keep for his time and troubles—not bad for a sixteen-year-old with nothing but a cell phone and a hand-me-down car to his name.

Billy had inherited this job from his brother, Albert Beachum, who had inherited it from his cousin, Stephen Beachum, who had inherited it from their uncle, Tyler Beachum, who had inherited it from who the hell knows because Tyler's dead now. Billy was discreet and didn't talk about his odd job with even his closest friends. He took pride in keeping secret his connection to the Man from Primrose Lane, as he took pride in delivering every item the old man asked for each week, a particularly hard game on the occasions when he asked for things like "a crisscross directory of Cleveland Heights, Ohio," "a shed cicada skin," or "a container, roughly ten inches square, that can persist in the elements of Ohio weather for fifty years." Mostly, though, it was easy stuff—groceries, paperback novels, jerk-off magazines.

The Beachums had kept their involvement secret for nearly thirty years. There was, in fact, only one thing that would permit them to break their silence—and that one thing had, apparently and unfortunately, occurred on Billy's watch.

"He won't answer the door," Billy said, by way of a greeting, as Sackett approached. "I think he might be dead."

The officer paused and sniffed the wet summer air. A dark tone of rot was unmistakable, though probably too faint for the boy to pick up, or he wouldn't be sitting so close to the door. Sackett, who had recently recovered the body of a man who jumped off the Y-Bridge, a body that had gone undetected for a week because no one at the homeless shelter had reported him missing, recognized the smell for what it was and felt his stomach lurch at the fresh memory of the maggots he'd found crawling out of the bum's nostrils, like living boogers.

He looked at the young man, at the grocery bags resting beside him (containing food, a copy of *Hustler*, the latest Winegardner novel, and a Geiger counter—which had been an extremely challenging request, for as much good as it would do now) and quickly deduced Billy's role. It explained a lot—how no one ever saw the old man at the convenience store, for example. Of course he had to have had someone running his errands. In a time when many teens text rumors and post salacious half-truths on Facebook, the policeman felt admiration for the young man—and those who had come before him.

He rapped his fist upon the door; a deep, hollow sound. He knocked again, louder. "Police," Sackett announced in a voice an octave lower than normal.

Billy regarded him with wide eyes but didn't move.

"Do you have a key?" he asked.

The young man laughed politely.

"I didn't think so."

Sackett peered through the misty porthole set in the front door. It was too dark inside to see.

Reflexively, he twisted the doorknob. The glass knob spun unhindered in his hands as the door clicked open with a shudder that seemed to ripple across the entire house. A puff of dust wafted through the narrow slit of dark between the door and the front wall, sprinkling the air with a galaxy of tiny motes. Was that the sound of a gentle sigh? Or was that in Sackett's mind?

"Holy crow," said Billy. "I didn't even try it. Sorry."

Sackett lifted a hand toward the young man. "Stay here," he said. "I'll be right back."

The house was a twentieth century Tudor, a large cottage-style home, and the front door opened into a narrow foyer. Beyond, Sackett saw steep stairs leading to a second floor. The smell was worse here. Rank and deep.

"Hello?" he said, his voice breaking in the middle like a teenager's. "Is anyone here?"

To his left was a thin coat closet that smelled of cedar. He knew what was in there even though he'd never stepped inside this house before. He couldn't help himself. He watched his hand stretch out from his body and pull the door open. Inside were boxes and boxes stamped MISCELLANEOUS. The top box was open, revealing an assortment of mittens, in every color of the rainbow. There had to be at least a hundred pairs in there.

By the time he turned back toward the stairs, his eyes had adjusted to the darkness well enough for him to notice the trail of blood leading from around the corner, where he assumed the kitchen was, into the living room a few steps forward and to his left. A body had been dragged across the dusty hardwood floor.

Sackett unsnapped his sidearm but left it hanging loosely at his side as he walked into the living room.

The trail ended at the body of the Man with a Thousand Mittens. The old man sat in a pool of dried blood at the center of the room, propped up against a toppled wooden chair. The only other furniture in the room was a single metal fold-out chair in one corner, beside an old lamp, resting on the floor. Each of the four walls was entirely concealed by stacks of paperback books that stretched to the fourteen-foot-high ceiling in tightly packed and ordered skyscrapers. The dead man's head rested on his chest, his legs splayed out in either direction. Someone had cut off his fingers.

Sackett leaned toward the body, carefully avoiding the pool of dried crimson surrounding it. The old man was dressed in a stained white T-shirt and khaki shorts. On the shirt was a black hole the size of a dime, a few inches below the sternum—a single bullet hole. Streams of maggots slithered out, landing on the hard film of blood with a sound that could have been a light rain against a window.

That sort of wound, he knew, makes a man bleed *inside*. Most of the blood on the floor had, no doubt, come from his hands.

Sackett stood and walked deliberately to the kitchen, following the trail of blood to its point of origin. It began at the blender.

"Are those fingers?" asked Billy, eyeing the chunky, mold-crusted contents of the blender from the other doorway. "Oh, God," he said. The young man heaved once. Twice. On the third heave, a half gallon of vomit shot out of his mouth and onto the floor, tainting Sackett's crime scene with partially digested ham and cheese Hot Pocket and red Kool-Aid.

"Feel better?" he asked.

Billy nodded.

"Next time someone tells you to wait outside, you think you might listen?"

Billy nodded.

"Good."

PART ONE

ELIZABETH

THE WORLD ACCORDING TO DAVID NEFF

David Neff missed a lot of things about his wife, but the thing he missed the most was the way she used to sit on couches, leaning against one giant pillow, her knees tucked up against her chest, her legs trailing behind her as she watched a Lifetime movie or some ridiculous reality show. He pointed out to her once, before she died, that no man ever sits on a couch like that, that it was a uniquely feminine trait. It was a little thing that delighted him. He loved the carefree way she moved her feet to the rhythm of the lights on the screen. When he finally went through her things two months after she was in the ground, he'd found a photograph of her as a child, curled up on her parents' sofa in the exact manner he remembered. He'd stuck the photo to the refrigerator. It was still there, next to the over-outlined caricature drawings of their four-year-old boy.

Like most Thursday afternoons, David was on the living room floor, in front of the couch—her couch—with a bowl of SpaghettiOs in his lap, a bag of Kettle Chips to his right, watching an episode of SpongeBob SquarePants he'd seen five times, but TiVo'd anyway. The boy, Tanner, napped upstairs.

David was a once-handsome man who had grown pudgy around the edges. His dark hair hung too long above his eyes, a bit too gray for thirty-four. Three-day-old stubble shaded his double chin. A dollop of dried ketchup was smeared across the front of his shirt, evidence of the barely won battle that had been Tanner's lunch.

The room around David appeared to be the remnants of a livable space that had been torn apart by some sort of laundry- and toy-filled IED. Every other week, Tanner's great-aunt came by and picked the boy's clothes off the mantel, lamps, and ceiling fan, laundered them, and returned them, folded, to the boy's bedroom dresser. She collected the broken robots into dustbins, sorted stuffed frogs and Legos into their assorted tubs, and replaced the batteries in the boy's plastic-ball shooter and tiny grand piano. It only took them two days to get the room out of order again. David didn't mind the mess. And neither did Tanner.

Because his wife's death had been ruled a suicide, her insurance had not paid out and David had not been able to work a single day since. But he and the boy didn't need the money. Royalties from David's first book—*The Serial Killer's Protégé*—had climbed to the seven-figure mark a couple years ago and sales remained strong, thanks, in part, to a *Rolling Stone* article that had forever labeled him as "the best true crime writer since Truman Capote." David no longer kept track of how much he had in the bank, but he knew it was more than he'd ever imagined making in his life.

After his wife's death and until just a moment from right now, David had resigned himself to the fact that *The Serial Killer's Protégé* would also be his only book, and that that was okay, because Tanner was alive and he could live out the remainder of his days keeping his boy safe and comfortable and happy.

But then there was a knock at the front door.

David wasn't expecting company. Tanner's aunt wasn't due for a few days. He assumed it was a neighborhood kid pushing school band–sale candy, so he ignored it. But then the knock came again, too loud to be anything but an adult.

He walked to the door and peered through the porthole. There was a man on his doorstep. A thin man with wire-rim glasses and a ring of hair circling a bald dome.

Paul.

David winced. He didn't want to see Paul. He didn't want to talk to Paul. It was Paul's fault that he wasn't able to grieve the way he sometimes felt he deserved—in a penniless gutter with other heartbroken souls.

Paul Sheppard was his publisher, the man who had read David's proposal for a book based on notes left behind by convicted killer Ronil Brune and recognized a modicum of talent. Before *The Serial Killer's Protégé*, Paul had been an exclusively local publisher, the sort that shipped glossy copies of *Cleveland Steelworker Memories* and *Cleveland's Haunted History* to local indie bookstores. Today, he kept an office in Manhattan.

Reluctantly, David opened the door.

"He's alive!" Paul shouted, raising his arms in the air like Dr. Frankenstein.

"Shhhh! You'll wake the kid," he said. He motioned for Paul to come in.

"Sorry." Stepping into the main room, Paul shook his head and whistled. "I saw this documentary on Discovery the other day," he said. "It was about this woman who lives in Manhattan and she's this ridiculous pack rat and never throws anything away. She had this path carved out in clutter she could use to get to the bathroom and kitchen."

"Yeah?" prodded David.

"You're like this far away from becoming that woman," he said. "Her family had her committed, you know."

"Thank God you're not my family, Paul," he said, smiling a little. "Don't sit on that!" He jumped to the recliner over which Paul was squatting and batted away yesterday's *Beacon Journal*. Underneath was a plastic dish that had once held a microwavable Salisbury steak dinner. David tossed it to the far corner of the room, where it landed next to a wastebasket. "I wasn't expecting company."

"I left you twenty messages. The only reason I knew you weren't dead is you keep depositing my checks."

Paul sat on the chair as David collapsed on the sofa, sending a mostly empty biggie-sized soda tumbling to the floor. "It is nice to see you," David said sincerely. "How's biz?"

"You know," said Paul, making a seesaw gesture. "*Protégé* is still selling. I think half the universities in the country are teaching it in their journalism programs, so that helps it move every semester. I just signed this new up-and-comer from Pittsburgh, whose manuscript knocks me out."

"It's not a memoir, is it? Tell me it's not another memoir."

"In fact, it is a memoir. It's about an alcoholic steel smelter who went to prison for grand theft and, when he got out, cleaned himself up by slowly constructing a jet-powered semi truck in his garage. It wouldn't kill you to blurb it."

"Is that why you came over?"

"Of course not," said Paul, a thin smile playing at one corner of his mouth. From his sports jacket pocket, the publisher pulled a bound galley of a book. He tossed it to David, who snatched it out of the air one-handed.

On the front was a grainy black-and-white picture of a grassy hill soaked in summer heat. Atop the hill sat a 1970s-era police cruiser, its driver's-side door ajar. Behind the car stretched a row of old-growth pine trees, gnarled branches like arthritic hands. David knew this photograph. He'd discovered it, in fact, tucked into a box labeled MISCELLANEOUS in the Press archives at Cleveland State. It was a picture of a crime scene, an artifact of one of the many unsolved cases he'd written about before he'd become completely obsessed with Ronil Brune. The title of the book was *The Lesser Mysteries of Greater Cleveland*. At the bottom was David's name.

"What's this?" he asked.

"Your next book," said Paul. "That's just a mock-up, but I wanted you to see it, to feel the weight of it in your hands. It's a good cover, no?"

"It's a great cover, Paul," he said. "Only problem is, I didn't write this."

"You did. It's twelve of your best true crime articles from your *Independent* days, Beverly Jarosz, Sam Sheppard, Lisa Pruett. I cleaned up the language and moved things around a bit here and there—don't look at me like that, you were still learning dramatic narrative structure back then—and I put them all together into this little trade paperback. Something for next summer's beach crowd, I'm thinking. Something to tide everyone over until the next David Neff book."

"I don't need the money."

"I don't, either."

"Then why?"

Paul glanced around the room, then back at David. "I think you need something to remind you why you were ever a writer in the first place," said Paul. "A little New England collegiate lecture tour? Some free publicity in the trades? *Groupies?*"

"True crime groupies are mostly middle-aged women who look like my high school home-ec teacher," said David. "Nobody wants to buy a bunch of old stories. Anyone who wanted to read them has read them online already."

"Ah," said Paul, raising a finger. "They're not all reprints. Check out the table of contents."

" 'The Curious Case of the Man from Primrose Lane?' "

"Your next project," said Paul. "It's the next mystery you're going to investigate, the new piece we'll use to market the book."

"The Man from Primrose Lane? Never heard of him. Who is he?"

"Geez, David. Don't you read the paper anymore?" Paul regarded his friend silently for a moment, studying his features, perhaps to discern if there was any trace of the old David Neff in there someplace. "You used to be the eternal optimist," he said. "You thought you could solve *all* of these mysteries, remember?"

"How'd that work out?"

"Are you fucking blind? Look around you. What paid for this house? These toys? The Volkswagen in the garage? Your four-year-old son's trust fund? You solved the Ronil Brune case. The most fucked-up case anybody ever heard of."

"I'm just a dad now."

"Four years is long enough to live in the dark. You told me once that you never felt better than when you were writing these articles and researching these cases. This is a new mystery to dive into."

"A little ironic, don't you think?" asked David. "You want to pull me out of my depression by making me investigate some unsolved murder."

"There's no dead kids in this one. At least not murdered ones."

"That you know of."

"Do you want to hear about it?"

David rubbed his hands together distractedly. Was he already feeling a little rush? His heart stutter-stepped in his chest. His neck itched. Yes, he remembered this well. A jonesing, a craving for something he knew he shouldn't accept. He imagined it was the way his mother must feel every time she saw a waiter pour a glass of wine in a restaurant. This was what almost ruined his marriage once upon a time. "Yes," he whispered.

"The Man from Primrose Lane was a recluse who lived on the west side of Akron, only about a mile from here, off Merriman."

"Right, I know Primrose. Wait. Are you talking about the old man who used to ramble down to the park in the middle of the summer sometimes wearing mittens?"

"I believe so, yes."

"I saw him a few times after we moved here. Strange dude. Walked like he had somewhere important to go, except I never saw him anywhere except walking. Never at the store or in line for Chinese takeout or stuff like that. Never made eye contact. Gave me the heebie-jeebies. I always thought he looked a little like my Uncle Ira on a bender. He's dead, I take it."

"Murdered."

"How could someone have a grudge against him if he didn't know anybody? Was it a burglary?"

"Doesn't look like it. It seems personal. Whoever did it hacked the old man's fingers off at the second knuckle and fed them into the blender. Sliced his palms to shreds. Then he was dragged into the living room and shot once in the stomach. Killer left him there to die. As much as they can figure, it took maybe a half hour for him to bleed out. The old man was forced to sit there and let it happen."

"Holy shit. When was this?"

Paul repositioned himself in the chair, suddenly uncomfortable. "They found the man's body on June twenty-first," he said. "June twenty-first, 2008."

"Two days after Elizabeth."

Paul nodded again.

"No wonder I didn't hear about it." David sighed loudly, then shook his head. "Suspects?"

"The police are clueless, and I mean that quite literally."

"What was the guy's real name?"

"Well," said Paul with a smile, "that's where it gets interesting. When he purchased his house in 1969, he used the Social Security number of a man named Joseph Howard King, but that isn't who he really was."

"What do you mean?"

"A year after they find the body, the police get a call from the bank. Turns out this guy had about seven hundred grand in a savings account and another three and a half *million* in stocks and bonds. Using the name Joseph Howard King, he invested heavily in technology—Apple, Google, stuff like that. But the bank can't find his next of kin, right? So they call the cops for help. By then, though, the detectives have been working the case for a year and they haven't found this guy's family, either. A probate judge gets involved because of the money. I mean, somebody's going to collect a big paycheck as soon as they figure out who it should go to."

"That money's probably the motive," said David. "Four million dollars means four million reasons to kill him, if you're an heir."

"Right. Except no family has come forward to claim it. So this judge appoints a man named Albert Beachum as executor of the estate. Apparently Beachum's family had been running errands for the Man from Primrose Lane for years. He allows Beachum to draw money from the account to relocate the guy's remains from his pauper's grave to a bigger plot in Mount Peace Cemetery. And when Beachum says, 'Screw the police, I want to hire a private eye to track this man's family down,' the judge says, 'Fine,' and lets him pay for his own investigator. The PI uses Joseph Howard King's Social Security number to get his birth certificate. That has the guy's parents' names and the name of the hospital where he was born. So the PI goes and pulls the records from the hospital in the years leading up to and following King's birth."

"He found Joseph Howard King's siblings."

Paul touched his nose with one finger and pointed at David. "Bingo. Another kid named King with the same parents was born two years earlier at the same hospital. It's the guy's sister, Carol. So the PI's really excited, right? He's about to call this woman up and tell her she just hit the lottery. Except, when he does, Carol tells him that her brother Joe has been dead since 1932. Died in a car crash in Bellefonte, Pennsylvania, at the age of six. The crash also killed Mom and Dad. Carol was at home with the babysitter."

"He stole a dead kid's ID and disappeared to Akron, Ohio," said David, his eyes wide and slightly unfocused, the look of a stoner in the afterglow of a good hit. "You know, I bet he came from Bellefonte. He probably read about the accident in the paper and remembered it years later when he needed to change his name for whatever reason. What are they going to do with the money now?"

"Everyone is fighting over it. Carol wants it, of course. Figures since this mystery man stole her brother's ID she has some right to it. She has a pretty big-time attorney working for her. The Beachums seem like nice people, but they've got a hand in this, too, and have retained their own lawyer. On top of that, you have the Summit County executive and the mayor staking claim. Law says if you can't find next of kin, money goes to the state, but the city and county want a piece of it, too."

"And the police?"

"The police haven't said peep. And there's one more twist to this, just to complicate the picture."

"Of course there is."

"Among the old man's very scant personal effects were a bunch of battered notebooks."

David leaned forward. "And inside the notebooks?"

"Inside is the life story of a girl he apparently never met, a record of every softball game she played in, every award of merit she won in school, every boyfriend, every minor traffic ticket. All the details of her life were collected in these notebooks in scrawled handwriting they can only assume belongs to the Man from Primrose Lane."

"He was a stalker, huh?"

"Of the highest degree."

"And this girl, she's going after the money, too, I take it?" asked David.

Paul shook his head. "Nope. She couldn't care less. Which is a shame, because those notebooks are like love letters in places. Obviously, the old man cared a great deal for the girl, sorry, young woman, in his own twisted way. He never names her as his beneficiary, but almost implies . . . well, you'll have to read the newspaper clippings."

David sat on the couch, staring into the air above the television. Periodically, he scratched at the stubble on his boyish face. Eventually his eyes settled on a picture of Tanner, resting on the mantel. The boy was about two in the photograph, his shaggy hair whipping about in the wind pulling out over the ocean behind him.

"It's a good story," he said at last.

"I know."

"Sounds like it's been mostly reported, though."

Paul waved his hand in the air. "It's been reported, but it hasn't been *written*. And there's still plenty mystery for you. Who killed him, who he really was, why he was stalking this girl . . ."

"I appreciate what you're trying to do," said David. "And if I was ready to start writing again, this would be about the perfect case. But I can't."

"Why?"

David stood up and motioned for Paul to follow. "Step into my office," he said. "Let me buy you a drink."

David's home was a sprawling high-ceilinged ranch built for an Akron homeopathic doctor in 1954. The architect had deferred to the bachelor doctor's sense of style: modernism with a hint of refined hillbilly. Rock gardens sat on either side of the fireplace, used, currently, as rough terrain for a phalanx of plastic army men advancing on the kitchen. The walls lining the long hallway leading off the living room were coated in horse-hair paper, soft to the touch but frayed near the bottom where the previous tenants' cat had rubbed against it. They passed Tanner's room quietly. He lay snoozing in the middle of his bed, his knobby knees tucked under him, his butt pointed toward the sky—it was the only way he could sleep. At the end of the hall, through an oak door, was the so-called East Wing of the house.

The East Wing was essentially two rooms connected by a wide threshold. David had converted the entire space into a workroom. Bookshelves lined the walls, many filled beyond capacity, paperbacks stacked three rows deep. Every so often the pattern of books was broken by *Star Wars* figurines David used for bookends. Han Solo kept a dog-eared copy of *The Dubliners* from slipping aside. Up front was a bar stocked with Dewar's, some gin, and a mostly empty bottle of Jameson, a gift from Paul. The fulcrum of the two areas was occupied by a Tron arcade game, which, sadly, no longer worked properly—the laser cars could not be controlled and the contraption had a habit of shocking you whenever you maneuvered your tanks. At the far end of the East Wing was David's desk, a monstrosity he'd found at an estate sale a week after his book broke *The New York Times* Top 15. Supposedly it had once belonged to the captain of the *Edmund Fitzgerald*. David thought it might be cursed. The *Edmund Fitzgerald* was at the bottom of the lake. His wife was dead. And he hadn't written a single page since he had paid five men to lug it inside. Mounted above the desk was the head of a brown bear, a curio that had come with the house.

David lifted the front of the bar and stepped behind it. He fished a shot glass out of the cabinet above his head and set it down in front of his publisher. Into the shot glass went the rest of the Jameson.

"Where's yours?" asked Paul.

"If I drink, I'll lose my liver," said David. "I'm up to a hundred and twenty milligrams of Rivertin a day. They tell me that if I drink on that, even a little, it'll wreck my liver quick. Hell of a side effect, huh?"

Paul blinked behind his glass.

"And I've discovered that, to some extent, it was my anxiety that drove my writing. My paranoia. And now I never feel anxious." David shook his head. "I've tried. All that comes out is trite garbage. I can't write an original simile to save my life. It's like . . . I dunno . . . it's like I'm comfortably numb. No more panic attacks, no more night terrors. But no more stories, either. I can't get to that place. And even if I wanted to come off it, I'd have to do it in stages. My shrink says it would take months to wean myself off the drug. So, when I say I can't, I mean, physically, I can't."

Paul upended the whiskey into his mouth. "Fuck," he said.

"Yeah."

A long silence settled in. After a while, the sounds of a child stirring could be heard drifting down the hallway, squeaky springs under gentle weight, low grunts and sniffles. Tanner would be awake soon.

"Look," said Paul at last, "everything happens—"

"Stop right there. Think about what you're about to say."

"There's a reason to things," Paul continued. "I mean it. I don't know why you were attracted to that story that gave you PTSD. But there's a reason. Gotta be."

"You can't say stuff like that to a guy whose wife drove her car into the side of a Dollar General at seventy miles an hour."

"The only reason you didn't join her was because you were on the meds. Am I right?"

David ignored him. "The universe is absurd. People want to make sense of it because we're hardwired to find reason in the randomness. We look for patterns in the chaos. See omens in coincidence. We look at the random distribution of stars in the sky and pretend they look like animals, call them constellations. For some reason, we want to give meaning to the meaningless. If you go looking for the number eighty-eight, you'll see it everywhere—the number of keys on a piano, the number of counties in Ohio—but it doesn't mean anything."

Paul wiped a tear out of his eye. Impossible to tell if it was from laughter or from the sadness he felt for David, who no longer believed, who could no longer even write. "About the constellations," said Paul.

"I always thought that God put the planet here so we would recognize the artwork He wove into the universe."

David drew in a breath. He was about to say something more, but then his son spoke from the doorway.

"Dad?" said Tanner. "I'm thirsty. Can I have a Fresca?"

The boy's head barely reached the doorknob, his dark hair crumpled and slept-upon. His brown eyes looked the size of half dollars below the ragged trim of his bangs. He was a skinny boy, four years old, with long arms and long fingers, piano-playing fingers. He looked more and more like his departed mother every day.

"Think about it," said Paul. "We've got time."

EPISODE TWO

SPARKO'S TALE

When David first met his wife—when David first *really* met his wife, because they'd been sitting in the same class for five weeks but had never had a conversation and she had never really looked at him, never *considered* him as a fellow human being—she hated everything about him.

It was at Kent State, in the basement of the music department, in a classroom that smelled of wet chalk dust. The class was Music Appreciation or Music as a World Phenomenon or something. They both forgot in the years that followed. But they both remembered that she really did hate him there for a moment. Him and everything he was about.

"Well?" the professor asked.

They were listening to a CD recording of "Fanfare for the Common Man" piped out of the tinny speakers of the teacher's stereo. For a moment no one spoke. The students avoided eye contact with their professor, lest they be called upon.

"How does it make you feel?" the professor asked. "What emotion is the composer trying to evoke?"

A suntanned young man in an armless T-shirt, sitting near the back, raised his hand. The professor nodded in his direction. "It makes me think of beef," the young man said.

Random chatter mixed with the deep sound of laughing approval.

"Right, it's from that beef commercial," said the professor. "Anyone else?"

From where he was seated, next to the door, David watched Elizabeth's face shrink into a scowl, her bottom lip puffing out in a childish, yet sensual, pout. She was waiting for the professor to notice, he knew. He had watched her from this safe corner of the room since their first day of class, hoping to catch her eye in exchange for a smile. But she never turned in his direction. He had memorized the contours of her profile, that bump of an upturned nose, her round ears, attached at the lobe, holding back a cascade of straight hair the color of dying embers. She was, as those Eagles once said, "terminally pretty." He had come to learn of her endearing idiosyncrasies, least of which was her desire—he assumed subconscious—for admiration and recognition. She finished tests ten minutes before anyone else. When it had been her turn to give a lecture on a major composer, she was the one who had picked John Cage and had actually scolded the poor boob who'd nodded off halfway through her presentation. She had flicked him, hard, on the right ear. But for it all, she was allotted a strange acceptance. David had been standing in the hallway, pretending to rifle through his backpack while he waited for her to pass by one day, and so had been present when the young man whose ear she had struck asked her to a movie. "Forget you," she had said. David couldn't stop the silly smile from stretching across his face as he remembered the way she had swished down the hallway without even looking in the jock's general direction, leaving him stunned and downright weirded out. David lay awake often, wondering what it was about her that he was so drawn to. The only woman he knew who could be so cruel and lovely at the same time was his mother. The mystery of why Elizabeth thought she needed to keep her distance from the rest of the world attracted him. He craved her mystery. On some level, he suspected the search for that answer was more attractive to him than she was. He was smart enough to realize there was some perversion in that.

"Miss O'Donnell?"

"It's a lie," she said.

"I don't follow," the professor replied.

Elizabeth waved her hand at the stereo as if she were motioning to the place on her carpet where the cat had just barfed. "That," she said, "is propaganda. Like religion. It's supposed to create passion in the common man, the blue-collar worker, to push them to serve their country, like to join the Navy or Marines, or even just to keep working those long shifts at Taco Bell. It's about the illusion of the American Dream."

David watched the quickening of her breath, the way her chest pumped up and down with anger, the flushing of her face. And suddenly he realized two unpleasant truths. One: this woman was crazy. And two: he was attracted to her in some way he did not understand, and could not control, and didn't that make him crazy, too?

"The American Dream is a myth," she continued. "The few who are at the top want us at the bottom to think that we can rise in the ranks through hard work. But that's just not true. This is like our version of Wagner. It's twisted. And dangerous."

"The American Dream is not a myth." It wasn't until the entire class—Elizabeth included—turned his way that David finally realized he'd spoken. He felt his face turn a dark crimson. *Shit*, he thought distantly, *I haven't done that since fifth grade.*

Elizabeth rolled her eyes at him. "Grow up," she said. "After your daddy finishes paying your way through state school, I mean."

"Ah, snap!" said a large white man to her left.

"My parents aren't paying a penny," David said. "And I think you're better than that, actually. I think that was just reflex and you didn't really mean to say something that bitchy, so I'm going to ignore it."

"What did you call me?"

"Okay," the professor said, raising both hands, palms out. "Okay, let's, you know, let's find—"

"The American Dream is *not* a myth," David said. "Not for me. Not for a lot of people in this room, I'm guessing. If you work hard enough, you can still make your mark in the world."

"And how will you do that?"

"I don't know. There's a million ways to get to where I want to be."

"And what if you get hit by a car or . . . or slip in your bathtub and break your neck on the way down, or you get cancer? There's a million more random things that can go wrong before you do."

"Look at Stephen Hawking," he said. "Guy's in a wheelchair. Can only move one finger. And he's changing everything we know about the universe. You don't have to be limited by the things that could go wrong."

"You're going to Kent State," she said. "Where did he go to school? You're proving my point. It's too hard to get there for people who start on our level. Don't you get it? We're not going to be celebrities, we're not going to be president, we're not going to change the course of history. We're the *workers*. *We're* the Morlocks. And our children will be their children's workers. And there's nothing we can do to change our future. But music like this makes us believe we can."

David shook his head. He wasn't blushing anymore, he knew. He felt strangely calm. "What happened to you?" he asked.

"What?"

"Was it a bad breakup? Did your parents just get divorced? What I mean is, who did this to you? Made you so sad?"

"That—that's enough," said the professor.

"Life," she said.

"Well, if it's just life, I don't see that you have any reason to complain," said David.

"You don't know me."

David opened his mouth to respond, but before he could, Elizabeth gathered up her books and walked out of the room. The class watched her go and then, in unison, turned toward David. He shrugged and sank into his seat.

He sat there for only another moment. And then, before he could think better of it, David scrambled out of his seat and ran after her. But she was gone. He searched the staircase on one side and peered in the women's room on the other. It was crazy, anyway. What would he have said?

"Over here, numbnuts," Elizabeth said. She was sitting at a desk in the dark in the empty classroom behind him.

He stepped inside and closed the door. "I didn't mean to offend you," he said. "Or maybe I did. I guess I did."

She sighed. "It doesn't matter. I don't know you. You don't know me. It's fine. Whatever."

"I do know you," he said, not daring to step closer. "I know that whenever you sneeze, you sneeze exactly three times into the crook of your left elbow. I know you're right-handed but write like a left-handed person, which tells me you must have had a mom or a dad who was left-handed and who loved you enough to teach you how to write before you went to kindergarten. I know that when you get nervous, like when we're learning something new, you whistle some Blink-182 song real low. I know you bite your nails but not in class. I know you used to smoke, because sometimes you pull out your purse and open the side pocket where you used to keep them before you realize you're doing that and then look around to see if anyone noticed. I know that necklace you wear has some special meaning because every so often your eyes get this glazed-over thing about them and you reach to the necklace, twisting it in your fingers to make it go away."

Finally, David paused. He felt light-headed, but needed to say a little more. There was a real chance, he realized, that he would never have another opportunity to do so. He knew how crazy he sounded. Crazy enough for a restraining order, maybe.

"The American Dream is not a myth," he said. "It offends me when you say that, because I've worked really hard just to get *here*. One day I'll do something that matters. I'll have a big goddamn house and people will know my name. Someday I'm going to have all that. And I don't really know how to prove to you that's possible unless you come with me."

Elizabeth didn't answer. It was impossible to read her. Her eyes were cold brown pebbles.

"I think you are just about the most beautiful woman I've ever seen," he said. "I am in love with you, even though we've never really even talked before. I'm in love with the way you *are*. Your bluntness. Your intelligence. Your *fragility*. You are . . . just . . . lovely."

Elizabeth looked back at him for a full ten seconds before saying anything. Finally, she said, "You can go."

Later that night there was a knock on David's dorm room door and he knew who it was without looking. When he opened it, there she was, her red hair bristly from the humidity. A cream-colored angora blouse clung to her body like a thin mitten. She set her book bag on the floor outside his room.

"I hate you and everything you're about," she said.

"No, you don't."

She stepped into his room. He closed the door. Even before it latched, her hands were on his body. They made love. When they finished, she took off her blouse and they fucked. Still later, they made love again, to the blue light of a television screen.

Lying in the dark, her head on his chest, long after he thought she had gone to sleep and he had passed the point of coherent thoughts, Elizabeth whispered, "I had a twin, once. An identical twin."

"Shhh," he said and stroked her hair. "I love you," he said.

"You shouldn't," she replied.

He awoke in the darkness and he was alone.

No note, no lipstick on his dorm room mirror, no sign at all that Elizabeth had even been there except for the faint lingering of her scent, soap and melon.

David found her name in the student directory, called her dorm at Prentice Hall, got no answer. The next day she did not come to class. He had a girl he knew from History of American Lit escort him to Elizabeth's room, but if she was there, she didn't come to the door. He left more messages on her answering machine.

Around nine o'clock, three nights after they slept together, the phone in his room rang. She was crying.

"What?" he asked calmly.

"David, I'm sorry," she managed. "I've been so mean to you."

"It's fine."

"I didn't know who else to call. I need your help."

"What's wrong? Did something happen?"

"I . . . I ordered pizza from EuroGyro. They always send out Catherine for me. She was supposed to work tonight. But when I called in my order, they sent some guy. I couldn't open the door. I just ignored him until he went away. I don't have anything left in my room to eat. Can you come and get me? Take me somewhere?"

David didn't question it. Didn't want to. This was her mystery, after all.

He picked her up five minutes later. Her lovely red hair was disheveled and he could tell by the clutter of her room that she hadn't been outside in days. He took her to EuroGyro, where he paid for her pizza—which they shared at the bar, over a pitcher of beer. Afterward, they went to Palcho's, a one-room donut shop on Main Street, near the university. Elizabeth listened while David talked about his family and his attempts at writing something meaningful. Whenever he asked about her childhood, she deftly spun the conversation in a different direction. He let her.

"I never answer the door for men," she said finally.

That night she stayed in his dorm room. And the next morning she was still there.

———

"No, no, no," she said, flipping through his CD case. "David, this is just awful."

"What?"

"Cranberries, Enya, They Might Be Giants. There's nothing in here older than 1990. It's like some horrible teen girl's CD collection."

He shrugged. They were on his bed and she was leaning back against his chest, his legs crossed over her pale thighs. He loved the weight of her against his body. When she was done, Elizabeth tossed the binder across the room and pulled away from him, slipping on a pair of Keds.

"I'll be right back," she said.

She returned twenty minutes later with a stack of CDs in her arms, held sturdy by her chin. She dumped them beside his radio, selected a disc, and turned the volume up louder than he'd ever pushed it. A gentle guitar riff; a tap-tapping of some percussion instrument—he pictured a man hitting a wooden spoon against his legs; a solid male voice, and the song broke into something more, a beat that filled his head with cool images and colors.

"What is it?"

"Led Zeppelin," she said. "'Ramble On.'"

He sat against the wall, his eyes trained on the space in the corner, while she selected more songs, rocking back on her legs and staring at him intently. "Free Bird." "Roundabout." "Sympathy for the Devil." "Time." "The Wreck of the *Edmund Fitzgerald*." "Brass in Pocket." "Bad Company." "Limelight." "Crazy on You." "Voodoo Child." "Take the Long Way Home."

"Thank you," he said. "Where have *I* been hiding all this time?"

Elizabeth's life was divided into manageable and repeating segments, and any derivation from her charted schedule seemed to lock her away into herself for a bit.

Every morning she drank a single cup of hazelnut coffee, which was dispensed from her single-cup machine. Then she signed online and checked the same four sites in order: the *Plain Dealer*, the *Beacon Journal*, Hotmail, and Drudge. Each afternoon, after classes, she got lunch from the Prentice Hall cafeteria, and took it back to her room on a beige tray, except for Wednesdays, when she treated herself to a take-out meal from Chipotle, eating in her locked car while she read the new weekly

Independent. One Wednesday, they arrived at Chipotle to find that all the spots in the lot had been taken, and, instead of driving to another restaurant, she had taken them back to the dorm and slipped under the covers, without eating, complaining of a headache until he went away. At seven-thirty, five days a week, she stopped studying and turned on *Jeopardy!*, but never said the answers out loud. For a snack, at ten o'clock, she ate cinnamon toast. She spent most of the weekends in the library. But on Saturday nights, she always disappeared.

For the first couple weeks, he didn't ask. When Saturday night came around and she told him she had plans, again, he found something else to do. But he knew she must leave campus because when he would go out to the bars with friends later, her car was always gone from the lot. And then, one Saturday night, just as he was steeling himself for the customary brush-off, Elizabeth said, "David, how much cash do you have on you?"

"About forty dollars," he said. "In the bank, I mean. Nothing on me."

She smiled. "You can borrow some of mine," she said, pulling him off the bed. She reached into her panties drawer and pulled out a folded wad of twenties and tens.

"Jesus," he said.

"It's my bankroll."

"Your what?"

"Bankroll. It's not . . . well, it's not real money. You can't think of it like that."

"It looks like real money."

She shook her head. "You only use it to get *more* money."

Elizabeth drove them to the Walmart in Ravenna, and parked behind a long charter bus surrounded by last year's sedans. "Red Hats," she said, as if that explained anything. "I like to play the ponies. Have you ever been to a track?"

David shook his head.

"Dark, smoky places. Full of men. But if you know what you're doing, the odds are in your favor if you play long enough. I needed a group to go with me, because I couldn't ever go alone, but I don't have anybody. So I found *them.*"

The Red Hats, it turned out, were a kind of sorority for retired women who wore red hats instead of fezzes. There were more than twenty on the bus and they waved at Elizabeth as she entered, and cooed at David as he followed her to a seat in the back.

The bus took them to Northfield Park, a wide concrete coliseum a half hour away. Elizabeth stayed in the center of the Red Hats, leading David by the hand as he watched prissy horses pulling little carts through tiny gates. Inside the restaurant, the air was thick with the smoke of cheap cigars and thin cigarettes. They took a section of tables by a window and ordered food and beer while Elizabeth read through sheets of what looked like random numbers to him.

Betting on harness racing, like all horse racing, like life, she explained, was something called pari-mutuel gambling. Unlike betting on football, the odds changed based on the number of people betting. She tried to walk David through the basics of handicapping—something about pacing and whether or not the horse had tripped in the last race—but it was too much for David to keep straight.

"Look at this one," she said, pointing to the stats on a horse called Santa Vittoria's Secret. It was at ten-to-one, but had placed in a quarter of its last dozen races. "It has good value." Instead, he put ten on Fatty Lumpkin, a horse at three-to-one, because he'd recognized the name from the Lord of the Rings.

Four hours later, they got back in the bus with the Red Hats, David in a daze, his head heavy on his shoulders. He'd lost $240 of his girlfriend's money. But she'd left happy, and $800 richer.

"Probability won out," she said. "It usually does."

She practiced the piano in a cramped room in the Music and Speech Building every Tuesday and Thursday. Sometimes he would arrive early to watch her through the square window, watch her lovely calm as she folded herself into some Poulenc or Chopin. That was when she was at rest enough to smile.

When they took a trip to Niagara Falls and she thought he'd gone out for booze, she had sung loudly in the hotel shower, sung with a girlish confidence that busted his heart. "Castle on a Cloud," from Les Misérables. He'd taped her performance with his microcassette recorder.

He stole glimpses of her when they got ready for dates in her dorm room, as she looked in the mirror at herself and made her lips into a silent whistle as she brushed her hair.

Only he knew these moments. Let others have their low-rent women, he thought. Elizabeth was worth more because only he knew how to find her. And only she knew how to find him.

—⊡—

"Where're we *going*, Dad?" asked Tanner.

David knelt in front of his son, tying the boy's Converse high-tops before zipping his coat and ruffling his hair. "Out," said David.

"But where?"

"On a little adventure." He took his son's hand and led him through the kitchen to the garage, where the restored canary-yellow Volkswagen was parked.

"Ugh!" said Tanner, trying to pull his hand away from David. "Is this like the museum trip where you wanted me to see Mayonnaise on the wall?"

"Manet," corrected David with a smile. "No, buddy. We'll suspend your art lessons until you're five."

"What does *suspend* mean?"

"It means 'delay' or 'wait until later.'" David opened the door and pushed the seat up for Tanner, who climbed into the booster seat in the back and buckled himself in.

"When do I get to sit up *front*?"

"When you're a little taller," David said. At the last visit to the pediatrician's, the doctor had said the boy was in the twenty-fifth percentile as far as height, small for his age. It had been weirdly alarming and David had stayed up well into the night wondering if he'd somehow neglected the boy's nutrition or stunted his growth by letting the boy sip his Coke whenever David had one with dinner.

The car's ignition fired with a noise that sounded like the coughing of a fat smoker after a flight of stairs. He didn't like taking her out of Akron, but he'd just had the Bug tuned and figured she could get them to Mansfield and back in one piece. In a moment they were bounding down Merriman, feeling each chuckhole and patched bit of pavement along the way. David stole a quick glance at the house on Primrose Lane as they passed—there was no sign of life there. The yard of Kentucky bluegrass was overgrown. Then again, so was his. He guessed it must still be empty—which would make it the only vacant property this side of town. There was no FOR SALE sign out front, though.

"But where are we *going?*"

"We're going to hear your mother sing."

After his book began to climb the charts, but before Tanner came along, David had been introduced to a lawyer in Mansfield, a gruff man of giant proportions who wore candy-cane suspenders and woolen slacks. Man's name was Louis Bashien, and he was a bit of a savant when it came to probate matters and financial planning. He was the first one who told David to sock away some cash and identification. He was the first one to tell David to buy a gun.

"Trouble comes to money like flies to shit," he'd told David four years ago. "Be a good Boy Scout. Be prepared."

And so David had given Bashien his money, to hide it, twist it, make it grow. He'd gotten a license and bought a gun. And he'd purchased a safe-deposit box at the bank across the street from Bashien's office in downtown Mansfield, an hour south of Akron. Elizabeth liked the idea of a little insurance against the future and so she went down with him when he filled the box. Inside went ten thousand in cash and their passports. He remembered how she'd spotted the neon sign to the robotics museum on the way home and how the sight of it had caused her to retreat into herself and grow silent, the way she used to in college.

When he asked her, later, what had upset her, Elizabeth's response had been as mildly amusing and maddeningly vague as the rest of her. "The robot in the window, on that poster in the window. Whoever made it is dead now and it has to live forever in that shitty museum, alone. It's sad."

After she died, he'd gone back to Mansfield, once. That time he had deposited his handgun, a handsome nine-millimeter revolver, the kind cops used to carry, and the microcassette player with her *Les Mis* performance tucked inside. It had not seemed like a hot idea to keep either one in the house with him.

He had forgotten the tape until today, until Paul had come inside his house, trailing memories. Now all he wanted in life was to hear her voice again and to share that with their son.

Tanner followed him inside the one-floor muni bank an hour later, skipping a few steps behind, tugging at the back of his jacket. They were escorted to a cozy alcove and after a minute a short woman brought out a long box and set it on the table in front of them. David waited until she walked away before he opened it.

"Whoa!" said Tanner, whistling approval and awe at the money stacked inside in bundles of twenty-dollar bills. Behind the money, the gun was still wrapped in a blue washcloth. He could smell its grease, an angry, paranoid stench. Resting on top of the money was the little recorder. He picked it up and handed it to Tanner. Then he locked the box and nodded at the woman, who came to reclaim it without a word.

They sat in the parking lot and listened to it five times. Nobody cried. In fact, Tanner was bouncing on the back seat in an excitable rush. "I love her voice!" he said. "I love the way she sings!"

Finally, David buckled his son back into his seat and pulled out of the parking lot, heading back through town. Tanner saw the sign's neon glow first, a dull pinkness against the buildingscape, which was falling into shade before the setting sun.

"What's that?" he asked.

"A robot lives there."

Tanner blew a loud raspberry. "Nuh-uh, Dad!"

"It's true. His name's Elektro."

"Is it a *dangerous* robot? Like General Grievous?"

"No. He's a friendly robot."

"Like WALL-E."

"Like WALL-E," David agreed. "But taller."

The Mansfield Museum of Circuitry and Robotics was located in an old bank downtown, past the abandoned and rusting buildings where Westinghouse had once produced affordable and durable appliances for consumers across the Midwest. The factory had employed half the town. When the late-seventies manufacturing bubble burst, it destroyed the local economy. Westinghouse's laboratories and office space were emptied and local businesses that fed off its employees—bars, convenience stores, retail—perished. That's one reason why a seldom-visited robotics museum could afford to rent a historic gothic bank, David supposed.

David had come across an article in the *Plain Dealer* years ago about the museum's curator and his efforts to restore Elektro and to rebuild Sparko, its trusty servant, a robot dog that had been run over by a car. According to the writer, Sparko's eyes had been photosensitive. If you waved a flashlight on the ground, it would follow the spot of light anywhere. Unfortunately, some engineer had left the door to the lab open one night and Sparko had been attracted to the headlights passing by outside. The idea that there was this odd man restoring a robot friendship here in Mansfield, where the biggest employer was a toilet factory, had always stuck with David like a burr on his sleeve, more so since his memories of Elizabeth were entangled with the place, too. What was it that had made her so sad about the notion of an eternal life?

David pulled into a diagonal space directly in front of the museum. Theirs was the only car downtown. Most of the nearby storefront windows had been newspapered or painted over long ago. Across the street, a homeless man warmed himself on a sewer grate. Above the door the neon sign pulsed rhythmically: MEET ELEKTRO THE ROBOT.

"Cool," said Tanner, unbuckling his car seat.

David helped the boy out of the car and took his hand, keeping a close watch on the bum across the street. But the bum didn't move.

Beyond the front doors, the air was brutally warm. Somewhere a heater shuddered against a wall, blowing dry air into the museum with its last ounce of strength. They stood there, David and the boy, for a few moments, looking about the lobby. Dozens of black-and-white framed photographs of the 1939 World's Fair hung on the scarlet walls. In each, a seven-foot-tall smooth humanoid robot performed some new trick. Here he was smoking a cigarette. There he was tossing a hot dog to Sparko as the dog sat on its hind legs, its mouth wide open. And here was one where Elektro was shaking hands with a man dressed as the Tin Woodsman from *The Wizard of Oz*. The Tin Woodsman might have been crying in agony.

After a while, David led Tanner to the ticket counter, behind which a doorway to some office or storage room was blocked by a black velvet curtain where dust bunnies clung, their tails dancing in the breeze of the dying heater. A brass bell rested on the counter next to a laminated hand-drawn sign: RING FOR SERVICE.

David rang the bell. Its sound reverberated in the shallow room.

From behind the curtain came the sound of metal things falling to the floor, as if the bell had set off some booby trap that had caused a box of tools to tumble from its perch.

"Is it the robot?" Tanner whispered, clutching his father's hand.

"No," David said. "It's the tour guide."

A little man trundled through a seam in the curtain. He stood just over five feet tall and had a wiry white beard that hung below his chin in a braid. The man was small, but not a midget. Old, but not ancient. A smell followed him out of the back room. Cinnamon? David watched as the man climbed onto a stepstool to better see his visitors from behind the counter. He noticed the man had something in his right hand. Something squarish and white. A cell phone?

"We'd like to see Elektro," David said.

The man brought the white object up under his braided beard. In a flash, David knew what it was. He had only enough time to realize this was about to be one of those moments Tanner would likely recall in therapy one day. There just wasn't enough time to explain before it happened.

The man behind the counter was the curator, of course. And the thing in his right hand was not a cell phone, but an electrolarynx he had used to talk since doctors at the Cleveland Clinic had removed a five-pound tumor—and his voice box—from his throat, in 2004. Because he was old and his hearing was going, he kept the box turned up to eleven, so he could hear what he was saying, too. What came out when he finally addressed his first guests in three weeks was both manufactured and loud. "JUST YOU AND THE BOY?"

Tanner had not let his father carry him for more than a year, but by the time the curator had said "JUST YOU . . ." the boy had scrambled up David's legs and had buried his eyes in the fold of David's right elbow.

David gave the curator a one-moment sign. The man nodded back. Obviously, he was fairly used to this sort of reaction from young ones.

Walking back toward the door, David slowly pried his son off him and set Tanner down. The boy peeked around him, spotted the curator, ducked his head back behind his dad, and let out a small moan. David felt pangs of guilt but knew it was important that he not just pack the kid up and turn tail for home. That would only compound the terror and the nightmares. He realized this was the first time he was going to ask his son to face a fear. Was Tanner old enough for such a lesson, at four?

"Tanner. Tanner, listen to me," David said.

"You said it wasn't a robot. He looks so *real.*"

"Tanner, that man is not a robot."

Still shaking, the boy gave David a look of reproach. That was new, too. And David felt it deeply. This was the first time he had told his son the truth and his son had decided that he was lying. Not just teasing. *Lying.*

"Sometimes people get hurt, their throat gets hurt in an accident or something," he said. "And sometimes, when they're fixed up, they can't talk like you and me. They have to use a little voice box, which they hold up to their neck. The box lets them sort of talk but it sounds really weird when they do."

Tanner stopped shaking a little bit. He stole another glance at the curator, who waved at him.

"How come I never saw anyone like that before?" he asked.

"Probably because we don't get out enough, kiddo," David replied. "My fault."

And then Tanner smiled and all was well with the world once more. "Can I have one?" he asked, already envisioning a scenario, no doubt, that included a sudden leap from the shoe closet with an electrolarynx pressed to his neck as Aunt Peggy searched for the duster.

"LUKE, I AM YOUR FATHER," the curator said in his mechanized voice.

Tanner laughed, but squeezed his dad's hand as he did. "Cooooool!"

David nodded a thank-you to the curator. "Just us," he said, handing the man a ten-dollar bill.

The curator shoved the money down the front pocket of his oil-stained overalls. He stepped off the stool and swung a section of the counter up so he could walk out from behind it, even though he could just as easily have ducked. "FOLLOW ME," he said as he stepped toward a steel door that had once led to the bank's gigantic vault, but which now held more priceless treasures. From his front pocket he withdrew a six-inch-long skeleton key, which he considered for a moment before handing it to Tanner.

The boy's eyes grew ever wider as he felt the weight of the key in his palm. David sensed that his son believed this to be a magical key, one that might open doors that led to other worlds. It certainly looked like a key from some fairy tale. Even David caught himself imagining the door opening onto a forestscape bathed in gold and green light from a star not unlike our own.

Tanner let go of his father's hand and walked deliberately to the metal door. The boy slipped the key in the hole below the glass doorknob and turned it lightly. What followed was a loud tumbling of gears from inside that seemed to go on for ten seconds. Finally, it ended with a grinding *THUNK!* and the door creaked open an inch.

"IT'S A GOOD THING YOU CAME," the curator said. "THAT DOOR ONLY OPENS FOR CHILDREN AND I LEFT MY HAT BEHIND THE LAST TIME I WAS INSIDE."

Tanner smiled and handed the key back to the curator, watching it disappear in that front pocket again, an adultlike expression of loss in his eyes. He was old enough, then, to understand that magical moments were rare and fleeting.

The museum was dedicated to the history of man's attempt to create a machine in his own image. A pathway snaked across the main room, past photographs and displays of early Westinghouse models, machines that vacuumed or served canapés, some with misguided names like Mammy Washington.

"Is Elektro here?" Tanner asked his father.

"RIGHT THIS WAY, YOUNG MAN, RIGHT THIS WAY," announced the curator, with a flourish of his hands that would make a carnival barker blush. "NO SENSE DELAYING THE MAIN ATTRACTION."

They soon arrived at the back of the museum, where a floor-to-ceiling black velvet curtain hung from the rafters.

"BEHOLD, THE APEX OF ELECTRICAL ENGINEERING. THE REALIZATION OF MAN'S IMAGINATION. THE WORLD'S MOST FULLY FUNCTIONAL ARTIFICIAL HUMAN. EEEEEEELEKTRO."

Pocketing his electrolarynx, he pulled at a long length of rope nearby and the curtain parted.

Slowly, slowly, a stainless steel frame was uncovered. It was easily more humanoid than the robots that had preceded it, and yet, less *human*. Elektro was seven feet tall, a barrel-chested giant with cool gray eyes and a mouth that suggested it was either attempting to smile or was gritting its teeth. It was frozen in time, its arms and hands extended outward in a gesture reminiscent of a model from *The Price Is Right* showcasing a new blender. There was a peculiar smell emanating from the robot; it smelled of waterfall mist, of positive ions, of ozone.

"Wow!" shouted Tanner, hopping in place excitedly.

David nodded. "Pretty cool," he agreed. "Can it still blow bubbles?"

The curator dropped the rope and returned the white box to its place under his wizard beard. "I'VE NEVER ACTUALLY GOTTEN UP THE NERVE TO PLUG IT IN," he said. "I'M AFRAID IF I DO, IT'LL FRY ITS INSIDES AND BURN THE PLACE DOWN."

Tanner looked distractedly down at the thick and tattered electrical cord trailing behind Elektro's left leg and at the wall socket a few inches away. David took a moment to get a better grip on his son's hand, before he got any sudden Frankensteinian ideas.

"AFTER THE 1939 WORLD'S FAIR, ELEKTRO TOURED THE COUNTRY AND MADE A DECENT LIVING FOR MANY YEARS. THE MONEY WESTINGHOUSE TOOK IN FROM HIS ENGAGEMENTS WAS SET ASIDE IN A SPECIAL FUND THAT COULD ONLY BE USED FOR HIS UPKEEP AND MAINTE-NANCE. THE INTEREST FROM THAT FUND IS WHAT KEEPS THIS MUSEUM OPEN TODAY."

"He had a dog, you know," David told Tanner. "He had a pet robot dog."

"*Really?*" The boy turned to the curator. "Is the robot dog here, too?"

"AFRAID NOT."

"The scientist made the dog so that it was attracted to light, so that whenever it saw a beam of light, it knew to follow it," said David. "Do you understand?"

Tanner nodded.

"But one day the scientist forgot to shut the door, and during the night the dog ran out into the street and it got hit by a car."

Tanner looked at the curator again. "Is that true?" he asked.

"NOT A WORD OF IT," the curator said, looking annoyed.

"Isn't that the story you told the reporter a couple years ago?" asked David. "I thought that's the story I remembered."

"SURE. THAT'S WHAT WAS WRITTEN. BUT THAT'S NOT WHAT HAPPENED."

"What's the real story?" asked David.

The curator looked up at Elektro, as if consulting with him before he continued. And when he did speak again, he did so nervously.

"THE TRUE STORY IS . . . STRANGER," he said. "WHAT RE-ALLY HAPPENED WAS THIS. ONE NIGHT, THE ENGINEER, WHOSE NAME WAS SAMUEL MCGEE, HE LEAVES THE LAB. GETS INTO HIS CAR. STARTS TO DRIVE HOME. SPARKO RUNS OUT INTO THE STREET. SAM RUNS IT OVER. DOG

GETS STUCK IN WHEEL WELL, SENDING THE CAR INTO A TELEPHONE POLE. THE CRASH KILLED SAM. KILLED WESTINGHOUSE'S ROBOTICS DEPARTMENT, TOO."

"The dog caused a crash that killed the man who invented it?"

"WAS IT REALLY SPARKO?" The curator shrugged. "SOMETHING ELSE THE WRITER GOT WRONG: SPARKO'S EYES WERE NOT PHOTOSENSITIVE. THE DOG WAS MADE TO RESPOND TO VOICE COMMANDS. BUT IT WOULD ONLY RESPOND TO ELEKTRO'S OWN VOICE."

"But how did Sparko get *out*?" asked Tanner.

"THERE'S THE REAL MYSTERY. THE JANITOR SAID HE LOCKED UP THAT NIGHT. IF HE'S TELLING THE TRUTH, THERE'S ONLY ONE THING THAT COULD HAVE LET THE DOG OUT." He glanced, coldly, to Elektro. To David, the robot suddenly seemed to be listening to them and pretending not to be alive. "ELEKTRO MUST HAVE PLAYED A PART IN IT. AFTER ALL, THE DOG COULD ONLY HAVE RUN INTO THE STREET IF ELEKTRO HAD CALLED TO HIM." And with that the curator continued walking down the length of the museum to the models of later robots built by other dead Westinghouse engineers.

"*Dad*," whispered Tanner.

"What, bud?"

"Dad, that was the best story!"

On the way home, they counted the stars. David had once heard—though he had no idea if it was true—that there were exactly eighty-eight constellations in the summer sky. "Can you name that one?"

"The Big Dipper!" shouted Tanner. "Duh. Who *put* the stars in the sky, Dad?"

David felt his blood chill. That had been his line, once. One of his first memories, actually: Riding in the car—in the front seat, beltless, natch—with his mother, when he couldn't have been more than two, two and a half, watching the factories of Cleveland belch fire as she drove them from Lakewood to his babysitter's in Bedford before work. As soon as they were away from the fire, the stars would appear. It had been five in the morning then, and not night. He'd asked that same question, every single day. To David, this was a bad omen. His worst fear, unsaid, was that his boy would grow up to be just like him.

Still, he used his own mother's old answer. "God," he said, though he no longer believed it to be true.

"Why?" asked Tanner.

"Some people think it's so that we can see how beautiful they are."

"Oh. They *are* pretty stars. I like them."

For a couple minutes there was silence. David was about to flick on the radio when his son spoke again. "Why do *you* think God put the stars in the sky?"

A stumper. No way to answer that one, for now. And the kid was only four. "So the Indians could read at night before electricity was invented, I think," he said at last.

Soon Tanner was asleep. As he snored into his shoulder in the back seat, David called Paul on his cell phone. He picked up on the first ring.

"I'm in," said David.

MENTAL CIGARETTES

"But where are we *going*?" asked Elizabeth. She slouched back in the passenger seat of his first car, a '79 Monte Carlo, bare feet resting on the dashboard as he drove them through the tangles of Kent's frat-row side streets. Her red hair was shorter, bobbed just above the white tube top she had bought for the way he looked at her exposed shoulders and the suggestion of breasts underneath.

"Palcho's," he said.

"Why?"

"Donuts."

"David, we're going to eat Chinese in, like, five minutes," she scolded. "Are you pregnant?"

It had been seven months since they had first visited Palcho's together, a formative evening that was already slipping into a gray jumble of forgotten episodes for Elizabeth, but which David still remembered in explicit and lovely detail.

They arrived and David quickly ran around the car to open her door. She stepped out and gave him a look of cold suspicion. "What's wrong with you?" she asked.

"I'm in love with you," he said.

"Cheesy," she replied. "Like, eighties after-school-special cheesy."

"Yeah," he admitted. "And this is probably worse."

David dropped to one knee as he pulled the purple-velvet jewelry box with the snap lid out of his pocket. He opened it. The ring inside was white gold, with bits of crushed diamonds set in the top. He'd had it sized for her already.

"Marry me?" He meant it as a statement, but couldn't help the rising inflection at the end that marked his insecurity.

She smiled. Not the plastered-on smile she gave strangers, but the wide-open childlike smile that pushed out her cheeks like a chipmunk and revealed the little gap between her front teeth. "No," she said.

He had expected this.

"You don't want to marry me," she said, shaking her head. But her smile was still real, still warm. She pulled him up to her and kissed him, hard, on the mouth.

"But I do," he insisted. "That's why I'm giving you the ring."

"It's really pretty," she said, pulling it out of its place and slipping it onto her left ring finger. It fit perfectly. And she left it on, placing the box back in her purse.

"It's the ring my father gave my mom when they got engaged," he said.

"That's really sweet," she said. "But doesn't that mean it's cursed? Aren't they divorced?"

"Maybe we could reverse it."

Elizabeth kissed him again, snaking her arms around his neck. She leaned in to whisper something important in his ear. "Let's get some Chinese," she said.

Five minutes later, they were seated at a table inside the Evergreen Buffet, a busy Chinese restaurant populated by college students and obese townies from nearby Ravenna. David felt weak and shaky, his fingers slightly numb, like he was on laughing gas, but he came to realize that he was not disappointed. She'd said no, but was wearing the ring. She'd said no, but was smiling as if he'd done something really swell.

Maybe it's a test, he thought, as they ate in silence. *A test to see how much I fight for it. Or maybe I'm not supposed to care. Maybe that's the trick. Maybe she wants me to get mad. Maybe . . .*

"I was a twin," she said.

He shook his head. He had forgotten that this revelation had come as she was falling asleep on his chest that first night.

"I was a twin," she repeated. "And when we were ten, I watched a guy take her. We never saw her again. It destroyed my family."

David realized that she was about to give him a peek inside her mystery and he was glad she was finally opening up. But there was a cold part of him, too, that wondered if she would remain as alluring to him once he knew the answer.

"There was a park around the corner from our house in Lakewood. It had a playground with monkey bars and this creaky wooden bridge and a hopscotch grid. Elaine was crazy about hopscotch. Anyway, we used to go there all the time by ourselves while my father cooked supper and waited for Mom to get home—she was an accountant in the city. One day we walked to the park and there was this van there, one of those white all-purpose vans contractors use? A guy was standing outside the sliding door on the side, pacing back and forth. Skinny guy. He had weird bushy hair. When he saw us approaching, he started calling out, 'Daisy! Daisy!' When we got closer, he waved to us. 'I can't find my puppy dog,' he said. 'Have you seen a little black Lab?' Of course, the only thing Elaine loved more than hopscotch was puppies, right? She goes running over to him and he's already opening that side door, swinging it down its track—I can hear it tumble down the shaky track, rumbling along. It must've been an old van. I'm right behind her as she reaches the van. I didn't think anything was really wrong, I just wanted to be with my sister. For a second he didn't do anything, just kind of stood there, looking at the both of us. I could tell he was scared. Isn't that funny? *He* was scared. And we weren't. And then we were. He grabbed Elaine's arm and flung her into the back of the van real quick, in one fast motion, just, boom, you know? And then he grabbed my arm and was pulling me toward the open door. But I had just a second more to take in the situation than Elaine and so I had the chance to brace myself and so he couldn't throw me in as easily. He got me halfway in, far enough for me to see Elaine kneeling on the metal floor back there, holding her head, which had opened in a long scrape above her left eye. Then I heard the honking. It was loud and constant, honk honk honk honk honk honk! He let go of me and I fell out, onto the gravel parking lot. 'Get the fuck in,' he said. I didn't say anything. I couldn't. I just sat there, in total shock. 'Suit yourself,' he said. He pulled the door closed and then ran to the driver's side and climbed in. All this time, the honking was getting louder. And louder. And then I saw a big Cadillac trailing down the road that ran along the baseball diamonds from the street, kicking up a trail of dust. It was going so fast, I could see it sliding all over the gravel. The guy in the van gunned it and took off through the baseball fields, cutting across to Clifton. When he got to the chicken-wire fence that marked the home-run line, he just kept going, tearing right through. The Caddy finally got all the way back to me and stopped on a dime. And another man got out and I remember thinking, *here we go again*, but what he said to me was, 'Are you all right?' I told him no, I wasn't all right. And I started crying. 'Where's your sister?' he asked. 'Where's Elizabeth?' I was crying so much I couldn't even correct him. All I could do was point at the van that was getting away. 'Shit,' he shouted. Then he got back in his car and tore off across the field after the van. I never saw her again. Or him. I ran back home. Told my dad what had happened. He left me alone in the kitchen and I climbed under the table with a butter knife, I remember, because I was sure that man was coming back for me. When my dad returned five minutes later, he called the police. They put men on every road leading out of Lake-wood, but he was already gone. I don't remember much about the next few months. A lot of it was spent in my room, reading, trying not to listen to them argue downstairs. When they got going, they said some pretty mean things. Tossing blame, you know? Back and forth like a tennis ball. Sometimes my mother put my name into the mix, too, even though I didn't have a voice and was only ten goddamn years old, anyway, and it was really her fault for being at work so late. Maybe she needed to blame me to deflect some away from her and the man she shared a bed with. I know she did, because that summer they sent me to live with my mother's sister. 'For a month,' they said. But it turned into forever."

"God, Liz, I'm so sorry."

Elizabeth waved her hand at him. "That's not why I told you," she said. "I should have told you that there would never be Thanksgiving with the fam. I haven't seen my mom in thirteen years. Haven't seen Dad in seven. And I'm never going to introduce you to them."

He reached over and took her hand. Her nails were chipped and bitten down to the quick. They shook a little.

"I'm not family material," she said.

She pulled the ring off her finger, looked at it a moment, then tried to hand it back to David. He pushed back her hand gently.

"It's for you," he said. "I'm only giving it once. If you won't marry me, you still have to wear it. You can wear it forever and we can date until we're seventy. Put it on a chain around your neck if you want."

Elizabeth pulled the necklace out of the tube top. It was a simple imitation sapphire set in silver, a child's thing. "I stole this from Elaine's dresser before my mother cleaned it out. I can't replace it until it falls apart, I guess." Instead, she put the ring back on her finger.

"When you change your mind, you can propose to me," he said.

A tear fell into her chicken and broccoli. She looked up at him and smiled. "Okey dokey," she said.

There was one thing that annoyed him. He could take the coldness, the negativity, the migraines she sometimes got that kept her in bed for two days. He could forgive her forgetting his birthday and for always saying 'effect' when she really meant 'affect.' He could forgive her for leaving her blow dryer on his side of the bedroom vanity and for making him spray that floral stuff in the bathroom. He didn't mind all this because he never took for granted the way her bottom lip puffed out a bit when she was drunk or the way she twisted his hair in her fingers when he lay in her lap watching television. The only thing that really annoyed him, the only thing he just could not get over, was her love of Christopher Pike, a late-eighties teen-lit horror novelist she'd become obsessed with in her sister's absence.

Elizabeth, who was up every morning at five-thirty making a pot of coffee so strong she might as well be snorting coke, could not, no matter how hard she tried, ever fall asleep before midnight. It had been this way since Elaine's abduction and did not abate in the slightest with the unexpected addition of David's love and security. By that time, anyway, it was habit. The worst part about it was that it kept her awake when everyone around her was asleep; it kept her alone. The only way she found she could endure this quiet time was to read. And the only thing she ever seemed to read was Christopher Pike. *Chain Letter 2: The Ancient Evil*, the *Final Friends* trilogy, *Remember Me*.

"Why don't you read Poe or Tolkien or Bradbury?" he asked once when he caught her reading *Last Act* for the sixth time.

"I don't have the patience for description," she told him, as if it were something dirty and tabloid. "I don't want to read about the history of Hobbit tobacco for an hour."

And so it went. Elizabeth would march through the entire Pike canon in the course of a year and start again with *Chain Letter* in early January. Well, almost the entire Pike canon. There was one book she'd never been able to track down. *Sati.* The story of a young woman who claims to be God. It was out of print. Whenever they passed a library book sale or Mac's Backs in Cleveland Heights, she was compelled to stop in so that they could spend twenty minutes searching for this rare hardcover.

One afternoon, a short time after David's awkward proposal, he found himself in Ravenna. He was working for a community biweekly newspaper that covered northern Portage County and the editor had sent him to the county seat to report on a nasty civil suit involving a development deal gone awry. It was not glamorous work, not the investigative journalism he'd dreamed of in college, but it was steady and he was grateful for the experience. On that particular afternoon, on his way to the Triangle Diner for a corned beef sandwich, he noticed a sign across the street that read GOODWILL BOOK SALE.

The place smelled of mildew, mothballs, and desperation. Rows of seventies slacks in shades of brown and orange hung on tall racks to his right, paisley blouses to his left. Taking up the center of the room were a dozen card tables topped with boxes and boxes of books. A milk crate full of hardcovers was mostly hidden under a lime-green shawl someone had tossed aside. Under the shawl, lying atop the other books, was *Sati.*

His fingertips brushed the cover. He felt dizzy inside. He never thought he could be so happy holding a Christopher Pike book. He still believed in signs, then. And what else could this be? All her life, Elizabeth had been dealt the universal equivalent of a series of seventeens when the dealer always came up aces. Her sister. Her mother. Elizabeth had become an acolyte of probability and she wouldn't allow herself to bet on him in the face of such a losing streak. But this was a bit of luck. How might that change her?

He thumbed open the front page and felt his breath sucked out of his lungs in one long sigh. *For Elaine,* someone had written.

On the way home, he stopped at a McDonald's, where he gently ripped the signed page from the book, leaving no evidence of its presence. He crumpled the page into a wad and tossed it into the garbage.

Back in their apartment, David wrote his own dedication. *For Elizabeth. Now you can move on.* He meant from Pike, but also from Elaine.

He wrapped the novel in polka-dot paper and got up at two in the morning so that he could secretly place it next to the coffeemaker before going back to bed.

David awoke at five forty-five to a strange twisting of his hand. He looked, to find a plain gold band on his ring finger. Elizabeth knelt on the floor beside him. Her eyes were smiling but her nose was pinched and wrinkly with emotion.

"One of the last things I remember," she said softly, measuring her words so they didn't catch in her throat. "Our eighth birthday party. Peggy got us grown-up gifts. The first time we'd gotten anything but toys, really. She gave me a magic set. With a top hat and little foam bunnies. I believed in magic then. She gave Elaine a book. *Sati.* Our parents pitched a fit. Said it would corrupt her mind or something. She hid it under her bed. But it disappeared. I think our dad pitched it." She began to relax. "I wanted to know what she knew."

"I get it."

"So marry me," she whispered.

—◫—

He missed the process. The process involved in reporting, in writing; that tactile experience in the preparation of his work. As Tanner napped, David returned to the *Edmund Fitzgerald* desk for the first time in four years to see if the magic remained.

He sat down on the expensive leather chair and it sighed around him, welcoming him into its grip. So far, so good. He clicked on the desk lamp, one of those classic green-glass types that adds its own ambience to a room. The bulb still worked, then. Next, he slipped open the shallow drawer above his lap. It smelled of pipe tobacco and cherry lozenges, delights of its original owner. Inside were several reporters' notebooks, narrow and thick pads of paper. His special pens were there, a box of them emptied into the well. Bic blues, inconspicuous tools he felt superstitious about—he'd used Bic blues during his seemingly endless reporting on the Ronil Brune case. To David, Bic blues held all the power of a magic wand that chooses its owner. Also in the desk was a half-empty pack of Marlboros.

David picked up a notepad and three pens. He felt their weight and smiled a little as he set the items on his desk. He took a pen and flicked off the top, sending it across the room and behind the bar. On the front of the notepad he wrote: *The Man from Primrose Lane*. He set the notepad back down and considered it for a long moment. He liked the sharp and solid look of his handwriting. It pleased him. He had forgotten this. The Marlboros, he remembered, served a purpose, too.

He opened the desk again and snatched up the packet. He slapped the cigarettes on their end, and that felt good. Smoking was a process, as well. And the process, the ritual, quieted the hum of his mind so he could write. Though he didn't smoke, these *were* his cigarettes. They weren't normal cigarettes; they were mental cigarettes.

Digging into the pack with one impatient finger, he drew out a slightly bent Marlboro and placed it between his lips. He leaned back into the chair and closed his eyes. He tasted the acrid bite of the tobacco-tinged filter on his tongue. He smelled the nicotine and tar and formaldehyde with his nose. He felt the cigarette's presence between his teeth. He imagined himself inside some hick bar, taking a long drag and exhaling the smoke in wispy circles. He exhaled and listened to his breath in the silence of the room. His senses were satiated and they thanked him. Nearer the end, when Ronil Brune had tormented him from the grave and the first fingers of depression threatened to drag him into the earth, too, this process had always brought him back. Mental cigarettes, he'd called them. Elizabeth had understood.

This might work, he thought. *I might be able to do this. This might be okay.*

He felt relief. But a part of him knew it was a lie.

On the limited occasions when David felt up to venturing into public alone—to catch an R-rated movie or to play poker with a couple chums from college he kept at arm's length—he left Tanner with the teenage girl down the street, Michelle. She was always available on short notice if he gave her $50 for a couple hours of her time. Tonight Michelle was "watching" Tanner at his house, which likely meant texting her boyfriend with an episode of *Grey's Anatomy* blaring in the background as Tanner fiddled with some new contraption in his room.

Though it was the closest library to his house, David hadn't actually been inside the Akron Public Library since it had been renovated in

2004. He'd done all his research on Brune in Cleveland because the library there was a nice place to walk to during his lunch break and because he loved combing through the old handwritten notes of the *Press* reporters at the archive over at Cleveland State. The new building in Akron looked more like an IKEA. It certainly didn't promise adventure like Cleveland Public did.

In a corner on the third floor, David found the microfilm department, a glass-walled alcove with a row of those nifty new computer-scanning readers. He could have done all this online but David was a tactile learner who retained information better if he could work a machine or flip a yellowed page. He needed to hear it, see it, feel it firsthand, or else everything was pushed to the back of his mind with the other junk.

He pulled a couple white boxes from the June '08 drawers of the *Beacon* archives and sat in front of an empty machine. His fingers had not forgotten how to wind the stiff film. He began to motor the film forward, scanning headlines as he went. He instinctively paused for a second when he saw his name.

"Writer's Wife Commits Suicide; A 'Heartbreak,' Says David Neff." Though he'd been quoted, he had never actually seen the article. He'd never seen this photograph of her car, a mangled mess of metal jutting out of a brick wall. It threatened to unravel him. He continued forward.

He stared at the front page of the June 23, 2008, edition.

"Who Was the Man from Primrose Lane?" the above-the-fold article demanded to know. "And who wanted him dead?" went the subhead.

There was a photograph in the center of the paper, once a lovely color photo of the hermit's house, preserved after publication in the black-and-white purgatory of microfilm, lending it a dense and palpable essence of evil, of dark.

The author was Phil McIntyre, a staff writer whom David had met once or twice, and whose beat had been crime until he was promoted to politics. David scanned the article for prescient details.

At long last we know the name of the Man from Primrose Lane—Joseph Howard King. But who was Joe King?

"He was always nice to me and my brother," says Firestone sophomore Billy Beachum, who delivered essentials to King. His brother has been appointed executor of King's estate until next of kin is located.

"That's all I really want to say. I don't know how he could have made any enemies."

"I always thought he might be a radical terrorist," says neighbor Lucille Youtz. "One of the Weathermen, like that Bill Ayers guy."

"Probably an old gangster laying low," figures retired FBI Special Agent Dan Larkey, who has consulted on the case. "The past has a way of catching up with these guys."

Further in the story, a hint of more clues kept from the public eye:

Yesterday, Akron homicide detectives were seen carrying several boxes from King's house but refused to discuss the contents. "This is an ongoing investigation," says Lt. Detective Mark Gareau. "The material taken from his home suggests a possible motive for his murder and may provide details that only Mr. King and his killer are privy to."

David combed through the front pages and local sections of a year's worth of *Beacons*. In September '08, McIntyre wrote a brief follow-up: "West Side Murder Still Has Officials Stumped." Not much in the way of new details, other than this cryptic statement from Gareau: "While it's true a young woman was recently interviewed by detectives, there is no indication she had anything to do with the crime. She is certainly not a suspect."

The real story came on May 17, 2009. It was a McIntyre special, a five-thousand-word Sunday feature that officially turned the Man from Primrose Lane into the stuff of legend. The headline read: "Police: 'Joe King Is Not Joe King. The Man from Primrose Lane Lived a Lie and Died a Millionaire.'"

David jotted down the salient facts of the case, circling each name as he went along. Before contacting any sources, he typically did a poorman's background check on everyone, Googling their names, seeing if they had any criminal histories or weird hobbies. He had once written a profile on a local chess wizard without realizing the man was once roommates with Jeffrey Dahmer and had always kicked himself for the missed opportunity to play with that, thematically.

As he read on, he could feel the mystery surrounding him, comforting him like a new drug. Somewhere in his brain a switch flipped "on" and instructed his adrenal glands to release epinephrine into his bloodstream. But the serotonin reuptake inhibitor—his daily dose of Rivertin—made sure he didn't feel the sudden rush he so desired. No downs, no ups for David. Just the mellow in-between.

Patrolman Tom Sackett discovered the body in the living room . . . shot in the gut . . . his fingers chopped off . . . the doorknobs and walls wiped of fingerprints.

". . . died with at least $3.4 million in stocks and bonds," says Mike Weger of Confidential Investigations, the private investigative firm hired by Albert Beachum. "And another $700,000 in a personal savings account."

Weger tracked King's birth certificate to a hospital in Bellefonte, Pennsylvania. Using the city's birth records, he located a possible relative, another King born to the same parents listed on Joe King's certificate, at the same hospital, in 1928, two years before King was delivered there. The woman's name was Carol. She has since married and has changed her last name to Dechant. Weger found her in Pennsylvania. "And that's when things got really weird," says Weger.

Dechant informed the investigator that her younger brother had died in a car crash, along with their parents, in 1932. Whoever the Man from Primrose Lane was, he wasn't Joe King.

Later:

Detectives were shocked to discover, inside the dead man's home, a box of composition notebooks that detailed the life of a young woman named Katy Keenan from age six to her eighteenth birthday. According to a source close to the investigation, Keenan claims she has never met the Man from Primrose Lane. She refused comment for this story. However, she posted this message on her Facebook wall: "I'd like people to respect my privacy. Something that hasn't been respected, apparently, for the last twelve years."

Though police do not consider Keenan a suspect, one detective, who asked to remain anonymous, believes she holds the key to this unsolved murder. He points to a passage from the notebooks in which the writer admits to following her into a movie theater because he wanted to protect her from other men who might be interested in her. In another, he admits to being in love with her. "I don't believe that the killer's motive was money—there is no relative who stood to inherit his fortune—so what is the motive? One possible motive might be someone close to Keenan finding out about those notebooks and confronting the man about it and then things escalated and got out of hand," says the detective.

. . . Keenan's father has refused to speak with investigators.

But that still doesn't answer the question on everyone's mind—just who was the Man from Primrose Lane to begin with? "Look, that's not my concern," says Lt. Gareau. "My job is to find out who killed this man. I don't care if the guy was running from the law, or from creditors, or a nagging wife. Someone murdered him. And we're going to find out who did it."

When David finished reading, he reached into his breast pocket for the pack of mental cigarettes he'd brought along. He placed a Marlboro between his lips and rewound the microfilm to the beginning so he could read it again.

"Sir, you can't smoke in here," warned the man sitting behind the room's reception desk. David noticed the man was reading a copy of *The Serial Killer's Protégé*. The thing about being a nonfiction writer, he'd discovered, was that most of your readers don't look at the author's photo on the back flap, the way they do with novels. Nonfiction readers seem to be less interested in the author than they are in the story.

"I'm not smoking," he said.

"Oh," the man said. "Well, good."

"What do you think of the book?" asked David. "I was thinking about picking up a copy."

"It's pretentious. Wordy."

"But you're almost finished."

"Well, I have to see how it ends."

David nodded and turned back to the newspaper article. "Fair enough."

Katy Keenan was not hard to find. Facebook. For a woman who claimed to covet privacy, she did nothing to help her cause. At least she didn't keep pictures of herself on her public profile—her avatar was a box of Count Chocula cereal. Katy Keenan was at the center of this mystery. He wanted to meet her tonight, while the thrill of the hunt was still strong. If he could win her trust from the beginning, the rest of his job would be a cinch—and he would have started with an exclusive interview, the best of omens.

At five after eight, David stepped into the Cuyahoga Falls Barnes & Noble. He always left a little bit of chance to his reporting, and so he had not called ahead to see if she was, in fact, working that night. It wasn't that he believed Katy would be there if he was "meant to" or "destined to" meet her. He enjoyed the gamble, the randomness and luck of it. He liked the risk of fucking up.

It didn't smell like a bookstore, this Barnes & Noble. It smelled like a Circuit City or a Target, that regulated-air and nothing smell. He missed the indie bookstore in Kent, where he'd gone once a week to pick up the latest issues of *Powers* and *Ultimate Spider-Man*, the one on Main Street that kept its door propped open even in the middle of winter—the aroma of binder glue, of cloth covers damp with humidity, of newsprint turned to dust.

He made his way toward the coffee nook. Behind the counter was a short man with a bad beard.

"Can I help you?" he asked. "Triple-snozzberry low-fat chocolate scone?"

"Is Katy working tonight?" asked David.

"Nah, Katy's not here, man," he said gruffly.

David turned away and wandered back through the aisle, toward the nonfiction shelves. His book wasn't turned to face out, like new releases and popular books were, but there were at least ten stacked in there.

Not really thinking—he was in a zone, a sort of autohypnosis that accompanied his early reporting, leading him to wander about in search of a narrative—David took a Bic blue from his pocket, pulled a copy of *Protégé* from the shelf, and autographed it. He took another one and did the same. If they wanted to, one of the managers could sell these copies on eBay for some beer money. He was signing his fifth copy when he got caught.

"Holy fuck, what are you doing?" the woman said.

He looked up to find a young woman staring at him, her face a mixture of alarm and disgust. For a second he was sure he was looking at the ghost of his wife. Then his mind cleared and he saw that this woman was younger. Brighter, somehow. Her bone structure was more angular. Still the resemblance was unsettling. The young woman was dressed in All Star high-tops, patched jeans, a red-and-white-striped WHERE'S WALDO? sweater. A pair of white kitten ears held back her shoulder-length straight-as-satin red hair. On her shirt was a name tag. KATY.

"Uh," he said.

"What did you write in there?" she asked. "Are you the guy who writes all that Christian shit in the Harry Potter books? Fuck, man. We have to refund those things."

Katy snatched the book from David's hands.

"Stay there while I call security." She turned toward reference.

"Wait," he said, reaching out for her arm and gently pulling her to a stop. She felt like velvet, like warm. "Look, this is really stupid. I don't . . . look . . . I don't . . . this is really awkward, but . . ."

"You're blushing," she said.

"Well, I'm a little embarrassed. I can explain about the book. I'm—"

"I know who you are," said Katy, a smile slipping over her face, pulling back to reveal her teeth in a decidedly Cheshire Cat, childish way. "I was just joshing you."

"Oh," he said, reaching out for the book. "Have we met?"

Katy rolled her eyes. "We're Facebook friends. You sent me an IM once. Don't you remember?"

David nodded. He had set up the Facebook account at his publisher's urging right before *Protégé* came out. He didn't maintain it anymore. But he knew who did.

"Matt said you were looking for me?" said Katy. "After the stuff came out in the papers, some TV reporters came in here and tried to get me on camera. Everyone was told to say I'm not here, if someone asks."

David nodded. His mouth was dry.

"In the back of my mind, I always wondered if you'd track me down," said Katy, tilting her head to the side to consider him. "I think I knew that one day you'd come walking back through that door." She paused. "Karen Allen. *Raiders*. Get it?"

"Yeah."

"Except I don't give interviews," she said. "I fucking hate reporters. They made my life a living hell."

"I'm not a reporter," he said. "I was an English major."

"That line usually works for you?"

"Actually, yes."

She gave him a once-over; shoes to his ruffly hair. "Where ya been, anyway? Where have you been hiding, David Neff? You write the best true crime book since *In Cold Blood* and then you disappear, pull a Dave Chappelle."

"Grieving."

"She was somethin' else, huh?"

He nodded. "She was."

"Okay, I'll talk to you if you want. But not here, okay? Come by my place tomorrow night. Six o'clock. Pick me up. Take me out to a nice dinner, maybe the Diamond Grille or something. You can afford it, right?"

Katy swiveled back on her feet, chasing a stray strand of red red hair away from her eyes. *Can anyone wear that much black eyeliner and not be goth?* he wondered.

"You ever get that feeling when you meet someone that your life is about to take a strange detour that maybe you'd be better off avoiding?"

He nodded again. "Couple times."

"Yeah," she said. "I bet." Katy reached behind David and pulled a book from the shelf. As she brushed by, he felt the whisper of her body. He smelled the lilac on her neck. These things should be making him feel light-headed and jittery, but he felt hardly anything. The meds were keeping this moment, this first real moment in four years, in check.

She grabbed the Bic blue out of his hand and began writing in the book. A moment later, she handed it to him.

"My cell phone and address," she said. "Call if you're going to be late. I mean it. I fucking hate waiting. For *anybody*. If you're late, I'm going to go to the movies with my toolbox fiancé. We'll go see something really crummy, too."

He stood there for a moment, just looking at her looking back at him.

"What?" she asked.

"Nothing," he said. "You're just not what I expected." He started toward the checkout. He couldn't help a half-smile from forming. There it went. It was a particular smile he'd forgotten, one he hadn't used in a long time.

"And fucking don't beat off to my Facebook pictures when you get home," said Katy from behind him, loud enough for the woman flipping through *Better Homes* at the magazine rack to glance over at him as he walked by.

Tanner was asleep by the time he got home. He paid Michelle and walked her to the door. Then he slipped back to his office, closed and locked the door, and did indeed spend the next twenty minutes jerking off to the Facebook pictures of his latest subject. When he was done, he felt spent and weird. But not guilty. Not even a little bit.

HIS SHERLOCK RUFFIAN

Once Elizabeth committed to the idea of getting married, a sucker's bet if there ever was one, she became enchanted by all the little ways she could gain control over the chaos of wedding planning. She saw the logistics of hosting a large party on their humble budget as a worthy challenge. There was not a cake-maker or caterer in all of Akron that she did not work over to some extent, no priest or minister she did not haggle with until their jaunty demeanors were frayed. One DJ, whom she instructed to meet her at a Wendy's in Cuyahoga Falls so they weren't on his home turf, was so insulted at her initial offering and rigid song list that he stood up and left without saying a word, leaving behind a tall Frosty and most of a cheeseburger. But what she put together out of five thousand dollars and persistence was more than either of them had imagined.

The ceremony was held at a Unitarian Universalist church in North Hill, on November 20, 2004. David arrived early, alone, in a slim tux, hoping to find a quiet place where he could review his vows. He started, for only a second, at the sight of smoke billowing from behind the podium. The air reeked of pot. But this was not weed. At least not that weed.

"Mom?" His mother's head popped up from behind the podium. She was a beautiful woman. Dark, raven hair. High cheekbones. Black-as-coal eyes. When she saw him, she stood quickly, the burning knot of wrapped leaves like a thick cigar in her left hand. "Hi, Davey."

"Sage?"

"I'm smudging the church," she said.

He nodded. She had done this for his high school graduation, too. Lynn Chambers, née Freemantle, was a reformed hippie with a ten-year sobriety token in her purse and the serenity prayer on a laminated square she kept in her shoe. She had learned sage-smudging at the annual AA Founders' Day powwow in Akron some years back.

"Come here," she said.

"Ah. I don't want to smell like weed."

"It doesn't smell like weed. Don't be a baby. Come here."

David walked to her. She placed a hand on his shoulder and waved the other, which held the smoldering sage, around his head. "Anything not here for the highest and best good, be gone," she said. "You are not welcome. You are not wanted."

And there really was something, a gentle shift in the air, he thought. But perhaps that was just his imagination.

His heart was conflicted about his mother. The booze and the drugs had possessed her when he was young, spirited her away, left him to mature with his father and an abusive stepmother. But there had been moments of such wonder during sober lulls. Trips to museums and symphonies and cheesy horror movies. Sometimes she had even fought for him—once she had kidnapped him from his grandmother's front yard while he played, some misguided attempt to regain custody. For all the drama she invited into his life, he loved her fiercely and did not care to understand or even to ask himself why.

"Thanks, Mom."

She kissed him lightly on the cheek and then walked down the aisle, waving the burning sage in the air, trailing a veil of smoke behind her.

By two o'clock, the church had filled; a hundred people, nearly all David's friends and relatives. Elizabeth's aunt was there, sitting with some of Elizabeth's high school chums. Some Red Hats, too. But her parents were not invited.

David stood at the front, on a riser of spotty red carpeting, next to his best man, Wally, whom he'd known since grade school but seldom saw much of anymore, and the minister, a plump woman in a flower-print gown. The congregation rose on some cue David had missed and suddenly Chip, a raggedy-haired man he'd met at summer camp ten years ago, was playing the "Imperial March" from *The Empire Strikes Back* on a synth he'd set up in the corner. Elizabeth stepped through the doors. As soon as Chip saw her, he dutifully switched to "Here Comes the Bride." The joke wasn't funny anymore, because the woman in that dress was not simply radiant or fetching, as those who were there would later claim; she was not glamorous or even lovely, as his father would tell him at her funeral—the woman in that dress was magical, and in an instant every last person in that little room knew and understood this, and more than a couple were moved beyond admiration into fear.

The dress was secondhand, from Once Upon a Bride. It was plain, straight, and had no train. It wasn't even white, really, but eggshell. But it fit as if it had been designed for her by a third-generation dressmaker at the end of a long career. The faux-satin fabric lay upon her form like a suggestion of a dress, slipping over her skinny tomboy hips, down her long slender legs. It slung around her breasts in a way that suggested the gentle firmness David knew, and wrapped around her freckled shoulders in thin strips of ribbon. Her hair, that wispy red hair he so loved to trace his fingers through, that hair was twisted up in a windy-do that revealed her milky-pale neck, her tiny ears. She wore no makeup. Her cheeks blushed with wonderful insecurity, her eyes sparkled in the flashes of ten disposable cameras as she walked, alone, to David.

He took her hand as she came to him and when she clasped to him he could feel her shaking. She felt like living lightning.

When it came time for his vows, he pulled the crinkled paper from his pocket with a shaky hand.

"I don't know why I love you but I do," he said, looking at her, at her eyes. "When I saw you that first day of classes it was like I had been waiting all my life just to meet you. It was like I finally understood my purpose. I will spend the rest of my life protecting you, Elizabeth, protecting you from all the randomness you see in the world, against all those probabilities. I swear I will never let anything happen to you or to us. Not as long as I'm alive."

"David," she said. "I've wondered a lot about whether I love you, because I never thought I could really truly love anyone. What they don't tell you is that love is faith and, well, faith is unpredictable. It has its own rules that I don't understand. I do love you, David. I know I do. I love you because in spite of the odds against any real happiness in this world, I believe we can be happy. You made me believe. Because you made me happy."

———

Besides the ill timing of a furry convention on the other side of the Holiday Inn Express off I-77 in Canton, the reception was a fine party. There was plenty of prime rib and chicken cordon bleu and a cookie cake and an open bar with middle-shelf liquor both dark and clear. By sundown David was buzzing on wine. He watched a line of nervous young men joking to each other as they awaited a turn with the bride for the dollar dance.

"I'm happy for you," someone said, from just behind him.

David turned to find his uncle Ira, an older man with wispy white hair and a long face. "Thank you."

"I got you a little something, kiddo," he said, handing David an unwrapped book.

It was a thin moleskin, filled with patient lines of thin-lettered hand-writing.

"When I was young, I was in love with words. Copied down my fa-vorite bits. Poetry, mostly," Ira said, his voice a powerful wind of whiskey. "Lots of Williams in there. He uncovered the rhythm of life, the balance of it. How reality is understood through imagery. The forms behind things. The light and the darkness there. If you're going to be a writer, you have to know this man."

David smiled, though he was unsure what exactly his uncle was try-ing to say.

He thumbed through it as Ira walked away, reading snippets about plums and red wheelbarrows. He waved a thanks at the old man, but Uncle Ira was already lost in some low conversation with David's mother across the dance floor. So he tucked it inside his tux and waited for his turn to dance with his wife again. He wondered if they might have kids one day and, if so, what they would look like. He thought of growing old with her, what sort of adventure that might be. He thought of all the va-cations and long Sundays he had to look forward to and felt the warmth around him, the warmth of the wine and the friends and the immediacy of the moment and all the promises of the future.

—▣—

He hadn't spoken to Jason Parker in several months, even though David kept the young man on salary. He thought of Jason as his "Sherlock ruf-fian." He was to David as the local beggar kids had been to Sherlock

Holmes: a source of unbiased information, a trusted ally, a proxy when needed. A writer's life, even the life of a writer in retirement, requires a couple close associates. When he needed someone to run to the drugstore to refill his psych meds, he called Jason, who didn't judge and wouldn't gossip. When he needed weed, he called Jason, who had friends who grew that sort of thing. Jason read and answered the emails that came in through the website and politely declined requests for interviews with David. Twice a week he picked the mail up from the post office and sorted through it, pitching everything David didn't need to know about. Sometimes threatening letters came in the mail and David would ask Jason to have his people look into it. Sometimes that meant background checks, which he was good at, and occasionally that meant showing up at the letter-writer's door late at night, which he was great at.

Sherlock ruffians are hard to come by. David had met his at a Black Keys concert at the Beachland Ballroom in Cleveland. It was his first journey out since the accident. He had wanted to clear his head, fill it up with music. Halfway through their set, a rode-hard hipster had tried to pick a fight with him, but then some Herculean blond-haired man had stepped between them and pulled David out the back door. "Bad press, man, punching a douchebag in a bar," the man had said. "I'd hate to have my sister see that on the news. She's a big fan." He had walked David back to his car and had handed him a business card (it read: *Jason Parker: Cowboy, Astronaut*). The next day, David mailed him a signed copy of his book for his sister. She wrote back. In her letter, she talked about her brother, who had moved in with her after her MS progressed. She casually mentioned he needed a job. David hired him immediately, dispatching him on errands at times created just to give him something to do. And when Jason's sister died a year later, David paid for the funeral.

The morning after he met Katy, David called Jason.

"Hiya, boss," said Jason. "What can I do you for?"

"Met a girl last night said she was my friend on Facebook."

"Ahuh."

"Are you using my Facebook to pick up girls?"

"Fuck, man. I didn't mean to do anything wrong. Look, they know I'm your assistant and not, you know, *you*, before I hook up with them. And it's not like it happens every day. It's a very rare thing. Like ten times I did it or something."

"I'm not mad," said David, though, to tell the truth, he was, a little.

His intern was using David's profile to mostly promote his dick and not the book. But why not? What was David doing with either his dick or his book these days?

"I'd be mad. It's a really shitty thing to do," said Jason.

"And you let them know you're you right away?"

"Oh, yeah. Right away. Right off the . . . whatever. You know, from the first email they know. Then, sometimes, they want to talk about what you're really like and because I know you they think I know what you're like so we start talking. I never tell them anything important, of course. Then after a couple more emails I'm usually like, 'Just come over and have a beer,' and sometimes they do."

"Do you remember a girl named Katy?"

"Fuck, yeah, I do. Redhead. Kinda goth. Or maybe new wave synth. She wants your junk, bad. I didn't get with her, though."

"Did she ever say anything weird? Anything about being on the news or anything?"

"Uh, just that the police wanted to talk to her father and he told them to fuck off. He's a contractor. A big redneck. Why you so interested? Should I get in touch and arrange something?"

"No," said David. "Actually, you should probably just let me work the site again. This is the kind of thing blogs—or, God help me, Gawker—would love to blow out of proportion if they got wind of your game."

"Coolio," said Jason, though David could tell he'd hurt the young man's feelings. "Gotta warn you about something, though."

"What's that?"

"Not all of the emails that come in are positive."

"It's okay. I'm used to bad reviews."

"Nah, man. Dark stuff. Especially lately. I think this one woman who is a witch or Wiccan or whatthefuck put a spell on you. Said she sent a demon after you. Oh, and you get gay stuff, too. A lot of English professors would like to polish off your knob. I get rid of that shit. Delete. Delete. Delete."

"Thanks, Jason."

"You got it. Anything else I can get for you?"

"Not right now. But soon enough, I think."

———

The detective bureau of the Akron Police Department was located within the crowded confines of the municipal building on High Street, a boxy brown office tower that appeared claustrophobic even on the outside. The bureau occupied the back corner of the sixth floor. It was painted a nauseating orange and beige that for some reason reminded David of corned beef.

"I'm here to see Detective Sackett," he said to the woman seated at the desk below the orange-as-a-plastic-tangerine counter.

"Take a seat," she replied, without looking up.

Detective Tom Sackett, David had learned, was the only police officer assigned to the Joseph Howard King homicide. A rookie. The youngest detective on the force. Obviously, he was someone the department could dump the case onto and still pretend they were doing something. Sackett was also the spokesperson for the case. Both the communications director for the Akron PD and the chief had passed the buck to young Sackett when David had phoned them earlier in the day. "Talk to Sackett," Chief Gareau, who had also been promoted since the original *Beacon* articles ran, had said. "He's your man. That's his case. Knows it better than any of us."

Doubtful, David thought.

When he got Sackett on the horn, the detective had sounded really eager to talk. And that was a plus. If he couldn't get any comment from the chief, at least he could get a lot of comment from the detective, even if it did turn out to be a bunch of Keystone Kops hyperbole. That had potential for good characterization.

Sackett had said he was available right away, if David wanted. So he had called Michelle, who readily agreed to another last-minute afternoon of babysitting—she was saving up for some kind of phone called an Android and a couple more shifts would put her over the top. Tanner had thrown a conniption when she arrived, one of those five-alarm screamers where his face turned blue and the world waited for him to breathe. It was David's fault, of course. He spent so much time with the boy, even these brief departures were wearing on his son, making the boy lethargic and slightly paranoid. Eventually, though, he had brokered a truce with Tanner in which he promised to build him a fort out of couch pillows and blankets if he would stop screaming. He had even told Michelle that Tanner could eat supper in there if he wanted—which he did. *Duh.*

A steel door beside David opened and Detective Sackett stepped out. He was dressed in a plain blue polo shirt tucked into blue jeans. On his left hip rested his sidearm, a weapon out of place on his boyish body, and his badge. On the other hip, his walkie-talkie and cell phone. If he was older than David, it wasn't by much. He didn't smile when he saw David, but David had a hunch he wanted to and only chose to remain stoic because he thought that was a part of his job that he wanted to experience.

"Mr. Neff?" he asked.

David stuck out his hand, which Sackett accepted. "David," he said.

Sackett nodded and introduced himself to the writer. "Nice bag," he said, motioning toward the large leather satchel slung over David's shoulder. It was wrinkled, beat-up, and a little dirty. "It's seen some action."

In fact, it had saved his life on one occasion, but that was a story for another day. Its weight was a comfort to him, like having his father's hand on his shoulder.

"Follow me," Sackett said, ushering David into the detective bureau.

Down a long, windowless, beige, and undecorated hallway, through a dingy wooden door, was the bureau: a square brown and orange container of a room with four empty desks piled high with paperwork and framed pictures of family. This room smelled of gun grease and old hot dogs. There were no windows.

Sackett sank into the chair beside a desk less cluttered than the others. Two pictures were tacked to a corkboard above his head. One, a picture of a slender woman with dark hair sitting with a pigtailed baby girl on a city park swing: the detective's wife and daughter, David assumed. The other, a school picture, slightly outdated, of a redhead beauty with soft cheeks and a galaxy of freckles tracing the bridge of her nose like a half mask. Katy, he thought. She looked about eleven, but he could see her adult self in the sharp set of her jaw and the Cheshire grin that twisted first up, and then down at the ends. Obviously, the detective believed she was a vital clue to the identity of the Man from Primrose Lane.

"So . . ." David began, digging into his bag and pulling out a reporter's notepad and a blue Bic.

"Wait up a second," said Sackett. "I just want to say that I've never done this before, spoken to a reporter or writer or whatever. Normally they don't let us do this. I'm open to sharing information with you because I think our leads have dried up and maybe getting some stuff out in the papers might generate something new. But there's some things I obviously can't talk about."

"Sure."

"And I haven't read your book, either. I hope you don't take offense. I'm not much of a reader. But my wife read your book when it came out and she loved it, so I'm sort of doing this for her. Against my better judgment."

"Okay."

"Also, I did some background on you. Asked around. Talked to the Medina County Sheriff's Department, who didn't have the best things to say about what you do."

"They wouldn't," said David. "They executed the wrong guy when they executed Ronil Brune."

"And now Ohio doesn't have capital punishment and so when we catch the real bad guys these days, we can't sentence them to death. Because of your book."

The Serial Killer's Protégé had set off a chain of events that had ultimately led to the overturning of capital punishment in the state. It was a fact that he actually took great pride in. "You're still calling him Joseph Howard King?" he asked, pressing on.

"I don't know what else to call him until we find his real name."

"Some people call him the Man from Primrose Lane."

"Well, I always called him the Man with a Thousand Mittens," said Sackett. "But what I wanted to tell you was, while those sheriff's deputies kind of despise you for what you did, they also have a great deal of respect for you, at least the lieutenant out there. He told me you should have been a detective instead of a reporter. He said you would have been a good one. That's why I'm talking to you."

David was surprised by this sentiment. Since the publication of *The Serial Killer's Protégé*, he had specifically avoided driving through Medina County, afraid of being pulled over for a burned-out taillight and winding up in some small-town gulag for the rest of his life. One retired deputy who had invested a lot of time in putting Brune away had written him a letter in which he had called David a "media whore" and promised to "rearrange" David's facial features if he ever saw him in town.

"So what do you want to know?" asked Sackett.

"Well, first of all, you gotta tell me why you call him the Man with a

Thousand Mittens," he said. "Then tell me about the day you found the body."

Sackett reached into his desk and pulled a cigarette from a pack of Camels. He lit it, took a long drag, and expelled the noxious smoke into the air, where it hovered, undisturbed, at the ceiling. He pointed to David's shirt pocket, where his traveled pack of Marlboros peeked out. "You can smoke, too, if you want," he said. "Promise not to give you a ticket."

It would take too long to explain his mental cigarette habit, so David just shook his head.

"All right," Sackett said. "Here goes."

For the next half hour, Sackett recounted his discovery of the dead body inside the house on Primrose Lane, how he had found hundreds of mittens in the closet, how he'd discovered the trail of blood leading to the blender, how the maggots sounded as they plopped out of the hole in the dead man's chest, how Billy Beachum had bolted in the kitchen. As he talked, he kept a steady chain of coffin nails in the corner of his mouth, such that, by the time he had finished, the room was a cloud and David's clothes were forever infused with the essence of cheap tobacco. Finally, Sackett flipped a switch on the wall and a fan turned on somewhere in the bowels of the building, sucking the fumes into ceiling vents, slowly clearing the air and replacing it with that odd fragrance of boiled hot dogs. David's notebook was half full of his blue-inked shorthand, a mishmash of cursive, print, and hieroglyphics. This, of course, was only a start and, David suspected, information that was no longer as relevant as it must have seemed to Sackett four years ago, in 2008.

"I've got a bazillion questions for you," said David.

"Shoot."

"What was Beachum delivering that day?" he asked.

"Some incidentals," said Sackett. "And a Geiger counter."

"A Geiger counter?"

"Yes."

"For what? Was anything radioactive?"

Sackett shook his head. "We had a team from Akron U come check it out. They didn't find anything unusual."

"It's a strange request, though."

"Yeah," said Sackett. "The guy made a lot of strange requests. Was there some method to it, some plan? Or was it just a guy going crazy from isolation? Nobody knows because nobody knew him, not really."

"Except the guy who killed him."

"Maybe it was just a robbery gone wrong," said Sackett.

David laughed. "But the fingers. Cutting off the man's fingers and turning them into pulp in the blender. That seems a little personal."

The detective leaned back and considered the writer for a long moment. "I hope I can trust you," he said. "We're building a relationship here. I'll give you some things, like I said, because we're in a corner with this one. But I got to know I can trust you."

"Do you want to talk off the record?"

Sackett nodded.

David set down his notebook. "Off the record," he said.

Sackett leaned forward and lowered his voice. "There's a reason why I'm the only one still on this case," he said. "The coroner is about to revise her ruling."

"To what?" asked David.

"Officially, it will be ruled 'unknown.' But we believe it was something like a suicide, in the end," he said. "The bullet missed the man's heart. Clean shot. Missed every major artery, bone, and organ. He would've lived if he'd called for help or walked to a neighbor's house. It was the loss of blood from his fingers that actually killed him. He just sat there and bled to death, waited to die. The coroner's forensic team determined that the man did not put up much of a struggle when his fingers were removed. The lacerations were smooth and definitely perimortem—that means they were cut off before he was dead. We think he cut off his own fingers. First with a knife. Then with a cigar cutter, one of those little guillotines, when there were not enough fingers left to hold the knife steady. He might have put the cigar cutter between his knees, put his remaining fingers in the holes, and squeezed it closed that way. Then he fed them into the blender, probably after whoever shot him left. That's just conjecture, of course. But we have the knife and bloodied cigar cutter and no gun."

"Shit," said David, rubbing his chin as he processed this information. "He was hiding his identity. He knew that if he went to the hospital, they'd find out who he really was. So he got rid of his prints. But what about his palms?"

"Sliced with the knife. We got a partial from one. But not enough to feed into IAFIS or anything."

"Is it true the house was cleaned of fingerprints?"

"As far as we can tell, Joseph Howard King wore those mittens every minute of the day. The feds spent a week in there. Spent a whole week and all they came up with were two latent prints. One on the back of the headboard of the man's bed. The other was inside the lip of the toilet's reservoir tank. They are from two separate individuals, we're sure. But we don't have anything to compare them with, so we don't know if either one is from our man or if they're prints from movers and plumbers."

"Weird."

"This man didn't ever want to be found," said Sackett. "What was he so afraid of? What was he so afraid of that he decided it was better to die than to reveal his identity? That's what I'm trying to figure out. There are few clues to go on. And now that it's no longer a straight-up homicide, the department doesn't really want to spend more of its resources tracking down far-flung leads. The FBI has lost interest. Well, that's not entirely true. There is a retired agent named Larkey. He worked on a number of missing person cases before he left the bureau. He's consulting on this case."

"What's your relationship with the FBI?"

"Shaky on a good day. Hard to say if they've shared everything they know about our guy. Bunch of overpaid accountants playing cop. A couple good ones, but they don't give those guys much of a leash anymore. That's all off the record, of course. On the record again, I would say that the Akron Police Department welcomes the FBI's help and cooperation."

"And there's no decent picture of this guy, huh?" asked David. "Other than the blurry photos they used in the paper?"

Sackett raised a finger and spun in his chair. He rifled through the desk behind him for a minute before coming up with a glossy photograph, which he handed to the writer.

The first thing David noticed was that the photo had been digitally altered, cropped, and enlarged from its original size until the pixels stood out like little circles of color, like those impressionist paintings, like a Manet. In the foreground was a shoulder draped in maroon rayon. Behind the shoulder was the profile of an old man with a long face. His skin wrinkled and sagged on the side in deep dark creases. His eyebrows were thick caterpillars, so white they were nearly iridescent. He stared ahead with a scowl set upon his face. Again, David was reminded of his uncle Ira.

"That's my little brother," said Sackett. "That guy behind him is the Man with a Thousand Mittens, Joseph Howard King, or whoever you want to call him in your book."

"You took this?"

Sackett nodded. "Only known picture of him," he said.

"That's a hell of a coincidence," David replied.

The detective took the photograph back. "Good detectives don't believe in coincidences," he said. "And I didn't think writers did, either."

David suddenly realized that Sackett was staring at him in a way that he didn't like, a deep stare that seemed to reach into his mind through his pupils, rooting around in there like a probe. "What?"

"Nothing."

"Is something wrong?"

"Nah," he said. "Well, I mean, you didn't know him, did you?"

"What do you mean?"

"It looked like you recognized him when you looked at that photo."

"You're good," said David, with a sense of unease. He felt their friendly connection starting to fade like an FM station around the first bend of Appalachian foothills. Sackett hadn't liked David's reaction to the photo. Not one bit. "He just looks like my great-uncle Ira. That's what I noticed. But, really, only as much as I look like Jim Carrey."

Sackett laughed. But the laugh sounded canned. So David changed the subject, quickly.

"Tell me about Katy Keenan," he said. "And this notebook you found in the house."

But the detective looked at the clock in the corner, which read a quarter past four. In the end it always comes down to time.

"We'll have to talk about that next time," said Sackett. "I got a few reports to file before five. Give me a call later in the week and we'll set something up."

"Thank you for your time," said David.

"Welcome."

He stood up but then the detective spoke again.

"David? What about the other photo? The one above my desk. Do you recognize the girl in that picture?"

"Sure," he said. "It's Katy Keenan."

"No, it isn't," said Sackett. "It's Elaine O'Donnell."

David recoiled. Because Elizabeth had always been on the outs with her parents since he'd known her, he had never seen pictures of her grade school years, never looked over her shoulder while she went through family albums. He had that one photo of her as a young girl, curled up on the couch, and then nothing until the ones he'd taken himself, while they were in college. But yes. That's what his wife—and her twin sister— surely would have looked like at ten years old. He didn't know what to say. "You're right," he managed.

"I've been working on her cold case for years. It's far outside my jurisdiction, so I do it in my spare time. It was such a big case when we were kids, remember? I was always drawn to it, even back then. A weird hobby. Anyway, they do look alike, don't they? Elaine and Katy."

"At that age, they certainly did." Now that he had been confronted with the resemblance for the second time, he was left wondering what he was truly looking for in Katy. The implications were unsettling.

Sackett nodded. "Don't fuck me over for helping you," he said.

David didn't say anything but waved goodbye instead. He knew better than to make promises this early in a story. Besides, he had to get ready. For the first time in many years, he was going on a date.

TANNER'S HOBBY

The honeymoon almost destroyed their marriage. The cruise was a present from Elizabeth's aunt, Peggy, a gift that David suspected her estranged parents had secretly contributed to. A week in the Caribbean; Jamaica, Belize, someplace called Charlotte Amalie. It was a week after their wedding, a month after they graduated from Kent State. She had just gotten a job working the circulation desk at the Kent Free Library; he'd moved from the community paper to an alternative weekly in Cleveland called the *Independent*. It should have been a nice respite before a new life. Instead it was hell, from the moment they boarded the *Carnival Elation* until Elizabeth stepped onto the aft deck three days into the journey, intending to commit suicide.

You had to call it a squall, a storm like this. It beat at the monstrous shiny-white ship as they boarded, rocking the gangway as they inched along. By the time they were halfway up the ramp, Elizabeth was rubbing at a migraine behind her temples. By the time they reached the top, David had ralphed his breakfast over the side, into the gulf.

"We can take a nap in our room," he said, rubbing Elizabeth's back as they waited to board. "It'll be okay."

Though they were large for cruise-industry standards, David found their quarters to be smothering. They couldn't take a Tums or a Tylenol because their luggage wouldn't be delivered for another hour, so they lay in the dark above the covers on the double bed and held each other. Outside, the squall took hold of the boat, pitching it slowly to one side and then the other. At times, the good ship leaned so far that David was sure it was going to flip like the *Poseidon*. He could feel the walls lean in on him and thought of his grandfather's claims that the walls of the submarine in which he served in WWII had bent inward during emergency dives as the pressure outside grew and grew, reminding everyone that nature, in the end, would eat them up, would swallow them whole.

Somewhere in the dark, he found sleep. He awoke in the dark, and he was alone.

"Elizabeth?"

He sat up and touched his eyelids as they opened and closed. They were open but he couldn't see the faintest trace of light.

"Elizabeth?"

He reached into the darkness but could not be sure his arms were even there. Slowly he walked forward, probing ahead of him. His left hand hit the door to the shower, stubbing his index finger. He felt around for a switch but could not find one. The ship tilted to port and he clunked his right knee against what must have been a chair pushed under a table. He rubbed at the bruise forming there and then collided with the far wall with a weak thud that smarted his nose. There, he felt something. A thin bump in the wall.

The light clicked on from above like the voice of God, full and brilliant and blinding. He looked around. No Elizabeth. What time was it? He felt as if he'd slept for days. There were no clocks in here.

David opened the door and peeked out. To his right, the hall seemed to stretch forever, dozens of identical doors on either side painted a dull, calming blue. To the left, more of the same. Still no luggage. He ducked back in for his card key, and set out to find his wife.

A map posted in the elevator promised this was the best route to the main floor, where the buffet and pool were located. Alarm set in as soon as the doors opened. The first thing he noticed was that it was dark on the other side of the windows that lined the cafeteria. Night had come, bringing with it rolling clouds illuminated by long streaks of lightning breaking like tree branches, above an angry sea. He must have slept for eight hours, at least. The second thing he noticed was that the buffet area was empty. No one was eating. No one was serving. He had not seen a single person since he'd left their room. Had he slept through an evacuation? Was he on a ghost ship?

A siren sounded from hidden speakers, a trilling noise. "Ladies and gentlemen," said a soothing male voice, "this is your captain speaking. The time is now nine-thirty. The Newlywed Game will begin in the auditorium momentarily. The casino has opened and there will be a Texas Hold'em tournament commencing at ten. Bingo at ten-thirty in the Blue Room. Also, there is a complimentary sushi bar in the library. It's still choppy outside but radar shows clear skies in our future. Hang tight and we'll have you through this soon. Thank you for riding *Elation*."

David let his instincts guide him toward the center of the ship. He became aware of a growing din of conversation that increased as he rounded a corner and found himself in the heart of the vessel. The middle of the *Elation* was a hollow canyon lined with retail shops and bars. A few hundred people milled about, taking pictures or buying drinks. On a hunch, David made his way to the library. Sitting inside, at a table facing the storm, was Elizabeth.

She did not look up as he sat down. In her lap was a plate of sushi. She shook her head.

"I can't do this," she said.

He felt a squeeze in his chest. "It's only been a week," he said. "Marriage is supposed to feel weird at first. Am I smothering you? Should I not be so affectionate? I'm still learning. I'm sorry if I—"

Elizabeth turned to her husband. She gave him a quizzical look. Then she smiled and held up the chopsticks in her left hand. "I can't do this," she said. "I've never used chopsticks in my life and they don't give you forks here like they do at the Evergreen Buffet. I asked every bartender and employee I could find and no one has a fork."

"Here," he said, taking the sticks. He twisted them around in his right hand, eventually arranging them into a pincer. He kept the bottom stick taut and used his other fingers to move the top stick as she watched. "Just takes some practice."

She took the chopsticks back and allowed him to help her place them correctly in her hand. With great care, she managed to lift a piece of sushi into her mouth. This small victory seemed to appease her immediately.

"No big deal," he said.

"No big deal," she agreed.

Three days into the cruise they ventured to the buffet and then to the main deck, bathed now in a thick blanket of sunshine, the planks burning their feet in a pleasant way. That evening they waited for the sun to set on a quiet balcony at the rear of the ship, watching the star sink slowly into the sea, where it became liquid fire. Starlight from eighty-eight constellations granted the sea a silvery outline that churned in the wake of the *Elation* as it made haste for Belize. The sound of the propellers was a low drone that David felt in his thighs. It was the sound of oblivion and it called Elizabeth's name.

David said he felt like a drink and led her directly to the closest lounge, a squat room filled by a glittering white grand piano surrounded by a waist-high bar and twenty leather stools. A young man with an Austrian accent and twisty yellow hair sat at the bench, playing "Piano Man" as if he enjoyed it. David and Elizabeth sat a few seats down from a bachelorette party and ordered double mai tais.

Several glossy music books littered the bar top and the Austrian motioned to them when he finished.

Elizabeth thumbed through a stack of songbooks. "Ugh. This is all junk. 'Desperado'? 'Tiny Dancer'?"

"Oooh! Oooh!" shouted a blond bachelorette. "This one!" Her friends laughed loudly and dared him to play their most favorite song.

The Austrian winked and confidently began a genuinely decent version of "Hey There Delilah," a song David had detested until just then.

"Ah," said Elizabeth. She yanked a white binder from beneath a stack of bound sheet music. A single word was written on the cover in black Sharpie: *Rachmaninoff.* "Yes. Here we go." Inside was a xeroxed copy of Rachmaninoff's Concerto No. 3.

To David, whose entire knowledge of sheet music was drawn from his experience playing the cornet in middle school, the concerto looked more like an abstract painting of mixed symbols than any coherent piece of music. The measures were loaded with sixteenth notes and key changes, filled with more sharps and staccatos than he could count. His head hurt just looking at it. Anyone who would choose to play Billy Joel and the Eagles, he realized, would most likely not have the practice, skill, or temperament to make it past the first page.

"He could use an ego check," she said.

"Come on. Don't be mean."

"I'm not being mean. I'm being real. They think he's brilliant. But I don't think he's played anything other than shitty rock in years. Probably ever."

David took another sip of his mai tai, rested his elbows on the bar, and fished around in his ice with the little umbrella while he waited for this lesson to play out.

The Austrian finished and before the blonde could suggest something by John Mayer, Elizabeth handed the man the binder.

He took it from Elizabeth without looking at her. His eyes were focused on the plain white binder. At first his expression remained unreadable. But David noticed a growing recognition roll over his eyes, followed by some emotion between longing and erotic pleasure.

"Thank you," said the Austrian. He wiped a film of dust from the cover, then opened the binder and placed it on the piano.

The bachelorettes had grown quiet. They watched him with concern.

The Austrian just sat there, staring at the first page.

Elizabeth laughed behind her hand.

David waited.

The Austrian breathed. In. Out.

He was waiting for the music to take him. And then it did.

His fingers crashed upon the keys and were lost, there, in a blur of motion and noise; the clunk of flesh on wood converted to the vibration of thin strings singing the most beautiful music. It was the sound of creation, of inspiration, of spirit let loose after a long imprisonment. It was the sound David heard, sometimes, as he drifted off to sleep thinking about the structure of an article. It was the sound of human accomplishment, the sound of a voice speaking over the din of a crowd. It was the sound of a child greeting a parent at the door. It was also the sound of a lover's gentle whisper.

Finally, the Austrian finished.

For a moment no one moved.

And then Elizabeth stood and walked out of the room. The crowd parted to let her through. The Austrian sat quite still, staring at the book of music.

"I'm done," he said.

He meant forever.

In Belize, the Austrian disembarked and was never heard from again.

Elizabeth did not return to their room. She wandered around the ship for the better part of an hour, aimless, past the tucked-away cigar lounge, past the crew's cabin, where a number of Brazilian women played table tennis on an old coffee table, past a massive laundry, until she found herself on a little deck at the very back of the boat that passengers were probably never supposed to find. The deck was empty. For the first time since she had boarded the *Elation*, there was no sign of human life, save for a slim bikini top slung over the back of one wooden deck chair. She stepped toward the railing.

Ever since the day Elaine was taken, Elizabeth had resigned herself to the cold random reality of the world, in fact had embraced this view as a way of surviving. In this world, there was no room for petty optimism. And maybe that was all right, she had thought. Maybe instead of hope, she could orientate her life using probability.

Unlike her twin sister, who had painted a still life of bananas at the age of six that could have hung in a SoHo gallery and been mistaken for an early Frida Kahlo, Elizabeth had always excelled in math, delighting in the way complex numbers fit together like the pieces of a jigsaw puzzle whose picture solved for x. By the time *she* was six, she'd recognized the formula of the Rubik's Cube, and had taught herself how to fix it blindfolded if someone told her how many times they had twisted it. More than anything else, she loved probability. She loved watching shows like *Deal or No Deal* and knowing that half of America was watching with anxiety when Howie Mandel asked the participants if they would like to switch their case for the last one held by the model onstage, when all along she knew and understood mathematically why there was a higher probability that the larger prize would be in the model's hands and that the participant's best bet was always to switch out. In college, she had taken David to Atlantic City, where there were still a couple casinos that played two-deck blackjack, and taught him the basics of counting cards. She applied this pleasure to her day-to-day routine. Before making a run to the grocery store, she charted out, in her mind, the probability of an accident, based on the time of day (how many people would be on the road? was it a weekend? had school just let out?

was there a local sports game or concert?), the condition of the road (had it just rained or snowed? was there construction in the area?), and the reliability of her vehicle (had David taken the Sundance and left the old Cavalier? when was the last tune-up? how old were the tires?). Then she would consider the necessity of taking such risk (can I do without peanut butter until the weekly trip to Giant Eagle? will the sauce still be palatable without the sherry?). Finally, she would weigh the probability of an accident against her need for the groceries. If that answer was somewhere south of an average person's daily risk of such an accident (which she had come to approximate, through newspapers and experience), then she would make the trip. She used similar formulas when buying a new car, trying a new restaurant, buying Christmas gifts for David, selecting a new song to download, applying for a job, etc., et al. And sure, you could say we all do this to some extent. But very few of us do it this precisely. In numbers, she found a slight advantage against the randomness of life. The Austrian was a bug, a worm, a flaw in her system of computation. What Elizabeth had heard in the piano bar was hope. And hope frightened her. Because hope suggested that the odds could be beaten. Hope suggested that the simple act of wanting might lead to safety and happiness. That, of course, was not acceptable. It would not compute. Because she had wanted Elaine to be alive and that's not what had happened.

The sea was black glass, shattered by the wake of the giant boat. On the horizon she saw another cruiser, destined for ports unknown, just globes of light at this distance. She listened to the churning of the propellers.

Three wooden posts ran horizontally across the open deck, providing a low railing. Elizabeth held on to the starboard wall and stepped onto the first rung.

She weighed the probability that anyone would see her (there were no cameras, no one above had the right angle to see where her body would connect with the ocean), the probability that if someone did see her, the boat could send a lifeboat in time (simple equation of velocity and mass of the cruise ship and reaction time of the captain divided by her willingness to drown). The odds were heavily in her favor.

Elaine's kidnapper had known about probability, too, hadn't he? He must have studied their movements for weeks, she had come to realize, learning their routines and waiting for that right moment when the odds of getting away with the crime were as high as mathematics would allow. How else could you explain it? There was always someone else in that park. Except for just then. How else could he have gotten away with it, if he hadn't planned it precisely? Of course, there had been a variable in the equation—the man in the Cadillac. Elizabeth had spent many sleepless nights as a child pondering who that man had been; how he had known about the abduction and why he had never come back to tell the police or her family what he knew.

She climbed onto the second rung.

This was inevitable, she thought. An equation with one solution, its first factor that man in the van who stole her sister. The only variable in that equation was time. But in this equation, time was not a constant. Time was the measure of her life as she waited and hoped for Elaine to come home, the time it took to accept this would never happen, the time it took to understand that her sister was dead, the time it took for her to love David, the time it took for her to realize he was really better off without her. Time was as long as she could hold on.

She stepped onto the top rail and leaned forward.

And then something seemingly random occurred.

"Elizabeth." A man's voice. From behind.

She turned and there in the doorway was an elderly man in a Panama hat.

"Elizabeth, come down," he said.

She shook her head defiantly.

"Elizabeth, come down," he said again. "Please."

"Why?" she asked. "What do you care?"

"Don't you recognize me?" he asked, taking off the hat. Underneath, his hair was thin and white. She imagined what he might look like with darker hair and a few less wrinkles and—and then yes, she did recognize him. His appearance here was no accident, but she could make no sense of it, either.

"You were there," she said at last. "*You* were the man in the Cadillac."

The old man held out his hand. "I'll tell you everything I know if you just come down from there."

Elizabeth took his hand and let him guide her back to the floor of the deck. They stared at each other in silence for ten seconds. Twenty, thirty. Finally, she smiled.

"It's so warm out here," she said. "Why in the world are you wearing mittens?"

───□───

He was in the bathroom, wiping off shaving cream and checking for nose hairs, when Tanner brought him the large ball bearing that was actually sort of a key.

On Tanner's third birthday, David's father had bought the boy Mouse Trap, the board game, the one where players build an elaborate trap that is set off by a chain reaction of tilting and twisting mechanisms triggered by a rolling ball. Tanner had taken it upon himself to improve upon the original design. Using Tinkertoys, a funnel, and cardboard tubes he'd fished out of the recycle bin, Tanner had extended the trap by several feet. One day David had come home and the trap had taken over the kitchen. Tanner placed a red plastic ball into an old wrapping paper tube and there was a pleasing low percussive sound as the ball rolled down the length of the tube and spit out the other end, into a funnel which he'd duct-taped to the dining room table, and then onto a stack of books the boy had tilted so that the ball was inclined to collide against the boot of the Mouse Trap game, where the rest played out as intended. It had taken David a moment to realize that the emotion he was feeling just then was fear, and another moment to figure out why. He had been frightened by the look in his son's eyes, that extreme focus that could only mean tunnel vision, obsession overriding physicality. He knew the expression well because it was the same one he made when he got locked into a piece of writing, a sort of vacant comatose stare that had unnerved Elizabeth so much she had made him write in the back bedroom when they had lived at the apartment in the Falls, just so she didn't have to see him like that. "Your zombie stare," she'd called it. Perhaps it was genetic. In the morning, he moved the Mouse Trap into Tanner's room. And little by little, Tanner improved upon it some more. The act of creating almost seemed to be driving the development of his mind, instead of vice versa. David even helped, when Tanner asked him to, or offered his input when Tanner ran out of fresh ideas. And now Tanner's room was one giant Mouse Trap, a machine that still was started by placing a ball in a tube—in this case a one-pound extra-large ball bearing David had found at a garage sale in Kenmore.

"Dad," said Tanner. "Let's do the Rube." The Rube, as in Rube Goldberg, the cartoonist who had once imagined such similar trifles for the newspapers of the early twentieth century. A framed copy of one cartoon hung above Tanner's dresser—David had found it online.

David led Tanner back to his room. These days it took the better part of an hour to reset the Mouse Trap and it was never, ever used for purposes of actually playing the game anymore. This was serious business. What it really was, was art, David had come to realize. Let the other kids make macaroni reindeer. This was what his kid did.

Scanning the room, David noticed his son had been tinkering with some improvements.

"What's it do?" he asked.

"It's a surprise," Tanner said.

Hesitantly, David lifted the ball bearing to the car track resting atop the dresser.

"One, two, three . . . go!" yelled Tanner.

David let go.

The ball bearing shot down the track, picking up enough speed to roll around a tall loop before coming down the far side, where it disappeared into a tunnel. A second later, it came out the other side and collided with the handle of a broom that had been placed upside down against the nightstand. The business end of the broom fell forward, yanking a string that wound through a small pulley. The string was attached to a Tinkertoy that was propping open a spring-loaded pint-sized baseball bat. The Tinkertoy was pulled away and the bat swung a little too hard against the "play" button of a stereo that Tanner had rigged to play one of his father's Jethro Tull CDs. "Aqualung" blared from the speakers as David watched the Tinkertoy rod continue a gravity-powered pendulum that brought it in contact with the lead domino in a methodically placed arrangement of brightly colored little bricks that, as they tumbled into each other, spelled out DAD. The final domino fell against another spring trap that released a plug in a bucket of sand. As the sand fell, the bucket rose in the air, lowering the shoe attached to it on the other side of yet another pulley. The shoe touched off another series of mundane but impressive devices that ultimately launched a stuffed cat across the room, where it fell through a basketball hoop and set off the original Mouse Trap endgame. Just before the trap lowered, though, Tanner reached down and pulled the mouse from underneath. David never questioned this habit—he understood his son well enough now to know that he would have felt genuinely guilty if anything he had constructed imprisoned something.

"That was spectacular, kiddo," he said, though he still felt a little unnerved. "Thanks," said Tanner. "It took all day."

"Your best yet. Can you reset it for Aunt Peggy?"

"Why are you leaving so much? Do you have a job again like Travis's dad?"

David turned his face sour. "It's just some writing. Some reporting like I used to do . . ."

". . . when Mom was around?" he finished.

"Yes."

"Was Mom pretty?"

"You know she was. I tell you all the time." Did his son sense, somehow, David's true intentions for the evening? On some level, yes, David thought he did. That the boy was protective of a mother he never knew was both touching and troubling in some way.

"Tell me how she was pretty."

"She was pretty like the sunbeams that dance through the windows in the morning."

"Aaaand?"

"And pretty as an angel's daydream."

"She was sooooo pretty . . ."

". . . that if you looked up 'pretty' in the dictionary, it would say . . ."

". . . Tanner's mom."

"That's right. That's exactly right."

"Can I make a confession?"

"Sure," said David. They were sitting in his Beetle, in the parking lot of the Diamond Grille. Katy had removed the cat ears. Her hair lay straight against her shoulders except for a few strands she had clipped around behind her head like some hippie tiara. She smelled like cheap shampoo and peanut butter. From the moment he had opened the door for her back at the apartment, she had been chewing at the nail of her left index finger. It was still at the corner of her mouth and he wondered, distantly, if she should be concerned about the amount of nail polish she surely must have ingested over the years. The first thing she'd done upon entering the car was turn his stereo to 91.3, the local independent music station. She'd sung along with an obscure Tori Amos song he'd never heard before. She wore a green dress over black stockings and a Ramones T-shirt. He knew she had never really listened to the Ramones. In spite of all this he found himself staring at her lips.

"I hate the Diamond Grille," she said. "Okay, not hate. Hate's a strong word. The steak was good, actually. But last time I was there I sort of tongued a state senator. A married state senator. Or he tongued me. Anyway, we tongued. And if we go in there, that's all I'm going to be thinking about and I'm afraid it might ruin the interview or whatever it is we're doing."

"So, Larry's, then?" he suggested.

She shrugged. "I don't know Larry's. But yeah. Anything but here."

Other than her appearance, Katy was nothing like Elizabeth. Completely opposite polarities, Katy was the positron to his dead wife's electron. No universe and no man could possibly withstand their combined forces. But both could be lovely on their own. Perhaps, he thought later, it was her differences that drew him in. Nothing about her reminded his heart of Elizabeth and so it didn't hurt him when they were together. And that was something new.

Twenty minutes later, they were seated at a booth inside Larry's, a small hardwood bar on Market known for its fried mushrooms and paninis. The owner decorated the place with around a hundred framed photos of customers wearing clown noses. David wanted to know what had started this tradition but had chosen not to ask because he didn't want to ruin the mystery. He had thought up his own explanation, that on the day the bar had opened, a clown had walked in after some Saturday afternoon birthday party and died of a coronary after eating a bowl of fried mushrooms and this was the owner's way of keeping the clown's ghost from haunting his bar.

"What's with the clown noses?" asked Katy, looking at a photograph of Don Plusquellic—Akron's mayor-for-life—wearing a Bozo nose, hanging on the wall to her right.

David shrugged. The waitress came with beer—Dortmunder for him, Stroh's for her—and then returned to the kitchen to check on the 'shrooms.

"Soooo," said Katy.

"So," he agreed.

"Don't you have a tape recorder or a notebook or something?"

"Nah. Whatever I don't remember, I just make up."

She smiled thinly.

"If I decide to use any of this, I'll call you up and get it on the record. I'm still fishing around on this. Not actively reporting yet."

"Sounds like a clever way to make me feel comfortable."

"You should have been a reporter."

"I could've," she said. "Ask away, Woodward."

"Did you know the Man from Primrose Lane? Ever met him?"

"Don't think so. But the detectives tell me I must have crossed paths with him a few times. Except . . . they showed me some of the man's biography or whatever on me. And there's a couple things in there that he couldn't have known. I mean, no way was he there. Like, for instance, there's details in there about a summer camp I went to out on Kelleys Island one summer. A 4-H thing. It was a small deal. Twenty kids. Five counselors. I know them all. I can tell you, he was not there. And there are details—what I ate, shit like that—from a vacation I took to Florida when I was eight. We stayed at my aunt's house on Perdido Key. It was the off-season. We were the only ones around. He could not have known that stuff. The detectives believe he followed me around my whole life, observing almost everything I did. I can't explain it, how he knows all that stuff, but I'm almost positive he wasn't following me. He couldn't have been. He doesn't even look familiar."

"What else did the detectives ask you?"

"They just wanted to know if I ever remembered seeing him. They showed me a photo of him. But he didn't look like anyone I remember. But maybe I did see him when I was really young. I don't know what I've forgotten, you know? But he's not someone who I saw enough of that I would recognize him. They even hypnotized me."

"Did that do anything?"

Katy pantomimed jerking off. The mushrooms arrived and she helped herself to the biggest, blowing away the heat with those cupid lips.

"Have you come up with any theories?"

"I've thought about it," she said. "A lot. It's weird thinking there was some stranger out there who knew everything about me. It's like I have no secrets with him. Like we shared some relationship I didn't choose. I think he must know the worst things I've ever done, the stuff I meant to keep to myself. Like, he probably even saw stuff like what I did with

Mr. Murphy behind the track utility shed when I was fourteen. And yet, I guess he was in love with me in spite of these things. Creepy. To the max. But theories? The best I can do is that somehow it's all just a big coincidence, that he was writing about some imaginary girl who just happened to have done everything I did in real life. Or maybe we were psychically linked or something. It's . . . ineffable, right? I always liked that word. Funny word. What about you? Have you figured it out yet?"

"No clue," he said. "But it's pretty cool."

"Not really."

He leaned back, rubbing his fingers through his too-gray hair. *How old do I look to her?* he wondered. "Other than this, what's the weirdest thing that has ever happened to you?"

She laughed. "In Cleveland Heights? Nothing weird happens in the Heights. It's the safest, most boring suburb of the city, haven't you heard? Maybe once some mother forgot to pack her princess a snack for lunch, but that's about it. Haven't you been there? I left to find weirdness. My life was sooooo boring. Until this. Be careful what you wish for, right?"

"No strange encounters when you were alone? No one peeping in your windows? No one being too aggressive?"

Katy reached out and grabbed his arm with both of her hands. They were warm. Clammy. He could feel her sweat on him and it excited him. "Oh, fuck," she said.

"What?"

"David."

She'd said his name. It was like an incantation, a seal closing, somewhere in his mind.

"David," she said. "I think I might have seen him. Once. Holy shit. How could I have forgotten? Yes. Yes, it might have been him."

"Who might have been him?"

"This guy. When I was ten. Or eleven. I was waiting for my mom to come pick me up in front of Big Fun in Coventry. You know, that cool toy store with the old lunch boxes and shit? I was twirling around this lamppost out front. And I look up and there's this guy walking toward me like he knows me. He has khakis and a windbreaker—one of those Members Only jackets. It was April. I must have been ten. I see him cross the street and walk past a couple other kids and come straight at me, watching me the whole time. And he opens his mouth to say something and I remember thinking, *Who does this guy think I am? Maybe he thinks I'm his niece or something*, because he looks like he knows me and wants to talk to me but I don't know him."

"He was the Man from Primrose Lane?"

"No. Shut up a second. No, he wasn't. What I was going to say was that this guy was almost to me and all of a sudden this old man comes running over at top speed out of nowhere and slams into the guy. Wham! Knocks the man right into the brick wall outside Big Fun. Scared the shit out of me. I ran inside and when I finally looked out again, the old man was chasing the guy across the street. At the time, all I could think was that maybe he owed the guy some money. But that old man. I think that was *him*. It could have been. He at least sort of looked like the Man from Primrose Lane as far as I can remember." She slowly let go her grip on his arm. "Sorry," she said. "I got freaked out a little. Goose bumps."

His mind buzzed with possibilities. Was this the reason Sackett was also interested in Elaine's cold case? Had the detective found other threads linking Katy to Elaine's abduction? "Did you fill out a police report?" he asked.

"No. I mean, I didn't even tell my parents. What would I have said? That I saw two men fighting in Coventry?"

"Don't you think it's possible that the man in the Members Only jacket wanted to harm you? And that the old man intervened?"

"Really? Looked like the guy remembered me. He probably thought I was someone he knew."

"So why did the old man attack him?"

"How the fuck should I know? I was ten. If the other man wanted to molest me or something, why didn't the old man come back and tell me so after he chased him away? Why didn't the old man go to the police?"

"I'm just thinking out loud here."

"I know," she said. "Right?" She drank her beer and looked at the photographs on the wall again. They were not amateur, after all, she noticed distantly. The lighting was too crisp and they shared the same fluffy cloud background. People were weird. Maybe that was the simple message here. "Why do you think Members Only wanted to hurt me?"

"Because it's a story I've heard before," he said.

"Shut the front door."

David nodded. "My wife. Her twin sister was abducted when they were ten. The man would have gotten my wife, too, if some strange guy hadn't shown up in a car and chased him away. No one ever saw the kidnapper or the strange man again."

"Is that why . . . shit. Sorry. None of my business."

"Is that why she committed suicide?" he asked. He saw the Cavalier bearing down on the Dollar General at seventy miles an hour, Elizabeth staring forward in a trance—or had she been smiling? "Postpartum depression was likely the trigger. But yes, I think so. Elaine's abduction . . . it was like . . ."

A *Rube. The ball clunked into a lever that set a domino tumbling forward and over a ledge.*

". . . it set off a chain reaction of events that inevitably led to my wife committing suicide. It was always in the cards. Just a matter of when, really."

"You miss her?"

"Every second of every day," he said. "At night I can still feel her lying next to me. And I don't mean I can 'feel' her lying next to me. I mean, I can feel her *skin* against mine. It's like an amputated limb, I guess. That ghost sensation that takes up the missing space of what was there before. She was cold. She was unkind at times. And she'd rather flip someone the bird than get to know them. But beneath all that was this warm being, this beautiful girl only I knew was there. And that's why I miss her. Because I've never met anyone else quite like that."

"I wonder if we crossed paths. Was she anywhere near the Cleveland Heights/Coventry area when this abduction happened?" Katy asked.

"No," he said.

"What else do you know about your wife's case?"

"Nothing. I never looked into it."

Katy laughed. "What? Why? I mean, that's what you do."

"Because," he said. "Because. Because. Because."

Katy let it drop. She was, in her own way, beginning to understand a little about him, too. This was an occupational hazard David did not love—the intimate bond that forms between a victim of circumstance and the interviewer. Frankly, it made him feel a little like a prostitute sometimes, all this trading of emotion for words, words, words.

"There's one big difference between my story and hers," she said.

"What's that?"

"Members Only didn't abduct anyone that day."

"Because the Man from Primrose Lane interrupted him," said David.

"It was so random, though. Why didn't he just go around the corner and get the next girl?"

"I don't believe it was random."

"I'm missing something, I think. You lost me," she said, laughing nervously.

Instead of answering, David pulled out his wallet. Inside was a picture of his wife on a rocking chair in their apartment, reading a Christopher Pike book.

"Oh, wow. Uncanny, right? If I just borrowed my mom's preppy clothes and cut my hair an inch and, you know, didn't wear makeup . . . maybe *you* wouldn't mistake me for your wife, but I bet other people would. It's the cheeks that make us look different."

"And the lips."

"There's some serious psychological shit going down here, David," said Katy. "Some fucking creepy-ass shit. Me and you. You and me. This cannot happen. Seriously. And not just because I have a fiancé. It's like if Hayley Mills drowned at that summer camp and her boyfriend shacked up with her twin when she came home. Have you even realized yet that, if you're right, about me being connected to this other abduction, you and the kidnapper have the same taste in women?"

"I was nine when Elaine was abducted."

"I'm not implying, I'm just saying. It's fucking weird."

"Yeah."

"You convinced me," she said. "There's a connection there, somewhere. So, what? The old man was this creep's partner and he had second thoughts at the last moment?"

"Both times?" asked David. He shook his head and shrugged. "I've got no explanation."

"Makes your job easier now."

"How's that?"

"All you have to do is figure out who knows me and your wife. Figure out where we crossed paths. The guy had to know us both. That has to narrow down your list of suspects."

"Good point. Assuming they *are* connected. It is possible it's a coincidence."

Katy waved her hand at him as if swatting away the notion of coincidence as a whole. This was a girl who still believed in fate. "Where and when was your wife's sister abducted?" she asked.

"Lakewood, 1989."

"Hmmm. West side versus east side. How many people frequent both ends? Not many. Delivery guys, taxicab drivers, reporters. So, what, after Elaine, this guy in the Members Only jacket was hanging around, waiting for another opportunity, for ten *years*, before he tried to take me?"

"Unless there are other missing redheads around here," he said. "Or maybe he was in prison."

"And somewhere, for whatever reason, the Man from Primrose Lane is keeping an eye on *him*? Are these things usually this complicated?"

"They only appear to be," said David. "The explanation is always elegantly simple. I guarantee that when we find this man, we'll smack ourselves for not seeing him sooner."

The waitress returned to ask about another round.

"Could you tell me something?" asked Katy. "What's with the clown nose pictures?"

The woman rolled her eyes. Obviously, this was the 347th time she'd been asked this question. David doubted the credibility of her answer, which, he believed, she had concocted as a banal autoresponse to customers who wished to waste her time. "Mitch, the owner, he just wore this clown nose someone left here one night. His wife took a picture of him and hung it behind the bar. Then he took one of her. And then it became a thing." The waitress shrugged and walked away.

"That was a simple explanation," said Katy. "But not exactly elegant."

"It was untrue."

"How do you know?"

"Truth is always simple but it's never that boring."

She lived in the "up" of an old house rented out to college students near the university. He parked the Volkswagen out front and kept it idling. It was warm inside, warmer than the fall air outside, which felt like early winter. Katy turned to him, and as she did, her hair brushed over his jacket.

"As far as first dates go, Mr. Neff, this is definitely one of my 'Top Five' weirdest."

"One of?"

"I once went to see *Rocky Horror* with a trans woman who thought she loved me, but that's a story for another day." She smiled at him and his mind was a void of pleasant light. "Can I tell you a secret?" she asked.

"Sure."

She leaned to him, to his ear, and he felt the swell of her breast against his arm. She cupped her hand around his ear. The touch of her hand against his skin lit up his senses as much as they could be lit, and he was suddenly sad again to be numbed by medicine. This was a peak he wished to experience in full. "This is just to say . . ." But instead of finishing the sentence, Katy pushed her lips against him, parted them with her tongue, and gently, briefly, licked his lobe. Then she was back in her seat, rummaging in her purse for her keys. "I'm going to go in now," she said. "You have my permission to jerk off to my Facebook albums tonight. Call me sometime? Let me know how your investigation is going, okay?"

He watched her bound up the front steps and disappear into the house.

There was a message waiting for him when he returned home. Cindy Nottingham had stopped by the house and left her card. Wanted to talk. About what, she hadn't told Aunt Peggy.

Cindy was a blogger—one of Ohio's most popular gossipmongers, a talking head on the cable news channels whenever a celebrity from Cleveland went to rehab or got a divorce. A few years ago, Cindy had worked with David at the *Independent*. It was his fault she'd been fired.

That she was showing up on his doorstep now, as he began work on his first piece of journalism in nearly four years, filled him with unease. He was worried about what she knew. He was worried even more about what she *thought* she knew.

It took the fun out of that nibble in the car. His sleep that night was broken and troubled. For that, and so many other reasons, he hated Cindy Nottingham.

For the record, though, he never wished her dead.

...

EPISODE SIX

ALL EXCEPT ELAINE

Elizabeth did not return to their cabin within the bowels of the cruise ship until well after two in the morning. She did not tell David where she had been and he did not ask. All David knew was that when she returned to him, she had changed. She glowed with a light he had never seen before. Elizabeth smiled. In the light of the bathroom, she smiled at the darkness where he lay as she brushed her teeth, and when she came to bed they felt and fumbled their way over, under, and into each other, laughing between long kisses until she fell asleep in his arms.

When they returned to Ohio, to their apartment in Cuyahoga Falls, Elizabeth began training for a marathon. She was up every morning at five for a run before heading off to the library. On the weekends, she did 5Ks and half marathons on the valley trails that follow the old canal towpaths to Lake Erie. Her newly discovered optimism motivated David. He began submitting bigger stories to the editors at the *Independent*, who, until now, had only known him as the young man who did the movie and concert listings. His first seventeen proposals were shot down. But the eighteenth, a short piece on a local group of film fanatics who got together once a month to crash a bad family movie and yell obscenities at the screen until a manager kicked them out, got through and made the cover. His next pitch, a profile on Bill Watterson, the reclusive artist behind *Calvin & Hobbes*, was approved immediately and he spent the next four months—the rest of Elizabeth's conditioning—working with the managing editor on a series of rewrites that left him feeling both mentally drained and emotionally fulfilled. *This is what I'm supposed to do*, he thought. *This is what I'm good at.*

Elizabeth landed a job teaching music at a public school on the south side of Akron and David began to hunt for the article that would make his name. A part of him had always known what this article would be, and that part of him had always been too afraid to actually put it into words. The story had found him, so to speak. It had sought him out. It was the best kind of story, too—a mystery, a murder mystery. It was an elegant game of chess against an opponent who had already bested every detective assigned to the case. David thought he could do better. There was no logical reason for him to believe this. And it was naïve, dangerous, and delusional for him to feel it so strongly. *The kidnapper is smarter than the cops*, he thought. *But not smarter than me.* After the marathon, he knew it was time to prove it.

"I want to write about Elaine," he said.

They were sitting at Aladdin's, eating a plate of hummus by the window overlooking Highland Square. Since their wedding, Elizabeth had burned off twenty pounds and her once-apple cheeks sat firmly against her bones in a way most men were drawn to. He liked her rounder. "I was wondering what you've been stewing about," she said.

"Stewing?"

"You've been away. Somewhere in your head for a couple days."

"Oh."

"I've seen that look before, you know? In the eyes of the detectives who stop by every couple years asking the same old questions—did strange men ever come over to the house, did your dad like to gamble, why do you think he took Elaine and not you—that's my personal favorite." She took another bite of pita. "It's a jonesing," she said. "Just like a drug. You go deeper and deeper and deeper, thinking you just need a little more and then it's done, but it never is."

"I just thought that maybe I could help," he said. "See what leads are out there, what the detectives haven't thought to look at."

Elizabeth reached out to him and took his hand. Before the piano bar, it had been like torture to get her to show affection in public. Sometimes it seemed she was making up for lost time. "I know. But I don't want to go down that road again. And I don't want to watch you go down there, either. Someone once told me that stories like this make ghosts out of the living. I think that's true."

"How will you ever get closure?" he asked.

"That's the thing, David. There is no closure for this. Closure is for buildings, not people."

A line from the movie *2010*, the one with Roy Scheider and John Lithgow in a spaceship bound for Jupiter's moons, bubbled up from his subconscious mind. *All these worlds are yours, except Europa. Attempt no landings there.* For David, it had always been this way—snippets of prose, dialogue from plays and movies, he was constantly bombarded with the echoes of other people's stories. He supposed it was like this for any beginning writer. On some level his subconscious was always in "story" mode, searching for ways in which life reflected art, how the art he knew reflected his own. His mind hunted analogies, craved meta-phor. That message from *2010*, for example. It had been God's warning to humankind, echoes of His first instruction to Man, the one about avoiding the Tree of Knowledge. *All these stories are yours, except Elaine. Attempt no investigations there.* When he'd learned about the Garden of Eden in Bible school, he'd wondered if God's warning hadn't been more of a dare, anyway, if deep down God had really wanted Eve to give that apple to Adam in order to set things in motion. Or what about this? Maybe He was just bored. Sitting there in Aladdin's, he wondered the same about Elizabeth. Regardless of her true intentions, he understood that each of these stories—the Tree of Knowledge, the warning to stay the fuck off Europa, the request to not dig into Elaine's case—eventually ended the same way.

Let that be another day, then, he told himself. Of course, he had other things to obsess over soon enough. A week later, he discovered the box.

The box was the size of a child's coffin. Heavy cardboard, the kind they don't make anymore, worn at the sides so that you could see the brown threads beneath. It sat on the cabinets above the copier in the editorial department of the *Independent* like a sleeping vulture, one word etched in thick magic marker on its side—BRUNE.

"Hey, Cindy, what's in the box?"

"Oh," she said, rolling her eyes in that decidedly Cindy way. "Don't even get me started on that box. It's a sick joke."

From the writers' den came the sound of Frankie Thomas's laugh—high and juvenile, taunting and loving. "Don't open the box, Davey. Don't open the box! Save yourself!"

He followed Cindy into the writers' den, where Frankie sat at a desk in the corner, his feet propped up while he read through a stack of legal documents. This was the beating heart of the *Independent*, the place where six-thousand-word feature articles full of bite and boom were written. Over its thirty-year history, the *Independent* had brought down crooked state senators and heads of business, the writers unafraid to follow the meager leads that the *Plain Dealer* reporters pitched into the streets as scraps. The paper was the voice of the struggling lower middle class of Cleveland, which is to say most of Cleveland. The writers who worked there wrote about the local boys who returned from the oil wars, about the toxins the steel companies dumped into the Cuyahoga, about the behind-the-scenes politics of the *Plain Dealer*—stories that would be left untold otherwise. These writers were underpaid, underappreciated, and loving it. These writers had never won a Pulitzer. They had never won a plaque from the local Order of Hibernians. The room smelled of old socks and McDonald's, of cigarettes and fresh ink.

Frankie's desk was orderly, his future stories arranged in separate folders to his right. Stapled to the wall beside him were the stylized covers for the features he had written—the one about the meth addict who kicked the habit and became a local rapper of some note, the one about a secret bar on the west side that only old mobsters and prosecutors knew about. Cindy's desk . . . well, Cindy's desk you couldn't see. It was buried beneath a pile of flotsam: empty iced-tea bottles; pantyhose; a stuffed zebra; notes on a story she'd pitched seven months ago; a half-eaten bag of chips; twenty folders that contained no paper; a single shoe. Once a month, Cindy cleaned off her desk by pushing everything into a large garbage bag. There were five such bags in her Camry. David's desk was next to Frankie's. There was nothing on his other than a photograph of Elizabeth taken at their wedding.

"What's in the box, Frankie?" he asked.

Frankie, a short guy with a light brown pompadour wagging constantly above his glacial-blue eyes, sat up and looked across his desk at Cindy. "Tell him about it."

Cindy's hair was a straight blond bowl and she had a round, dimpled face and childlike buck teeth. "Fuck you, Frankie," she said.

"What?"

"Fuck you, Frankie."

David lifted an eyebrow at the young man in the corner.

"Inside that box," said Frankie, "is the greatest story never told. It's the one Pulitzer this paper will ever publish. Many writers have tried to solve its secrets"—he nodded his head toward Cindy—"but so far it has only driven them insane for trying."

"What's in the box?" he asked again.

"In that box, my friend, are the last notes and personal effects of Ronil J. Brune, the Back Road Strangler, the man who raped and murdered perhaps as many as seven young girls in the early eighties. When he was executed in 2002, he had everything from his death row cell shipped here, in that box. Attached to it was a letter from Brune himself, in which he proclaimed to be innocent of the crimes for which he was executed. He said that the clues leading to the real killer were contained within the box. And if he's telling the truth, and the state of Ohio murdered an innocent man, then it's a once-in-a-lifetime story."

"It's a sick joke," said Cindy. "Brune's idea of revenge. He wants to use the media to cast doubt on his guilt, use us to torture the families of his victims. He wants to exert control on them even after his death."

"He *wanted* to exert control, you mean," David corrected.

"Wants."

Frankie fidgeted in his chair, the smile gone from his face. "There's a reason the box is not in the writers' den," he said. "There's a reason we put it way the hell up there. And if you decide to open the box, you have to respect our . . . superstitions, and keep it out of the room."

"It's a haunted box?" David asked.

"Yes."

"C'mon."

But Frankie didn't laugh.

"*C'mon.*"

"Look, all I know is that when we kept the box in here, some strange shit went down. Maybe it was the box. Maybe it wasn't . . ."

"Right," said Cindy.

". . . but when we put the lid back on the box and moved it out of the room, it all stopped."

"Stuff like what?" David asked.

"Like, every time I tried to fart, I sharted instead," said Frankie. This busted David up and the three writers laughed until David's side started to hurt and Frankie had snot dribbling out of his nose.

"When I opened the box, I got the worst headache," Cindy said, her eyes going unfocused. "That night, when I went to bed, I dreamt I could feel a man's hands on me."

A few stray chuckles spat out of Frankie's mouth before he could clamp it shut.

"I miscarried the next morning."

"Jesus, Cindy!" said Frankie. "Too much. Too much."

"There was a spot in my bedroom, that if you stood in it, you could smell a man's cheap cologne for a week after that."

"What happened to you, Frankie?" asked David, trying not to envision everything Cindy had just said.

Frankie shrugged. "Stuff," he said. "I got mugged—beat to shit—outside by a homeless guy who the police later informed me was legally blind and couldn't lift a hat. I woke up one morning and my dog had swallowed its tongue. All that's incidental, though. There is, the best way I can describe it, a *darkness*. There's a darkness in that box. You can feel it on you. Like something standing on your chest. I thought I might be getting clinically depressed or something. But when I closed up the box and put it away"—Frankie jumped up and held out his arms—"ta-da! Right as rain."

"Seriously, David, leave the box alone," said Cindy.

So he did what no other writer had been stupid enough to do: he took it home.

It weighed 78 pounds, making it a struggle for 145-pound David to first bring it down from atop the cabinets in the editorial wing—using a ladder he found in the storage closet—then from the eighth floor of the Western Reserve Building to his Sundance parked out front. He could feel the added weight in the trunk altering the performance of the car on the way home, down I-77. The car didn't swerve in and out of traffic the way he had taught it to. It veered, rather than corrected. It hesitated when it should have punched through a hole in the rush-hour traffic. To David, it felt as if he had a sumo team sitting in the back.

He brought it into their first-floor apartment in Cuyahoga Falls, and set it on the table in their kitchenette with a dull thunk. Elizabeth had called him to say she was staying after work to catch up on grades and lesson plans (these late nights had increased steadily in the last few months but he didn't think to question if she was really where she said she was). He was alone with the secrets the box contained.

His stomach rolled with excitement. It was the way he felt when a new Robert McCammon novel or Richard North Patterson mystery novel was published, an excitement for the information within. Except this was better. This was a mystery no one had read before. Sure, Frankie and Cindy had sorted through the papers and had begun to develop stories of their own, but their interpretation of the material would have been quite different than his. The story he would glean from the documents would be entirely unique.

The lid slipped off with the slightest hint of a sigh.

———ⓠ———

"Do you remember what you said to me when we first met?" asked Dr. Popodopovich, the thin woman sitting behind the mahogany table.

"Yes," said David.

"Then you understand my concern."

"I can't feel anything."

"So let me take you off it gradually."

"How long?"

"Three months."

"No."

"This isn't like aspirin," she said. "It's much more like heroin."

"You said it can't kill me, the withdrawals."

"David, before it's over you'll wish it *could*."

Her name was Athena Popodopovich. She dressed in paisley prints that hadn't been manufactured since the late sixties—God only knows where she bought them. Years ago, Dr. Popodopovich had worked as the traveling counselor and nanny for a fairly well-known rock band that had turned sober in the years since they had topped the charts. She understood ignominy better than most. She'd been there for David after Brune. She'd been there for him after Elizabeth had taken her life. She'd brought him back. Until now, he'd always followed her advice.

"You run the possibility of undoing everything we've worked on," she said, a touch too firmly. "If your body hasn't relearned how to manufacture the chemicals you need to not be sad, you could potentially become severely depressed before you recognize what's happening. I'm afraid a crash like that might cause you to become dependent on this drug for the rest of your life. I'm afraid of what else it might cause you to do. And, frankly, I'm concerned for Tanner."

That stung.

"Tanner's going to stay with my father while I dry out," said David. "I'll be out of town, anyway. Working on this article."

"Where are you going?"

"Bellefonte, Pennsylvania. Near State College."

"I thought this guy you're writing about was from Akron."

David shrugged. "No one knows where the Man from Primrose Lane was from. We know he died here. But he got his fake ID in Bellefonte. So he has some connection to that town, too."

"Do you think it's a good idea to be in an unfamiliar setting while you go through withdrawals?"

"Why? Would I enjoy them more at home?"

"You're five minutes from the hospital here. You know your surroundings. What if you become disoriented? Have you ever heard of dissociative fugue? It's where you experience something so stressful your mind reboots and you forget who you are, sometimes forever."

"How likely is that?"

"Rivertin is a new drug," she said. "It's the best thing we have for PTSD, but there's a lot we don't know about it yet. There's a lot we don't know about the side effects of coming off it so quickly. There is something called hypnagogic regression, an episodic memory—what you might call an intense flashback—which is quite unpleasant for the person experiencing it. The person reliving it."

"You told me there was a, what, ninety-five percent chance I'd be sterile on the Rivertin, too, and now I have a four-year-old kid."

"You're sort of proving my point."

"I'm sorry," he said at last. "But this not feeling anything is making me feel like an invalid."

"Have you stopped taking it already?"

"No."

Athena shook her head. "I don't understand the rush. Three months isn't that long. Let's do this right."

David didn't want to wait. Suddenly it felt like all he did was wait anymore. He was beginning to sense how he had squandered the last few years of his life. No more waiting. Not for one day. He gathered his jacket and stood. "I'm sorry. I am. But I think this is going to be all right."

"You're not thinking rationally."

"I know." He turned to leave.

"David."

He looked back at her. For the first time since he'd made up his mind to quit the pills, he felt nervous. He felt nervous because Athena looked scared. She'd always been so confident, an anchor to the real world for him. But he could see that she was afraid.

"When you crash, there's going to be a time when you will want to reach for that phone and call me to save you. By then you're going to have forgotten all these reasons you have for doing this. You'll be in so much pain the only thing you'll want is for me to come and save you. But here's the thing. By the time you get there, you will have crossed a point of no return. If we give you the drug while your body is revving up to replace it, you'll go into coma and we'll probably destroy your liver while we're trying to get you back."

He smiled. "Give it to me straight, Doc. I can handle it."

Her cheeks pushed back in a grin. "It's going to feel like dying. Do you understand?"

He didn't say anything.

"I hope you know what you're doing," she said.

"Me, too."

David cheated.

He took Tanner in the middle of the night, dressed in footie pajamas and wrapped inside the blue blanket that he used to sleep with in the crib. He didn't want to explain to Tanner, who could not yet grasp the concept of time enough to consider the passage of a week, that he was going to be away longer than he'd ever been gone before. *It's better for him this way*, he told himself. *He'll miss me less if he doesn't see me leave.*

David wondered how he'd feel when he saw his son again, unfiltered by the drug. He knew he loved the boy more than he ever believed was possible. What would that be like without anything blocking that bond? It was something else he looked forward to. *I could be a better dad. A dad who would know better than to go off like this in the middle of the night.*

David's father carried Tanner to the bedroom on the second floor of his large country home in Franklin Mills, a little town in the hills of eastern Ohio. He followed with a bag full of clothes, sippy cups, Yogo Bites, Tinkertoys.

It was past eleven and his father's third wife, a tender woman he'd met five years ago at a Christian singles dance, was asleep and the house was silent but for the tick-tocking of the clock above the kitchen sink. They crept quietly back downstairs to the dining room table, a slab of driftwood oak that Berlin Lake had given up one Saturday afternoon. This was not the house David had grown up in. There were no memories here for him in the walls. To him, it had the feel of a vacation home or a place for convalescence, a cabin in the woods, a Walden Pond tuckaway. David's father pushed a pie tin at him. Inside was apple betty and a runcible spoon.

"Thanks," he said.

"How long will you be gone?" His father's voice was deep and husky and it filled up the room to its last hidden nook, even in whisper.

"A few days. Maybe longer. Not more than a week."

"I thought you were done with writing."

"Me too."

"What's the story?"

"Mistaken identity. I guess you could call it an unsolved suicide. This old hermit was shot once in the stomach and then it appears he chopped off his own fingers and fed them into a blender. He bled out instead of calling an ambulance for help."

"The Man from Primrose Lane?"

"You've heard the story?"

"On the weener radio," he said. WNIR was the talk-radio station based out of Ravenna, a bastion of local gossip and prognostication. "They said the man was probably an old mafioso who snitched. They're saying that the coroner might change her ruling."

"I know. The bullet missed everything. In, out. He would have survived if he hadn't cut off his own fingers."

"How do you know the guy that shot him didn't put the gun to his head and make him cut off his fingers?"

David shrugged. "The CSI people seem to think the way the fingers were severed suggests he did it."

"That's disturbing," his father said, shaking off a shiver. "What about you? Are you doing okay?"

"What do you mean?" he asked.

"You know. Where's your head at?"

"I'm fine," he answered. "I'm going off the drugs."

"Your doctor know?"

"Yeah. She's cool with it." His father looked at him over the table, that certain long look of study he'd perfected as a father over the last thirty-four years. *You can fool some of the people all of the time,* he used to say. *And you can fool all of the people some of the time, but you . . .*

"But you can't fool Dad," his father finished. Reading minds, another mostly useless trait parents pick up without meaning to.

"She's not cool with it, no," he said.

For a moment, his father didn't say anything. The gears inside turned and turned, processing an appropriate response. He knew his son was, generally, a responsible person. He'd picked himself up after the death of his wife, had raised his son and asked for little help. He was allowed the occasional bad idea. *An odd kid,* his own mother had warned him. *Always wants to touch the stove to see if it's still hot.* "Well," he said, finally, "I kicked cocaine cold turkey. You'll get through it."

There was a message on his cell phone when he returned to the Bug. It was from Detective Sackett.

"David, sorry about the late call. If you could, please stop by the station tomorrow morning. I'm in at eight."

—▣—

You stupid poser! Who the fuck is this?

It was a little past two in the morning. He was in his office rediscovering his Facebook profile. He was touched to see that he had over twenty-five hundred friends now, even if he didn't know most of them. Several of his high school classmates were on there. Even Brian Pence—the football hero who'd once knocked him into a locker so hard he'd passed out. The instant message popped up next to a picture of Count Chocula, Katy's avatar.

It's me, Kate. I repatriated my profile. Long story.

Why r u up so late, old man?

It's hard to sleep the night before a trip.

Where r u going? Can I come?

Bellefonte, PA. I'm going to try to track down someone who knew the MFPL.

Kool. Thanks for the shrooms and beer the other night.

Welcome. Why are you still up?

I'm 22. I'm just getting in.

Right.

How's your toolbox bf?

If we're going to have a "thing" you can't ask about him.

Are we having a "thing"? Did something happen that I don't remember?

I mean, if you want to.

Could you define "thing"?

It's ineffable.

I should hope not.

? Oh. OK, maybe a little eff-able. ROFL. Seriously, can I come on your little trip? I don't have to work again until Wednesday. ;)

Man. Man oh man. As much as I hate to say no, I think I need to do this part alone.

You sure?

Not really.

Well let me know if you change your mind.

Will do.

Sleep tight, professor.

You too.

Was that a butterfly fluttering inside his stomach? He wasn't sure. It had been, after all, a very long time. But he thought it might be. And he thought that lone butterfly might be joined by friends as the medicine wore off. He hoped, anyway.

Our greatest moments of truth take place near toilets. The final purge of an alcoholic at rock bottom; the recognition of an eating disorder; a child's first introduction to death, as his mother flushes the goldfish; and, here, David's first step to reclaiming his mind.

Maybe this isn't such a hot idea, he thought. *Why can't I just be happy with Tanner and the life we've made? Why do I have to go back to this dark stuff?*

Because you love it, said a stronger voice—his true shadowed soul.

Still, if it had just been crime writing he missed, he could have sacrificed that and stayed on the meds.

I want to fall in love again.

She's not Elizabeth. You'll never get her back.

That's true. But maybe it could still be something good.

Three weeks' worth of Rivertin plopped into the water. He looked at the pills for a moment. He felt nothing.

Sackett made David wait twenty minutes before he opened the reinforced door and led him toward the detectives' office. "We're in here today," Sackett said, ushering David into a small room to his right.

The room was cliché. Square. Plain. Drab. The only furnishings a steel table and three chairs. On the wall to their left was what appeared to be a large mirror, but which David knew must have been one of those see-through kinds they use in cop shows.

"Cool," said David. "This is a real interrogation room, isn't it?"

"It is," said Sackett. The detective motioned for David to sit in the single chair on the opposite end of the table.

As David sat, a second man entered the room and closed the door. He was a husky dude with a thick white handlebar mustache. He was dressed in jeans and a polo shirt snug around his biceps. A large gun with a bone-colored grip sat in a holster under his left arm.

"This is ex–Special Agent Dan Larkey," said Sackett. "He's working the Joseph King case with me, a consultant with the Bureau."

"What's up?" said Larkey, shaking his hand. The man's voice was gravelly, his handshake firm and brief.

"Nice to meet you," said David.

Sackett took a chair. Larkey remained standing, slowly rubbing his hands together as if he were warming them.

"Has there been a development in the case?" asked David.

"You could say there's been a significant development," said Larkey.

"What happened?" he asked.

"We identified the fingerprint the FBI pulled from the bed board," said Sackett.

"Wow. That's . . . that's awesome," said David. "Who is it?"

"Guess," Larkey said with a smile.

"Hmmm," said David. "Was it the Beachum kid?"

"No," said Larkey.

"Hang on a second. I gotta check this out," said David, standing up and walking over to the two-way mirror. "They really use these, huh? I thought everything would be video by now."

"We're still behind the curve," said Sackett.

David cupped his hands to filter out the light and peered into the glass. He could make out a row of chairs and a desk and . . .

"Shit!" yelled David. "Christ, that scared me."

"What?" asked Sackett.

"There's someone in there," said David.

"No shit," said Larkey.

Suddenly David's face flushed. His heart raced, speeding up his metabolism, pushing the last of the Rivertin through his system. He turned to face the men in the room. They stared back at him.

"Whose fingerprint was it?" asked David.

"The fingerprint belonged to your wife," said Larkey.

David's mind was a blank. His ears suddenly throbbed as if they were infected.

"You know what makes a good detective, David?" asked Sackett. "Don't answer. I'll tell you. What makes a good detective is being able to recognize when a suspect does not act naturally. You have to notice when someone acts hinky. You know? Sometimes it's the only warning you have that the guy you pulled over is going to draw a gun on you. The troublemakers, the guilty guys, they all act hinky. Not guilty. They don't act guilty, necessarily. Just, you know, hinky. When I showed you the picture of the Man with a Thousand Mittens, the normal reaction would have been curiosity. But that's not how you acted. You acted hinky. You acted like you knew him already."

"I didn't. I told you I didn't."

"But I didn't believe you. And I got to thinking. Maybe . . . maybe . . . And I had a hunch. I expanded our fingerprint search to include the state educator's database that catalogues public school teachers' identification. That fingerprint we found on the bedpost matched Elizabeth's. And then your reaction began to make sense."

"It was her left middle finger, David," said Larkey, climbing onto the table like an old tomcat. "But it was found on the right side of the bed. She'd have to be laying on the bed like this . . ." The agent lay back on the desk and reached his left hand behind his head, grabbing an invisible bedpost. "Get it? She's on her back and holding on to the post like this. She's fucking him."

"I don't know about fucking him," said Sackett. "Probably another explanation, right? I mean, Elizabeth was a beautiful woman. And he was such an old man. I can't picture it."

"The fingerprint got us a warrant, which got us into your secret lockbox in Mansfield," said Larkey. "We found your nine-millimeter. Same caliber used on the Man from Primrose Lane."

"There was a lot of cash in there, too, and passports," said Sackett. "You getting ready to leave? Taking a vacation?"

"The gun's in ballistics right now," Larkey continued. "We'll have the results tomorrow."

"Give me something," said Sackett. "Elizabeth wasn't sleeping with that old man. Couldn't have been. What really happened, David?"

He didn't say anything. His mind wouldn't move fast enough. Every time he tried to form a thought, something fizzled against a connection inside his head.

"Maybe she did give it up to him," Larkey suggested. "Did you find out your wife was a whore, David?"

David balled his fists. The light in the room grew gray, sparkling around the edges of his eyesight. He moved closer to the FBI man.

"Back the fuck up," said Larkey, rolling off the desk.

"We disagree on the specifics, David," said Sackett. "I know she was a good woman. I'm sure there's an explanation. Maybe you could help me understand."

He looked at the glass. The man he'd seen behind it had been dressed in a sharp suit. The prosecutor? Was he about to be arrested? Was this actually happening?

"Why was she on his bed?" asked Sackett. "Help me out, David. Why'd you do it? What did you find out?"

"Allow me to spin a yarn," Larkey interrupted. "Famous writer figures out his wife's having an affair with the village idiot. Writer surprises them at the man's house. Shoots the guy. Wife kills herself out of shame and guilt and maybe just to get back at the writer. It's a rough draft, but it has potential, doesn't it?"

"It's ridiculous," said David. "No fucking way."

"David," said Sackett, leaning forward over Larkey's body, "where were you on the night of June nineteenth, 2008?"

He knew better. He didn't say a word.

"I know you killed this man," said Larkey. "He may have cut off his own fingers for some fucked-up reason, but you put the bullet in his chest. And now *you* know *I* know." He leaned to David's ear so that his voice could not be picked up by the three audio recorders whirring in the next room. "I'm going to nail you for this, you fucking elitist *fuck*."

How many times had he written this scene? David wondered. At least a dozen. Every murder story had a scene like this. And once you got the suspect in this room, he knew, the questions would come like this, rat-a-tat quick, for hours, until he broke or asked for a lawyer. Sometimes, if it went on long enough, innocent men would confess just to be done with it. With his mind already compromised, he could not risk it. Of course, if he asked for representation and they already had an indictment, they'd cuff him, put him in a holding cell, and then take him to court to be arraigned. He'd have to post bond, but who knew how quickly Bashien could gather the money? He didn't think they would have had time or evidence to present to a grand jury yet, though. Either way, he was done here. It was an acceptable risk. One Elizabeth would have signed off on.

"I want to talk to my lawyer," he said.

Sackett exchanged a look with Larkey and then sighed. Sackett nodded and Larkey stepped to the door and opened it for David.

So no cuffs. Not yet. But he could tell they thought it was inevitable.

"Thank you," said Larkey.

"For what?"

"This one thought you'd break. I bet him twenty you'd make it a challenge."

INTERLUDE

THE BALLAD OF THE LOVELAND FROG

1986 Halfway through Johnny Carson, the rotary phone on the side table by his father's recliner rang out. Everett Bleakney, age nine, looked forward to these interludes in the middle of otherwise normal evenings. That particular phone had its own extension. It only rang if there was trouble. And when it rang during the weekends, Everett's father had to take him along for the ride. That was the deal they had hashed out long ago.

"Bleakney," his father said into the phone. "Uh-huh. Uh-huh. Huh! Hurm. Uh. Uhuh. Yes, thank you."

Everett, lying on the living room floor, looked up.

"Get your coat," his father said.

"Yes!"

His mother, a gaunt woman who was reading *Flowers in the Attic* at a seat beneath a lamp in the corner, gave a curt sound of disapproval. "It's late, hon."

"It's just a drive-by," his father said, standing up and drinking the rest of his Yuengling in one quick gulp. "Lana Deering saw some animal out on Twightwee."

"What kind of animal?" she asked without looking up.

"Frog."

"A frog?"

"A big frog."

"Okay, then. But don't stay out. And don't take him into Paxton's."

"They don't mind."

"I don't want my son hanging out in bars."

"All right. No Paxton's," he said. But he winked at Everett in a conspiratorial way.

Everett sat in the passenger seat of his father's cruiser, warming his hands against the dashboard vents. It was cool out tonight, too cool for early September. There might even be a frost on the corn come morning, the newspaper warned.

"How big was the frog Mrs. Deering saw?" asked Everett.

" 'Monstrous' was the word she used, I think," said his father. "At least that's what Dory told me." Dory was the Friday night dispatcher. "I guess it's just sitting out there on Twightwee, out by Camp Ritchie. She thought it was dead, hit by a truck. Got to clear it off. Apparently, it cannot wait till morning."

Everett, who had imagined putting the frog in a bucket and bringing it back with them to live at the house, was visibly disappointed.

"Might not be dead," said his father. "Who knows? We'll see."

Downtown Loveland was dark. The streetlights cut off at eleven p.m. every night, throwing the false-fronted retail stores into shadow. Everett was always a little unnerved to see his town like this. It was always so busy during the day: adults window-shopping, teen lovers strolling over the bridge that crossed the Little Miami, his classmates organizing games of pick-up in the park. But at night, it was like everyone had evacuated the place, like they knew something Everett and his father didn't. Out by the river, though, two streetlights were always kept on: the one in front of Paxton's Grill and the one in front of Stacey's Drive-Thru. Everett's father pulled into Stacey's and drove around back to the entrance.

The light inside was garish, an overly bright depot in the darkness, full of beer and tackle and chips. Stacey—a spindly thing with stinky cigarette smoke hair—was working, of course. She always was. And according to her version of this story, Everett's father looked just fine when he pulled up to her register.

"What'll it be, Ev?" His name was Everett, too. Everett, his son, was actually Everett the Third.

"Mountain Dews and Slim Jims, please. And a bag of pork rinds."

She gathered the goods and passed them along to the police chief. He handed her a five.

"Where ya two headed?"

"Twightwee, I guess."

"How come?"

"Lana seen a frog out there, size of a Doberman."

"No kidding."

"That's the word, Thunderbird."

"You know, my uncle once noodled a catfish as big as a mastiff. Ain't never heard of a frog that big."

"Think your uncle was probably drinking some of that white lightning he makes in his shed, Stacey."

Everett giggled.

"No doubt. No doubt," she said. "Hey, Ev."

"Yes'm?"

"You suppose it could have anything to do with that boomin' we heard the other night?"

"Boomin'?"

"Yeah, like a thunderclap. Real loud. 'Round midnight. Some people over at Paxton's said they heard it a couple nights in a row, but it was loudest the last time, two days ago."

"Nobody called it in to the station."

"No?"

"No. Least not that I heard. And I didn't hear it anyway."

"It was real loud, Ev. Some of us were thinking maybe it was a jet or something, 'cause Roldo was in the navy in Nam, you know? Anyway, Roldo says it was a sonic boom. I don't know, 'cause I never heard one, but do you know of any jets coming down from Dayton or anything? Out of Wright-Pat, maybe?"

"No, I ain't heard nothing about that."

"Well, anyways. Sounded like it was coming from the direction of Twightwee Road. Just thought they might be, I don't know, *connected*."

"You never know."

"No, you don't."

As they drove out of Stacey's and into the dark toward Twightwee Road, Everett sat up in his seat, smiling.

"What?" his father asked.

"You talk different around some people," he said.

"Part of the job," he said, ruffling his son's hair. "She'd think I was puttin' on airs if I didn't slip an 'ain't' in every so often. People need to trust their police chief. It's even okay if a couple of them actually think they're smarter than me." He laughed. "Now hand me a Slim Jim."

Twightwee was a gravel road that bisected the Little Miami over an antebellum bridge. Everett's father slowed the cruiser as they approached.

"Spotlight," Everett said.

His father whirled the large spotlight around so that it pointed straight ahead and then pinged the "on" switch. The night retreated several yards around the bridge. The harsh light saturated the roadway, stealing color from the stones and scrub grass lining the edges. The road was empty.

"Maybe it hopped back in the river," said Everett.

"Little farther."

The car edged forward. Everett rolled his window down. The sound of the tires pinching the gravel was loud but it was also an empty sound, a lonely sound. The air bit his cheeks and earlobes. As they passed over the river, the boy smelled the muddy water churning below—earth and grit and . . .

"Dad?"

"What's up?"

"You smell that?"

There was something new, something alien in the air. Everett thought it smelled a little like a movie theater. His father's first thought was of a wedding reception, carrying an Amaretto Sour back to Everett's mother.

"Almonds," his father said. "And something else. Wheat? Beans?"

"Alfalfa!" Everett said.

"Yep. Alfalfa. Odd."

The car rolled on. There were no houses out here and the woods were slowly devouring the road; tufts of bluegrass reached for the car and scraped gently along Everett's door like soft fingernails.

"Wait!" said Everett. "Wait. What's that over there?"

His father pivoted the spotlight to the left. There *was* something there, leaning against the berm.

"Just a bag of garbage."

"You sure?"

"Yes, I'm—"

It moved. The back of the black round thing heaved up in what could only be a deep, labored breath, and then settled back down. Everett reached out and grabbed his father's arm.

"Dad?"

"What?"

"What is it?"

"It's not a frog."

"What is it?"

"I . . . I don't know. Could be a dog that was hit by a car. Or maybe a small bear."

"A bear?"

"Maybe."

Everett's father reached into the glove compartment and came out with his stubby Smith & Wesson nine-millimeter, which he quickly unlocked and loaded.

"What are you doing?" asked Everett.

"I have to see what it is," his father said. "Looks like it's suffering. I should put it down."

"No, Dad. Call Horace in. He'll still be up. Have him bring out his shotgun."

His father smiled. "It's okay, Scout," he said—a nickname he hadn't used in over a year. "Whatever it is, it's too sick to hurt anyone. This'll just take a minute. Stay inside." He left the driver's-side door open and rambled slowly toward the creature at the side of the road, the gun low in his right hand.

Still strapped in his seat, Everett watched his father approach the animal and circle halfway around it before stopping to pinch his nose with his free hand.

"What?" shouted Everett.

"It stinks!"

"What is it?"

In the beam of the spotlight, his father slowly moved to the form and pushed it with one shoe. It rocked a little, but didn't turn over. He pushed again and this time it nearly rolled before collapsing back. On the third push it suddenly came alive. Everett watched the black shape leap to a crouching position, its red eyes fixed on his father. It really did look like a frog for a moment—its face wide and wet and squished, its skin a greenish black muck-colored organ with holes for a nose and a gash for a mouth. That gash opened and what came out was a cry full of human anguish. It lifted a hand, webbed, covered in black foam, dripping pollution onto the blacktop of the road.

His father lifted his gun at the animal but as he did, the frog-thing wrapped its hand around the weapon and snatched it from his grip, tossing it into the woods. It reached to its waist and Everett noticed for the first time that there was a metal rod attached to some sort of belt there. The monster's hand closed around the rod and pulled it out. It began to emit brilliant sparks of blue-white light, hissing like a road flare. The smell of alfalfa grew sickeningly sweet. All he could see of his father now was his backlit form against the overpowering light of the monster's wand.

"Dad!" cried Everett.

The light abruptly quit and Everett peered into the darkness for the shape of his father. But the light had been so strong, he saw nothing for a few seconds. He felt the car lunge to the side and he knew that the frogman was inside with him, opening its gash of a mouth for his throat.

"Everett."

His father. It was his father. Yes. He could see him now, lifting his legs into the driver's seat and closing the door behind him.

"Everett," he said again.

"Dad?" he said through tears.

And then his father's body pitched against the steering wheel. The horn blasted away the quiet with a droning wail.

Everett unbuckled himself and pushed his father's body back against the seat. His father's skin was gray and cool, his eyes rolled back into his head. One hand clutched at his chest. His doctor had warned him three years ago that it was time to quit the drinking and the red meat, that one day his ticker would get a shock and dislodge a buildup of plaque and then that would be all she wrote. He'd told the doctor the most excitement Loveland's police chief was likely to see was the Memorial Day parade. If he had known of such things as frogmen with laser sticks, he might have heeded the doctor's advice.

Everett would forever harbor a dirty guilt over his father's death. A Bear in the local Cub Scout troop, Everett had purposefully skipped the meeting in June when a paramedic had taught the boys basic CPR. He'd skipped it because it hadn't sounded fun.

Eventually, Everett would think to call in to the station on his father's

CB radio. But for a long while all the boy could think to do was cradle his father's head against his chest and stroke his cheek the way his father had done for him as a toddler.

By the time Horace arrived, the monster was gone. And when Everett told the story of what had happened to his father, no one believed him. It was easier to believe the boy's mind had overloaded at the sight of his father's untimely death. Easier for the boy to blame a frogman than a clogged artery.

In fact, he should have blamed a writer named David Neff.

PART TWO

BRUNE

EPISODE SEVEN

WITHDRAWN

"Your Honor, state calls David Neff to the stand."

Elizabeth squeezed David's hand before he got to his feet. Assistant Prosecuting Attorney Brice Russo, a paunchy fellow with curly gray hair, a seasoned vet of the criminal court of common pleas, greeted him with a friendly pat on his arm and directed him to the witness stand.

"You okay?" he asked quietly.

"Fine," said David.

He took a seat at the stand to the judge's right and looked back at the courtroom as Russo made a show of gathering his notes, though what he was really doing was allowing the jury a moment to take in the author, to see him as the polished young professional he appeared to be—a man not unlike their own children or favorite nephews.

To David, the jury, seated in two rows along the wall to his immediate right, looked like a hastily assembled Mouth-Breathers Anonymous meeting: the fat old woman who drove the bus for the Independence Schools District; the thin black man dressed in a borrowed polo, fighting as hard as he could not to fall asleep; the armchair detective/pet store clerk who had already been reprimanded by Judge Jerald Siegel for rolling his eyes during the coroner's testimony. Closest to him was an astute woman with sharp features who taught social studies to fourth-graders at Parma Elementary. She would be the foreperson, when it came time to elect one. There was little doubt of this. *Make eye contact with her early on*, Russo had instructed him. *Smile.*

He met her eyes, partially obscured behind bifocals, and smiled. She did not return the salutation.

David turned his attention to the room. It was squat and square, the walls covered in cheap wood paneling. To his left, Elizabeth sat next to his father, who looked out of place and quite uncomfortable in one of David's suits. His uncle Ira was standing in the back today, he noticed. Russo continued searching through a box of police reports at the desk in front of them. Directly in front of David was Riley Trimble, the man David's words had put behind bars, a man who appeared to be a simpleton but who was, himself, playing the part. The defendant appeared out of his element here in this Cleveland courtroom, pulled from his rural setting due to the special circumstances of his crime that had resulted in a change of venue from Medina (where the majority of that county preferred a lynching). Flanking Trimble was his team of lawyers, led by Terry Synenberger, a former assistant federal prosecutor who had since made a name for himself defending some of Cleveland's most prominent businessmen, including Scott "The Man of Steel" Shick, busted in 1999 for bribing inspectors to overlook the carcinogens his refinery was dumping into the Cuyahoga. He was a muscular man with a large bald head, tanned to a light beige. Behind him, David was disappointed to see, was the family of Sarah Creston, the dead girl who just wouldn't die for good. In this upside-down world, they actually supported Trimble—the Medina County detectives had convinced them years ago that Brune was responsible for their daughter's murder. They believed David's motivation for accusing Trimble of the crime was fame and fortune.

Russo stopped his busywork and turned to David, a yellow legal pad in his hands. There were a few things written on it, but it was just another prop for the jury. The jury watched *Law and Order* and expected certain things like lawyers holding legal pads and coroners testing DNA in less than twenty minutes (not six months, like the Medina County coroner had tried to tell them).

"State your name for the record."

"David Joseph Neff."

"Where were you employed in 2007, David?"

"I was a reporter for the *Independent*, Ohio's largest alternative newspaper."

"Could you please describe for the jury what, exactly, an alternative newspaper is?"

"I'm still trying to figure that out myself," David said. *Keep it light*, Russo had told him. But his throat felt dry. He felt a coughing spell coming on. "An alternative newspaper is just that, an alternative to the daily news. The paper comes out once a week. It's one of those free magazines you find at the bar. College kids pick them up to see what band is playing at the Grog Shop on Saturday or what art film is showing at the Cinematheque. It's edgier than the *Plain Dealer*. Some people call the writing 'snarky.' The articles are usually longer and told in the New Journalism style, meaning they have a narrative structure instead of an inverse pyramid like the daily papers' articles. They read like good fiction, sometimes."

Russo winced. *Bad choice of words*, David realized.

"But it's all factual reporting, just like the *Plain Dealer*," prompted Russo.

"Of course," he said. "What I meant was, it's a little more fun to read because it's told in the structure of a short story."

The prosecutor nodded, then paused, glancing at the jury.

"Mr. Neff, this isn't going to be a short interview. Would you like water or something?"

"Water, please."

Russo nodded at the bailiff, who produced a carafe of water from under the judge's bench and brought it over to David, who poured himself a glass, his fingers jittering. He did not drink it.

"Ready?" asked Russo.

"Yes."

"Mr. Neff, could you please tell the jury . . . what led you to accuse the defendant of being a serial killer?"

"I'll do my best," said David. He looked at the schoolteacher, made eye contact. "Everything kind of got rolling when I talked to another reporter about the Ronil Brune case. His name is Frankie Thomas. We were sitting in the writers' den at the *Independent* one night and I said to him, 'I think Ronil . . .

. . . Brune might have been innocent," said David. It had been three days since he'd taken the box home.

At the desk beside him, Frankie rubbed the bridge of his nose and sighed. "No, you don't," he said.

"I think I might."

"Why?"

David nudged his chair closer to Frankie, who was at least feigning interest. "Let's look at the facts. What we know, for sure, about Brune. Guy's about forty-five. He's an intelligent—some say *brilliant*—accountant for a large Akron firm, right? In 1984, he's living by himself in a small ranch house in Bath. Woman shows up at his neighbors' house one morning. She's mid-thirties. She's naked. And there's a handcuff dangling from her wrist. She tells the older couple who live there that she's been held captive by Brune, in his house, for two days, that she escaped after he went to work on Monday morning. Police arrest Brune. She identifies him as her abductor, as the man who tortured her, who sexually violated her over and over. And after his face appears in the *Beacon Journal*, three other women, all in their thirties or forties, come forward saying Brune kidnapped and raped them, too."

"You're right!" said Frankie. "He does sound innocent."

"Just listen. No doubt, no doubt Brune was a serial rapist. He admitted to it. He admitted abducting and raping those adult women. We can agree that he's—that he was—a very bad man."

"Agreed."

"The police search his house and find all these newspaper clippings about Sarah Creston, an eight-year-old girl who was abducted from Medina in 1982. Creston had been raped and strangled to death, then dumped beside an oil well drive. On her body they found several cat hairs, gray tomcat hairs. The hair matched samples taken from clothes and carpet in Brune's house. The cat itself was never found, but it was obvious it had lived there at one time. So they go back and look at other unsolved murders of young girls in the area. Detectives soon finger Brune for two more murders—the 1980 murder of ten-year-old Donna Doyle, who was wrapped in plastic that had once contained a bedspread purchased by Brune, and the 1980 murder of ten-year-old Jennifer Poole, who was covered in those same gray cat hairs."

Frankie looked back at David with a touch of concern. He shrugged. *And?*

"Doesn't fit," said David. "Haven't you seen those A&E interviews with FBI profilers? The ones who study these predators? They always say that serial killers become more violent over time. A serial killer wouldn't kill kids and then start abducting and *releasing* adult women. And they would stay with one age group."

"C'mon. Nobody knows what really goes on in a killer's mind. They're sick. They don't make sense."

"Brune admitted to the rapes. Why not the murders? He already knew he was going to die. I'm sure the prosecutor offered him a deal. Life in prison if you fess up, for the families' closure."

"Have you talked to the prosecutor?"

"No."

"Then how do you know?"

"I guess I don't."

"Then don't guess," said Frankie. "You can't guess stuff like that. If a woman comes in here and tells me she's my mother, I'm going to get my father to verify it, you know? No guessing in journalism."

"I wasn't going to write it without checking."

"Good. And, oh, by the way, how the fuck are you going to explain away the evidence at Brune's house that links him to these girls?"

David smiled.

For the first time, Frankie perked up. "What? What did you find?"

"Did you guys ever read what was in that box?"

"Just a couple pages," he said. "Cindy read about half, I think. What?"

"Like I said, Brune was living alone in 1984, when the woman escaped from his house. But from 1981 to September 1982, during the time of Sarah's abduction and murder, Brune had a roommate."

"Why didn't that come out in trial?"

"It did, sort of, but Brune's lawyers didn't do anything with it. They didn't connect the dots for the jury. I think maybe Brune even told them not to."

"Who was it?"

"A nineteen-year-old man he'd first met through scouting. Brune let him live there, rent-free, so he could save some money. And get this. The kid abruptly quit his job and moved out of that house a week after Creston's body was found."

Frankie stared blankly into the air to David's right, deep in thought. "It's another suspect, I guess. But you're a long way from being able to suggest he was involved."

"I know. But it's something, right?"

"It's something," admitted Frankie.

"It's nothing," said Sergeant Hugh Boylan, turning a piece of fish with his fork. Boylan had been a patrolman on the Medina police force in the fall of '82, when blond-bobbed little Sarah Creston was snatched off her bike just outside of town. Later, he'd walked the line, looking for evidence in the field where her body was found. In the years since, he'd risen in the ranks and was now facing retirement after recently turning down an offer by city council to become the next chief. "You're five years late," he'd told them in a secret meeting that had occurred in the back room of this mildewed honky-tonk. "So fuck you, fuck you, and fuck you. I got a piece of land out in West by-God Virginia and as soon as I have my pension, that's where you can find me."

The dining room of the restaurant—a saloon called the Inn Between, which was neither an inn nor actually between anything—was dim, and David and Boylan had it all to themselves at three in the afternoon.

"What do you mean, it's nothing?" asked David.

Boylan shrugged. "No evidence. What do you got? A guy that might have lived with him around the time Sarah was murdered?"

"If he was there at the time, he would have to have known what Brune was up to."

"Yeah?" Boylan looked up from his plate. David felt the man was trying to figure out just how stupid this young reporter really was. "Because of the cat hair they found on that girl? Because the hairs match the samples taken from his house, that means Sarah was in the house? You're assuming too much."

"Help me out."

"Those cat hairs were all over his van, too. Maybe he just kept her in the van that whole time." Boylan shoveled another forkful of scrod under his mustache.

David rubbed distractedly at the back of his head. "Mr.—Detect—I mean, Sergeant Boylan? I was hoping you'd let me take a look at the police reports, incident reports and stuff from that case."

"Why do you want to see all that stuff?" he asked, wiping his mouth.

"Well, what if Brune really didn't do it?"

"Brune did it. I was there for the whole thing. The arrest. The trial. He was a monster. He raped those women. And he killed those girls. Look, this is still a small town. Everyone knows the Crestons. Everyone knew Sarah. You weren't here. That murder nearly broke this town. Its spirit. Closing the case healed that a little. I don't know what would have happened if they hadn't caught Brune, if they didn't have the evidence to tie him to Sarah's murder. We don't need anyone picking at the scab. I like to think I have an open mind, so I might be interested in anything you find that would show this Trimble character knew it was going on. Maybe then we could get him, too. But I don't want you suggesting Brune was innocent. I watched his execution. And I slept like a baby that night."

"So can I—"

"Fuck, man. Can I see the reports? Can I see the reports? Yes. You can see the goddamn . . ." Boylan trailed off, looking across the room. "Sorry," he said. He shook his head. "He couldn't have sex with her. He couldn't manage to get it up. So he molested her with a screwdriver. It was still in her when we found the body. He put metal clamps on her tits and wired them to a car battery. It burned her skin off. That stuff stays with you. That's the stuff you're going to read about in those files, David." Boylan made eye contact with the reporter. The man was depressed, David saw. No, not depressed. Haunted. "You really want to have that in your head?"

While he waited for Boylan to copy the police reports, he hunted down the prosecutor's notes from the trial. "Haven't looked at the file myself for about twenty years," said County Prosecutor Martin Baxter, through a window at reception. "They're probably in the microfilm now. You're welcome to take a look."

The microfilm contained much more material than David had expected. Too much to be just witness statements and transcripts. It didn't take him long to discover why—the grand jury testimony was included as well.

Testimony presented to a grand jury in the state of Ohio was kept secret, an exception to the generous public records laws there. Reporters were expressly forbidden to view these documents. Prosecutors claimed they needed this privilege so they could present confidential informants to the grand jury without compromising their safety. The real reason was the grand jury often serves as a rough draft of the trial, a chance for the prosecutor to test a particular strategy to see if it might be accepted by a regular jury. This system allows prosecutors to present a case to a grand jury over and over and over again until they find a strategy that grants them an indictment. In Ohio, there's an old saying: prosecutors can indict a ham sandwich.

David played it cool. He printed each page, skimming the testimony as he went along, praying he'd have enough time to print everything he needed before the office discovered the mix-up.

Trimble had testified in front of the grand jury. A young, ambitious assistant prosecutor named Martin Baxter had led the questioning.

BAXTER: Did your friend, Ronil Brune, ever talk about kidnapping girls?

TRIMBLE: Not girls, but women.

BAXTER: What did he say?

TRIMBLE: He'd say stuff, like, all women have rape fantasies. That, secretly, they want to be taken and it was an okay thing to do so long as you put them back.

BAXTER: Did he say how he would do it?

TRIMBLE: We both came up with ideas. Like, you know, I suggested to weld the hook into the floor of the van.

BAXTER: What?

TRIMBLE: But I thought it was all talk, okay? A fantasy of his. I liked to go cruising with him, looking for girls on bikes out in the country. Just for fun but not for real. Just drive by. Kind of like catching and releasing trout. I thought we was just telling stories.

BAXTER: Tell us what Brune did.

TRIMBLE: Well, I never saw him do anything, but he talked about it a lot.

The testimony continued for over forty pages. Each time Trimble incriminated himself, Baxter deflected his answers and implicated Brune. It was clear the young prosecutor was trying a strategy on the grand jury, one that painted Brune as an overbearing control freak, and Trimble as his malleable protégé.

BAXTER: Did Brune ever bring women back to the house?

TRIMBLE: Oh, just, you know, girls he was dating. Women, I mean.

BAXTER: And was he having sex with these women in the house? Was he rough with them?

TRIMBLE: He couldn't have sex with them. Had something to do with some football injury. He would ask me to have sex with them. A lot of them were into it. He'd watch. He liked me to put things in them.

BAXTER: Things?

TRIMBLE: Vibrators. The top of a bowling pin. Stuff.

Printing the last page, David realized he'd lost all track of time. It was a quarter to four in the afternoon. He'd never checked in with his editor. He'd forgotten to pick up Boylan's reports. And he was going to be late getting back to his apartment to meet Elizabeth—they had planned to go running in the park at five.

As soon as he stepped out of the microfilm dungeon and his cell phone could find a signal again, it beeped. Andy, his editor, had left several messages. The last text read simply, *Hey, Fuckhead. I'm drinking at the Harbor Inn. Find me.*

By the time he arrived in Cleveland and made his way through the Flats across the swing bridge, to the little brick bar with wood benches and everything on draft, Andy was hammered and angry. "This Brune shit has got to stop," he said, after buying David a shot of Irish whiskey. "Cindy told me what you're working on. Fine. It's a waste of time, but fine. Only, do it in your spare time. I need shorter pieces. And I need more. I need something this week, or we don't have a paper. And if we don't have a paper, my kids don't eat. You don't want to take food out of my kids' mouths, do ya?"

"No."

"Good. Then give me twelve hundred words on this science wiz who's coming to Kent. Tonight."

Elizabeth was upset. He was missing dinner again, another lonely night for her in their apartment. He felt himself getting angry, in defense. As if any of this were her fault.

Back at the office, he thumbed through the notes Andy had copied for him. The scientist was a man named Ronald Mallett. He was a theoretical physicist who had dreamed up a way to twist the fabric of the universe into a loop using high-energy laser beams—much like stirring a cup of coffee until it creates a vortex. He was in town pushing a book.

It was hard stuff to digest—David had taken Intro to Astronomy at Kent, but this was far more advanced. Essentially, what Mallett was attempting to do was to send a subatomic particle—"information," he called it—into the past. Moments, mere moments, mind you. But if it worked . . . well, how fucking *cool*.

To his surprise, David discovered Mallett's number listed online and was able to get the physicist to agree to an impromptu interview a little after eight that evening. Mallett spoke of his father's sudden death at an early age and how that event had motivated him to pursue this quest for time travel. Unfortunately, Mallett's device allowed for travel only as far back as the device was turned on. No going back fifty years to save his dad; it was a bittersweet revelation.

There was only one question David posed that the scientist considered worthy of a little regard. It was this:

"If this machine you build can one day be made to send information back in time, would you necessarily even need to send it? For instance, I make up my mind to send today's stock listings back in time to the beginning of the day, so that I can take advantage of the markets. Well, when I turn on that machine at the beginning of the day, that message should already be waiting for me, right? Because I will eventually send it. Now, I use the info to play the markets but then decide not to send that info back at the end of the day. Why do I have to? I already used the information."

"What you're talking about is *intentionality*," said Mallett. "You have to have made up your mind to send that information back no matter what."

But David wondered.

He turned in a draft at 1:17 a.m., a little past deadline, but he didn't think Andy would care that much. It was titled "Master of the Universe." It wasn't anything to tack to the fridge. The science talk was too dense even with his generous use of blue-collar metaphor, and the writing could be kicked up a bit. But it was finished.

The next afternoon, as David sat at his desk in the offices of the *Independent*, his eyelids pulling toward the floor by invisible weights, his face unshaven, his mind full of misery following a morning spat with Elizabeth, his heart beating dreadfully as he feared he was letting Brune's mystery sneak away while he was occupied by other things, Andy walked by and patted him on the head.

And that felt good, didn't it? To be liked again? Sure. Sure it did.

Besides, there was still time left in the day to do a little research on Brune. He could make it to Medina before the records room closed if he left right now. He wondered what secrets he might . . .

. . . discover in the police reports Boylan copied for you in Medina?" asked Russo, leaning slightly on the partition that corralled the jury. "What did you find?"

"An interview with Riley Trimble, the man sitting there." David pointed over to the defendant, a gaunt man not yet fifty, with gray hair, cut short. He wore an orange jumpsuit a couple sizes too large but his hands were not cuffed. David could still feel the animalistic terror he'd felt when he'd first spotted Trimble's face in the dark, outside the window of his car, floating, ghostlike, across a dirty lawn.

Russo walked to his table and picked up a few sheets of paper. He handed one to Trimble's lead attorney, Terry Synenberger, and walked another to Judge Siegel. "State's exhibit, H. Police report taken by Medina Detective Shane Somersby, dated October 27, 1984. David, why was that report of particular importance to you?"

"I found it interesting for a couple reasons," said David. "At the time this report was taken, Brune was a suspect in the murder of Sarah Creston, which is why they were interviewing his roommate, Trimble. The police were told that Trimble had lived with Brune that summer and they wanted to know if he had seen anything strange at the house. According to that report, Trimble told the detective that he had moved back to his parents' house in Marietta on September tenth, 1982. I found that interesting because Sarah was abducted on September sixth. Her body was discovered September ninth, and the turtle trappers who found the body said it must have been dumped that day, because they had been in the area the day before and had seen nothing. If Brune had kidnapped Sarah and taken her back to his house like he did with the women he later raped, then I thought it was very likely Trimble knew about it, or was possibly even an accomplice. I thought it was interesting that he moved out of the house the day after Sarah's body was dumped. That suggested to me that maybe he wanted to distance himself from a crime scene. Also, the detective at one point asked Trimble if he'd be willing to volunteer his fingerprints and take a lie detector test. Trimble refused."

"It was shortly after this that you met Riley Trimble for the first time, is that correct?"

"Yes."

"Mr. Neff, could you tell the jury, please, about that first encounter?"

"Yes, I can," said David. "The first time we met, he asked me if I wanted a blow job."

———□———

How long before I'm back in a courtroom? David wondered, four years later. *How long before it's me in that orange jumpsuit?*

He was in a rental, a blue compact vehicle that was less a car and more a Japanese torture device of some sort, zooming along I-80 toward the smooth foothills of western Pennsylvania—the Bug would never make it through the mountains. The wheel was uncomfortably low and the seat dug into his spine. If there hadn't been more important things to worry about—such things as *I'm the only suspect in the attempted murder of the man I'm researching* and *Did Elizabeth have an affair with the Man from Primrose Lane* and *When do the withdrawals start*—he'd have been a little more consumed by it. He'd already put Synenberger on retainer. And even though Synenberger knew well that he could afford the blue-blood rate now, the lawyer would only take $2,500. "After the Trimble debacle, I owe you one," he had said. "Besides, this is going to blow over. It's silly."

He had considered, briefly, ending his quest to find the true identity of the Man from Primrose Lane. If Sackett learned he was still digging, he might be mad enough to arrest him for obstructing justice or intimidating witnesses. Might be persuasive enough to get the prosecutor on board. But if this became a thing . . . if the bottom dropped out and they indicted him for attempted murder based on circumstantial evidence . . . it was important to gather all the information he could about the victim before that happened. If he could figure out who the Man from Primrose Lane really was, before he'd started calling himself "Joe King," maybe a more likely suspect would present himself.

And much like the Sarah Creston case, he realized, he didn't think he could quit if he wanted to. His wife's fingerprints had been found on the man's bedpost. Fuck the real identity of Joe King's killer—the real mystery he was compelled to solve was how Elizabeth came to be in that house on Primrose Lane. He didn't believe his wife had cheated on him. Not with an old hermit. Anyway, cheating wasn't in her nature. He was the only family she really had, other than Aunt Peggy. Would she risk that? He didn't think so. Then again, he'd never imagined she could commit suicide.

The gun from his safe-deposit box was a bit of luck, actually. Sackett and Larkey were so sure it was the murder weapon, perhaps they'd rethink their investigation when ballistics proved it hadn't been used in the crime.

He was halfway to Bellefonte, on the edge of a mountain, when the withdrawal began to take hold. It happened suddenly and he knew at once what it was. It started with a sense of vertigo, as if he were leaning his head against the window of a very high apartment, looking at the cars below and feeling the distance that separated him from the ground, imagining the sweep of the wind that would cradle his body if he fell through the glass. He pulled to the shoulder of the interstate highway, opened the door, and puked onto the gravel. The remnants of an Egg McMuffin and a large coffee became an abstract painting on the ground. When he sat up, he felt lighter, as if his brain had shrunk an inch in diameter and was swimming around inside his skull, bumping into bone.

David stopped for a ginger ale and Tylenol at the next rest stop and for a while the symptoms subsided. It wasn't until he neared the Bush House Hotel that he felt the first warm rush of fever drift across his forehead.

David trucked his luggage inside and secured the largest apartment in the hotel—a four-room suite on the top floor, overlooking Spring Creek. There was no elevator and he felt too sick to climb the three flights of stairs to his room just now, so he left his bags with the concierge. He asked for directions to Zion Elder Care, current residence of Carol Dechant, last surviving relative of the Man from Primrose Lane's alter ego, Joe King.

"She's visiting with her son right now," the receptionist told him. "Room 119, end of the hall."

It was a small and yellow room. Carol Dechant lay in her bed, which was raised so that she could see Dr. Phil on the television. In a chair beside her sat a thin man, fortyish, with large bifocals: her son.

"Mr. Dechant, your mother has a visitor," said the receptionist, a largish man with a lisp. Then he quickly left. It was obvious to David that he did not care for Carol's son.

"Who are you?" the man asked.

David ignored his tone and put on a smile—hard to do when he felt so much like throwing up. He put out his hand over Carol's body. It was shaking slightly. He couldn't hold it straight. "David Neff," he said. "I'm a reporter from Akron working on a story about Joe King."

The man took his hand. "Spencer Dechant," he said. "Do you know my mother?"

David sensed alarm in Spencer's voice. Why was he afraid?

"No," he said, and looked to Carol for the first time.

She was at least eighty years old, and her skin had taken on the translucent sheen of the aged. She stared at the television but David could tell she wasn't processing anything. Her right eye was a mottled cataract. Gone was the sparkle of life but it was clear she had once been a stunning young thing with long blond hair. He understood at once the reason Spencer was afraid—his mother was senile. It was the boy who must be directing the lawsuit for the Man from Primrose Lane's assets. Soon Carol would be dead, and as the sole heir, Spencer stood to inherit millions. Perhaps he justified it by believing it's what Carol really wanted as he scribbled his mother's signature on the forms their lawyer left for her.

"She's having an off day," said Spencer.

"Does she have any on days anymore?"

"Of course," he said. "All the time. Just yesterday she beat me at rummy. She's very lucid most of the time. Just an off day. Like I said." He paused to swallow. "So what brings you out here? If you'd called first, I could have warned you about this. I just hope she's feeling better tomorrow. I'd hate for you to waste such a long trip."

"Uh-huh." David rubbed his chin. He looked at the TV for a moment, pretending to be interested in Dr. Phil's assessment of teenage newlyweds, but in his head he imagined pulling out a cigarette from the pack he kept in his pocket, the pack he could feel pressing up against his thigh at that very moment, imagined placing it in his mouth, tasting the poison, the sweet chemicals soaking into his tongue. His stomach lurched again. There was nothing left to throw up, though, and it passed.

"Did your mother ever tell you if she knew who the Man from Primrose Lane really was?"

Spencer shook his head.

"Did you even ever ask her?"

"No," he said.

"Identity thieves prey on family and friends first. Did your mother have any close friends who disappeared? Any friends of hers have sons who disappeared years ago, in a weird way, unannounced?"

"If she did, she didn't tell me."

"Are you sure?"

"I'm sure."

"Spence," said David.

"Spencer."

"Spence. I admit that I'm a little out of practice. Haven't reported on a story in over four years. Wasn't particularly good at it when I was doing it regularly, to tell the truth. But I think you're lying to me about something."

"I . . ."

"Maybe not lying, Spence. But you're holding something back." David began to walk around the bed. As he did, the man hunched in his seat, possibly expecting the writer to punch him. "I can see it in your eyes. It's the same look my kid gives me when I catch him doing something wrong. You think that if you tell me your secret, I'm going to make it so that you don't get a piece of that money. But, Spence, I don't give a shit about that money. I don't care who gets it. I don't even care, not really, that you're taking advantage of your invalid mother to get at that money. It's every man for himself, anyway. Isn't it, Spence? Besides, she'd do it herself if she weren't so far gone, wouldn't she?"

Spencer opened his mouth to answer but closed it again, slowly.

David stopped a foot away from the man in the chair. "Here's the thing, Spencer. I don't give a fuck what you're up to. You're not the first kid to get impatient. I promise you this, though. Nothing you tell me will affect your case in court. I'll keep it in confidence. Strictly off the record and on the QT, as they say. In exchange, I'll be sure to keep you out of my next book."

"A guy came by the house," he said quickly. "About five years ago, before she got sick. My stepdad told this to me before his heart attack, in '08. This man that came by the house asked the same questions you was asking. Except polite, you know. He was trying to find the Man from Primrose Lane. This would have been about a year before the guy was shot in his house in Akron."

"Who?"

"Said his name was Arbogast."

"Fake name."

"Yeah. The guy from *Psycho*, right?"

David nodded.

"What did your mother tell him?"

"Said he should go see Frank Lucarelli."

"Who is Lucarelli?"

"He owns the pizza shop on top of Lamb Street."

"Why did she tell him to go see Frank?"

Spencer shrugged. "She dated Lucarelli back in the day, before my dad come along."

"Your stepfather tell you anything else about this guy?"

"Not that I remember."

"Okay. Thanks for your time, Spence." David started toward the door.

"David." The voice came on a breeze, like the fluttering of a heavy curtain against an open window.

She was sitting upright in bed, reaching out for David with pale fingers. The blanket had fallen away. She wore a thin pale green hospital gown underneath, spotted with old food. Or was it blood?

He looked to Spencer, who had tucked his feet under him in some defensive move. "She doesn't know about me, does she? Did she read my book?"

"David was my biological father," said Spencer.

"David," she said again.

"She does this," said Spencer. "Talks in the night. Calling out names."

"David," she whispered, leaning closer.

"What?" he asked.

"You were always so handsome."

She lay back in the bed, then, and her eyes drifted back to the television.

"What happened?" asked the receptionist from the doorway.

"Another one of her spells," said Spencer.

"You should probably let her get some rest. Both of you."

Without saying goodbye, Spencer walked out of the room, and David followed, keeping space between them as they traveled the hallway to the exit.

"I'd never hurt my mother," he heard the man whisper.

He considered driving to Lucarelli's, but returned to the hotel instead. He had a hunch he was about to feel much worse. He was right. As he flipped on the television and sat upon the queen-size bed, the first brainstorm hit him like a seizure. A wave of electricity rippled across his neurons like an internal aurora borealis, misfiring axons as it went, causing him to simultaneously piss his pants, raise his right hand, and sneeze. Somewhere deep inside his amygdala, the wave washed up against an arrangement of neurons that housed a distant remembrance. For several minutes, David's consciousness was elsewhere, reliving this memory in five senses:

It was dark. And warm. And he was enveloped by the sweet smell of his mother's shoes. He sat upon them, a mound of heels and flip-flops and high-topped leather boots. The door was ajar and let in just enough light for him to see the redhead seated in the closet beside him, Melinda, his cousin, and she was about three years old. And, if she was three, that meant he was four.

What is this? he tried to say, but nothing came out of his throat. David tried to move his hands. Though he could feel them, they would not obey. His pudgy little-boy fingers remained where they were, holding Melinda's. They were hiding. He had always used the shoe closet for games of hide-and-seek, he remembered. This was the shoe closet inside her apartment, in Garretsville, the one-bedroom efficiency she'd rented after the divorce.

Her voice carried across the apartment from the living room. One end of a conversation: "No. No. I know. Yes. What do you want me to do? He won't take me back, goddamn it! He knows."

What if I'm trapped here? he wondered. *What if this is like TiVo or something? What if, somehow, I hit "start over" and now I have to watch my life play out in front of me, again, for the next thirty years?*

He concentrated on opening his eyes (even though they were already open), on willing himself to wake up as if this were all a dream and not one of those episodic memories Dr. Popodopovich had warned him about.

Wake up. Wake up. Wake up.

Whoever his mother was talking to, she was really worked up.

"He knows," she said again. "No, not about that. About us. He just doesn't know who. And I wouldn't tell him."

Melinda held his hands tightly and he felt his body lean forward of its own accord and bring his eyes around to the slit in the door. Outside, in the kitchen beyond the living area, his mother was pouring Wild Turkey into a bright red plastic cup. She was crying.

"You know something?" she said. "You can go fuck your apologies, okay? You should have left me there. You should have left it alone."

He didn't want to see this. Didn't care about the nasty details of the divorce. (Except, he must, right? Because why did his mind bring him here? Here of all places?)

Wake up!

He felt his body rise into the air. He heard the sound of the ocean, of a violent rushing wind.

Wake . . .

. . . up!" he yelled at the empty bedroom.

He didn't open his eyes, for they were still open. One moment he was rising into the darkness, the next he was sitting up in bed. The vertigo caused by the change in perspective was too much. He stumbled to the bathroom and collapsed in front of the commode. He heaved. Bile trickled from his mouth, dripping into the toilet. His throat stung.

His forehead felt too hot for a normal fever. Someone knocked on his door. Loudly.

"Who—"

He vomited again. The knocking grew urgent. His entire body shook.

The desk clerk, he thought. *Someone must have heard me screaming and called the front desk.*

Knocking. He pulled himself to his feet and started for the door. He felt another one coming, another brain storm, a pulse of electricity behind his eyes, threatening to break like lightning. He knew he had to reach the door to unbolt it, to let help in. But he did not think he could get there before the storm hit.

Here it comes, he thought.

If it took him away, his body would fall to the ground, he knew. He might not wake up in time to eat or drink. He might fall on his back and suffocate on his own bile. Dr. Popodopovich had warned him it would be bad, but David had never considered the withdrawals might really kill him.

He reached for the bolt just as the thunderhead broke in his brain. As he fell, he was unsure if he'd managed to unlock the door and turn the handle. He thought his odds were something like fifty-fifty. *Ironic*, he thought as he fell into another memory. *I might be killed by the medication I took to keep from killing myself.*

He thought of Ronald Mallett, that physicist he'd interviewed for the *Independent* so long ago. Mallett had told him about a frightening theory, something called Zeno's paradox, a lovely little physics conundrum: If an object falls, it must first reach a halfway point before it connects with the ground, and from there must again reach a midway point between that location and the ground. And half and half and half, etc. Was it really even possible to connect with the floor? Shouldn't he only travel halfway there for infinity? To David, it didn't matter. He was unconscious long before he collided with the floor. David's mind was overtaken by another brain storm triggered by the depletion of Rivertin in his system. Halos of electricity danced around his cerebral cortex and across his brain stem. It swallowed him up, consciousness and all, and delivered him into the realm of memory, a cascade of remembrances lost over the years but which the withdrawals rediscovered easily.

He was falling again, but slower. He looked around, as he had then, and found himself wrapped in the blanket of the bed he shared with his father. David was, what? Three? Four? After the divorce. He was wrapped in a cocoon of blanket that had caught him as he rolled off the bed and was now holding him suspended, inches above the floor, while his father slept the sleep of second-shift men. He could smell the bitter stank of Pabst, his father's dinner, and wondered why he never drank the stuff now, because it was a smell he loved. He listened to his father breathing, his inhalations dragging on for longer than David's little body could match. Sometimes it seemed like his father wasn't breathing at all, and that scared him, he could feel the fright in him, because his father was all that was left. His mother had moved on. Was elsewhere. Sometimes he saw her, he knew, but the time, the space between those meetings was immeasurable and might as well be an eternity. His father could not die and leave him here alone. Please. Please. And the breathing began again. It always did. It always would, he reassured himself. He was thirty-four now, not three, and his father was very much alive. This was a memory. Not a dream. But dreamlike. It felt good to be here, wrapped in these blankets. He wished he would stay.

In the back of a Volkswagen now, a yellow thing his mom called a Bug.

"Keep your head down, Davey," she said, a beautiful thin thing with obsidian eyes, sitting in the passenger seat, holding him against the back seat with one hand. Her hair fell down her back, over a leather-braided jacket. Uncle Ira was driving. The car smelled like pot. He had just been abducted from his grandmother's front yard.

"We're taking you home, Davey," Uncle Ira said. "Don't cry."

But he was crying, he realized. Big, sobby, choking gasps. He wanted his dad. His dad was at work and didn't even know he was gone! What if he came home and forgot he had a son because he wasn't there? What if he didn't know how to find him? *Please take me back!*

"Don't cry, hon," said his mom. But she was crying, too.

College. The first hot day of spring. May 4 at Kent State.

David stood vigil in the Prentice Hall parking lot, on the spot where William Schroeder was shot and killed by a member of the Ohio National Guard in 1970. This was his hour to stand in Schroeder's place before he was to be relieved by another member of the May 4th Task Force. Alumni on their yearly pilgrimage walked by in quiet reflection, some with children.

"What's he doing, Dad?" a little red-haired girl asked.

"He's paying tribute to Bill," the man said. "Standing in his place. Bill was my friend. The one I told you about."

"It's so sad," she said.

"It is. Come on, Katy, I want to find my old dorm."

And then there was that *tugging* sensation again, as if a great wind were pushing at him, pushing him back. David wondered if this might be what certain brain damage was like from the inside. Was this what they meant when they said, "My life flashed before my eyes?"

David wondered if he was dead. He wondered, after a while, if there really was such a thing as death.

"I hate you," he said to his stepmother, standing in the kitchen, papered walls, and yellow.

"I love you," Elizabeth whispered in his ear. The smell of his old car: oil, leather.

"I love you," his dad said to him, carrying David in his arms.

"I hate you," said Riley Trimble as two police officers pulled him out of the courthouse. "I hate you forever!"

In bed. Sunlight on the sides of a dark curtain. The room in shadow. A shape beside him.

"Elizabeth," he whispered.

David reached out at the shape and found that his hand worked. He was no longer a prisoner inside his own body. Somehow, he was manipulating this memory. Did that make it a dream?

His hand found her body under the covers, her skin warm and alive, soft and covered in a thin and lovely down. She turned to him and he saw her outline in the dim light and he pulled her to his mouth. He kissed her. Gently. Then more. Her lips parted and her tongue set out to find his. He climbed onto her and she took him in her embrace, her lithe legs wrapping around his frame.

"I've missed you," he said. "God, I've missed you."

"I've missed you," she replied and reached down to his stiffened prick. She guided it quickly and he pushed into her. She moaned.

"Elizabeth," he whispered.

Suddenly she stopped writhing beneath him.

"What?" That voice. That voice was not Elizabeth's.

"What?" he said.

An arm reached over to the bedside and clicked on the table lamp. Katy stared back at him, naked, with something close to actual alarm.

EPISODE EIGHT

THE FORGER'S TALE

"He offered to fellate you?" asked Russo.

David felt the eyes of the jury. He knew the old woman in the back row must be picturing the defendant going down on him and, to his horror, he felt the beginnings of uncontrollable giggles.

"Yes," he said.

"Could you describe the encounter for the jury?"

"One night in November last year, I parked outside Riley Trimble's trailer down in Steubenville, intending to basically stake out his house."

"And why would you want to do that?"

"Well, by then, based on the files in Brune's box and the grand jury testimony I had uncovered, I had become convinced that Trimble was at least an accomplice in the abduction and murder of Sarah Creston. Unlike Brune, though, Trimble was free to continue killing. I went to his place to see if I could catch him stalking young girls."

"And what did you see?"

"I saw . . ." David clapped a hand over his mouth as a giggle bubbled up and out. He was quick to cover it with a cough. No one noticed except Elizabeth, who stared back at him with a look of concern he'd never seen on her face before. He tried to think of something sad. He thought of the autopsy pictures he'd seen of Sarah, the way the blood in her body had pooled on her back, painting it forever the color of a ripened eggplant, in sharp contrast to her alabaster face. That did it. He began again. "I saw . . .

. . . a company truck for a heating and air-conditioning business parked outside Trimble's garage.

An advertisement on the side promised HVAC SPECIALS! HEAT OR COOL YOUR HOME FOR LESS! He had hoped to find Trimble working in some butcher shop or shaping steel in a factory by the river. He hadn't expected this. He had never considered the man he suspected of being the real child killer might have secured a job giving him easy access to thousands of homes. He felt sick.

This is too big, he thought. *I should turn this over to another reporter. Someone who's been doing this for longer than a couple months.*

Problem was, nobody believed him. And it wasn't a tidy mystery. Too hard to explain. A man had already been executed for the crime. Physical evidence was found on Sarah Creston that matched samples taken from Brune's home and van. And now, after Brune is long dead, a rookie reporter thinks it was actually one of his scouts who was the serial killer? It was a tough sell.

In for a penny, he thought, and sat back in his seat, eyeing the house across the street from the shadows.

It's difficult to keep track of long stretches of time when nothing happens to separate one moment from the next. How long had he been sitting there? Two hours? Five? He didn't want to turn the car on to find out, didn't want to risk Trimble seeing the dash lights from his home, where the flickering glow of a television set danced in a dark room beyond a picture window. He could have checked his cell phone but he was in the boonies of southern Ohio, a cellular black hole, and all the roaming had drained its battery. Minutes began to feel like seconds, hours like minutes, speeding up just to get to something, anything, until he noticed the TV was off.

It was one of those country nights utterly devoid of light. A cloudy sky under a new moon, far from any city of note. He had to concentrate to pick up the faintest shadows across the street. He saw the outline of Trimble's house, the tree in the front yard, the truck in the driveway. And something else, something nearer the door . . .

David felt the wind suck out of him as if a ghost had punched him in the gut.

Trimble was standing there, staring back at him, fifty feet away.

Ever so slowly, Trimble was shuffling his feet toward the car, in a straight line, without lowering his shoulders, creating the effect of a man hovering in the air, floating to David rather than walking.

If I move, will he come after me? wondered David. *Or will he run away?*

Hell with it. He wasn't going to let him get close enough to pounce. David reached over to the passenger's seat where he had set the keys. In his haste, his fingers knocked the keys to the floor with a loud jingling. He bent down, fishing around the floor amid cans of soda and rolled-up McDonald's bags.

When he sat up, Trimble was at the window, staring back at him, his ruddy mouth open, his dark tongue lolling around inside like sentient cancer. He lifted a hand, shaped in a gaping circle, and moved it up and down like a piston. David's head was so awash in numbing terror that it took a moment for him to realize Trimble was pantomiming a hand job.

"Want me to touch you?" asked Trimble in a low voice. "Do you want me to suck your dick? What do you want? Do you want to watch me jerk off?" Trimble lifted his shirt and David saw that the man was not wearing any pants. A narrow, long, and erect penis rubbed a soapy trail of pre-cum against the window of his car.

"Mr. Trimble," David said, through the window, as loudly as he could. "Mr. Trimble, please stop that."

Trimble's penis disappeared under the shirt in an instant. Trimble stared back at him, a look of anger at David's supposed trickery. "Who the fuck are you and how do you know me?"

"I came down to talk to you about your old scoutmaster. About Ronil Brune."

"Why the hell you outside my house at two in the morning?"

David didn't know how to answer that. He hadn't prepared for this. His mind was a dark void. And still he hadn't managed to start the car. The door wasn't even locked, he realized.

"Are you stalking me?" asked Trimble. "What the hell do you want?"

"Do . . . do you think Ronil Brune really killed Sarah Creston and those other two girls?" he asked.

"What?" he crinkled his nose at David as if he smelled sewage. "You a fucking reporter? Get the fuck out of here." Trimble turned toward the house and started walking away.

David rolled down his window. "I don't think he killed anyone."

Trimble stopped but didn't turn.

"Obviously, Brune raped those women. But he wasn't a murderer. All those women he let go, even when he was supposedly killing these children. That's not how it works. Serial killers don't suddenly start *not* killing their victims. Their violence escalates."

Trimble looked back at him. "I know he didn't do it," he said. "I tried telling the prosecutor. But he was so sure. Said he had cat hair or something that showed Creston was at his house."

"But when Creston was abducted, you lived there, too. And a day after she was found, you moved back here, to Steubenville, to be with your parents. What made you leave so quickly?"

"I got a bad case of shingles," he said.

"That's what you told your boss at work?"

"Yeah."

"If I track him down, is that going to jibe with what he remembers? What was the name of your doctor?"

"I didn't see no doctor."

"Well . . . that doesn't make much sense," said David. "How do you know it was shingles if you didn't see a doctor?"

"You're confusing me," he said, and he was turning now, walking back toward the car. "I remember now. Yes. I saw a doctor, yes. Company's doctor or something. The fuck is it to you, anyway, Encyclopedia Brown?"

"Did you kill Sarah Creston?" There. It was out. Like dice thrown from a cup.

Trimble smiled. "C'mere," he said. "Get out of the car."

David rolled the window up quickly and started the car. Something hit the window, a loud *THUMP*. He looked over. It was Trimble's dick, still hard and dripping. Had the talk of murder turned him on more? David thought so. Trimble started pumping his body against the car.

Finally, David clicked it into drive. The moment the car lurched forward, Trimble shot his load, trailing semen along the side of the reporter's car like a racing stripe from hell. David found an all-night wash in the next suburb and spent a half hour disinfecting his car, trying not to puke.

David returned to the apartment in Cuyahoga Falls just as the sun peeked over the horizon. Elizabeth was in the shower, preparing for another day of teaching. The dining room smelled strange. Like liquor or some musk, like a strap of leather lying in the sunshine. He couldn't place it. He assumed she had read one of those thick, glossy mags the night before, the kind with the pull-tab cologne samples.

His notes were spread over the table, arranged into piles labeled by Post-it-note tombstones: Sarah Creston, Donna Doyle, Jennifer Poole. There was a new stack, too, pages of new reports on the unsolved abduction and murder of a girl from Steubenville that had occurred two years *after* Brune was already in prison. She had lived two blocks from Trimble's house.

How many more girls should there be? he wondered often. *How many am I missing?*

He thought, again, of Elizabeth's sister. It was tempting to let the pull of his obsession take him there, to believe Trimble may have abducted Elaine as well. He understood the allure of trying to lump every little girl abduction to one bogeyman. Sometimes even good detectives did that. Better to think one man was responsible for all the horror. But there was no sign that Trimble had even scouted the region north of Akron. And he would have stood out like a transient in the ritzy section of Lakewood where Elizabeth had lived.

David spent his spare time searching for some bit of circumstantial evidence to connect Trimble to Donna and Jennifer. Though Sarah's was the only murder for which Brune was convicted, David had spoken to the detectives in charge of Donna and Jennifer's cases and had been told their files had been closed, their deaths long ago attributed to Brune due to the fact that those animal hairs were found on Jennifer's body, hairs identical to those that had come off the carpet in Brune's house and van, and Donna had been wrapped in a plastic bag that had been traced back to the bedspread in Brune's master bedroom. "You can't kill a man twice," one detective told him.

How long do you look for something that doesn't exist before it becomes a delusion? Before it becomes an obsession?

"You're home," she said from the doorway of the bathroom, naked but for a terry-cloth towel wrapped around her hair, diamond drops of water on her small breasts reflecting the light from the window.

"Sorry about last night."

"You need to sleep."

"I need to go to work."

"But you haven't slept. You look like crap."

"I'll be fine. I'll grab some coffee."

"It's dangerous to drive like that. Why don't you lie down for a half hour?"

God, her voice was grating sometimes, wasn't it? It bit into his head with sharp teeth. He could feel the headache growing behind his eyes. "Can't," he said. "I have an article due today."

"Then why did you drive to Steubenville?" This was the tone she used with him all the time now. Why couldn't she see how important this was?

"I had to meet him. I had to see Trimble."

"What's the hurry? The girl was murdered over twenty-five years ago."

He shook his head. "We're talking in circles," he said.

"You're being stupid about this."

"Do you think I want to spend all night on the road?" *Shut up*, he thought. *Shut up. Shut up. Shut your pie-hole before you give me a migraine.*

"So stop."

His field of vision collapsed into a gray dot. Motes of light danced at the edges. "Goddamn it, I can't."

She walked into the bedroom and slammed the door.

David returned to his notes, tall sheets full of his longhand, summaries of Brune's files. He never heard her leave, even though she must have walked right by.

Two hours later he still sat at the dining room table. He had gone through Jennifer's file again and found nothing he could use to place Trimble in her path the day of her death. But a few pages into Donna's paperwork, he caught his breath at the sight of one word: Hap's. He set that report aside from the others. Then he rooted into the box for a detective's interview with Trimble he'd found in Medina. Hap's. There it was again.

Hap's was a meat processing plant in Marshallville. In 1982, the year Sarah Creston was murdered, Trimble had worked as a butcher there. And in 1980, the year Donna was murdered, the man who had discovered her body had written, under occupation, *Meat Cutter, Hap's* on the statement he gave to the detective.

The man's name was Burt Wrenn and David found him still listed in the white pages.

"'Lo?" said a frail voice on the other end of the line.

"Hi, Mr. Wrenn? I'm a reporter who is researching the Donna Doyle case."

"Yeah? They catch him?"

"Well, the police executed Brune four years ago and—"

"Not Brune. The fella that lived with him. The guy that worked next to me. Girlish name."

"Riley?"

"Yessir. Riley Trimble. He . . .

. . . done it,' he told me," said David.

"Objection, Your Honor!" yelled Synenberger, standing. "Hearsay."

"Mr. Wrenn is unfortunately dead and cannot be subpoenaed to testify for this jury," said Russo.

"Your Honor, please," said Synenberger. "This is ridiculous."

"In 1980, Mr. Wrenn reported his suspicions about Trimble to the police," said Russo.

"No such document has been entered into record," countered Synenberger.

"Because none exists, Your Honor. We believe it was purposefully 'misplaced' by the Medina County prosecutor in order to deflect doubt during Brune's trial."

"Your Honor, now this man is impugning the integrity of a respected county prosecutor in order to squeeze this hearsay into record," said Synenberger. "Can we draw the line here, please?"

"State of Ohio would like to enter into record a video deposition of Mr. Wrenn, conducted shortly before his death earlier this year."

"Objection, Your Honor. The defendant, at that time, had just been charged and had yet to obtain legal counsel."

"That is incorrect," said Russo. "Trimble was afforded a public defender, who was present for the deposition. It clearly satisfies the requirements set by *Crawford v. Washington*."

"Objection overruled," said Siegel. A young woman wheeled a TV stand in front of the jury.

"Mr. Wrenn's deposition," said Russo, "taken in the presence of the public defender, two weeks prior to Wrenn's death due to lung cancer."

The screen crackled to life. Members of the gallery craned their necks to get a better look. On the television, the body of a weathered old man sitting on a hospital bed came into focus. Burt Wrenn's nose was obscured by some breathing apparatus that gave his voice an off-putting nasal whine. He spoke at the camera, appearing to address the jury directly. "I, Burt Wrenn, being of sound mind, do offer the following testimony and swear that it is the whole truth, under God.

"In 1980, I worked beside Riley Trimble at Hap's in Marshallville. He and I separated out the different cuts of meats from the body of a cow. Or pig. Deer in the fall. We spent a lot of time in close quarters, talking about family and where we were from. On several occasions I know I talked to him about the spread of land I have in Marshallville. There's nothing on it except an oil well and an access drive. I told him how I would go there in the fall to hunt and I told him how it was the perfect place to get deer because it was on a road that wasn't much used, and out of sight of any house. There's a field of bluegrass there that the deer like to congregate on around dusk. Couldn't have been three weeks after we talked about it that they found that girl, Donna Doyle, lying on the grass by that access road.

"I was suspicious of him, right away. He was always sort of shady. Too smart to be working at the meat market, for example. And he pretended to be stupid. A couple times he'd accidentally say a word that was way over everyone's head and he'd blush and say he'd heard it on the news and the other guys would rib him about it for days. It just creeped me out, though. I remember one word—*verisimilitude*. Who uses a word like that in conversation? I had to look it up.

"When the cops questioned me after they found the girl on my property, I told them about Riley. But I never heard from them again.

"And then I saw on the news that his roommate was arrested for raping all those women and my first thought was, *I bet they did this together. I bet they killed Donna together.* I'd never met Brune. But Riley knew all about my field. After David Neff told me that Riley was living at Brune's house back then and had moved back to Steubenville the day Sarah Creston was found, I was sure of it. I just don't see how Riley couldn't have been a part of these girls' murders. He certainly knew how to cut his meat."

The video ended.

Synenberger shot out of his seat. "Your Honor, is this a deposition or a testimonial? I didn't hear a single question posed."

"Defense council didn't ask any," said Russo. "But they were present. They had their chance."

Synenberger raised his hands at the judge. But Siegel only shrugged. "It is what it is. Take your seat, Terry."

Russo let the room fill up with silence for a moment as his assistant wheeled the TV cart back to the corner of the room. "What did you do after Mr. Wrenn relayed this important information to you, David?"

"I immediately took it to the police, the Canton police, actually, because that's where Donna was from."

"We of course have already learned from prior testimony by Canton detectives that they quickly reinterviewed Trimble. They also had the Bureau of Criminal Investigations and Identification compare a finger-print found on a plastic bag that had been found near Donna's body. That fingerprint, we now know, matched Riley Trimble," said Russo, pointing dramatically at the defendant, who stared back at David. "Did that surprise you, David?"

"No," he said.

"Why not?"

"By the time the results came back from the lab, I was already con-vinced that Trimble was the man who murdered Donna Doyle, Jennifer Poole, and Sarah Creston."

"Thank you, Mr. Neff. No further questions, Your Honor."

"That's lunch, folks," said Judge Siegel. "Defense will cross when we return in an hour."

David looked to Synenberger. Caught his eye. The lawyer winked and then turned away.

—▣—

"Where are you, David?" asked Katy, drawing the sheets around her naked body. "Where do you think you are?"

"Shit, Katy. Where the fuck *am* I?" He rolled off her and sat up. He looked around the room, his rooms, that is, at the Bush House Hotel.

Katy sat back against the headboard, using her left hand on the frame to pull herself up. "I came out here to surprise you," she said. "Only one hotel in Bellefonte. But when I opened the door, there you were, passed out on the floor like some heroin addict. I thought you were dead. I al-most called for an ambulance but then you started talking in your sleep and I knew you were okay, more or less. Anyway, I cleaned you up, got you in bed. You stopped talking around five in the afternoon. But you kept me up all night so I guess I dozed off after that." She looked at the clock on the nightstand: 11:32.

"I've been asleep for twenty-four hours?"

"Longer, hon," she said. "It's eleven-thirty in the *morning*. You passed out Friday night. It's Sunday now."

He'd never slept so long in his life. He wondered if there really might be some brain damage involved.

"Kate, I'm sorry," he said.

She blushed. "Don't apologize," she said. "Why do you think I came out here? I just don't really like you thinking I'm your dead wife when we're bumping uglies. So let's cool it until later." She laughed but he could also see that she was, in some very basic feminine way, quite shook up over their sudden and weird first sexual encounter.

"I'm famished," he said at last. "How about some pizza?"

Lucarelli's Pizzeria was located in a one-story rock building atop Lamb Street, in an allotment overlooking Bellefonte proper. Frank resided in the apartment above the restaurant and his son, who hand-rolled dough beside a large oven as David and Katy ate, brought him down after their plates were cleared. He was a tiny man, covered in liver spots the size of large freckles, bent over an aluminum cane. He wore suede slippers and a long tweed coat tied around his waist. Carol had once been this man's lover, sometime before her dead brother's name had been used by a hermit from Akron. Frank sat in the booth beside Katy without acknowledging her presence.

"Some baked ziti, Dominic," he said. "And a coffee. Not decaf."

Dominic disappeared into the kitchen, muttering something from the motherland under his breath.

Until his son returned, Frank stared at the table in silence, his bottom lip moving slightly of its own accord. *He has some palsy*, thought David. *Something degenerative like Carol, but not Alzheimer's, and not that far along.*

As soon as the fumes from the high-octane coffee hit his olfactory center, drifting up from a ceramic mug in spindly fingers, Frank awoke. His dark eyes opened and surveyed his neighborhood as he sipped the drink loudly. When his eyes found Katy, he winked. He set the mug down.

"I knew when I did it I'd be haunted by the decision my whole life," said Frank, looking up at David. "Ever since I was a little kid, when faced with a decision, I listen to my heart and my heart tells me if I should do it or no. And all my life, if I get a feeling of unrest in my heart, I choose no. Every time except that day. But he was so goddamned *insistent*."

"Who?"

Frank smiled. "I am not as senile as I appear," he said. "I thought of going to the police. Don't know why I never did. I guess I got a little scared. I made a deal with the devil one day, forty-some years ago. Summer of '69. I sold the identity of my girlfriend's dead brother to a man in bed with the Philly Mafia."

"Did you get his name?"

Frank leaned forward. "As a matter of fact, I did."

"Back in the sixties, the Italian Mafia that ran those parts of Philly not controlled by the Irish had a capo who scouted this area for protection rackets, bookies, and small-time poker games," said Frank, between bites of baked ziti. "Name was Angelo Palladino. Ruddy little fella. Couldn't grow a beard. Just a thin mustache. Why they made Ange, I don't know. Fucking stupid move on their part, I thought at the time, because Ange was a real mouth breather, you could tell. Figure that's why they set him out on the far territories, the little towns like Bellefonte, here. Used to come in to my shop, used to come in here and expect a tithe. Like I needed protecting. But I go along to get along and I will say I had use for them a few times in my life and they was always forthcoming when I needed certain services, so que fucking sera, okay? Okay.

"Came a time during that summer of '69, when the hippies were tearing up college campuses across the country, and we had a skirmish here in Bellefonte. These three longhairs from State College come down and put a rock through the window of the recruiter's office. Did it after dark, too. Cowards. Lot of old-country folk called out to Philly saying, 'Hey, buddy, we pay you for protection, remember? Maybe we should stop.' And so the boss, he sends out Ange and a couple a men and they take up stake down at the Bush House, where, no doubt, you're staying. Got to know Ange and his men well that week. Hot as fuck, it was. End of August, Africa hot. Even the niggers stayed inside. Big Ange and his crew would lunch here every afternoon.

"Eventually, they caught up with those hippies. I'm happy to say they never came south of State College again. Point is, I got to know Ange's men. It got to where they trusted me a little and to where I let them in on my side project. I think I did it just to be friendly, but it was a fucking stupid move because now they wanted a cut of that action, too. What I did was I made a couple hundred bucks a month making fake IDs for the local high schoolers. And yes, I altered some documents for the hippie draft dodgers on occasion. It wasn't my war. I didn't begrudge them their protests on principle, but I do get a little upset when they start trashing places. Anyway, I made fake IDs. I was good at it. Shoulda been an artist. My mother, God rest her, in the ground forty years, my mother— my mother always said I drew like da Vinci himself. Mothers, huh?

"So one of Ange's men, his name being Sal, Sal says, 'Hey, Ange, maybe he could help with the McGuffin situation.' And I says, 'McGuffin situation?' And Ange is quiet for a moment, right? He's sizing me up, but it hurts his brain too much, you can tell. He tells me all about this guy Sam McGuffin. Some smartypants who showed up in Philly and asked for the don's help. 'But McGuffin's an Irish name,' I says. But Ange, he just shrugs. Big galoot. McGuffin wanted papers. Documents. Wanted to change his name. And wanted it done right. In exchange, he promised to give the don some financial advice. To prove his worth, this McGuffin character, he tells the don to invest into a certain company several thousands of dollars. The company split twice that week and the don became even richer. More to the point, he became indebted to this stranger.

"So we make a deal, yes? You see it? They let me keep *all* of my earnings in exchange for making this McGuffin disappear forever. They were my masterpieces, these papers I made. When making fake IDs for kids, I usually just grabbed a list of Social Security numbers from the office of vitals here in town. Or a birth certificate. You know, something good enough to buy them beer or get them into Mexico or Germany or what have you. But this man wanted a new life and papers that would hold up under the greatest of scrutiny. There is only one way to do this. You must find a person of roughly the same age, within five years will do, but a year is better, of course. Someone who died at a young age, young enough so that they had not yet applied for a Social Security card, young enough that they had never paid taxes. So that the only paperwork they have is that birth certificate. That's when I thought of Carol.

"I never dated Carol, all right? I know she says this. But it's not true.

I have only ever had eyes for my beloved Anna, God rest her soul. But yes, I did fuck her. Excuse me. Pardon my fucking French. But I am old and there's no reason to lie. Yes, she was my goomah, my mistress. Carol, as I'm sure you know, had a brother who died in a terrible car accident when he was just a little boy. More, had he lived, he would have been just as old as Mr. McGuffin claimed to be. Was perfect. So there it is."

"So you never actually saw him?" asked David.

"No, I never did. Ange's men took the papers back to Philly. A notarized birth certificate, a high school diploma, college transcripts, employment documents from several out-of-state businesses, and a Social Security card, a *real* one. Didn't need to doctor that. Back then, you had the birth certificate, you could get a soash. Easy-peasy, Japanesey. McGuffin—he liked the papers so much, he writes me a letter. More financial advice. Invest in Sony, he said."

"I spoke to Carol's son. Says she sent a man to talk to you in 2008. Did you tell all this to that man Arbogast when he came by asking questions?"

Frank shook his head.

"Why not?"

"That man was trouble," he said.

"What do you mean?" asked Katy.

"I asked him why he wanted to know, what business of his it was, and he tells me this story about how the guy I helped was an uncle of his and he needed to find him to let him know that his sister was deathly ill. Been around liars long enough to know a good one, and this fella was terrible. Obviously, this guy was in cahoots with whoever it was sent McGuffin into hiding in the first place. So I told him to go pound salt. When I seen the report on the news about the strange murder of Joe King, it didn't take me long to realize it was *my* Joe King they were talking about, the identity I created. As I live and breathe, I am sure that Arbogast or whatever his name is had a hand in his murder. How he tracked him down, I don't know. There are ways. But they are beyond my means these days, I'm afraid."

And the trail was cold again.

"What answer are you pursuing, Mr. Neff?" asked Frank. "Arbogast's identity or the reason behind McGuffin's secrecy?"

"Arbogast's real name is probably more important," he said. "I'm the main suspect in the other man's attempted murder at the moment and so I'd sort of like to find who's really responsible before it gets out of hand."

"There is one more thing, now that I think about this man. But it's probably not important. He parked in the crippled space. Had one of those permits but there didn't seem to be anything wrong with him. Like I said, probably doesn't mean anything. I used to make crip permits, too. But it's different."

EPISODE NINE

FEEDING HIS GHOST

"How are we doing?" David asked Russo, the assistant prosecutor. Elizabeth was at his side, her fingers intertwined with his, as if he might suddenly be blown away, his father walking behind them. They headed for the elevators that would take them to the third-floor cafeteria.

"We're doing fine," he said, clapping David on the back. "Eat something light. Drink something caffeinated. Go over your notes before we head back in."

Moments later, they were seated at a table in the lunchroom, a salad and a bag of Cheetos in front of David.

"It's so surreal to see you sitting up there," said Elizabeth. "It's like you're the one on trial. I hate it."

"It's the only real defense," he said. "To tear me down."

"Heads up," said his father, nodding toward the door. Trimble's mother was making a beeline for their table.

"Hello, Grace," said David.

Trimble's mother was a lanky woman with hair the color of some sea monster's ink. Her voice was ruptured and nasal. "You are a selfish prick," she said. "Making money. That's all you care about. You don't care about the truth. You'd probably write that your own mother was a murderer if you thought you'd make a hundred dollars."

"Oh, come on," said Elizabeth. "He hasn't made anything off the book. He put more money into the research behind it. Get away from us, lady. Go talk to your son. He's the one who's hurting your family."

"If you were telling the truth, you wouldn't need to be medicated like a crazy person," she said.

"Grace, go sit down," David said.

"You're psychotic," she said.

"A little bit," he said. "Because of your son and his scoutmaster. Because of what they did to those girls, the stuff I had to read about. Maybe I am. Yeah. Maybe. So do you really think it's smart to piss off a crazy man?"

Grace no longer looked angry. She looked concerned, the way a woman would look if she suddenly realized she had accidentally walked through a staff door at the zoo and found herself in the lion's den.

"Davey," said his father, shaking his head.

"Go back to your table, Grace," said David. "Go . . .

. . . fuck yourself, you talentless hack!" The voice was thin and loud and full of rage. "You don't have it and you never will."

"What?" asked David.

Cindy peered over the top of the cubicle that separated her desk from Frankie's. "I didn't say anything," she said and popped back down. Frankie was out covering a county commissioners' meeting. The room was theirs.

David stared at his desk. It was littered with stacks of documents from Brune's box. A packet of autopsy pictures lay half covered by a stack of police reports but he could still see the ghostly shape of Donna Doyle's naked backside. Her killer had carved two large gashes across her body there.

Had he dozed off? Had he been dreaming of Brune's voice?

Outside, the sky had grown dim over Cleveland. The setting summer sun hit the Cuyahoga and painted it a deep orange that looked like fire. (As it was the Cuyahoga, it was not outside the realm of possibility that it was, in fact, fire.) He looked at the clock on his computer—almost seven, another lost dinner with Elizabeth.

He hadn't called. And he still needed to come up with something to send along to Andy this week, a part of the job that felt like a chore. He was trying to make the most of it. He'd started honing his writing skills on other true crime stories about some of the city's famous unsolved murders, which he fed to Andy at a semi-steady rate between smaller news pieces on local activists or how much the county was spending on voting machines that could be hacked by retarded monkeys.

From behind Cindy's desk came a dramatic sigh.

"You okay, Cindy?" he called.

"No."

"Wanna talk about it?"

"No."

"Okay."

She was already walking to his desk, though, and there was a look of exaggerated exasperation on her face, a look she had long ago perfected. "So," she began (she was the sort of young woman who often began conversations with the word *so*, as if you had just been waiting for her to start), "I've been reporting on this story for, like, five weeks now and uhhhhhhg, David, I can't finish it. It's too confusing."

Sometimes when Cindy was nervous, like in pitch meetings with Andy, she rubbed the back of her right ear and then smelled her finger. She thought no one noticed this compulsion, but David had spotted it during his third pitch meeting. He could tell she was getting nervous talking about this story and he hoped that she wouldn't start rubbing the waxy garbage behind her ear, because he knew that there would be no way for him to hide the fact that he had noticed. And then they would have to talk about it. And David did not ever want to talk about that.

"What's the story?" he heard himself say.

"So there's this family, right? Rich family. Old money. Something to do with carpeting. So the patriarch dies. But he doesn't leave a will. He has a little over five million in the bank and the guy doesn't leave a will. I know, right? Anyway, they think he did it on purpose to punish everyone who was sitting around waiting for him to die. And now the family is tearing itself apart. Brothers fighting brothers. Mothers fighting daughters. Everyone with their own lawyer, everyone sure that they should have the biggest piece of the inheritance. They've been fighting each other for fifteen years. That's the story."

"Awesome," he said. He wasn't being patronizing, either. There was a lot of room to write about strong characters in a story like that. "Are you looking for a hook?"

"Yes."

David took a moment to think of something to peg such a story on. "What about the house?" he asked, thinking aloud. "They've been fighting over all this money, but there's got to be a big goddamned house somewhere, right? Who's in the house?"

"Nobody," she said. "A judge appointed his oldest surviving heir, a son, as executor of the estate and he got everyone to agree to sell the house and divvy up the profit—it's the only thing everyone agreed to, actually. But that money is in escrow until everything is figured out."

"They can do that?"

"I guess."

"I thought maybe you could make the house a character," he said. "I saw something like that in *Esquire* once, I think."

"No house," she said.

"Hmmm. What you need is a neutral, omniscient character. Something you can use as a filter, as a point of view. You know, something that can comment on each of the people subjectively. What about . . . what about a gardener or maid or something? Did they have one of those?"

"I think so," she said. "I saw something about a maid in one of the filings."

"Try and track down their maid," he said. "Someone like that could tell you everything you need to know about this family. It'll be someone the reader can relate to, too."

She giggled a little. She looked relieved. Other writers had quit rather than disappoint Andy by dropping an assignment. "Okay," she said. "That's good. Thanks, David."

Poor Cindy.

Why do demons choose to hide in plain sight? David wondered as he drove up to Brune's house the following afternoon. Dahmer, Gacy, Ridgway. Like Brune, they'd all lived in workaday homes. Not like the movies, not in dungeons or old Victorians poised above run-down motels.

It was a drab, low-slung ranch, a vinyl-sided bungalow with a postage-stamp front lawn and a mailbox in the shape of a fish. It sat in a run-down allotment in the no-man's-land between Akron and Canton, near the regional airport.

He didn't know what he hoped to find here. He certainly didn't entertain any notion of finding conclusive proof of his emerging theory: that Brune had been a rapist of women, his protégé the serial killer of young girls. He doubted such evidence existed; Riley Trimble was not the type to keep a diary.

Still, he was drawn to the place. There was a thought playing at the back of his mind, a romantic, thematic thought. And it was this: the only thing that separated him from absolute truth now was a single dimension, Time. He stepped out of the car. Here he was, in the exact location—in three dimensions—where Trimble, presumably, had driven into his garage with Sarah Creston in the back of his van. The only thing keeping him from witnessing the crime was Time; a single, but very necessary, ingredient in both absolute truth and soft-batch cookies.

David knocked lightly on the door and a shirtless man with a paunch and a stubbly goatee answered. David did his best to explain his interest in the house, and then asked a crazy question. "Could I take a look inside?"

"I don't think so, boss," the man said.

"Did you ever look in the crawl spaces? Ever find anything unusual?"

"That's about all I have to say." The man closed the door.

David returned to the car and drove around the block to a tiny cemetery situated behind Brune's house. The cemetery was separated from the home by a thick swatch of forest a quarter mile deep. Again, he had no real hope of finding anything. Again, he was flying on instinct. Wouldn't a serial killer bury things in the woods? Didn't that happen on TV? It did. But in real life? He thought it was worth ten minutes of his time. He parked in the back, near a tilting tombstone from 1897, dedicated to some guy with only a first name, Tanner. Tanner. He filed it away for later use. He liked the sound of the name. Strong. Underused.

It was the beginning of a hot summer and the air was heavy, rippling with gnats and midges and horseflies, the ground saturated from recent thunderstorms. He hadn't prepared for the briars and burrs and berry bushes that lined the forest and they bit at his khaki pants and stung his ankles, but when he was through, the going was easier. Skunkweed and ferns grew to his knees, but bent as he passed. After a while he became acutely aware of the silence. He heard no birds, no deer crackling the bracken under hoof, no squirrels fighting in branches overhead. He heard no crickets or frogs. This patch of old-growth forest was utterly silent except for his intrusions. And it *was* old-growth. The oaks were wide as cabins, their canopies blocking out the sun almost completely. It was dark, but there was also a *darkness*. He felt it in his bones, in a dull aching in his head, the taste of copper in his mouth, like dried blood. This place had remained untouched throughout modern human history, undeveloped by white man. Had the Indians avoided this place, too? Was it some hallowed or evil ground that people avoided subconsciously? How much was David imagining simply because he knew how close this place was to a den of true evil? Not much—even the birds felt it.

As he was about to turn back, David happened upon the clearing.

It was lined with giant white elm trees that had miraculously avoided the disease that felled their Ohio cousins: great, formish, idyllic elms, the likes of which David had never seen and never would again. It was a large circle, perhaps a hundred feet in diameter, carpeted with bluegrass that bended and lolled in the dank, wet hot. It was so bright in the center that David's eyes hurt and he was forced to squint so much his vision was reduced to a thin slit. It was several minutes before he noticed the stuffed animals.

The animals were crucified upon the elms.

Brown bears, sock monkeys, a child's furry tiger. Someone had nailed them to the trees that lined the clearing, every single elm, so that they faced the center. David inspected the closest tree, where the tiger was crucified. Its paws, he saw, were not just nailed to the tree, but also stapled and tied. A swatch of duct tape had been applied to its mouth. Two roach clips were secured to the fur where the tiger's breasts would be. There was a gaping hole where its private parts were located. As he watched, a hornet crawled out of the hole and zipped away. The tiger had been there a long time, its once-orange fur mottled with fungus and brown as sewage. He couldn't tell if the animals had hung here long enough for Trimble to have done it. It was possible some other troubled boy had lived nearby and discovered this clearing one unlucky afternoon. For a moment he caught an image of a blond-haired boy dancing in the clearing, naked and singing a nonsensical song in a foreign and lost language David thought might be Aramaic.

His imagination could get away from him if he let it. Especially when he was scared. If he let the fear in, if he let in the fear that had tightened its grip around his heart the moment he stepped into the clearing, if he let that fear run around inside him, there would be a cascading of delusions like this, he knew, and he would find himself running back to his car half out of his mind.

His father had taught him how to control his fear. When he was twelve, David had stayed up through the night after watching *The Exorcist* on TV. The next day, his father had made him walk through the woods behind their house alone, all the way to the end of their property and back, to prove to David that there were no demons waiting for the opportunity to kill him. It had been a particularly frightening hike because the neighborhood kids had believed those woods to be haunted. Legend had it that the Native American tribe that had once occupied the area believed a demigod lived there, an imp that took the form of a cat and who would allow passage only by subjecting travelers to degrading acts of corruption and humiliation. But he had returned unscathed. Little had frightened him since.

But now he was sure that something was watching him.

Still, he couldn't leave without seeing what was in the middle of the clearing.

It was a stump, the stump of a gargantuan oak. He wanted to touch it, to feel its oldness, to find out if it was petrified. He didn't dare. Whatever was darkening these woods came from this stump, from the roots that still thrived in the ground below.

A single word was carved into it: BEEZLE.

The word meant something to David, but not in this context. He knew of beezle from Dr. Seuss. *Horton Hears a Who.* The animals in that little gem of a story had planned to commit genocide on the Whos of Whoville by throwing their world (which existed on a speck of dust perched atop a flower) into boiling Beezle-Nut oil.

He felt an urge to say the word aloud, to hear the sound of the word, the *name*, in this clearing. But the thought of the repercussions stopped him. What would happen here if he muttered such an invocation? He did not care to know. If this was the place Beezle called home, he didn't want to meet him. Or *It*. And he certainly did not want to call it.

And through the wrongness of the clearing, he felt something else. Or imagined it. The sensation surfaced as a picture in his mind as he tried to draw out the analogy. He thought of two bar magnets, placed such that their opposite polarities were close to touching. Slowly, the magnets scooted toward each other, gathering speed, and collided, then rested, at last. In some way, he was one of those magnets. And this clearing. No, this stump, the Thing it represented. This darkness was the other magnet and it pulled at him, promising a final rest for his soul if he would only surrender to it.

David awoke to himself, just as he was about to step onto the stump.

He blinked the daze out of his eyes, turned, and walked out of the woods. He forced himself to go slowly.

In the car, David kicked it into gear and macht-schnelled the hell right out of there. He stopped at the nearest gas station and bought a pack of Marlboros. He unwrapped the pack and placed a cigarette in his mouth. He was too afraid of emphysema to smoke it, so he just rubbed his tongue around the filter and felt the weight of it between his lips. It calmed him immediately.

She's cheating on you, David. She's fucking the band director. They share an office, you know. She always stays after work so late. What is she doing there? She's not grading papers, I'll tell you that.

Brune's voice, nasal and meek, the voice of a good accountant.

David looked at the clock above the kitchen sink. It was almost eight.

He's fingering her right now. He's knuckles-deep, digging.

"Stop it," he said.

He looked down. Brune's Box of Fabulous Files was spilling over. David had gathered police reports from every jurisdiction that had cases of missing or murdered girls from the early eighties and nineties, trying to find a link, something definitive to tie Trimble to the crimes. He realized, sickly, what he was really doing. He was *feeding* Brune's box. Adding evil to it. New tales of murder, added and mixed with Brune's own handiwork. And as he added to the box, Brune's voice grew louder within his head. He was feeding a ghost and the ghost was becoming more real.

Why are you still wasting your time on this? I left these notes behind for a real journalist. Not you. Not some kid. You don't have the stones.

He had written one word on a blank sheet of printing paper.

Beezle. Ha, Beezle. You don't know what you're talking about.

He heard Elizabeth's key in the door's lock and shuddered because he knew what Brune had in mind, what Brune really wanted.

Do it.

Never.

She's a cheating cunt. Take her.

No.

Then do the world a favor and cash out.

I might.

You're a coward. I don't believe anything you say.

"David?" her voice, her hand on his head, twisting his hair, loving.

How he wanted to twist that hand behind her until it broke, until she couldn't fight back. He didn't have roach clips in the apartment, but he had tweezers that might work. And he had some spare wire and his car battery.

"Go away," he said. "Elizabeth, please. Go away for a bit."

"What are you talking about?"

"Go to your aunt's. I'll call you."

"David, talk to me."

"Get the fuck out of here," he said. "Get the fuck away from me. Leave me alone."

She left. He never looked at her.

Coward.

She'll be back.

You're getting weaker.

She'll be back.

Let's read some more. What do you say? Let's read some more about my favorite Boy Scout, the apple of my eye.

"I'm planning to kill myself," he said.

Athena Popodopovich, the thin psychiatrist whose name he'd randomly picked out of the phone book earlier that afternoon, a week and a day after he had made Elizabeth leave their apartment, looked back at him with genuine concern and interest. "How will you kill yourself?" she asked.

"I'm going to jump off the Y-Bridge."

"Well, that'll be messy."

He watched for a hint of a smile at the corners of her mouth but she wasn't being cheeky. She was being blunt, being true.

"You wouldn't be the first of my patients to take a swan dive off the Y-Bridge," she said. "I just figured a writer would be a little more imaginative."

"I thought about eating hot coals but that's been done. Most suicides are clichés. The running car in the garage, the gun in the mouth, the hanging—"

"The jumper."

"See," he said. "It's hard to find a new angle. Besides, the whole reason I'm at this point is because I can't think original thoughts anymore. I can't write anymore. My editor is going to figure that out soon. And then I won't have a job."

"Why can't you write?"

"I need to hear my voice, in my head, you know, when I write. Sounding out the words, telling the story. That's part of my process. I can't hear my voice anymore."

"Why can't you hear your own voice anymore?"

"All I hear is Brune. Ever since I opened that box, I hear his voice. I think about him all the time. From the moment I wake up until the moment I fall asleep and then he's in my dreams. I can't get Sarah Creston's face out of my head. Donna and Jennifer are there, too, but it's Sarah mostly, because I have so many pictures of her."

"Are these voices telling you to harm yourself? To harm others?"

David buckled. His chest heaved. He started to cry. Heavy sobs. "Yes," he said. "There's something inside me. I can feel it burrowing in."

Dr. Popodopovich sat up in her chair and wrote on a green form. "David," she said in a calm and friendly voice not devoid of amusement. "It's possible you're suffering from post traumatic stress disorder brought on by your exposure to these horrific stories. In a sense, you're reliving these tragedies. I've seen this before in journalists who've covered the wars in Iraq. David, you're going to spend the night at the Glenns; it's a mental health facility just a few miles west of here. When someone tells me they intend to harm themselves I must do this, you see. But I will promise you that the nature of everything you have told me and everything you will tell me in the future will remain under the strictest of confidences. Do you understand why I have to do this?"

"Yes."

"The fact that you sought me out tells me you are stronger than you believe yourself to be. We'll get you through this. And the first step begins right now."

He stared at his feet.

"Look at me, David. We're going to get you through this. David, look . . .

. . . at me," Elizabeth said, as they walked back into the courtroom. "Just look at me, if they start attacking you, okay?"

He nodded and walked to the witness stand. A moment later, the jury entered, and then Judge Siegel, and everyone stood. "Be seated," he said.

Synenberger was out of his seat in a flash. Out of the corner, he unleashed a hard punch.

"Mr. Neff," he said. "Are you crazy?"

"Objection!" shouted Russo.

Synenberger waved him away. "I'll restate the question. Mr. Neff, are you suffering from any psychological impairments?"

"I suffer from post-traumatic stress disorder, but it's never been an impairment," he said. In a room on the ninth floor of this very building, Russo had grilled him just like this, so he knew what to expect and how to answer. It had felt a little like training for a fight—but no matter how many times you punch a bag, it's still difficult to avoid flinching when you're up against the real deal.

"But you are taking medication for this, correct?"

"Correct."

"If it's not an impairment, why do you need to be medicated?"

"Well, Mr. Synenberger, it's sort of like being an alcoholic," he said. "Some alcoholics can function, can do their job very well before their livers turn on them. In my case, I always managed to hit a deadline but I could feel something wrong inside."

"Like an alcoholic's liver, except it was your brain, your mind that was not right?"

David cringed a little. "Basically, yes."

"You were hearing voices. Hearing people who were not there."

"Yes."

"Isn't it possible you were also seeing people who were not there?"

He thought of that awful night, of the homeless man outside their bedroom window, the one with the knife and the lame eye. But there was no way Synenberger could know about that. That was buried deep in his shrink's notes, inadmissible in court.

"No," he said. "I don't think so."

"I'm speaking about Gary Gonze. Your secret source for the book. Gary Gonze is not real, is he?"

"Unfortunately," he said, "Gary Gonze is very real."

—▣—

They drove back to Ohio in Katy's car, a ten-year-old Saturn stuffed with CDs and vinyls of bands David had never heard of: Salt Zombies, the Decemberists, Neutral Milk Hotel.

He'd returned his rental to the Enterprise in State College and paid the fee to have them ship it back to Akron. There were few perks to being silly rich, he'd come to realize, but convenience was one of them.

Somehow, being in Katy's car, in the passive passenger seat, he felt closer to her, closer even than during the seven times they'd had sex since she had arrived in Bellefonte. Sitting in the passenger seat of a woman's car—that's intimacy.

At a stoplight in State College, she had leaned over and licked his lips. He had felt so dizzy he thought he might faint.

"So what now?" she asked, pulling onto I-80 West.

"We can take this all the way home."

"I mean what next, what next? What next with you?"

"Oh." He looked out the window, at the foothills of the Appalachians sweeping east in an impressionistic blur of green and gold. "Well," he said, "not much, really. I just, you know, have to find a better suspect in the attempted murder of the Man from Primrose Lane so that I'm not put on trial. To do that, I have to, somehow, figure out who this 'Arbogast' guy is. The only guy we can assume had motive to kill the Man from Primrose Lane, if your memory is reliable, and memory so often is not, is the man who approached you outside that toy store in Coventry, only to be intercepted by the Man from Primrose Lane. Logically, that man was this 'Arbogast.' But logic is on vacation these days. You and Detective Sackett both believe that you are somehow connected to the abduction of my wife's sister, Elaine, that perhaps the man who attempted to abduct you was the same man who took Elaine, and tried to take Elizabeth, only to be interrupted by . . . who? The Man from Primrose Lane again? I'd also like to know why my wife's fingerprints were on that guy's bed. Also, Tanner has swimming lessons Wednesday. So, there's that."

"Do you still think the solution is elegantly simple?"

"It always is," he said.

"Well, we at least have a last name to start with."

"What do you mean?"

"McGuffin," she said. "That old man said the guy he made the IDs for was named McGuffin."

David laughed. "That's not a real name, either," he said.

"How do you know?"

"It's a bad writer's device. A McGuffin. It's the object that everyone is after in a caper, or in a crime story or mystery. It's something the plot centers around but which, in itself, is not of any real importance. It's like the Maltese Falcon. Or the Arc of the Covenant, in *Raiders*. Or what's in Marcellus Wallace's briefcase in *Pulp Fiction*."

"So no leads, then, on the Man from Primrose Lane's true identity?"

"Actually, the best clue to who he was is still in Akron. His house."

At a rest stop east of Pittsburgh, one of those transient depots full of tchotchkes and fatty foods, they stopped to eat and to call home.

"Dad!" yelled Tanner. "I painted Shadow green!"

Shadow was the cat.

"All of him?"

"No. A little. It was an assident. He has a green spot now."

"Good."

"Are you coming home?"

"On my way, buddy."

"Yay! Oh, Papa wants to say something." There was a loud rumble as Tanner transferred the phone to David's father.

"'Lo?"

"Hi, Dad."

"Everything work out?"

"It did."

"Good. Hey. There's, uh . . . there's stuff on the news out here. It started on the blogs. That girl, Cindy. She has pictures up on her site with you and a young woman."

"Great."

"Did you know that the woman you're with in the pictures is the fiancée of Ralph Rhodes?"

"I'm guessing that's Joe Rhodes's son."

"Right-o."

"Huh," he said. *Yes*, he thought, *Ralph Rhodes certainly is a toolbox.* What did Katy see in *that* guy?

"Well, the newspapers picked it up and figured out who the woman was."

"What do you mean?"

"That she's the one the Man from Primrose Lane was stalking."

"Uh-huh?"

"Today's headline from the *Beacon*: 'Famous Writer Key Suspect in Death of Mystery Man.' And below that: 'Dates Woman the Victim Stalked.'"

"Nice."

"Are you in trouble, David?"

"No, Pop. It's a misunderstanding. Build you up, tear you down. That's the media's job. I have Synenberger on it. Nothing to worry about."

"Are you sure?"

"Mostly."

"Well, come on home."

"Be there in two hours."

Katy was closing her cell phone as David approached her in the colossal lobby. The look on her face said everything he needed to know.

"Fuck," she said.

"Yeah."

"I mean, *fuck*! None of this would have happened if I hadn't gone out with you," she said. "That bitch got a picture of us in your car, dropping me off. I'm the one who cheated on my fiancé. I'm the one who that creep from Primrose Lane was obsessed with."

"Why didn't you tell me who your boyfriend was?"

Katy shrugged. "I don't care about that stuff."

"His father is the leader of the Summit County Republican Party, owns the biggest lumber business in Ohio. Powerful family."

"I know."

"I'll give you this," he said. "You're certainly not boring."

"Ditto."

"Shall we, then?"

Katy tossed him the keys. "Your turn."

From the website ClevelandChic.com, posted October 18, 2012:

YOUNG BOOKSLINGER CAN'T GET E'NEFF
OF LOCAL WRITER
Exclusive by ClevelandChic

Who is this mystery woman smooching up to the ear of Akron's famous true crime writer? According to neighbors, the YOUNG woman, seen in this picture with her tongue in <u>David Neff's</u> ear, is a twenty-two-year-old Barnes & Noble employee named "Katy." The young woman herself could not be reached for comment. Neither could Neff, for that matter. It appears the two may have escaped to a lovers' retreat, where they can canoodle far from the gaze of ClevelandChic's cameras.

Neff, who was widowed in 2008 when his wife <u>committed suicide by driving a car into a convenience store</u> the day she was to be released from the hospital after the birth of their boy, Tanner, has remained in self-imposed isolation since the tragedy. Is this a sign that Neff is back in the singles scene? Or did Katy work her way into his heart through correspondence of some kind? Neff is easily reachable through <u>Facebook</u>, where Katy is one of his "friends."

Full disclosure: Yours truly worked with Neff for a spell at the now-defunct *Independent*. It is true we have our own history. While I thought we were friends, Neff stabbed me in the back and made up stories about me to the editor, eventually leading to my termination. He's got a lot of fans, but ClevelandChic is not one. Take it from me, Katy, this guy's a skeez.

Twenty-two-year-olds, David? Really?

UPDATE: Whiskey-Tango-Foxtrot! "Katy" is <u>Katy Keenan</u>, the same Katy who was the focus of the <u>Man from Primrose Lane's</u> secret obsession. She's also ~~married~~ engaged to Rhodes Lumber heir apparent <u>Ralph Rhodes</u>. Ouch! What a social climber. Looks like Neff has met a kindred soul.

UPDATE 2: Holy twist, Batman! The <u>Beacon Journal</u> just revealed that Neff is suspect #1 in the "attempted" murder of MFPL. As they say on Drudge, label this "developing."

By early evening, David was home with Tanner. There was another card from Cindy in the door. She had written *We should really talk!* on the back. Cindy had also left a voice mail on his machine. There were messages from Phil McIntyre at the *Beacon* and Damian Gomez at the *Plain Dealer*, as well. He figured it wouldn't be long before one of the television stations came knocking.

They ate a quick supper—mac 'n' cheese and hot dogs. Afterward, Tanner escaped to the living room to watch *Wow! Wow! Wubbzy!* while David cleaned up. As he reached for the refrigerator door to put the leftovers away, he noticed the picture of Elizabeth as a child, rolled up on the couch, hanging on the side, and stopped abruptly.

He'd felt grief over Elizabeth's death, as much grief as the Rivertin would allow. What he felt building inside him now, at the sight of his wife for the first time since kicking the drug, was something new. It was a cascading of madness, as if a great gate inside himself had opened and the stored sadness of several years was rushing out to overwhelm his senses.

He felt the loss of her, the missingness of having her nearby, the aloneness she left behind.

Elizabeth, he thought. *Why did you have to go away? Why couldn't you stay with me? With us?*

It was impossible to tell, later, if the last brain storm was triggered by all this new emotion, or vice versa. It enveloped David before he recognized it for what it was. One moment he was standing in the kitchen, staring at Elizabeth's photograph and the next . . .

. . . he was jogging next to her, through the zigzagging dirt paths that wound between giant boulders inside Nelson Ledges Park—a place she had liked to go when she was training for a marathon.

"Keep up, old man," she said.

"Wait," he heard himself say. "Just a minute. I need to catch my breath."

"Can't!" she called, pulling ahead of him. "I have to keep pace."

He watched her disappear behind a thirty-foot-tall rock left behind by a glacier ten thousand years ago. He smelled her sweat in the breeze and he came to a rough stop and bent over, gasping for air.

She's gone, he thought.

But then she was back, jogging in place, with a hand on his back. He stood up again and she paused momentarily to kiss him gently. Inside his memory, David felt his heart break.

"Just a little farther, David," she said, a crooked smile full of teeth. "I love you. But you have to keep up. Come on!"

She pulled his arm and they were jogging again. But as they turned the corner David . . .

. . . came back to himself, more easily than with previous flashbacks. In fact, he was still standing, still holding a Tupperware container of macaroni. He felt better, though he remained keenly aware of Elizabeth's absence for the rest of the night.

In order to stave off further attacks, he decided to keep himself busy. There were things he could do to get at more information about the Man from Primrose Lane. At the top of that list was one task he shouldn't put off any longer. He bundled up the boy and a few minutes later they were heading down Merriman in the yellow Bug. The journey, this time, was less than a mile. They parked in front of a modest Colonial and David helped his son out of the car and led him up the brick driveway. For once, Tanner didn't ask questions. He just held his father's hand tight.

Albert Beachum arrived at the door before David knocked, the overwhelming fragrance of freshly baked cookies drifting around him. He was a very tall man, at least six-five, with a scraggly red beard in need of a trim. His face was stretched and gaunt, the face of a man who had worked out-of-doors his entire life and had enjoyed every minute of it.

"Hello?" Albert asked.

"Mr. Beachum, my name is David Neff. This is my son and partner, Tanner Neff. Our newly formed realty company would very much like to make you an offer on the house on Primrose Lane."

"And a cookie, please," added Tanner, in a businesslike tone.

Albert laughed. "Come in, then."

"I know you didn't kill him," said Albert, setting a plate of cookies on the coffee table in front of Tanner and David. His wife, "Keek," a reformed Hells Angel, sat in a chair across from them. She didn't seem so sure.

"Thanks," said David. "I didn't. So I guess that makes two of us."

"I called the police after I saw your name in the paper and told them that. They were not interested in what I had to say."

Tanner held up a cookie the size of his head and contemplated where to begin. As he did so, he scooted closer to his father.

"What *did* you have to say?"

"As I'm sure you know, my family has looked after Joe King, or the Man from Primrose Lane, if you want, since at least the late seventies."

"I didn't know it went back quite that far."

"At least. At least that far. You see, no one really remembers anymore how my family got dragged into this. We kept it so secret, even from each other, until he died, and the Beachum who first had the job is now dead."

"I see."

"I inherited the job of getting things for Mr. King when I was fourteen. Used to walk down to the grocery store and back for him or have someone drive me into Chapel Hill for his stranger requests. On very rare occasions, he instructed me to drive him places. Bellefonte, for instance. Overall, it was pretty uneventful . . ."

"Except for one time."

Albert nodded. "Except for one time. This was the fall of 1989. End of October sometime. Not yet Halloween. A Friday. I come to his house like normal, a bag of groceries in my bike basket. I go to set the bag down and pick up my money—he paid me in cash, in envelopes, always a little too much—but then I hear all this noise inside. Stuff being thrown against the wall or onto the floor. Sounded like the old man was fighting someone in there. I try the door. It's unlocked. I run inside. And there he is destroying the place. He's throwing all his books onto the floor. He had a TV then, and it was on the floor, busted. He fucking *annihilated* a chair. Guy was pissed. 'What happened?' I say. He's so scared that someone is in his house, he jumps and it takes him a second to figure out it's me. But then he calms down, real quick. He says, 'Albert, you can't come back for a while.' 'Why not?' I say. 'Because I fucked it all up.'"

"What did he mean?" asked David.

Albert shrugged. "Hell if I know. Something important. I asked him but all he said was, 'Albert, it's not safe here right now. I've made a very dangerous man very angry with me,' he said, 'and I don't want anyone else to get hurt because of me. You have to stay away.'

"Then he goes to a drawer in the corner and fishes out a wad of money. Over five hundred dollars. 'Here,' he says, pushing it at me with his mittens. 'Keep this. Consider this your severance. I may not need you again. But if I do, I'll write to you and ask you to come. It's very important you and your family stay away from here until I contact you. Do you understand?' I told him I did. He thanked me. And then he did something really out of character. The old man hugged me.

"Five months later, I get a letter in the mail. Two sentences: *Safe to return. See you Friday, if you are still interested.* Obviously, that episode had something to do with his murder. Cops told me memory is too un-reliable to be trusted. Whatever, man. We never saw your wife over there. Me or my brother Billy. No one was ever over there except the old man." Albert's eyes wandered away from David's and found a space in the corner of the room. "If it's true that they found her fingerprints in-side, then someone must have planted them. You need me to testify to it, I will. I don't care."

"Thanks."

For the first time, Albert's wife spoke up. "You said you wanted to buy the house?" she asked.

"Yes. As executor of the estate, Albert, it's in your power to sell the home as long as all parties with a claim agree to it. I would pay into an escrow account set up by the court—my attorney can arrange all this, free of charge, of course—and those funds would accrue interest while you wait for the judge to make his ruling. It's an old house, not likely to fetch much on the open market. I checked online. Its assessed value is a hundred and twelve thousand. I'd be willing to pay twice that. Then at least all you'd be fighting for is money and not property. Might make things easier."

"What if we want to keep the house?" asked Keek.

"Honey, shush."

"Well, Albert, it's obviously worth a lot to this man."

David sighed. "All I can tell you is my interest in the house is less about money than it is about covering all my bases. I need to find the guy who shot the old man. Maybe there's something in there that will help me out."

"We've been all through there," she said. "Nothing but a bunch of old books and dirty clothes and about ten thousand mittens."

"Well, you never know," he replied. "I'd also be willing to have my lawyer look at your claim to the estate and see if he can't move things along in your favor."

Suddenly the old biker seemed more attentive. "We could use a good lawyer, Albert."

"You know I don't care about the money," Albert said. "But we have no use for the house, either. I think I can get everyone on board for this. One thing everyone can agree on is the more money, the better." He shot a glance at his wife.

"Great. I'll have the guy who handles my accounts call you in the morning. His name is Bashien. He's going to create a realty business with me and my son as primary stockholders and silent partners. For reasons you can understand, I need to keep my name off this transaction as much as possible. And I know, from your work for Joe King, or whoever he was, that you will keep my involvement in confidence. This is probably the last time we'll meet. In fact, all communication from this point on will come from McGuffin Properties Limited, and as far as you know, some guy named Bashien is in charge of the operation."

Albert laughed.

"What?" asked David.

"Nothin'," he said, shaking his head. "Just sounds like something he'd have said. How does my family keep getting involved with people like you guys? No offense."

"Luck, I guess."

"Mr. Neff, I don't think luck's got anything to do with it."

One thing troubled David as he led Tanner back to the car—Beachum's expression when he'd said the only person he'd seen at the house was the old man. The avoidance. He was hiding a piece of information. David knew this as if it had been written in a caption over the man's head. The question was whether or not it was an important piece of information or just some random memory he wished to keep private. Some part of the man was still protecting the Man from Primrose Lane's legacy. But Beachum also seemed invested in finding the man who'd shot his employer. Whatever the secret was, David believed it had nothing to do with his investigation. He had to trust the man. Confronting him with such suspicions would likely bring a quick end to their relationship, and at the moment their relationship was more important.

"Boss?"

David could hear the primal *thump-thump* of loud music diminish as Jason stepped away from whatever dance club he was cruising to take his call. "I need some information."

"That's why you pay me the big bucks."

"It's probably nothing, but I can't root around after this guy myself without making certain people angry with me."

"I'll be conspicuous."

"Inconspicuous."

"That's what I meant."

"You remember that redhead? The one from Facebook?"

Jason laughed. "You getting some strange? Good for you, man. About goddamn time. You, what, want me to look into the boyfriend or whatever?"

"No. I want you to do some digging on her father. I don't know anything about him. He wouldn't talk to the cops about the Man from Primrose Lane business. So it's a loose thread."

"I'll tie it up. Give me a couple days."

Sleep eluded him.

Had Elizabeth really known the Man from Primrose Lane? Was there an innocent explanation for the fingerprint? Was he a victim of happenstance or was someone trying to frame him? Why was he attracted to the same women targeted by Elaine's abductor? Why did his life intersect with the dead man's in tenuous ways? Were they even intersections or was he inventing a pattern that wasn't there, making constellations from random stars?

Was it possible Riley Trimble was behind all this? A paranoid thought. Riley didn't resemble the description of the man who kidnapped Elaine or the man who had gone after Katy—the man in the Members Only jacket had been well dressed and put-together, Riley was always a mess. And, while Riley was technically a free man, he was far from free. But it was not entirely outside the realm of possibility, was it?

Certainly Trimble had motive for revenge.

THE HOUSE ON PRIMROSE LANE

"I'll be lucky if we get a hung jury at this point," said Russo, pacing around the conference room adjacent to Siegel's court, hands on his hips. After a relentless attack by Synenberger, the judge had called a short recess so that David could collect himself. The jury had not looked at him as they exited the courtroom. "We went over this. We went over and over and over this. You knew how to dodge his questions. What happened in there?"

"I'm tired of spinning everything," David said. "If we just explain how it is, the jury will see I'm not trying to hide anything."

"The jury thinks you're a nutcase. I would if I were on the jury. Everything you testified to"—Russo raised his hands in fists and opened them—"gone! Poof. Over."

"There are other witnesses who—"

"You were the case, David!" said Russo. "You were the case. Remember that when we lose." The assistant prosecutor marched out of the room.

David sat there for a moment, feeling rotten and corrupted and poisonous. He searched within himself, a quick journey into his inner psyche, to determine if he'd done the wrong thing. But his soul was still. He could live with his decision to tell the whole truth, even if it did kill the case.

He stepped into the hallway. It was a short recess, so Elizabeth and his father had remained in the courtroom. Cindy Nottingham had not.

"Alone at last," she said demurely.

"I don't have anything for you, Cindy."

"If you don't feed the media, it will eat you, you know."

"Then go ahead and eat me, Cindy."

"Nice."

"What would you have done in my place?" he asked her. She knew what he meant.

"I would have come to me."

"I didn't have that choice. Andy walked . . .

. . . over to David's cubicle in the writers' den. It was after eight and outside the Warehouse District was aglow and bumping, Cleveland's last bit of social equity. The editor had spent much of the day sleeping off a migraine. The rest of the staff had already gone home.

"Whatcha readin', Davey?" Andy asked.

David held up several pages of double-spaced manuscript. "Cindy's story," he said. "I took it off the shared folder. I like to read the covers before they hit the streets."

"That's a good habit," said Andy. "I used to do that. So, whaddya think?"

"It's good. She made the whole family dynasty thing work without bogging the reader down in all the legal details."

"That's the third draft. Lot of heavy lifting all the way up to deadline. It's been a rough edit."

"Well, it's working now. Especially how she uses the device of telling the story through the eyes of the maid."

"You like that?"

David nodded.

Andy picked up on a subtlety of expression. "What?"

"No. Nothing. I like it."

"Don't bullshit a bullshitter."

"I'm not."

"Then what?"

"Nothing. I just suggested to Cindy that that might be a way out of the hole she'd dug herself. That if she had some outside observer, it might read better."

Andy's expression didn't change. But David watched the color drain out of his editor's face. Finally, he exhaled one long, "That fucking bitch!"

David was so surprised, he jumped. "What?"

"You told her to find a maid to use as an observer?"

"Yeah."

"And then she finds a maid she'd never interviewed before, just like that?"

David started to see where he was going. "That's not what I was trying to say."

"I know," said Andy. But he was already punching numbers into his cell phone. "Cindy?" he said. "Cindy, where are your notes on this family thing?" Andy turned to her desk, a scaled-down version of a garbage dump. "Where?" he shouted. He rummaged under a sweater. He tossed an empty iced tea container against the wall so hard the plastic dented. Finally, he came up with a stack of notes. "Where's your interview with the maid?" A pause. "Why is it at home if everything else is here?" A longer pause. "Don't you fuckin' lie to me, Cindy, not after everything I've done for you." Pause. "Just tell me . . . you know what . . . you fucking know what . . . tell me, Cindy." Pause. "Do I need to spike the story before it goes out tomorrow?" Pause. "God-fucking-damn it! Goddamn it! You stupid bitch! You have any idea? *Any* idea what could have happened? You're lucky David figured it out. We're lucky. You stay the fuck away from me if you know what's good. Send someone for your stuff. You have a day before I throw it all out. Yes, you're fucking fired!" Click.

Andy stood in the doorway, panting like a boxer on the ropes. He looked to David. "Good job, kid," he said. "We got a hole to fill in this week's issue. Write me something good." And before David could tell him he didn't have anything ready, that he'd gotten distracted again with the Brune story, Andy disappeared into his office behind a locked door.

Twice-a-week sessions with Athena had helped. And his two-night respite inside the Glenns suicide ward had been enough to frighten him into fighting harder against the symptoms of PTSD—the renovated Victorian mansion-cum-loony-bin had smelled like dried puke and Clorox. But Brune's voice had not been silenced entirely. David discovered quickly that the more stressed he became, the more susceptible his mind was to a full-blown Brune invasion, or, if you like, an "episode" in which his id manifested itself as Brune's voice in order to wreak havoc upon his conscience. He hadn't made up his mind on which explanation he believed. For now he had convinced his doctor to keep him off pills, but she had threatened to lock him away again at the first sign of mania or depression, and then he would have to be medicated.

And he was getting stressed again.

The first thing he did was call Elizabeth, but she didn't answer. This was a little odd, given the late hour, but she might have told him that she was staying after work to help with the school musical. He couldn't be sure.

He'd gotten Cindy fired. He didn't feel good about that, even if he had caught a crafty act of fiction. Now Andy wanted him to fill the hole in the paper created by that silent explosion. And he didn't know where to begin.

He scoured the local dailies for a hint of a story. Nothing. It was too late to call what few sources he'd kicked up in the nine months he'd written for the *Independent*. He thought about calling Frankie, but he had just written the cover for the previous issue—a five-thousand-word piece on a minority front company skimming money from an airport contract.

The techno-tone of his in-box chimed. Someone named Deep-Throat2@hotmail.com had just sent him an email. He clicked it open.

> I hear you're looking into Riley Trimble.
> I can prove he murdered Sarah Creston.
> Let's meet. Edgewater Yacht Club. Now. (I know you're still at work.
> I can see you sitting at your computer.)

The shock of being spied on struck him like a slap. He looked out the window, across a condom-littered parking lot where hoboes grazed, to the row of apartments that marked the beginning of the Warehouse District. He saw people milling about, but no one seemed to be watching him.

He heard laughter. Brune. Somewhere deep inside.

"Shut up," he muttered.

Is it a trap? he wondered. *Is it Trimble?*

He was a junkie, he realized. Too hooked on the mystery to think logically. A part of him enjoyed this.

By the time he stepped into the elevator, David had already forgotten he owed Andy an article.

The parking lot of the yacht club was empty except for a couple cars near the restaurant and an SUV idling near the walkway to the piers. It was late summer, but the wind off Lake Erie cut briskly across the city. Most of the yachts and smaller boats were covered. The SUV flashed its high beams as he rolled into the lot. Definitely not Trimble. He couldn't afford a ride like that. David drove out to the vehicle, ready to gun the accelerator at the first sign of trouble.

The SUV's window rolled down. A bald black man in an expensive suit sat behind the wheel. He wore an ascot instead of a tie. He was old, his skin wrinkly as a pug's around his cheeks and chin. "Get in, David," he said, a voice full of glass shards and old smokes.

"Can we talk outside?"

"No."

This is a bad idea, he thought as he killed the Sundance's engine. *No one knows I'm here.*

He's going to slit your throat and fuck your mouth as you die, Brune whispered.

"Stop it," he said to the empty passenger's seat.

If Elizabeth really cared about you, she'd be home right now. You knew she didn't have the strength for this. You knew she was broken. That's why you picked her. You and Riley, you're not so different.

As if he were sleepwalking, David stepped out of his car and climbed into the SUV. The old man reeked of bad weed and Sucrets.

"Thank you," said the old man. "That shows good faith, David. And respect. I knew I could trust you."

"Trust me with what?"

"Trust you with my secret."

"What is your secret?"

"That I'm a practicing pedophile."

For a moment David said nothing. His heart beat against his chest like an angry landlord.

"Sucrets?" The man tilted an open tin toward him but David waved it away.

"Why did you tell me that?" he asked. His mouth was dry as sandpaper.

"Because I know how you can prove Trimble murdered Sarah Creston. But the only reason I came to know what I know is because we, for a while, were part of the same exclusive club. Not a formal club, but I think you know what I mean."

David stared back at him. He wanted to leave. But he still didn't have his answers. And he thought this would be the closest he might ever get to proof.

"You have to ask yourself, I guess, if you really want to hear what I have to say. I will have to tell you things no one wants to hear. Is knowing what really happened to Sarah worth taking a pedophile into your confidence? Hiding his secret so that a more dangerous man goes to jail? The only consolation I can offer you is that I never killed anyone."

On some level, David knew the old man was speaking in the same reserved tone he used when grooming his victims. "Tell me what happened," he said.

"There was a video-production warehouse hidden in the basement of a bicycle shop in eastern Michigan in the seventies and early eighties. It was the second largest dubbing and distribution center for child pornography in the United States. The Russian Mafia had a hand in the operation, enough that they fronted dividends to the local cops so that we didn't have them breathing down our backs.

"I was what we called a 'talent scout.' I cruised the inner ring of Cleveland. West side, mostly, between 117 and the Market. Our clientele preferred white kids, so the east side was out. I did some scouting in Parma, too. It comes so you recognize a kid no one's gonna care about. You find them playing out front in fenced-in yards gone to dirt from the scraping of mutt dogs. Kids playing on the tracks, in the empty lots, while their parents shoot heroin at home. These kids were our bread and butter. You could pick them up for the weekend, drive them to Detroit, and send them back with a fifty in their pocket for the trouble and you could guarantee no one would call the cops.

"There are 'talent scouts' and there are 'moonlighters.' A moonlighter is like a freelance talent scout. Maybe they don't bring you any props for a couple years and maybe then they bring you three. These guys liked to dip their wick but not live the dream, you know? Trimble was a moonlighter.

"This was my territory back then so he comes to me, right? I'm sitting at home on a Tuesday evening and it's not even dark yet and he pulls his van into my driveway. And he's got this girl inside. I thought I was done for. I mean, if a neighbor had peeked their head outside at that moment, it would have been all she wrote. That's the problem with moonlighters. They take stupid risks.

"Anyway, I opened the garage and he pulled it in. I go out there, and there's Sarah Creston. He's got her cuffed to some metal ring set into the floor and I can tell right away that she's not one of these kids that go home and keep our business to themselves. This is a kid someone cared for, you know? 'Fuck,' I tell him. 'You gotta drop this girl off. Get her away from here.'

"But then he says, 'I want it on film.' And he's willing to pay a thousand dollars for me to set up the equipment. I know I can copy it and get ten times that from the bike shop guys. And they'll make fifty-large selling cassettes at flea markets—we had this system back then where all the kiddie stuff was sold out in the open, in fake cases that showed adults. The way you knew the difference was the kiddie stuff was always marked with a green X. It gave you deniability. The bolsheviks taught us that. I was a workingman and that sort of money didn't come around every day.

"So what I did was I drugged her. Sodium pentothal. Got it from a dentist client of mine. I gave her the drug so she wouldn't remember anything of the experience. There was even a good chance she wouldn't remember me. That stuff messes with memory, man. If you can believe it, I did care about her well-being.

"It only took me fifteen minutes to set up. Then a half hour for Trimble to do his thing. Got it on film, which was dubbed to cassette—better for duping that way, less generation loss. 'Take her back home,' I says.

"'I can't do that,' he tells me. And I know what that means. But I don't want to know any more so I pretended I didn't hear him. We got the girl back in the van. I dosed her again. One for the road. And they took off."

David opened the SUV's door and stepped out onto the parking lot with legs that threatened to fail him. He bent over and heaved twice before puking his dinner. He felt a hand on his back. It was the old man.

"Don't touch me," David said, recoiling.

The old man withdrew the Sucrets again and took one for himself, which he swished between his teeth loudly. "I know what I am," he said after a moment. "But I have morals, believe it or not. I would never kill a kid. Never."

"Do you have the tape?" David asked.

"No. All the tapes were destroyed after Sarah Creston's murder became front-page news."

"So what good is any of this to me?"

"The original film still exists," said the old man. "It's being kept in a boat at the end of that dock." He pointed to the farthest dock from the parking lot, where a massive sailboat was moored.

"Who owns the boat?"

The old man shook his head. "Won't tell you that. I think I've said enough." He turned back toward the driver's door.

"Wait," said David. "What if I need to get in touch with you?"

The old man shrugged. "I done all I could," he said. "You could probably get my name from my license plate, David. But remember, I asked you to keep me anonymous, in your confidence. I would never kill a kid. No, sir. But you. If you came to my doorstep? Yeah. I could kill you."

David never ran the license plate. He didn't want to know the man's real name. For the book, he simply called him "Gary Gonze," after a villain in a pulp sci-fi novel he'd read as a teen.

David's body pulsated with adrenaline as he walked the length of the docks. He felt the vertigo of the undulating waves pushing and pulling at the boards beneath his feet. He considered, briefly, calling the tip in to the police. But he knew the tip was not good enough for a warrant. Not without the old man sticking around to talk to the police himself. There were issues such as breaking-and-entering and chain of evidence to think about, but the need to know was too great to resist. It controlled him, his very being. He could not come this close and not at least *look*. The need to know, to really know that Trimble was the serial killer and not Brune, was more important than avoiding jail, more important than closure for the Creston family, even.

It was easily the biggest yacht in the entire club, a towering white schooner with presidential-blue trim. Three portholes were set into the port side, facing David. It was utterly dark beyond the glass. The sails were snugly wrapped. It had every appearance of a ghost ship. He looked to the aft and shuddered at the sight of the ship's name: The *Beagle*, it was called, after the boat that spirited Darwin to the Galapagos. But some-one had spray-painted over the *a* and the *g* so that it now read BEEZLE.

David looked over his shoulder, back down the dock. No one was running after him. There were no lights on in any of the other boats' cabins. He turned back to the *Beezle* and jumped onto the ladder dangling from its side like some deep-sea creature's trap.

The deck was sealed off from the weather by a transparent tarp secured to the boat by grommets. He unsnapped one end and slipped inside. Too dark to see. He felt around the floor and eventually came across the Hobbit-sized door leading to the cabin. Beside the door was a switch. He clicked it on. A row of lights set into the floor illuminated the deck around the ornate steering wheel, a nondescript area carpeted blue, a place for sunbathing and steering. Attached to the wall was a heavy flashlight. He snatched it up, clicked it on, and doused the floor lights.

The cabin door led into a kitchen and dining area. At the back of this room two doors were set into an oak-paneled wall stained the color of fresh mud. The kitchen reeked of mothballs.

He shone the beam of light around the room, catching circles of countertop and cabinets and the outline of a large fridge. There were cubbyholes in the walls beside the dining table. He opened up the first he came to. Inside were a flare gun and several maps. Inside another were two folders full of kiddie porn. Momentary flashes of the pictures contained within burned into his mind like a virus, insisting that this is the way the world is, this is the way the world is.

I smell your decay, whispered Brune.

He set the envelopes down, keenly aware that his fingerprints were now all over them, and sickened by his unconcern. Quickly he scanned the rest of the boat. Nothing. He opened the portside door at the back. It was a large bathroom with a glass shower. He wished he had not seen the Hannah Montana scrunchie wrapped around the showerhead.

He opened the second door. The bedroom. The bed was a canopy, wrapped in sheer pink silk. A mirror on the ceiling. Beside the bed was a nightstand, its cupboards full of tubes of something called Love Gel and magnum-sized condoms. He combed the drawers of a dresser. Clothes in adult sizes. Sweaters that cost more than he made in a month. One drawer, however, contained a pile of little-girl panties.

Soon he had searched every nook and cranny in the room and had found nothing more incriminating than the photographs. Defeated, David sat on the silk bedsheets. He felt it under his ass and knew immediately what it was—he had once worked at a movie theater and knew the general size and shape of a film reel.

This one was smaller than the sort David had once threaded into projectors, by about half. The film was thin and brittle. It smelled of vinegar, a sign this was old stock, prone to disintegration. It was labeled with black marker on white tape: S.C.

David held it in a tight grip and started for the ladder.

There was the shadow of a man on the threshold of the door to the kitchen. David was too stunned to feel fear. His first thought was that it was the old black man, come back to spring the mousetrap, but as David swung the light up, he saw white, manicured hands, wrinkled hands, sticking out of a flannel shirt.

"Keep it off my face," the man growled.

David froze. There was, of course, no way out.

I'm going to die tonight, he thought.

I'll be here for you on the other side, said Brune. *And I can't wait . . .*

. . . to meet this mystery source of yours," said Cindy, as David came out of the men's room. "I find it really hard to believe an anonymous 'old black man' told you right where you could find a snuff film starring Sarah Creston. Too convenient. Of course, no one will ever get to see the film, since it was destroyed on that boat." He started walking toward the courtroom. "I don't suppose you'd like to at least tell me who owned the boat? I might be able to backtrack the connection and at least verify some of the things you've accused Trimble of doing."

"Not everyone is like you."

"At least I had the courage to admit when I fabricated a source."

"Only because Andy figured it out first."

"There was no Gary Gonze, was there? There was no snuff film. There was no boat, was there, David?"

Several people loitering in the hallway turned to see what all the commotion was about.

"The police have a *piece* of the film."

"Why didn't the prosecutor enter it into evidence?"

"Go ask him, Cindy."

"Because it wasn't Sarah, was it?"

"Believe what you want."

The time it took Cindy to ambush David in the hallway was just long enough for her to lose her seat in the packed courtroom. As David entered, she was directed back out, to wait with the other standbys.

"But I'm a reporter," she whined.

"Lady, I don't care if you're Angelina Jolie," said the bailiff, a chubby Irishman. "Wait outside."

Before returning to the witness stand, David leaned over the partition and kissed Elizabeth. As he did, she slipped something into his hand. It felt like a long spoon. He didn't look at it until he was back at his seat. There, he unfolded his hands. It was a pregnancy-test wand. It showed a pink plus sign. He looked over at her and smiled when she gave him the A-okay sign.

A miracle, in a way, considering the dangerous side effects of Rivertin. His virility thrilled him. And that was good. He needed a bit of grandiose confidence for what came next.

———□———

The house on Primrose Lane sat above a postage-stamp yard, unmowed since Jimmy Carter was president, a minuscule field of bluegrass swaying in the chill autumn breeze weaving around Merriman Valley, along the Crooked River that flowed all the way to Lake Erie, thirty miles north. David and Katy stood beyond the lawn for a moment, holding hands, looking up at the curtained windows, imagining what lay inside. Today Katy wore a Chippewa princess headband, a thin strap of rope wrapped around her head that held three blue feathers in place behind her right ear.

"What are you going to do with it?" she asked.

"Dunno," he said. "Make a cool B&B. Aren't all those places supposed to have ghosts for the tourists anyway?"

"I don't think many people summer in West Akron."

"Yeah, well. Maybe I'll rent it to college kids." He tugged her arm. "C'mon. Let's check out the things he left behind."

A lockbox hung on the front door. David's lawyer had given him the code this morning, after the sale was finalized for an even quarter-mil. He entered the code, withdrew the key, an old steel key heavy like a secret. It tumbled the locks and the door clicked open with an audible *ahhhhhhhhhhhhhhhhh.*

To the right was a light switch, which David tried. It didn't work, but it was high noon, and Akron was enjoying a rare cloudless day. The light through the curtains illuminated the rooms a bit. David led the way. Katy held his hand tightly and followed, keeping the door open behind them.

They looked in the closet, at the boxes of mittens. David took out a reporter's notepad and jotted down the name of the company written on the sides of the boxes—Nostos, Inc., Dublin, Ireland. He also took a pair of mittens and tried them on. They fit. Wearing the dead man's mittens made him feel queasy, though, so he stuffed them into his pockets.

He turned toward the foyer. On the hardwood was the dried blood of the Man from Primrose Lane, long streaks trailing into the living room, ending in a crimson stain the shape and color of a wax seal.

The room had remained relatively untouched since the coroner's team had removed the body in 2008; Akron homicide detectives had taken the notebooks about Katy along with a few other items in 2009. Stacks of paperbacks still lined the walls. Mystery novels, mostly. Everything from Conan Doyle to James Patterson. Some horror novels. Some do-it-yourselfs—*Wordworking for Dummies, Guitar for Dummies,* even something called *Surviving the Apocalypse for Dummies.* A copy of *Ulysses,* spiral-bound, open to Episode 10, rested on the mantel below a dark square that suggested a mirror once hung there.

"It smells like the library at Roxboro Elementary," said Katy. "Do you think he read all these books?"

"I'd bet on it," he said.

A single painting hung on the western wall, a reproduction—likely illegal—of *The Persistence of Memory,* the one with the melting clocks and the weird dead fish monster that was supposedly Dalí's self-portrait.

They traced the trail of blood back to its place of origin: the kitchen. The blender was gone, but David recognized the outline of the machine in a pool of petrified blood on the counter by the window. Katy investigated the cabinets. The Man from Primrose Lane had labeled everything. There was a specific place for rice (brown and white) and peanut butter (crunchy and not) and spaghetti and soup. The fridge had a shelf labeled MILK and ICED TEA but had been overcome with some form of bacteria or moss that smelled of living death. They didn't open the fridge again. Katy pointed to something on the fridge, a magnet in the shape of a cat. It held a letter to the door. David recognized the handwriting at once.

Baby's coming. I'll be by to see you asap. Get your walks in. Keep a smile on your face. Loving you. E.

Had the police missed it or had they taken a picture of it for the file and moved on? David didn't know for sure, but he thought it had probably been overlooked. He'd almost not seen it. There was something to be said about hiding in plain sight.

Inside, David felt the unfamiliar grip of doubt tickling his heart. *Welcome, my old friend.* He pushed it away. No time for that. "I can't explain it," he said to Katy. "But there *is* some explanation. I don't believe she was cheating on me. You'd have to know her. She just didn't have it in her."

"Not like me, you mean?"

"I didn't mean that."

"It's okay."

"I didn't, you know."

"I know."

There were two rooms upstairs, not counting the tiny bathroom. To the right was a small studio. An easel stood in the center of the room upon which hung a half-finished canvas that David suspected had been stretched and framed by the mystery man's own hands. It was a surrealist expression of a still life—an egg, hanging in midair, like Dalí's clocks. But this egg was black and large. It was set against a half-rendered background that looked a little like part of the Cuyahoga Valley, but one where the trees were not organic but somehow mechanical. His brushstrokes were almost nonexistent. This was the painting of a patient man.

In grade school, David had loved art class. He was surprised to recognize a sudden longing inside himself for the feel of a paintbrush in his hands. And the smell. He missed this smell of thick paint and cloth. It was as he remembered Miss Wolf's art room in fourth grade. How much he had forgotten about his childhood. What else had he once enjoyed? If he ever again had time enough to spare for a hobby, David thought he might like to paint again. *Maybe even finish this painting,* he thought.

It was the only painting in the room. The entire studio was bare except for this single work-in-progress and a squat table on which rested a pallet of earth-tone oil paint, dried to stone.

"Where'd he store the *finished* paintings?" asked Katy.

David shrugged.

The other room was a bedroom. Orderly. Efficient. Two button-down shirts hung inside the thin closet next to a pair of slacks and a full-bodied worker's suit spotted with paint. Atop the dresser was a bottle of Old Spice from the seventies. There was nothing inside the drawers except a ratty pair of shorts and a dead mouse. The sleigh bed was covered in three layers of sheets that were once tan but were now a mottled gray. The headboard had been removed, David deduced, by the Akron police.

David walked over to the bed and put his face into the pillows. He paused, nodded grimly. "She was here," he said. "I smell her perfume." His chest hitched. He sighed loudly and steeled himself as best he could. A single tear streaked down his left cheek before he could catch it. "I'm sorry," he said.

"Don't be sorry, David," she said.

"I really thought . . . I don't know. Christ, this looks bad for me."

"You didn't do it," she said.

"Doesn't matter," he said. "Innocent men are convicted all the time. Guilty men go free."

"Trimble got his."

"Did he?"

The Man from Primrose Lane kept his treasures in the basement.

The concrete floor was warped and cracked, pieces jutting out so far it looked like it had survived an earthquake or two. But everything appeared to be dry and he smelled no mildew.

"I'll have to fix that floor if I ever decide to sell it," he said.

"Might be easier to level it and start over," said Katy. "I know a guy can get you a good discount on lumber."

"Funny."

The room was full of turn-of-the-century essentials: boiler, fireplace, coal bin, sink. Arranged throughout were half a dozen rectangular shapes shrouded in bedsheets, leaning against oak support beams. Canvases, no doubt.

He pulled the linen off the painting closest to them, with a ta-da flourish. He had expected a landscape. He had hoped for a self-portrait. What he got instead was . . .

"Oh, shit," said Katy.

It was a painting of a girl who appeared to be about ten years old. She had a round face full of sunshine freckles and red hair cut in a bob. She was seated in a ride called the Whirling Dervish. David recognized it from Cedar Point, an amusement park an hour west of Cleveland. He'd been there many times himself as a teenager. The girl wore a white halter that fluttered in the ride's jetstream. Her eyes radiated youth and serenity.

"That's you, isn't it?"

Katy nodded, cringing. "Fucking creep."

"It's beautiful."

"Yeah. That's somehow creepier."

"Look." David pointed at the bottom right corner. The painting had been titled, simply, *Katy.* "I think these are all going to be you," he said. "You want to keep going?"

"Definitely. I have to see if there's one of me in here painted from outside my bedroom window when I was sixteen. I can't wait to have nightmares about it."

But that was the only one featuring Katy. The next revealed two identical twin girls, hand in hand, walking down a sidewalk, sipping Icees from opposite hands. It was labeled *Elaine & Elizabeth.*

"Apparently, this one is my nightmare," said David. There was no question anymore. Elaine's disappearance was linked to Katy in some way. The Man from Primrose Lane had known it before anyone else. How? How could this hermit with no friends have found a connection that had eluded detectives for decades? And why was he interested, anyway?

"Actually, this one is," said Katy. She stood by another canvas, a portrait of a young man standing in a parking lot, holding a candle. It was *David* at Kent State.

"What the fuck, Katy?" His head spun. He searched for meaning and found none. Because what meaning was there? And yet, he wasn't surprised to find himself in a painting, too. Not really. After all, wasn't he also a link between Elaine and Katy?

"David, I think . . . I know this. I . . . I think I was here."

"Yeah, I think you were." He didn't care to discuss having relived that particular memory during his withdrawals. He just let it be. It was to the point that she accepted this. "Apparently so was the Man from Primrose Lane."

The next one looked like an advertisement for some Dirty Harry movie. It was a painting of a police officer standing in front of an outdated cruiser, pointing a pistol at the observer. David saw the shape of someone sitting in the cruiser, but couldn't make out enough detail to determine if it was a passenger or a prisoner. The car was parked on a bridge. It was night inside the painting, the darkness broken only by the headlights. What was the cop aiming at? he wondered, but he was glad whatever it was had been left out of the picture—this particular painting scared him more than the others for reasons he could not grasp. It was labeled *Incident on Twightwee Road*.

"Where is Twightwee Road?" she asked.

"Don't know. But that cop looks mad."

Only two canvases remained. Katy walked deliberately over to the one propped against the far wall and yanked off the blanket.

This oil-on-canvas was titled *Tanmay*. It showed a middle-aged man of Indian descent, dressed in a white lab coat, his arms crossed and a smile on his face. In the background was an oddly shaped building of metal and glass that appeared to be melting, a familiar architectural wonder to anyone who has lived in northeast Ohio for a spell.

"That's Case Western," said David.

"He shouldn't be hard to find." Katy pointed to the scientist's name tag. It read DR. TANMAY GUPTA. PROFESSOR OF ENTOMOLOGY. "What's entomology?"

"The study of insects." David braced himself. "Are you willing to trade in all these prizes for what could be behind curtain number six?" he asked.

There was a man behind that last curtain. And this painting was not titled.

It was, David realized at once, a passable police-artist sketch, but with much more depth and color. It was the face of a handsome man with shaggy hair pushed below the line of his forehead in a queer way. He wore wide glasses and was dressed in a Members Only jacket. His eyes were the color of the spring sky but harbored no emotion. His mouth was pursed in a thin slit.

"That's him, David. That's the man who came up to me in the plaza back in 1999, the one that old man jumped."

He nodded. "And likely the man who took my wife's sister. The only man who had motive to kill the Man from Primrose Lane."

Later, outside the house, he put an arm around her and looked back at his investment. It stared back at him with black-window eyes full of contempt. He might own it now, but David was still—and forever—a trespasser here. Unwelcome. Whatever secrets the house held, whatever had happened inside, he was never supposed to uncover. This was something he felt deep in his soul and worked to ignore.

"Am I being paranoid," he said, "or were those paintings placed there after the fact?"

"What do you mean?" asked Katy.

"Well, I mean, how did the police miss them? Did they really never go down to the basement?"

"I don't know."

He shook his head. "There's no reason for me to be in one of his paintings," he said, so quietly it was as if he were speaking to himself. "I'm not some girl he kept tabs on. I didn't even know him."

"Can we please go?" asked Katy. "I feel like we're being watched. Can't you feel it?"

David scanned the streets. An expensive Cadillac idled across the street in a driveway a few houses down. Otherwise they were alone. He led her back to the yellow Bug. "Dr. Gupta should be easy to find, at least," he said. "The Man from Primrose Lane thought he was important. The question is, why?"

"There's no Dr. Gupta in Entomology," said the receptionist at DeGrace Hall the following afternoon.

David had taken Tanner with him since he couldn't wrangle a babysitter on short notice. Katy was slinging coffee at Barnes & Noble, which was fortunate because David still felt funny about the idea of going someplace with both his son and his, what? . . . girlfriend? . . . not-so-secret mistress? . . . paramour? As far as he knew, she had not formally canceled her engagement. She wasn't talking about that part of her life and he was not asking. Maybe soon, he thought. But not today.

Tanner was happy to tag along and had dressed the part—in the basement he'd found an old fedora that had belonged to David's grandfather. David had helped him craft a "press badge" to stick in the band. Tanner carried a large notepad and a pen with him as he followed his father, who toted his old writer's satchel.

It had been a while since he'd been to Cleveland, longer still since he'd been to Case Western Reserve University. The campus was situated on the east side of town, just beyond the ghetto, near the symphony and museums. It had the look of a New England prep school, dotted with brick and sandstone buildings lousy with ivy. There was, however, one glaring bit of modernity. In the mid-nineties, CWRU commissioned renowned architect Frank Gehry to design its new school of management building. Its melting steel structure and overabundance of glass always made David feel as if he were staring through a window into an alternate reality, where the laws of physics were just a bit different.

But no Dr. Gupta. No surprise there. This case was an endless Russian nesting doll: twist one piece apart and you find only yet another, and inside that one yet another, and another, and another.

"We have a Tanmay Gupta, though," the receptionist said as they started to leave.

David stopped. "Yes. Tanmay. That's him."

"He's not a doctor," she said.

He shrugged. "I've never met him."

"You're in luck. He's right down the hall, in 101. I'll get him for you." She exited the office and was gone for only a minute before she returned with a boy who appeared to be all of thirteen.

A wave of vertigo washed over David. Though this was obviously not the man from the painting, this young boy felt familiar to him. He wouldn't even call it déjà vu. More like the memory of a memory in a dream. Something about this moment was very similar to the brain storms caused by the Rivertin withdrawals. The present had begun to feel like an episodic memory.

"You're Tanmay Gupta?" he asked.

"Yes, sir, I am," he replied in a thick and slippery Hindi accent.

"You have a father named Tanmay, who's a doctor somewhere?" he asked.

Tanmay shook his head. "No, sir. My father, his name is Bevin. He resides in Mumbai."

"How old are you?" asked Tanner, raising his pen to his lips.

Tanmay laughed. "I turn sixteen this year. I graduated high school in Mumbai at fourteen."

"And you don't know any other Tanmay Guptas?" asked David.

"No, sir. Not in America, that is. It's a fairly popular name back home."

"Weird. I'm a writer, right? And I'm looking into the death of this guy from Akron. He had this . . . okay, I know this sounds a little strange . . . but he had this painting in his basement of some doctor at Case named Tanmay Gupta."

"I know no one from Akron. I am sorry."

"It's all right. Maybe it wasn't Case. Maybe I got the university wrong." But he knew that was untrue. The Gehry building had been in the background. No. It was Case in the painting, he was sure of it. And didn't the man look similar to this young boy? Similar enough to be related? They must be. His mind tried to make sense of it, but his thoughts dissolved into white noise behind his eyes. It was too much to figure.

"It was nice to meet you," Tanmay said. "Sorry I could not be of help." Tanmay shook his hand and then turned toward the door.

"Just out of curiosity, what do you study here, Tanmay?"

Tanmay turned back to the writer and his son. "I am studying the hibernation cycle of the cicada; how their biological clock is set, how they subsist for seventeen years underground before springing forth from the earth. I am not sure this information would be of use to your murdered man from Akron."

"No. I suppose not. I was just curious."

Tanmay nodded. "Of course, there may one day be real-world application for my work," he said, defending his own apparent obsession.

"What sort of application?"

"If we can come to understand the mechanisms behind hibernation, perhaps we can apply that knowledge to the biology of man. It is, after all, such a long way to Mars. Astronauts, they have to eat so much. But if you could trick them into sleeping the whole time, you could save so much on supplies, not to mention cabin fever."

David felt a chill run through his body. He shivered. "Sounds like coma," he said.

"No. Very unlike coma. Coma we can induce. But coma patients must be fed. In true hibernation, the metabolism slows down such that the body may need very little energy to survive. And this energy may be extracted from the body itself or, quite possibly, from a liquid solution of nutrients into which it could be submerged. We all did this at one time in our lives. Think of the womb."

"You couldn't pay me enough to try something like that," said David.

Tanmay smiled. "I won't call you when looking for test subjects, then."

THINGS ELIZABETH NEVER TOLD HIM

"Come on, man, you've got us on the edge of our seats," said Synenberger, rubbing his bald head distractedly, as if he were trying to keep David's preposterous story inside his skull in some semblance of order. "What did the man in the shadows tell you on his boat? I mean, obviously he didn't kill you. Wait. What happened to the snuff film, anyway? I almost forgot about that. You had it in your hands, is that right?"

"Yes."

"So where is it?"

"I don't know."

David looked over at Russo and was surprised to find him smiling. He gave David a nod and turned to his assistant excitedly. The young woman raced out of the room. David didn't have the slightest idea why Russo was suddenly happy. To him it still felt like Synenberger was doing a stand-up job of eviscerating him—and the state's case against Riley Trimble—on the stand.

"Well?" asked Synenberger. "Go on with your story."

David cleared his throat. Russo made his hands like he was pulling taffy. He did it quickly just as Judge Siegel blew his nose into a hankie.

Stall.

"He told me not to shine the light in his eyes, so I never really got to see his face," said David.

Synenberger rolled his eyes. "Of course not," he said.

"'Give me the film,' the man said to me, 'Give . . .

. . . me the film."

He handed the reel of old film stock to the man who stood in the darkness of the captain's bedroom. As he did, David bumped the nightstand to cause a little noise. Still, he thought the man might have heard his sleight of hand, the brittle snapping under the shifting of objects upon the table.

"How did you find this?" he asked. "How did you know about this?"

David said nothing.

"I have a gun," the old man said. "Tell me."

"No," said David. He didn't know if the man had a gun or not. Quite possibly men like this carried weapons meant for killing. But this man sounded weak, like his grandfather used to sound after climbing a couple steps. David knew that the man did not have a gun in his hands at the moment, anyway—he could see them both and one was holding the film reel. In the waistband of his slacks? Maybe. But how quickly could he get to it?

Apparently the old pederast sensed his doubt. He launched himself at David. The film tumbled to the deck and suddenly the man was at David's neck with his scrawny hands. If his body was weak, his hands, at least, were quite strong. They choked David's throat closed. Long nails pinched into his neck.

Kill him! Brune shouted. David heard it not in his mind this time, but in his ears. *Kill him! Kill him!*

"Oh, I will," said the old man, leaning against him. He could feel the old man's growing hard-on under the thin slacks.

David scraped at the old man's chest, ripping open the button-up flannel shirt. The man's chest was devoid of hair and slippery with lubricant. David had nothing to grip. He couldn't kick him, either; the old man had pushed him against a bureau and there simply was not enough room. He did the only thing he could think of; he grabbed the old man's nipples and twisted.

The old man screamed, letting David go. As soon as those cancerous hands released his throat, David shoved him away. He heard him smack against the wall. As David made for the door, the man scampered after him in the dark. There was no time to stop for the film. David ran for the ladder and the docks beyond.

"No!" the old man screamed. It was a high-pitched scream, the scream of the insane.

You fucker! shouted Brune.

"I'm sorry!" the old man screamed, and for a moment David thought he was still talking to him. "I'm sorry, Beezle! He's too strong! I told you he was too strong! No! Please, no! Beezle!"

David slid down the ladder so quickly he stumbled and fell the last five feet, cracking his ass on the dock. He didn't look back. He ran to his car, panting, afraid he was about to die of a coronary. And as he ran, he clutched at the thing in his pocket, the secret the old man didn't know about: four frames he'd managed to snap off the beginning of the reel.

He pulled off the highway halfway to Akron and rolled into a McDonald's parking lot. He walked inside and locked himself in the men's room. Then he brought out the film and held it to the light.

The four frames stood out like zoetrope drawings, freeze-frames of a despicable action that occurred in the past and could not be changed. Four single pictures. But that was enough. They were sitting on a couch. Sarah was on his lap, her pants stripped away. Her head lolled to the side, away from the camera so that only her chin and part of a cheek were visible. But it was her, without a doubt. There was no mistaking Trimble, either. He was looking at the camera and smiling.

Elizabeth kissed him on the forehead the next morning before she left for work. She didn't ask where he had been all night. They were separating. He could feel it. On this trajectory, separation was unavoidable.

He watched her walk out of their bedroom and wondered if this was the last time or if he could disappoint her again before she cut her losses and moved on, moved back into exile with Christopher Pike.

Only one way out, Brune whispered. Was his voice a little more distant this morning? David thought maybe. Also, it was in his head again. Not his ears. And David sensed desperation in the tone.

Already his body was beginning to tense up, preparing for the psychological assault of another day under Brune's spell. David leaned over the side of the bed for a moment, digging into the pocket of his jeans

that lay on the floor, and returned to the pillows with the pack of Marlboros, his mental cigarettes. He stuck a coffin nail in his mouth and imagined himself lighting it, imagined himself inhaling the nicotine and tar
and formaldehyde, and when Brune spoke again his voice sounded like
it was coming through a transistor radio tuned to an AM station.

Jump off the bridge, David. It'll feel like flying.

It was that moment that David made up his mind to quit the paper.
It would be, he knew on a basic level, a first step toward some kind of
salvation.

He drove to Cleveland with the car's radio tuned to 90.3, a local
NPR affiliate. He was not surprised to hear the news update, "Emergency crews this morning are responding to a fire at Edgewater Marina
that has already claimed three large yachts, including one owned by retired county sheriff Gregory O'Reilly. No word yet on the cause of the
fire, which started sometime around three a.m. Unconfirmed reports
suggest O'Reilly may have been living on his boat. His family, when
reached by phone, declined comment."

The editorial room at the *Independent* was bustling with young copy
editors and music writers scrambling to push the latest issue to print.
This excitement usually thrilled David, who liked to imagine himself
walking through the *Daily Planet* on a day when renegades from Kryp-
ton threatened Metropolis and only *he* had the exclusive scoop from the
Man of Steel. Today, however, the cacophony faded into murmur. He
no longer felt a part of it.

"Mother*fucker!*" yelled Andy.

David entered his office and shut the door behind him.

"Where the holy fuck have you been?" asked Andy. "Where's my
story? It better be in your little man-purse there. Because, what the fuck?
We got a cover to lay out and this baby gets sent to the printer at noon."

"I quit," said David.

Andy looked at him for a moment, his face a blank, as if something
inside had shorted out. Then he smiled. "Ha! Fuck you. That's good.
That's good. Funny guy."

"I don't have your story, Andy," he said.

"All right. Cut it out, man. You wanna give me a heart attack?"

He didn't say anything. Just stood there and gave his editor a moment to catch up to reality. David suddenly felt boneless, held together

by tape and wishes. Andy jumped up and came around his desk. *Here we go*, thought David. He prepared himself for the punch.

"You get points for coming down here and saying it to my face," he said, through clenched teeth the color of coffee. "But all that buys you is about another thirty seconds. If I were you, I'd get gone."

"What are you doing home?" asked Elizabeth as she returned to their apartment to find him on the couch at four-thirty that afternoon. She was dressed in a smooth Erin-green sundress, a sweater tossed over her shoulders to make it school-appropriate. Her neck, he noticed absently, was splotchy and red. Usually only he could make that happen. *She must have run up the steps*, he told himself.

"Where have you been?" he asked casually.

She shook her head. "Staff meeting. What's up?"

"I'm done with the *Independent*."

"They fired you?"

"I quit."

Elizabeth came around the table and snuggled up to David on the couch, where he sat watching a rerun of *Unsolved Mysteries*. She kissed him. "I'm so happy, David," she said. "You have no idea."

"I have to write one more story, though," he said. "I've got to do something with this Brune thing."

Elizabeth scrunched her eyes at him. "I hate that story. You've been weird ever since you brought that box home." She took his head in her hands and turned him toward her. "Why do you want to live in that world?"

"It's the real world."

"No, it isn't. These things are like lightning strikes. It's like you're only talking to people who have been struck by lightning and assuming everyone else has been."

"This guy is still out there. Trimble is still out there."

"Let the police deal with him."

"The police don't believe me."

"Then promise me it'll be your last," she said. "When this one's done, promise you'll never write about this stuff again."

It felt like a lie, but he said it anyway. "I promise."

———

The first thing he did the next morning was visit the Medina Police Department, where he gave the strip of film to Sergeant Boylan. He spent the next hour and a half explaining to Boylan how, exactly, it had come into his possession. An assistant county prosecutor was called in. After he explained the story again to her, the county prosecutor graciously opted not to charge him with obstruction of justice (for tampering with a potential crime scene and fucking up their chain of custody).

"I'm still not sold," said Boylan. "All it proves is that Trimble is a creep. You can't see the girl's face. It's impossible to tell if it's even a child. Her chest isn't exposed. I'm not sure this is even pornography."

"We could never present this in court," said the young APA. "The chain of custody is broken. Which is why reporters shouldn't run around playing cop. The rest of the film, I'm sure, was destroyed in the fire."

"We'll follow up on this," assured the policeman.

It was the response David had expected, the response he needed to push him to turn the story into a book. He would have to go after Trimble himself, the only way he knew how—with words.

And so when David left the station he drove to the nearest Barnes & Noble. He'd never before given much thought to writing a nonfiction book. As a teen, devouring fantasy fiction from Tolkien to Stephen King, he'd considered writing similar stories one day, but all he had to show for it was a binder of hackneyed short stories, printed on typing paper that was turning yellow in the closet. He knew he could kick around for years searching in vain for an agent—he'd heard horror stories about the submission process from college professors. He hoped there was a way to bypass that, even if it meant publishing in a narrow market.

The "local interest" section was dominated by three companies. He found the names of the editors on their websites and emailed queries to them as soon as he returned home. His instinct, that a local publisher would be more apt to give an unproven writer a chance, was spot-on. David got offers from each, but in the end chose Sheppard Publishing mostly because he liked the cover designs for their series of ghost story paperbacks.

The next day, Paul Sheppard bought him lunch at a Chinese place on the east side and listened intently as David walked him through the murders of Jennifer Poole, Donna Doyle, and Sarah Creston; through Ronil Brune's arrest and conviction on the rape charges, and his execution by lethal injection for Sarah's murder; through the evidence he had uncovered that implicated Brune's young friend Riley Trimble.

"Whew," Paul said when David finished. "It's a good story. A long one, I think. It's probably going to take you nine months."

It took David three.

He set a grueling pace for himself, eager to rid his soul of Brune. The act of writing became a form of exorcism. Ten pages a day at first. By the end, he was writing fifteen pages in eight-hour shifts starting the moment Elizabeth fell asleep. She never saw him write a single word.

Brune's voice dissipated at once and by the third week was gone altogether. David's nightmares subsided. He gained twenty pounds, due in no small part to late-night writing sessions at Steak 'n Shake—he had discovered he craved fatty foods when he was "in the zone."

On July 19, 2007, David stopped writing. The manuscript was five hundred pages long, easily the longest project he'd ever worked on. He had no idea if it was readable. He wasn't about to let Elizabeth take a peek. A nagging voice in his head—his own, this time—suggested his book might read like crazy talk, like a terrorist's manifesto. He expected Paul to take one look at it before asking him if it was some kind of joke.

He copied it to disc and printed it out into a thick folder and mailed everything to Paul. He heard nothing for three weeks. He had just made up his mind that Paul had indeed thought the book was nothing but insane ranting and supposition when the phone rang and Paul's assistant, Heather, asked if he would drive up to Cleveland for a meeting.

"We're printing four thousand copies, hardback," said Paul, clapping David on the back as he walked into the office, located in an old Twinkie factory near Chinatown. "I don't know if it's going to sell or not. It's not going to be what people expect and that could turn off some true crime fans. What we're going to have on our side, for once, are the critics. They're going to love this."

"Yeah?"

"That stuff in there about how this story hurt your relationship with your wife. That's going to affect people. But one thing . . ."

"What?"

"We have to come up with a name for the old man in the boat."

"You mean, other than O'Reilly?"

"We'll never know for sure if that's who you saw."

"It was his boat."

"Maybe," said Paul. "But he's not dead. You know that. They found him alive, wandering around Lakewood. He's institutionalized but he could still sue. And you never did see his face."

"No. I didn't."

They settled on the hard-boiled moniker "Mr. Shadow" for the mysterious old man on the boat. David didn't like it, but he accepted it. He also accepted the $2,500 advance Paul gave him that day. He used part of the money to take Elizabeth out to dinner.

But that night, long after David had begun to believe the voice of the executed rapist had been nothing but his troubled subconscious all along, Brune sprang his trap.

It happened while they were having sex.

Elizabeth was perched atop his lap, naked but for a pair of striped ankle socks, sitting back so that he could watch her taut body move around his prick. Her breasts pulled up and down as she moved; her pale nipples, nearly as white as the rest of her, were erect and beady with sweat. Her eyes were half closed, watching him push into her.

It felt like he tripped.

One minute he was sitting on the edge of the bed, inside her. The next, it felt like he had stumbled during a walk. It was that feeling you get sometimes as you're just falling asleep and something in a dream jerks you awake again. Except he didn't feel awake. It felt like he was falling. His vision drew back and Elizabeth's body shrank inside a sort of darkened tunnel, not unlike the tunnel vision he sometimes experienced when he was focused on writing, except much more complete. He tried to move an arm, but discovered he could not. He tried to speak and nothing came out.

I'm having a stroke, he thought.

But then he watched his arm move. It was not the one he had commanded, not the right one he favored, but the left. He watched his left hand cup her right breast and knead it, hard. Elizabeth moaned louder.

"I want to tie you up," he heard himself say. "I want to hear you beg." But it was not his normal voice. It was different. Gravelly. More nasal. The voice of a good accountant. "Tell me you want it."

"Yes," she said, daring.

What the fuck is happening? he cried out in his mind. *What the fuck is this?*

"C'mere," he said. The perspective changed as his body moved from inside her, from the bed, and pulled Elizabeth after him. He saw himself remove several neckties from his closet, which his hands used to bind his wife's wrists together. He made the knots tight. Another tie became a blindfold. He made her kneel on the bed so that he could tie her to the frame. He smacked her ass with enough force to leave a pink blossom behind. Elizabeth bit her lip and moaned.

His body stepped around to the large window beside the bed and drew the curtain back. David felt his blood turn to slivers of ice at the sight of the large, hulking homeless man standing in the dark outside their window, his face illuminated by the sparse light of the bedroom lamp. The bum's teeth were gone, except for a single bicuspid. One eye was milky. The other one stared back hungrily at the naked woman tied to the bed.

He watched his hand reach to the floor. His belt lay there.

"Fuck me," said Elizabeth.

"Soon," he whispered. He brought the leather strap down across her upper legs.

"David," she panted. "David, not so hard."

He hit her again.

"Ouch! David!"

I'm going to make her bleed, the voice of Brune said in his mind. *And I'm going to make you watch.*

Except it wasn't Brune, he knew. No ghost, no ordinary psychosis could be this powerful. There were two explanations, he realized, and both options were equally frightening. This was either a complete nervous breakdown or . . .

Say it.

. . . or a possession. A possession by the darkness that haunted Brune's box. That thing called . . .

Beezle.

He watched his left hand reach for the window latch.

David focused his energy at the end of that funnel, on the vision of his hand unlocking the window and pushing it open for the diseased human on the other side. He willed himself to control that hand, like a quadriplegic might try to summon movement out of a finger. As far as he knew, he was trapped in his body forever unable to control himself, a bystander to another consciousness that now controlled his flesh.

The homeless man leaned in the window and reached for Elizabeth. He reeked of rotted meat and somewhere in that ratty black jacket, David knew, was a knife.

NO!

With mad confidence, he stepped forward inside himself and, quite physically, felt his being push aside this *Other*. He fell forward, colliding with the man, who was already partway through the window. The bum reacted in fear and yanked his arm back out of the window with a low grunt. David slammed the window shut.

"David, what the hell was that?" said Elizabeth. "Was that the window?"

Shaken, still testing the limits of his repatriated motor skills, David didn't say anything as he quickly freed his wife. She slipped the blindfold from around her head. She was sweating, panting from the unreleased tension.

"Close the curtains," she said, wrapping her arms around her breasts.

He didn't want to, didn't want to go near that window. But he pretended that there was not a monster outside and forced himself to close the curtains. A quick glance revealed nothing but hedges and a single sodium light across the street illuminating the parking lot of a softball field.

"If you want to finish what you started, I'm game," she purred, offering to put one of the ties around her eyes again.

But David just sat on the edge of their bed until she sighed and turned away. When she fell asleep he went into the bathroom and stood below the hot water until it turned tepid. Of course, there was no washing off the darkness.

In the morning, he waited for Elizabeth to leave for work, loaded the Brune files into his Sundance, and drove to a flooded rock quarry in Franklin Mills where teenagers built bonfires in the summer. Once it had been a community swimming hole, with a food stand and lifeguard towers, but now the snack shack listed to the side, its whitewashed walls gray and speckled where the paint had baked off. Claytor Lake, they'd called it. Private now. A good place to disappear cars. As good a place as any for an exorcism.

With the care of a chef preparing a last supper, he hunted down the most perfect kindling from the surrounding woods and built up a pyre made of cedar and oak. It ignited on the first match and in a few minutes fingers of flame reached to the sun above. He returned to his car and lugged the box to the fire. Page by page, he fed the papers to the flames.

As each new piece was destroyed, he regained a little courage. And he needed some courage before he could bring himself to do what came next.

"David, look at me," said Athena. It was an emergency session and she had come in on her day off after he had called her cell phone.

He did.

"Post-traumatic stress disorder is serious stuff. There are veterans of war who come back and sometimes wake up to find they've accidentally bludgeoned their wife to death. Loss of control—these psychotic episodes, like the one you experienced last night, are not uncommon. Your brain chemistry is out of whack and that cannot be helped with therapy alone."

"I don't want to be a zombie," he said. "And if it was all some mental breakdown, how do you explain the homeless guy? Something *summoned* him to that window."

"David, in all probability the homeless man was never there. Just like Brune. Or Beezle. These things are not real. It's your own voice you're hearing inside your head. These are hallucinations. If they are allowed to progress, there may come a time when you will not be able to separate reality from the fiction you are creating. The world of your delusions will quietly replace reality. We have to help you, now."

"How do we do that?"

"I want you to go back to the Glenns. For a week, at least. I want you medicated. There's this new drug, Rivertin, that shows promise for treating depression and anxiety. I was in on the trial study and if you really want to get better, this is the drug I'd recommend. It's not something you can go on and then off again. Rivertin will get your chemicals balanced, but it takes time to prime your pump, to get your brain to start making those chemicals on its own again."

"How long?"

"Years, David. Years."

"Will I be able to write?"

Athena shrugged. "There's no way to know. I'm sure that would be subjective and dependent on each patient. Will it make you think differently for a while? Yes."

"Do I have any choice?"

"Sure you have a choice, David. You can choose, today, to start getting better. Or you can choose to put your loved ones at risk. You could choose to let it go until you are no longer in control, until you no longer know that up is up and down is down."

He didn't cry. He didn't have it in him.

"Fuck it," he said. "Let's . . .

. . . rock and roll," said David, into the microphone set into the witness stand.

"So you went away to a psych hospital," said Synenberger. "How long?"

"A month."

"A month. That's a long time."

"It is."

"So you were actually still in the hospital when my client was arrested for these crimes after your old employer, the *Independent,* ran an excerpt from your book? A little essay that disgraced the Medina County prosecutor and forced the state's attorney general to move the trial to Cleveland."

"Andy brought me a hard copy to edit from my room, in between group therapy sessions."

"You think because of your candor about your mental disorder the jury is more likely to believe your earlier statements about Mr. Trimble?"

"I don't know," he said.

"But you fully admit that you wrote the book *The Serial Killer's Protégé* at the height of your madness, before you sought treatment?"

"I was in therapy."

"But not medicated."

"No."

"And we're supposed to believe that a man whose own therapist warned him that he might confuse reality with fiction . . . we're supposed to trust that that man was going after the truth?"

"I never made anything up."

"Of course not," said Synenberger. "Not on purpose." He turned to Judge Siegel. "Nothing further, Your Honor."

Russo stood. "Redirect?"

Siegel motioned to the floor. As Russo came out from behind his table, his young assistant returned with a manila envelope, which she handed to him. Russo passed it along to David.

"David, would you please open that envelope and explain to the jury what is inside?"

He unclasped the envelope and tilted it upside down. A piece of sixteen-millimeter film, four frames long, tumbled out.

"Objection!" shouted Synenberger. "That is inconclusive and prejudicial. There is no way to determine who the girl in the photo really is or how old she may be."

"You opened the door, Terry," shot Russo. "We weren't going to enter it into evidence. But since you started down this road, the jury can decide what it really shows."

"You've been given a lot of leeway," Siegel said to Synenberger. "I don't know why you went down that road, but it's done. Go back to your table. Objection overruled."

Synenberger rummaged through a stack of papers at his desk.

Siegel twisted in his chair to look at David. "Mr. Neff? Mr. Russo asked you if you recognized the object in your hand. Please answer his question."

"This is the piece of film I snapped off the reel that was in the yacht. It is four frames of sixteen-millimeter film that clearly shows Riley Trimble having sex with a blond girl who appears to be underage. I believe that girl is Sarah Creston."

Two days after visiting Case Western, David loaded Tanner into the Bug and drove toward Lakewood, on the other side of Cleveland. It was a forty-five-minute haul, so he packed a few video games and a snack to keep the boy busy. He was taking his son to meet his grandparents for the first time, Elizabeth's mom and dad, two people whom David had never met himself.

Aunt Peggy, the sister of Elizabeth's mother, had set it up for David. Had, in fact, been happy to do so. "Something that should have happened when Lizzie was still alive," she'd said. Tacit in her statement was that it was partly David's fault that it had not happened sooner. He did not tell her the real reason he needed to meet them now had more to do with the mystery of Elaine's abduction than any family reunion.

The O'Donnells still occupied the three-story Colonial on Edgewood in which Elizabeth had lived for eleven years. Elaine, ten. It was on the very west end of Lakewood, not far from the park. Ivy had taken three-quarters of the facade. Giant oaks kept it shaded during the hottest months. It was October now, and the wind cutting off Lake Erie was alarmingly frigid; the windows were already shuttered and wrapped.

"Here we go, buddy," said David, bringing the car to a stop against the curb out front.

"Do they look like Mom?" he asked, eyes wide. Tanner unsnapped his belt and shimmied off his seat and out the door.

"I don't know," he said, catching up to him and taking his hand. He was touched by his son's fearlessness. This meeting was not awkward for him. That might make things go a little easier. "I've never met them." Never even seen a picture, he realized.

Mike, Elizabeth's father, was at the door. He was a tall man with a full head of thick white hair. He wore a red sweater vest over a button-down shirt, khakis, and slippers. David thought he looked to be about sixty-five years old. Distinguished. A man with a quick smile for young children.

"Hey ya!" he said, crouching down to Tanner's height.

"Hello," said Tanner.

"You look just like my little brother Tim."

"How old is he?"

"Well, he's fifty-eight now."

"Do I really look that old?"

Mike laughed. "No. I mean, you look like he did back then, when we were little."

"Well, I'm not little," said Tanner, who was conscious of his short stature, especially when he was among his library reading group peers. "I'm lots taller than some kids."

"Of course you are," said Mike. "I can see that now." Then, to David, "I see he's inherited Elizabeth's sharp tongue."

"No kidding," David agreed. He shook Mike's hand. Mike shook back firmly and met his gaze.

"You better come in and meet Abigail," he said. "She's in back."

Mike led them through a large sitting room furnished with a mini-grand, two sofas, and a fold-out card table that appeared to be the battle-ground of some recent gentlemen's poker night.

"Your mother was an excellent piano player," he said to Tanner, and as he walked past the piano his fingers glided across the keys. "Do you play, Tanner?"

"No," he said. "I have a recorder. And a harmonica. I can play the first measure of 'Stairway to Heaven' on the guitar, but Dad has to help."

"Well, then you're learning the essentials."

Beyond the sitting room was the dining area. A large table made of polished walnut took up most of the space, with just enough room left for a set of high-backed wicker chairs. A large abstract painting hung on the far wall.

The kitchen came next: a high-ceilinged affair with two ovens, two dishwashers, two islands, and refrigerated units behind squarish wooden doors set into one wall.

"Do you ever get lost in here?" asked Tanner.

"Once," said Mike. "And I'm still looking for the way out. So let me know if you find it."

A door at the other end of the kitchen opened onto a glass-walled twentieth century addition. On a wicker chaise, wrapped in a heavy blan-ket, reading a dog-eared copy of *The Immortal Life of Henrietta Lacks*, sat Abigail.

"We have company," said Mike.

Abigail sat up and looked to her grandchild. She was a thin woman, her arms long and bony. Her hair held a hint of auburn and was twisted up with chopsticks. David saw some resemblance to his wife in her sunken cheeks and her diminutive upper lip. From behind thin reading glasses, she regarded Tanner sternly. "Come here, young man," she said, pointing to the floor in front of her with one wrinkled finger.

Tanner hesitated only briefly, then walked to her.

"Turn around."

He did. When his back was to her, she winked at David.

"Let me see your teeth."

He opened his mouth and waved his head around.

"Are they okay?" asked Tanner.

"Oh, yes," she said. "No concerns there. Now tell me, little one, do you know any poems? I delight in poetry. A fine poem always makes me smile."

"'This is just to say, I have eaten the plums that were in your icebox and which you were prolly saving for breffast. Forgive me. They were delicious. So sweet and so cold.'"

For a moment her sternness persisted. Then she chuckled. "Brilliant," she said, reaching out and touching his cheek. "Williams is one of my favorites."

"Are you really my grandmother?" he asked.

"Yes," she said.

"Well, how come I've never seen you before?"

"That is a very good question for which there is no good answer. Silly grown-ups. Silly, silly grown-ups with their silly grown-up problems. I'll make you a deal, Tanner. I'll tell you all about it someday. But right now I have to talk to your father a bit. I have to talk to him about some of those silly grown-up things before it gets any later. Then we'll all have supper. But for a couple minutes do you think you could go with . . . do you think you could go with Grandpa over there? He wants to show you the pool table in the cellar."

"Ever shoot pool?" asked Mike.

"Never," said Tanner.

"Then I'll show you some tricks." He held out his hand and Tanner took it without a second thought and let his grandfather lead him out of the room.

When they were gone, Abigail turned to David and removed her glasses. "You passed a wine rack on your way in. There's a corkscrew hanging above it. Find us something red."

David obliged. As he returned, Abigail was lighting a thin cigarette with a match.

"Do you smoke, David?"

He shook his head.

"Good. Bad habit. Especially with kids in the home."

He poured them each a tall glass, then sat in a wicker chair facing Abigail. She finished the cigarette, staring at the great lake outside as if she might be waiting for the *Edmund Fitzgerald* and its load of iron ore to come gliding into the harbor, just a little off schedule. When she finished, she picked up her glass with a shaky left hand and urged it to her lips.

"I look back, David, and my biggest regret is not telling you about the history of depression and suicide that runs in my family. I feel that if I had, maybe you would have recognized the signs . . ."

"I was being treated for post-traumatic stress disorder. I wouldn't have been able to recognize the signs if she had been waving them in my face. I knew she was sad. Thought it was typical postpartum stuff. Then it was over."

Abigail nodded. "My uncle Steven was so determined, he took a bottle of aspirin, tied a noose around his neck, stood on the barn rafters, and then shot himself in the face with a Kraut handgun he stole off a dead German in World War II."

David waited for her to continue. He knew some things needed airing before he could start asking his questions.

"I read your book, by the way. I watched the *Dateline* special on TV. Did she ever read your book?"

"No."

"It's a little too close to home," said Abigail, nodding. She took another sip of the wine. "I'm so glad I got to meet Tanner. You have no idea. I know you probably hate me. That's fine." When he tried to reply, she waved his words away. "Hush. I know what I know. They were identical twins, David. She looked exactly like Elaine. It was hard enough seeing my dead girl's face every day—there's no closure with that arrangement, ever. But what was worse was her voice. Every time I heard her playing in the other room, talking to her My Little Ponies, on some basic level my mind always insisted that it was Elaine I was hearing, that she was back and her abduction had just been a nightmare."

"She knew your reasons," he said. "She understood. But she didn't accept it. I don't think I could, either."

"I wonder," said Abigail, eyeing him with something close to amusement. "I think maybe you could, if you found yourself in that situation. I bet you'd be surprised."

"Fortunately, we'll never know," he said.

She looked away. "You're up against the wall out there in Akron," she said. "Read the papers. Read the blogs. Are you going to face charges in this man's death?"

"I don't know. I don't think so. There's a better suspect. I didn't do it, if that's what you're asking."

"One blog is saying the police found Elizabeth's prints in the man's house, somewhere."

"It's true."

"Was my daughter stepping out on you, David?"

"I didn't think so. I don't know."

"Would it make you mad if she had?"

"Of course. But I wouldn't kill him. Or try to."

"I told Mike, when my sister called and told me you wanted to meet, I told Mike that what you really wanted was to ask me about Elaine's murder. He said I was being paranoid. That you just wanted to reunite Tanner with this side of the family. I was right, wasn't I?"

"You were right."

"You think the man who murdered my Elaine is the same man who shot the Man from Primrose Lane."

"I think it's possible. I've come across some evidence that shows someone was trying to track down the Man from Primrose Lane. A man who fits the description of Elaine's abductor. I'm almost positive the Man from Primrose Lane was the man who saved Elizabeth's life back then, the guy who interrupted the abduction too late in the game to save Elaine."

"Another mystery," she said. "I was never any help to the police. Did Elizabeth ever tell you that?"

"She never talked about it."

"I couldn't give the police anything useful. That's what they told me. It was my fault, I guess, since I was a casual drinker and couldn't even remember what clothes Elaine was wearing that day."

"I don't think it was a crime of opportunity," said David. "The man was waiting for them to cross through the park. I think he knew they were coming. I bet they went there every day after school."

"They were at the park all the time."

"So he must have crossed paths with your daughters at some point before the abduction. I think this guy has a thing for redheads. I think picked Elaine and Elizabeth out of a crowd somewhere, targeted them."

"FBI thought so, too."

"What was going on in the girls' lives the week before Elaine was taken? Did . . . I don't know, did you change up your routine in any way, go someplace you didn't usually go with the girls—dry cleaner's, pharmacy?"

Abigail shook her head. "Nothing like that. They swam at the Y twice a week. They had gymnastics on Saturdays. We'd gone shopping that week to pick out clothes for school pictures. But they went with me to the store all the time. The night before the abduction, we went out for ice cream. I know the police questioned everyone who saw my girls in the weeks before he took Elaine."

"Any suspects?"

"Not officially."

"Unofficially?"

"There was a man who did some work on our house a few months before it happened. He built this room we're sitting in, actually, him and his crew. I guess he used to be some big-time consultant in Indonesia. He was the first guy I thought about."

"Why?"

"He was creepy. Didn't talk much. To adults. But when the girls were playing outside, he would always make an excuse to talk to them. He wasn't married. Lives in an apartment near Rocky River. Harold Schulte. I know the cops have been out there to talk to him about it. More than once."

"Did the police tell you anything?"

"Guess he got in trouble in high school for indecent exposure on the school bus. That was it."

"Did Elaine keep a diary?"

Abigail shook her head, but as she did, she stood up and walked over to a bureau near the sliding glass doors. She opened the top drawer and rummaged under some papers before she withdrew two items and returned to her seat.

"Elaine was my artist and poet," she said, handing him a piece of wide-ruled notebook paper filled with a young girl's loopy handwriting. It was titled "Dead Cat." *Dead cat on the road. Killed by Mother Nature. Or maybe a truck.* "It's a haiku."

"I see."

Abigail handed him the other item, which was already familiar to him; he'd seen it hanging on the wall in Sackett's office. "Her last school picture," she said.

"They really do look so similar." He traced his fingers over a black scratch on the top of the picture. He meant Elaine and Katy. "Any other hunches after all these years?" he asked. "Anyone else you feel could have done it?"

Abigail shook her head again. "We don't even have a body, you know?

That complicates things. You want to hold out hope she's still alive. But I knew in my heart she was murdered the day she was taken. I could feel it. Mike didn't accept it until probably five years after she was gone. He cried with me one night and then he didn't wait for her anymore. We both came to accept that our daughter was dead. And, believe it or not, you sort of move on after a while. You move on or you die. Elizabeth, I'm afraid, was lost in that struggle. By the time her father and I were sane again, we'd just been apart too long. I was too ashamed to reach out to her and she was too stubborn to come to me." She fought back an eruption of emotion and then stuck another cigarette in her mouth. "*C'est la vie.*"

David heard the front door close. Abigail looked at him with a start. "Expecting company?" he asked.

"David, take another drink. You think that you couldn't have made the same decision I did back then. That you couldn't have sent Elizabeth away just because she looked like her dead sister, that maybe you could have learned to live with that."

"I don't understand. Who's here?" He heard footsteps in the dining room, approaching. High heels slapping against a hardwood floor. He turned to look.

"Eventually, I did get used to it," said Abigail.

She walked into the room, unassumingly, bouncing on her feet. David's breath caught in his chest.

"Hello," she said, smiling under her red bangs. "Hi, Mom. I didn't know you had company."

"David, this is my daughter Eloise," said Abigail. "She just turned twenty. She's attending Ohio State, but comes home so much we shouldn't really be paying for her dorm room."

"Shush," said Eloise. "Who's your friend?"

"This is David Neff, Lizzie's husband."

"Shut *up*," she said. Then she grabbed him in an embrace. She looked remarkably like her dead sisters. Her cheeks were higher. And her eyebrows a shade darker. Her lips were a bit fuller. But the resemblance to the woman he had fallen in love with at Kent State was unwelcome and disturbing. "I'm so glad to meet you. I always wanted to meet Lizzie."

"Her son is downstairs with your dad," said Abigail.

"No way," she said. She kissed her mother and then ran out the way she had come, shouting back, "Stay there, David! I'll be right back."

When they were alone again, David looked over to Abigail, who stared back, trying to read his emotions.

"Peggy never said anything."

"I told her not to."

"Why?"

"I didn't want Lizzie to know until I got a chance to tell her myself. I wanted a boy. Instead, I got another spitting image of the girls I lost. God has a sick sense of humor."

"I think I should go," he said.

Abigail nodded.

They pulled him over as soon as he crossed the Summit County line on 77 South. Two cruisers, a black sedan, three news vans, and two civilian cars he assumed were print reporters. For just a second he considered gunning it. But then he remembered Tanner in the back seat and that kept his mind thinking logically. He pulled over.

"Tanner, listen to me."

"Whoa, are those cop cars? Dad, were you speeding?"

"No, I wasn't speeding."

He could already see Sackett and Larkey climbing out of the unmarked sedan. Even from this distance he could see that giant gun under Larkey's armpit, the one with the bone-colored grip.

"What happened?"

"I don't have time to explain it right now, kiddo. I'm very sorry, but whatever happens next, you have to just believe me that everything is going to work out."

"What's gonna happen?"

"In a second those guys are going to take me with them. And, I think, someone else is going to . . . let you ride with them."

David snatched a piece of paper from his glove compartment and furiously wrote a name and number on it. He handed the note to his son, whose eyes were wide with fear and filling up with tears.

"Look, buddy, it's going to be okay. You give this to whoever you go with. It's Grandpa's cell phone number. He'll come and get you."

"Dad?"

"Get out of your seat, Tanner. Come here."

The boy unbuckled his belt just as the detective and the FBI agent reached the car. He leapt into the front and onto David's lap.

"I love you."

"I love you, too, Daddy."

A tap on the window. It was Sackett. David rolled it down.

"Mr. Neff, we've got someone here who can take your son. This is Pamela Swanson, she's from the Department of Job and Family Services." He motioned to a young woman with a pleasant face. She smiled at Tanner warmly.

"Tanner? My name's Pam. We're going to take a little ride and let your father talk with these men."

"No, Dad," he whispered.

"It's okay."

Tanner gripped him tightly around the neck. He kissed his son and somehow managed to pull him off his body and hand him to the social worker through the window. He knew there wasn't much time in situations like this before the police grew impatient. Tanner just hung his head and cried. The woman jogged back with him to one of the civilian cars and placed Tanner in the back seat with her.

No one said anything for several long seconds.

Finally, David said, "I am a man who doesn't care about money. I am also a man who has a lot of it. And now I am a very angry man with a lot of money who doesn't care about spending it. I will use every penny making your lives miserable for as long as I can."

Larkey smiled. "There he is," he said. "There's my killer."

"Mr. Neff, step out of the car," said Sackett, his voice cool as an Arctic breeze.

David got out.

"Turn around."

As he did, there were flashes of light. Two photographers crouched at the back of his car, snapping pictures for tomorrow's papers.

"Why?" David asked.

"That other print?" said Larkey. "The one from the dead guy's toilet? We figured it could only have been left by a plumber or the Man from Primrose Lane himself. When we found a match on the barrel of your gun, we knew it wasn't left by the plumber."

"Mr. Neff," continued Sackett, "you are under arrest for the murder—"

"Murder?"

Handcuffs slapped around his wrists. More flashes went off.

"I didn't kill the Man from Primrose Lane," he said.

"You tried," said Sackett. "So we're charging you with attempted murder, too."

"What are you talking about? Is this a joke? You can't charge me for murdering and trying to murder the same man!"

"You fucker," said Larkey. "Stop playing mind games. We're charging you for the attempted murder of the John Doe. You're being charged with *murder* because you strangled your wife and staged her suicide. Or did you forget about that, too?"

CONFESSIONS

"Why do you love me?"

They were in Tanner's room, pasting big foam letters on the wall above his crib. A mobile of brightly colored hot-air balloons spun slowly above them. They'd purchased it at FAO Schwarz on a trip into New York to meet with a foreign rights agent who was selling David's book overseas (twelve countries, and counting). The toy had cost more than David had made in a week working at the movie theater in college. The big house still smelled of fresh paint and Elizabeth's belly was enormous under her sweats.

"What are you talking about?"

"Why do you love me? Have you thought about it in a while?"

David laughed. "I love the way you whistle when you're nervous. I love the way your toes play with your sandals when you're sitting in a restaurant. I love the way you sit on couches. I love your big fat belly."

She smiled. "Those are things you notice about me. Writer things. Incidental."

"I don't think they're incidental."

"I was thinking about the way we met," she said, pretending to straighten the letter *T* on the wall, without looking at him. "You didn't know anything about me. Other than what you observed about me."

"Yeah?"

"I think you fell in love with what you didn't know about me. I think you made up a story in your mind about me. You wanted to know why I was odd. Why I was so mean."

David turned her around gently, tugging at her shoulders. "What does it matter? I love you, stupid. I love you."

Elizabeth kissed him lightly on his lips. "I was in Atlantic City once, before I met you. I was at this roulette table. Counting the reds and blacks. I saw a run of reds. Fifteen in a row. A couple other people saw it happen. They got real excited. Thought it was some sign. Some streak of luck. But it's just probability. Eventually it had to balance out. I started betting on black. Let my money ride. It took a while. But I was patient. I went home with three grand."

"You know I get lost with all this math mumbo jumbo," he said.

"Sometimes I think this terrible thing that happened to me—to Elaine—I think maybe you were the thing that came into my life to balance that out. That you were the good the universe sent to me to get me back to equilibrium."

"Sounds good to me."

She nodded. She smiled again, but her eyes remained sad. "And I think about Brune. And how it all ended in court with Trimble. And it was so good what you did, David. It was so oddly good, what some would call lucky, that I wonder what the universe might do to balance that out."

"It doesn't work that way," he said.

"Doesn't it? Sometimes I think of the odds of anyone making it all the way through life and it seems so impossible."

"Whatever happens," he began . . .

. . . "I'll be here with you," said Elizabeth. Judge Siegel entered the courtroom. Everyone stood.

Following David's testimony, which had ended shortly after identifying the frames of film to the jury, Russo had rested the state's case against Riley Trimble for the murders of Sarah Creston, Jennifer Poole, and Donna Doyle. They had made a strong argument, a compelling argument, but their case remained entirely circumstantial. Nothing linked Trimble to the murders directly. But when you looked at everything that implicated him, you came to see that it was mathematically impossible for him not to have done it—there was just too much circumstantial evidence to explain away. Brune himself had been convicted and sent to the chair for less. Still, the prosecutor had his doubts. "Sometimes justice is just getting the guy in the courtroom," Russo had told him.

"Be seated," barked Siegel, taking his place behind the bench. "Has the jury reached a unanimous verdict?"

The jury foreperson, the teacher from Parma, stood. "We have, Your Honor," she said.

Elizabeth leaned to David's ear. "Whatever happens, everything is going to work out," she whispered.

He squeezed her hand.

"What is your verdict?"

"On the charge of murder in the first degree, in the death of Sarah Creston, we, the jury, find the defendant not guilty."

David's ears rang loudly. He felt the tension of the trial collapsing around him, threatening to bury him. Hopefully, he thought, the Rivertin would do its job. *I don't want to feel this.*

"On the charge of murder in the first degree in the death of Jennifer Poole, we the jury find the defendant not guilty."

Wordlessly, Russo stood up and left the courtroom.

The jury foreperson read through the remainder of the forty-seven charges. Trimble was acquitted on each count.

Russo stood before a pool of reporters camped out in the hallway. He denounced the verdict and insinuated that the jury's instructions had been too complicated for them to understand.

When the reporters saw David, several of them broke from the pack and reached toward him with large microphones.

"Mr. Neff, Tim Pohlman, Channel Five. Can you tell us how you feel about today's verdict?"

"I think the jury is a bunch of idiots," he said. Elizabeth tugged at his arm, urging him toward the elevators.

"Mr. Neff, are you afraid Riley Trimble will use today's verdict to support civil charges against you?"

"I'm not afraid of Riley Trimble," he said. "He's a serial killer. He's a coward. Let him come after me."

"We can't air that!" said a reporter from Channel Three.

David shrugged.

Pohlman pulled him aside a few steps from the elevator. Elizabeth and his father waited a few feet away. The other reporters, catching a glimpse of Trimble walking out of the courtroom still in his orange jumpsuit, but free, left them. "Hey, I believe you, kiddo," said Pohlman, a fortyish investigator who reminded David of a childhood friend. "Just give me a little sound bite. Everyone else is going to paint it black. We'll make you look good. No worries. I thought the evidence was overwhelming."

David looked back at Elizabeth and gave her a one-minute sign.

"Put this on," said Pohlman, twisting a wireless microphone around David's lapel. His cameraman was setting up the tripod. "I'm just going to ask you a few basic questions. Let you tell your side. But watch out for the defamatory stuff. Blog that or something. We can't air it. Stick to the facts. I'll make it look good."

David nodded. "Is the mic working?" he asked.

The cameraman gave a thumbs-up. He saw the red record light click on.

David was suddenly struck by a dangerous idea.

"I have to use the men's room," he said, and before Pohlman had time to protest he walked into the lavatory behind them. No one else was inside. He stepped to the sink and waited.

"Hello, Dave," said Trimble.

"Hello, Riley," said David.

They stared at each other.

"I thought you might want to apologize," said Trimble.

"Why would I do that?"

Trimble chuckled.

"What's funny?" asked David.

"Nothing."

"No, really. I want to know. What's funny?"

"This," he said, waving at the walls, in the general direction of the courtroom.

David smiled. "Yeah."

"I can never be tried again, you know," he said.

"That's the way it works."

"Double jeopardy."

"Double jeopardy," David agreed.

"I could even tell you how I did it," said Trimble. "And ain't nothing you could do about it."

"That's true."

"Does that bother you?"

"No."

"It does."

"You don't scare me, Riley. You know that, right?"

Trimble looked cross for a moment. Then he smiled and wagged his finger at the writer. "You. You're scared. I can tell."

"Why would anyone be scared of you, Riley? You just proved to everyone that you're just a white-trash air-conditioner installer who never hurt anyone."

"I don't care about *them*," he said, stepping closer to David. "Just you. You know what I done. You're smart enough to be scared."

"Which part am I supposed to be scared of, Riley? The part where you couldn't man up and face the music so you let your scoutmaster take the rap for Sarah? The part where you couldn't get a hard-on for grown women so you gave up and went after easier prey? The part where you were too scared to touch the dead bodies so you had to roll them out of the trunk?"

Trimble stepped to David and grabbed the writer by the throat, pushing him back against the mirror. He leaned in toward David's ear. "How about the part where I stuck a screwdriver up Sarah's pussy and carved out her insides? How about the part where I taught Ronil how to kidnap his holes and not get caught? How about the part where I pierced Jennifer's tits with copper wire and plugged her into the wall? How about now? Are you a little afraid now, you sarcastic little shit?" He shoved David backward, hard enough that David saw stars dance in his periphery for a few minutes.

"No," David said. "But if I were you, I'd be afraid of what happens next."

"What do you mean? I'm *free*, you dumb fuck."

David tapped the microphone bud on his lapel.

"Is that on?" Trimble asked.

"I'm not sure," he said. "It was when I came in. But the cameraman could have turned it off."

Trimble looked at the bathroom door, as if expecting a team of police detectives to come tumbling through it to take him back to prison, double jeopardy be damned.

"You're lying," he said.

"I'd never lie to you, Riley."

"You're trying to trick me." Trimble's hands were shaking.

"Now who's afraid?"

"Fuck you," said Trimble, and he walked out. David followed.

Pohlman's eyes said it all. That and the fact that he and the camera-man were sharing one pair of headphones.

Behind them, the jury foreperson was giving an exclusive interview with Action News. "I just didn't believe the reporter, that Neff guy," she said. "I never trust reporters. Especially *him*. He looked like a snotty kid. If he was their best witness, then they never really had a case."

Trimble leapt at Pohlman's camera, tackling it to the floor as if it were a person who had wronged him. "Ahhhhhhhhhhh!" he shouted, tearing at the compartment that contained the videotape.

Everything in the corridor came to a sudden halt. No one spoke. All eyes were on the exonerated killer as he assaulted the camera.

Then the cameraman from Channel Five snapped to it and grabbed Trimble by the back of his shirt. "The fuck off my gear!" he said.

Instead of surrendering the camera, Trimble tossed it at the nearest wall, where it collided with the brick inches from a woman's head. It fell to the floor, intact. He looked at David. "You motherfucker!" he yelled and launched himself at the writer.

David didn't think. He just balled a fist and planted it straight out as Trimble ran forward. It connected with the man's nose with a loud smack.

From the crowd of people, two police officers rushed out and grabbed David's arms.

"He came after *me*," said David.

"Just stop," said one of the officers.

He suddenly realized how this must look to everyone except the team from Channel Five: an angry journalist punching the man he had wrongly accused.

"No," shouted David. "He admitted it."

"Can't you leave him alone?" yelled a stout woman David recog-nized as some distant relative of Trimble's.

"He's telling the truth," said Pohlman. "Jerry got it on tape. Why do you think he just kicked the shit out of our camera?"

"I'm innocent!" said Trimble.

Trimble jumped at David again, but this time the police officers were ready. They tackled him to the ground and pinned his arms behind his back.

"You tricked me!" shouted Trimble, trying to wrestle away.

"Cut it out, Trimble, or we'll use the Taser," said the older policeman.

"Arrest him, already," someone shouted. News cameras repositioned to catch B-roll of the struggle.

"For what?" asked the older policeman. "He was acquitted."

"That's bullshit," shouted a teenage boy in front of the pack.

"It's the law," the policeman responded.

"Christ," said a deep voice from the back. Except it came out as kind of a "Kee-riced." The audience parted to let Judge Siegel through. His face was ashen and he was in jeans and a polo, having discarded his robe. He put his hands on his hips and took a moment to think, clicking his tongue against the roof of his mouth. He looked at David and Pohlman and said, "You just killed my legacy." He shook his head, then addressed the crowd of lookee-loos. "I cannot order this man arrested. However, this outburst demonstrates to me that Trimble is a man who could likely be a danger to himself and others should he remain free at this time. The safest place for you right now is a psychiatric ward. At least for a while. As it happens, the nearest psychiatric-care facility is next door at the county jail. Officers, please escort Mr. Trimble to lockup."

"No!" shouted Trimble. "I ain't no nut! Fuck you, Judge! I ain't no nut."

"Get him away from me," said Siegel. The officers yanked Trimble toward the elevators.

As he passed, Trimble glared at David, marking him. "I hate you," he said, simply. "I hate you forever!"

The Serial Killer's Protégé had only sold 2,452 copies when Trimble confessed to murder on the day of his acquittal, in December of 2007. It was, after all, a local book. But later that night, Pohlman aired an exclusive on the local ABC affiliate and a series of events quickly propelled David into a new and strange life.

Pohlman's piece was rebroadcast on the national newscast the following evening. *The Morning Show* picked it up. A week later, *Primetime* did a story. A month later, *Dateline NBC* scooped everyone with the revelation of a long-lost witness in the Donna Doyle case who positively identified

Trimble as the man he had seen with Donna before she disappeared. The Ohio legislature, smelling free publicity and recognizing the turning tide, began to consider an end to the state's death penalty. One grandstanding state representative proclaimed, "Brune's wrongful execution should serve as a constant reminder that we can never be entirely sure of a criminal's guilt. That does not mean justice does not work, but rather, like each of us, that it is imperfect and fallible. Therefore we cannot in good conscience continue to mete out that ultimate punishment. Let God be the final judge." An argument started—mostly by Fox News pundits—for the end of double jeopardy laws, but, to David's great relief, that was quickly quashed by more intelligent voices. Paul fielded paperback offers from several New York publishers. *Vanity Fair* published a new introduction that David wrote for the paperback edition. Sam Mendes's production company snatched up the movie rights.

Three months after the verdict, the book had sold a hundred thousand copies. Six months later, it was half a million. By then Elizabeth was dead.

It was impossible for him not to become distracted, he told himself later. He should have noticed Elizabeth's gloomy moods returned as her belly grew. Initially he chalked it up to stress—the baby was going to change every part of their life, wasn't it? He should have been stressed, too. But he was medicated. And yet, he felt that everything would be okay now. And it wasn't just the money or the Rivertin talking. He didn't think so, anyway. And he tried to explain this to Elizabeth. And she would smile and nod.

He thought the house would cheer her up. He hired movers. He hired a decorator. She pretended to be happy.

Looking back, he would come to realize how often she had made excuses to go out, "to the store," "to the bank," "to the library." Where had she really been? And why?

David distracted himself with things like the big goddamn desk from the estate of the *Edmund Fitzgerald*'s captain and the yellow Bug he'd always wanted as a teenager. He spent a great deal of time reading things like *What to Expect When You're Expecting* and *Fathers of Boys*. He almost didn't notice she never picked up these books herself.

When she broke down crying in the middle of the baby shower, he told his family it was because hers was not there. But had he believed that? Not really. Do you want to know his secret fear, the thought that troubled his mind while he waited for sleep at night? His real fear was that she had caught his darkness like a cold, that Brune or whatever it was had transferred to her, that the demon in the box had even, somehow, impregnated her.

"Are you okay?" he had asked the night before she went into labor. But by then it was way too late.

"Yes," she had said, forcing a smile. "I'm . . .

. . . just fine!" exclaimed the young male nurse. "Ten fingers and ten toes."

David was relieved at the mere sight of his boy. The books he'd read had warned him that the baby might look strange at first, slimy, its head shaped into a cone from the pressure of the birth canal. But Tanner just looked like a baby. He'd been swaddled in blue cloth and lay with his eyes closed in the warm bin atop the cart that would take him to the nursery. His little face, wrinkled like an old man, almost looked contented. Soon they were finally alone. A family.

"David, I don't think I can do this," said Elizabeth.

"Can't do what?"

"I don't feel a connection, any connection," she said. "I don't feel anything."

He held her hand in one of his and brushed her hair with the other. "Shhh. You just went through a lot. All this takes a while."

She shook her head. She mumbled something.

"What?"

"I told you I wasn't going to be good with family stuff," she said.

"You'll be fine. You're going to be a great mother."

She looked at Tanner strangely. David could not read her thoughts. "What if I wasn't supposed to become a mother? You know? What if I was *supposed* to end up like Elaine? What if I was meant to be murdered? That guy that interrupted the whole thing . . . what if he changed my destiny or fate or whatever? What if I was never supposed to grow up and have this kid?"

"But he did interrupt it," said David. "So it must have been what was meant to happen."

He could tell she didn't believe him. "What if he grows up to be bad?" she asked.

"That could never happen," he told her.

Later, in the hall, the nurse spoke to him in an accusatory tone. "I'm concerned about your wife," he said.

"She's fine," said David.

"I think she has postpartum depression. She doesn't like being with the baby."

"That happens, right?"

"To a degree."

"What do you want me to do?"

"Talk to her," he said. "See if you can get her to spend some time with our counselors up on the fourth floor."

"The psych ward?"

"There's a special section for postpartum patients."

"No," he said. "She'd never go for that. And she'd think I was attacking her."

"Mr. Neff, your wife needs help. Let us help her."

He nodded. "I'll talk to her."

"I swear to God, I will kill myself if you make me go up there," she said. "This isn't postpartum depression. I'm just sad."

"Listen to what you're saying," he said.

"I'm fine. Please. Just give me some time."

Her cell phone rang. She looked at the display. "It's work," she said. "Let me take this. It'll just be a minute. Can you go get me a salad from the cafeteria and a Coke?"

He was gone less than ten minutes. When he returned to the room, the nurse was standing there with Tanner in his hands looking panicked.

"Where's Elizabeth?" David asked. The bed was empty. She had cut off her wristbands. They lay on the table next to a pair of snips.

The baby went back to the nursery. The police were called. He searched for her in the hospital for the better part of an hour. David's yellow Bug, the car they had driven to the emergency room when she had gone into labor, was still in the parking garage. When the police drove by their home, they discovered that Elizabeth's car was missing.

At 8:16 that evening, while he sat on her hospital bed feeding Tanner, two officers stepped into the room and he could read their faces well enough to know that it was over.

The sorrow he should have suffered was muted. The officers who had delivered the news, however, did not know that David was medicated for PTSD. They noted in their report that he appeared unemotional, disaffected. Years later Tom Sackett would read this report and begin to wonder if Elizabeth's death really had been a suicide.

—— ◧ ——

The courtroom had not changed. Only this time he was standing where Riley Trimble had once stood.

"How do you plead?" asked Siegel.

"Not guilty, Your Honor," said David.

An assistant prosecuting attorney named Jacqueline Day stepped forward. She was two years out of law school and hungry for her first big case. "Your Honor, the defendant has unlimited resources, the know-how to alter his identity, and the means to hide forever. The state believes he is a serious flight risk."

"C'mon!" said Synenberger. "My client is a famous author who cannot disappear and go unnoticed. His assets are not liquid. He has a son he must take care of. He will not run."

"He is a cold-blooded killer who has managed to fool everyone close to him for four years," she snapped.

"My client remains innocent of the charges put before him."

Siegel held up his hands. He looked over to David and couldn't help but smile. "Every time you step into my courtroom, you test the boundaries of this bench," he said.

"I did not kill my wife."

Siegel looked away. "You will surrender your passport," he said. "I'm setting bail at one million dollars."

"Your Honor, with all due respect, a million dollars is nothing to this man. He'll be out of jail by the end of the week," said Day.

"Court dismissed."

Synenberger was right. David's manager, Bashien, had diversified his money into bonds, stocks, and real estate. He recommended mortgaging the house. Still, cutting the county a check for a million dollars would take a few days. Maybe a week. David thought that might be too long. Too long without Tanner.

He was returned to his sixteen-by-five-foot concrete room with its plywood ledge, painted gunmetal-gray, that doubled as a chair and a bed. The night before his arraignment had been a kind of torture he had never before experienced, a total lack of control, separated from his son, unsure where Tanner was or how he was doing. He kept picturing Tanner in the home of some foster parent who seemed pleasant enough during the day but became something else at night, something akin to Riley Trimble. And when he wasn't thinking of Tanner, he was thinking of Elizabeth. Strangled. Picturing her accident had been hard enough, but now his imagination created images of her murder in his mind. A faceless man wringing the life out of her, her eyes wide with terror, the agony of suffocation. She had suffered. She had been murdered, and for four years, no one had cared. That anyone thought he could have done such a thing was too much to take in. His heart was too full of grief and shame to make room for self-pity.

In the morning, he had been allowed a phone call. He had called his father, who told him Tanner had made it to him the night before, after spending three hours talking to Family Services. Tanner had stayed up half the night but was sleeping finally, so David's father didn't wake him. "I don't have to ask you if you did any of this," his father had said.

"Thanks, Pop."

After the arraignment, he ate lunch—corned-beef hash and beans— and returned to his cell. He lay on the blanket they had provided him and began to count the imperfections in the plastered ceiling.

He thought about Elizabeth. Murdered? There were, he realized, only two explanations for this: she had been killed by this man who called himself Arbogast or by the Man from Primrose Lane himself.

With these thoughts overwhelming his mind, exhaustion found him and stole him away into a fitful and troubled sleep.

He awoke to the sound of his cell door opening.

"Neff," said the guard. "Somebody bailed you out. Let's go."

Bashien had worked faster than expected.

David followed the guard through a large chain-link fence and into a room where he changed back into his clothes.

Dressed, he was led to a window where he signed for his things— wallet, keys, watch—and was told his car had already been towed back to his house. "Your ride is waiting in the lobby," said the woman inside the window, pointing an acrylic nail toward a set of double doors. She buzzed him through.

The man waiting for him on the other side of those doors was not

Bashien but a young man, about twenty-five years old, with shiny blond hair gelled back against his head in a very Gordon Gekko way. He wore a dark tailored suit, his spectacular cuff links catching the reflection of the fluorescents set into the ceiling.

"Mr. Neff, my name is Aaron Zumock," he said, shaking David's hand. "Please follow me. I'm told we're running late." He waved David through the front doors and into the stark bright sunshine of late October. When his eyes adjusted, David saw that a stretch limo was parked at the end of the walkway.

"Do you work for Bashien?" he asked. He had never known his manager to be so flashy. Certainly this show of wealth would not help his case.

"I don't work for Bashien, sir."

"Who do you work for? Who bailed me out?"

Aaron smiled warmly. "I've been instructed not to say anything more. I'm supposed to bring you to the car. My employer is waiting inside. I'm sure he will explain everything."

"Kid, I'm not getting into that car unless you tell me who's in there waiting for me."

"Well, that's the thing, Mr. Neff. I don't really know, myself."

"You don't know the name of your employer?"

Aaron shook his head. "No."

"What sort of work do you do for him?"

"This and that," he said. "My biggest asset is my discretion. So I couldn't really get more specific. Today I'm his driver. Tomorrow?" He shrugged.

David nodded. "Everyone needs a Sherlock ruffian, I guess."

Aaron laughed. "Funny. That's what he calls me, too."

David crouched down and stepped inside. The door closed behind him.

It was too dark to see.

"Have a seat, David," said the voice of an older man.

David stretched out a hand and felt around. He found a leather couch at the back and collapsed into it. He squinted his eyes. There was a shape sitting in a leather seat facing him. Aaron climbed behind the wheel.

"Home. And some privacy, please."

Aaron raised the window separating the driver from the passengers.

"Who are you?" asked David.

He heard a sigh. "I think you know."

"I don't."

"You should. After everything you've found, everything you've gone through in the last few weeks, you have enough clues to put it together. It's the only explanation that makes sense, even if it's crazy."

David could see a bit more detail now. The man in front of him was dressed in a sharp suit, a sleek navy-blue number. His hair was white and thin. His cheeks hollowed. His skin worn. He knew this man.

"You're the Man from Primrose Lane," he said.

"No. Well . . . not really."

"Who are you?" David asked again.

"David, there's a lot we have to discuss and there really isn't that much time. I need to know you're with me for what happens next. I need your mind to be sharp. I've given you enough time to work it out, I think. I left those paintings for you to find. To think about. You really have to come to this yourself. You need to trust your instincts. You have to have a little faith again. You know who I am."

David didn't say anything.

"Who am I?"

And then David put it into words. "You're me," he said.

"Good," I replied. "Now let's get you up to speed."

INTERLUDE

THE BALLAD OF THE LOVELAND FROG

1996 He was in the park, under a magnolia tree, making out with Hannah Belcher beneath the empty summer sky, when it happened again.

Everett Bleakney was twenty, a lanky, dark-haired version of his father, the former police chief of Loveland, a beloved lawman who had died of a massive coronary out on Twightwee Road in 1986. Hannah, a blond-haired beaut with somewhat of a snaggletooth, was the middle daughter of Stacey Belcher, the old skank who ran the drive-thru. They had met in high school biology (during—of all things—a frog dissection) and had been going steady for two years. Everett was taking criminal justice classes at the community college; Hannah was a waitress at Paxton's Grill. He had his hand up Hannah's T-shirt when he heard it.

The sound was not merely percussive but invasive, a dull rhythmic drumming he felt in his fillings.

"Do you hear that?"

Hannah looked at him. "Somebody watching us?" she asked. She pulled him back down. "Let them."

The fact that Everett had heard the sound and Hannah had not did not necessarily mean anything important. Over the years, Everett had trained himself to automatically distinguish between normal ambient sounds of everyday life and those sounds that were, for want of a better word, *alien*. The reason for this was simple: though he had never dared to put this thought into words, Everett believed his father had been killed by something from another world. He still had nightmares about that night in 1986 when his father got the call to drive out to Twightwee to investigate what he thought at the time was some abnormally large frog in the middle of the road. He remembered in vivid detail how the thing stood up, almost six feet tall, covered in a black goo that smelled of alfalfa, a creature that looked reptilian and carried a stick that emitted blue sparks like some fake wizard's electrical wand. The sight of the monster, or perhaps the wand itself (Everett suspected the latter), had caused his father's arrhythmia and he had died in Everett's arms as the beast raced back into the forest. The frogman was never seen again. But Everett knew that a series of loud noises had preceded the creature's appearance, explosions like thunderclaps when there had been no clouds. He reckoned if the thing should ever return, the sounds would return with it.

Everett didn't allow Hannah to redirect his attention. He focused on that steady beat, waves in the air, like shock waves from some distant explosion. Over a period of ten seconds it dissipated, disappeared.

"We have to go, sweetie," he said, kissing her quickly and pulling her up.

"Why?"

Because, he thought, *I have to go shoot the monster that killed my pa.*

Everett dropped Hannah off at the drive-thru, where her mother expected her to stock forties of Schlitz and bags of pork rinds before going home. He told her that he had forgotten tonight was the night his mother needed him to drive her to St. James for bingo.

He drove to the trailer his family had moved into after his father died and the mortgage became an issue, a double-wide on the east side of town with a yard and a well-kept garden. It was a home. His mother didn't look up when he came in—she was deeply entranced in *Wheel of Fortune*—and she did not notice Everett removing his father's sidearm from its case in the cabinet over the fridge.

"Hot Rod Serling!" she shouted at the tube.

In some other world, in some other universe, he knew his father had not taken that call and was still alive. He wished he lived there.

I will kill this thing, he thought.

He heard it again, through the open window. It sounded like someone hitting an empty fifty-gallon water drum with a sledgehammer. The humidity of the air hanging stagnant over this desolate stretch of Twightwee seemed affected by the sound in some weird way. The sky rippled like a pond after someone had tossed in a pebble. Except that wasn't exactly right. The sky didn't ripple. Everything in his perspective rippled. It was as if the three dimensions Everett perceived rested upon an invisible medium that acted like water and wobbled the trees and the air like inflatable toys in a pool.

He parked his car just beyond the bridge, a quarter mile from the old entrance to Camp Ritchie, as close to the spot where his father had died as he could recall. The sound came from the woods to his left. He guessed it had originated a few hundred feet in, past a thick hedge of briars, somewhere among the evergreens.

Everett checked the safety on his father's gun. There were ghost chasers, he knew, who sometimes came out here with their ectoplasmic catchers and Geiger counters to try to find the frogman. The story of what he had seen that night had trickled out of Loveland over the years, until some author had collected all of Ohio's strange legends into a compendium two years ago. Since then, seekers of the Loveland Frog remained fairly steady—they were instantly recognizable by their funny hats and X-*Files* T-shirts—and picked up considerably around Halloween. He didn't want to accidentally shoot one of these delusional nerds. For all he knew, it could be one of them making the sound, in an attempt to summon the beast.

The briars grabbed at him and dozens of trefoil seeds stuck to his jeans, little green triangles that looked like scales. Beyond, the woods were dark, the tall pines creating a cool canopy that shielded the sun and kept undergrowth from running amok. The forest floor here was a bed of spent pine needles, soft and pungent. He could see for what seemed like miles down long corridors in the trees. It would be easy to get disoriented here, he knew; there was no discernible way to tell one tree from another.

The sound came again.

It was so loud that it forced Everett to clap his hands to his ears and moan weakly. He watched the air vibrate in nauseating waves from the direction of the base of a particular tree a few feet away. The waves doubled over themselves until it was impossible to see what was at the center anymore.

Suddenly it was over. And there, at the epicenter of the disruption, was a large black egg. It was about ten feet high and four feet at its widest. There were no markings or scratches on its surface; there was no writing of any kind. It was so shiny, Everett saw himself reflected in it.

His first thought was that the object was an extraterrestrial craft or probe sent, perhaps, to locate the creature that had arrived ten years ago. And he asked himself a crazy question: Could he really kill an alien? Was that what he came here to do?

For several minutes nothing happened. Everett didn't move a muscle, so transfixed was he on the vessel. He stood fifty feet away, the handgun pointed at it.

He thought about touching it, to see what would happen. But he remembered *The Blob*. He had stayed up late with his father watching it on the Midnight Movie when he was six, and it had scared the living shit out of him. He knew better than to touch something that might be from space. Fuck that.

A high-pitched electrical sound emanated from the craft. It sounded like an electric can opener.

A thin line appeared around the top of the black egg. Something was hatching from it. Something was breaking out.

Everett clicked off the safety.

The sound stopped and the top popped off. A hiss of trapped air rushed out from within. A thin vapor wafted out of the hole. It smelled like rotted meat.

A hand appeared on the lip, a humanoid hand covered in thick black goop. It was impossible to tell how many fingers it had.

Everett hid behind the closest tree. He didn't want to die out here, eaten by some monster. He no longer even wanted to kill it. He was too scared. His flight response had kicked in. He just wanted to get out of the woods alive. But if he moved now, maybe the thing would hear him. Hear him and start chasing. Because maybe it had been in there long enough to get hungry.

Another black hand appeared and pushed upon the lip of the egg. Its body rose up and out of the hole, an indistinguishable mass of blackness, like living oil. It collapsed upon the ground, struggling against the harsh and unexpected gravity of another planet. He did not have to worry about this monster chasing him; it could barely stand up.

In fact, it took almost five minutes for it to pull itself up onto its ganglion legs. It leaned against a tree and cried out in some fierce language, "Ahhhhhhnaaaa!"

It was a weak and confused sound and Everett realized he was no longer afraid of this feeble creature. Well, okay, he was. Afraid enough to keep his distance. But not so afraid that he wasn't going to find out once and for all what it was. He stepped around the tree and moved forward.

Two black eyes looked up at him in surprise. The creature's frog-fish lips drew back in a snarl. It tried to speak. "Nahop. Nahhh oppp!" it said. It lifted a hand and Everett saw that it, too, had one of those spark-wands.

He reacted before he was aware he meant to. A single shot: boom! The bullet hit the monster's left leg. It roared and fell to the ground. Then it lifted itself on its elbows and looked at him. Quite clearly, but quite slowly, it said, "You dumb motherfucker."

Everett's heart stopped—literally stopped—from the shock of hearing the alien speaking in English. It started up again with a rusty flutter that made him feel dislodged from his body. Obviously, it had tapped into his mind and had learned the basics of human speech. And if that was the case, what else could it do? *Could it*, Everett wondered, *make me turn the gun on myself?*

He turned and fled.

Back in town, he would arrive at Paxton's, where he would try to convince the patrons that a frogman from another planet had crashed in the woods. Reinforcements had come to get the thing that killed his old man. They had to go back with guns. They had to kill *it* before it killed *them*.

He spent that night in the psychiatric ward. The first of many.

PART THREE

ME

EPISODE THIRTEEN

THE BLACK EGG

In the back of the limousine, David sat quietly as I finally shared the story of my life. Which, in a way, was the story of our life.

I fell in love with Katy Keenan not long before her body was discovered lying facedown in an Ashland County wheat field. I fell in love with the girl from the MISSING poster. The first one. The school photo with the cloud background. The one with her in that ponytail. She had some kind of light about her. An inexplicable and unfortunate sensuality. What I'm saying is it was very difficult for any man, age five to ninety-five, not to fall a little in love with her at first sight. I was twenty. I mention this only because I believe it became her undoing.

It was not a crime of opportunity, not some random kidnapping by a guy cruising the suburbs in a dirty van. She was targeted. Katy, I learned from the newspaper accounts, had encountered the man outside Big Fun (a toy shop in the village of Coventry, about a mile from Cleveland Heights) at about three o'clock on a Sunday afternoon. A classmate saw a man walk up to her, whisper something into her ear, and then lead her into a car and drive off. In broad daylight, he had walked past half a dozen other kids before he reached her. Any other day, Katy would have been with a friend or her parents. But that day, her mother had been late to pick her up. It was as if this man had stalked her, waiting for just such a moment to whisk her away.

I became obsessed with the crime.

It was the knowledge that if I had met this girl when I was a kid in school, she would have been the one I passed notes to behind Miss Kline's back. This was a girl I would have loved. A girl who could have loved me. I was sure of it.

To me, the case was a giant puzzle. The kind where, even if you get all the pieces in the right places, you still have to look through the picture to see the three-dimensional solution hidden within. I thought I was smarter than the detectives working the case. I thought I could figure it out before they did. I thought I could figure it out in enough time to save her.

On May 15, 1999, a man walking his dog along County Road 581 in Ashland County, about sixty miles from Cleveland Heights, discovered Katy's body ten feet off the road, in a harvested cornfield. She had been strangled. And raped.

As tragic as the discovery was—I couldn't sleep for two nights—it was a bit of luck for investigators. They had a crime scene. And, from the desolate location of the dump site, they could logically infer that who-ever had murdered Katy had been familiar with both Cleveland Heights and Ashland County. That narrowed their search a little.

A year later, I used my notes on the case as research for my senior project at Kent State. I wrote a thirty-thousand-word paper. At the prod-ding of my professor, I submitted a proposal to a local publisher. The thesis became a book. Ten years later, I wrote a sequel.

The problem with Katy's murder was not lack of evidence—on the contrary, we had several clues left behind by the killer—it was the vast number of men who had the means, motive, and opportunity to commit the crime.

There was the principal at her elementary school, a man named Burt McQuinn, who had called in sick that day. His family owned a hunting cabin not two miles from where Katy's body was found. And when authorities took a close look at his hard drives, they discovered that he'd been sending digital pictures of his penis to several girls at his school, some as young as twelve.

There was the paper man, an odd fellow named Kevin Sweeney, who delivered the Keenans' daily copy of the *Plain Dealer*, and who, the

FBI found after some digging, had once lived in Florida under the name "John" Sweeney, but fled when he was caught sodomizing a Girl Scout behind a playground slide.

There was the well-known lawyer, a partner at Cleveland's most prestigious firm (you know the one I'm talking about). I won't name him—after all, the man *is* a lawyer. This particular barrister had a side hobby of flashing joggers in the Metro Parks. He was also a closeted polygamist.

There were a dozen or so men like this close enough to Katy to have committed the crime, each with weak or nonexistent alibis.

Over the span of twenty-eight years, I interviewed all of them except Kevin Sweeney, who had committed suicide before anyone could ask him questions.

After I graduated, I became a journalist, and about once a year I'd update Katy's case for whatever publication I worked for at the time. Whenever I caught a spare moment between stories, I dug some more. I could not allow this murderer to think he was smarter than me. There must be some puzzle piece yet unfound.

By 2014, I came to believe I had exhausted all conventional methods of solving this crime. I began to consider unconventional methods.

In 2018, I spent a week in Tibet—ostensibly to work on a freelance piece on the effect the Dalai Lama's return had on the region, but in reality to study with a particular brother the art of transcendental meditation. But the answer was not in the spiritual realm.

And then there was a fabulous breakthrough in 2022, in the study of the properties of light, and I came really close to solving Katy's murder. A scientist at MIT had invented a method to slow down photons. Actually, she was able to not only slow down light, she found she could stop it . . . and reverse it. I took a sabbatical from the paper and, through a grant from a wealthy upper-crust Manhattan family who had reason to thank me for the revival of their patriarch's cold case—a story for another day—I was able to work alongside the scientist and her team as they developed a practical application for their discovery. After many nights, I proposed the idea for the first Light Collar, a device that has now become a standard tool for homicide detectives. If the scientists could capture light they produced in a lab, I figured they could modify their instrumentation to capture light in the field. What they built was a sort of collar, about the size of a dinner plate, which could be bolted together

and taken apart. It could be wrapped around an existing beam of light.
Can you see the importance of such a contraption for my obsession? Let
me explain. You see, I knew Katy had been abducted in front of Big Fun
in Coventry, a toy shop with big floor-to-ceiling windows out front. We
rigged the collar to wrap around the light reflected off the glass. Its digital innards relayed a feed to a nearby computer, which converted the
patterns of light pulled back through it as images, frames, pictures. Essentially, we were able to play back the reflections. We saw images of
people and cars and bugs moving by the window up to five years in the
past, back to the point when management had replaced the window. It
was very promising. We tried every window in nearby shops. But the
furthest back we ever saw was 2009.

I became depressed after this failure. I was no longer a young man.
More than half my life had been spent chasing a killer who eluded me
and, I'm sure, laughed at every article and book I wrote about the crime.
I had sacrificed any real life for myself. Though I had been married
three times, none of the women I brought home accepted my obsession.
Each eventually became jealous of the time I devoted to Katy. I don't
blame them. I know it was unhealthy. Believe me, I have tried to stop. I
have.

Then I heard of a man named Tanmay Gupta, an entomologist from
Case Western, who, through studying the unique chemical reactions
that take place within cicadas during their seventeen-year hibernation
underground, developed the first viable method of sustained human
stasis. He had a simple shot that could put a person into a deep sleep
indefinitely and another shot, an antidote, if you will, that woke the person back up. During the hibernation, the body's metabolism slowed down
so that it only needed about fifteen thousand calories a *year* to survive.
Gupta was funded by an eccentric entrepreneur who owned several un-
derwater hotels and properties in the Gulf of Mexico, but whose secret
love had always been outer space. Anyway, this weirdo, on live iRis, injected himself with Gupta's cocktail, immersed himself in a sealed vat
of protein goop, and pointed his private shuttle toward a star thirty-five
light-years away that may—and I stress *may*—have a planet roughly the
size of earth rotating around it. If he makes a return trip, he won't be
back for two hundred years. After his ship passed Pluto, most people lost
interest.

When I learned of Gupta's discovery, and watched the launch on my iRis, I thought about another theory that was the big to-do of the physics world at the time. For a century, we had accepted that the universe had begun at the Big Bang and was enormous, but finite. For instance, if some matter was ejected from the epicenter of the Big Bang at near the speed of light, and we know the Big Bang was about fifteen billion years ago, the universe must be something like thirty billion light-years across, if matter is somewhat evenly dispersed. But a growing number of theoretical scientists were suggesting the physics during the first moments of creation allowed for an infinitely large universe. And, in physics, *infinite* is the magic word. With infinity, you get all kinds of cool things. In an infinitely large universe, where matter and energy are arranged in infinite ways, there must be worlds out there not just like our own, but mirror images of our own. Think of the old cliché, if there were an infinite number of monkeys sitting at an infinite number of typewriters, one of those monkeys would be writing the collected plays of Shakespeare. If the universe is infinite, there is an earth out there in which Katy's murder has been solved—or, even better, has not yet played out. With Gupta's discovery, it might only be a matter of finding that lost world. Unfortunately, on earth, our vision is limited by the speed of light—we only see fifteen billion light-years in any direction. In an infinite universe, chances were that the earth on which Katy's murder had not yet occurred was beyond that horizon.

Blah, blah, blah, science, science, science, right? I know. I was always a writer, not a physicist. My mind got bogged down in the details, too. But I had many years to study these theories and I was bent on finding a solution at any cost.

A few weeks after my fifty-eighth birthday, in the summer of 2036, I learned of a man named Victor Tesla. Tesla was a distant begotten decedent, or so he claimed, of Nikola Tesla, who designed some weird electromagnetic wonders around the turn of the twentieth century. Victor Tesla was a scientist and protégé of a theoretical physicist named Ronald Mallett. In 2019, Mallett and his team had attempted to send a single neutron five minutes into the past. While the project was an inspiring success, the energy requirements appeared too great a hurdle for any large-scale device. Tesla had solved the problem, he claimed, in an interview with the *Times*. He was set to make a major announcement in the new issue of *Science*. As luck would have it, Tesla's lab was located in Ohio, not far from where I grew up.

It took some doing, but I convinced my editor to let me write the profile that would be appearing on the Slipstreams, Sunday, beamed to five billion iRises instantly.

The drive to Tesla's lab took me farther north than I'd traveled in many years, into that part of Ohio between Akron and Cleveland that had come to be called the Scrubber Barrens.

The roads were empty. What was once Interstate 77, a six-lane highway, had surrendered to nature. It had become a two-lane road of sparse gravel thrown atop cracked blacktop. Gargantuan Russian thistle grew like green cliffs on either side. There were no trees. They had been replaced by endless fields of more efficient Lockheed Scrubbers: man-made towers as tall and wide as redwoods with branches of triangular nanofilters that scrubbed the carbon dioxide from the air and replaced it with breathable oxygen. The government had reclaimed this land after the Fed foreclosed on Cleveland and five other failing cities in order to avoid another countrywide depression in 2019. President Boehner had likened it to amputating a limb to save the body. The state evicted the entire city. Refugees moved south, into Akron, Columbus, Marietta, disappearing into patches of clapboard slums wherever they finally landed. Demolition crews leveled houses and factories all along the east side, replacing them with fields and fields of these hauntingly mechanized trees.

Where the exit sign to Independence once stood, a dirty marker hung crooked on a single bolt. NEW CLEVELAND, COMING 2027, it read. But Cleveland was never coming back. Too expensive to clean up. It was a vacant wasteland now, like Detroit and Baltimore, lost to the excesses of the twentieth century, its only inhabitants vermin—animal and human. Though there was no sign advertising Tesla's lab, I turned off here, and headed due east along a winding dirt access road set between rows of scrubbers. Their nanofilters fluttered like synchronized leaves.

My car was so quiet I could hear those damned scrubbers doing their thing above me. *Shooshshooshshooshshoosh.* The Barrens creeped me out, to tell the truth. It was like they were telling me to be quiet. I hated driving up there. I always had the feeling these machines were aware of my presence. They were too big. They would still be standing, scrubbing up the greenhouse gases we put there, long after we humans had finally managed to completely destroy ourselves. That seemed to make them condescending somehow.

Tesla's lab, a sprawling warehouse that had once been a post office, appeared over a rise. Mounted surveillance cams captured my approach. As I neared, a gate opened and shut behind me. Two men sat on stools inside a guardhouse, watching some reality show on an old wall screen.

I parked in the lot and strapped on my old leather satchel, which held my earwig, voice recorders, notepad (mostly for show), and a few other items I needed for this particular interview.

It occurred to me that there was a real chance I would die here.

I thought that was acceptable.

"Mr. Neff, it's a real pleasure to meet you," said Victor Tesla, taking my hand and pumping it three times. He was a harsh-looking character with ebon eyes and a jutting chin so sharp it could cut meat. He had dressed the part, with a long white lab coat.

"Pleasure's mine, Mr. Tesla," I said, meaning it.

"I can't wait to show you my egg," he said. "You're the first civilian to see my presentation. Please, come with me."

He led me through a set of double doors at the back of the marble entryway and into a gallery that reeked of ozone and roses, of sterility masked by human comfort. Tesla's assistant, a waif of a woman named Ilsa, glided behind. She wore an earwig and occasionally muttered to it as she recorded our meeting for the lab's legal team. The gallery was high-ceilinged and sparse in décor. A military-issue gunmetal-gray desk sat to one side, topped with neatly piled paperwork. A new Apple Boomerang hung suspended in the air above, relaying the day's local news feed. The center of the gallery was occupied by a pedestal that looked quite Draconian in this tech-heavy setting, a squat Doric column. Above this objet d'art rested a wide circular mount made of heavy metal with tiny displays of some sort set into its rim.

"Not quite what I expected," I said.

Tesla laughed. "The greatest inventions tend to be underwhelming, at first glance," he said.

"What do you imagine Einstein would think of Tesla's Egg?"

"He'd have a coronary," said Tesla. "Come." He ushered me to the pedestal and motioned for me to set down my satchel on a chair beside it. He cleared his throat and adjusted his coat as if preparing to pose for a picture. Perhaps he thought I did that sort of thing. "Would you care to hear a little of my history and how I came to work for Professor Mallett?

It is a long story, but I believe a necessary one if you are to understand my inspiration."

I held up my hand. "If you don't mind, could I see a demonstration first? I'd hate for your life story to prejudice my expectations."

"Of course, of course," he said. He pointed at the empty space above the circular contraption. "The egg is there. Probably."

My heart sank. Another crazy. I'd been here many times during my relentless and damnable search. I never expected this scientist, whose credentials appeared solid, to be part of the company of madmen and psychics who pretended to know the unknowable.

"Do you believe?" he asked.

"No," I said shortly.

He shook his head. "You must believe. Otherwise the egg will never appear."

"I'm sorry," I said. "I think you've got the wrong reporter. I don't have time for this." I turned from him and started to leave.

"What we're talking about here, Mr. Neff, is intentionality. Your intention, your faith in your future actions, is key to this little experiment we're conducting."

I stopped. "Intentionality?" Once, a millennium ago, it seemed, I had argued against intentionality with this man's mentor.

"Mr. Neff," he said. "You have to decide now that you will, no matter what, follow my instructions to the letter, no matter how bizarre. Nothing will hurt you. I promise. Just a few simple steps. If you decide now to follow the instructions, I guarantee you that the egg will appear."

I looked back at the pedestal. It was still empty.

"Will you do as I say for the next five minutes?"

After all these years, what was five more minutes?

Tesla smiled. He reached toward the empty space above the pedestal. When his fingers crossed the top of the circular disc, something odd happened to the air there. It wrinkled. It bent. Suddenly there was a loud *POP!* as if a pistol had fired. Then a louder one. Then the rippling abruptly ended and standing motionless in the center of the disc was a black egg, about the size of a goose's egg.

"There," said Tesla.

"What . . ." I began but could not get my words in order.

Tesla reached out and took the egg. But didn't. Or did. All I knew for sure was that Tesla now held an egg in one hand, while another remained atop the pedestal. It was as if one egg had suddenly become two.

"Listen closely," he said. "In a few seconds I will ask you to walk over to my desk and open the top drawer. In that drawer is the egg. It has been there all day. You will bring the egg over to this pedestal. Then"—and here Tesla handed me a device that looked like a garage door opener—"you will push this button. The button is what turns the egg *on*. When the egg is turned on, it stops moving forward through time and begins to exist—that is, to move—*backward* through time. Go now."

I was numb. For just a second I could not move. Then I pulled myself forward and toward the man's desk. There, in the top drawer, was what looked like a third black egg. I picked it up. It was heavier than I had expected. Dense. And shiny.

"Come here," he said.

I did as told, carrying the egg in one hand and crossing the room slowly, mindful of any small bump in the concrete floor that might cause me to trip.

"Place the egg on the pedestal," he said.

"But there's already an egg on the pedestal."

Tesla shook his head. "It's the same egg, silly. Not to worry. It will exist in wave form until you place the egg on the pedestal. There will be no crashing of eggs and eggs dropping to the floor."

I didn't understand what he was saying, exactly, but I had promised to follow his instructions and so I gently reached out with the egg toward the other already there. As I felt they were about to touch, I watched the two merge together, as if the one on the pedestal were but a hologram of an egg. I let go. Two eggs had become one. But Tesla still held a black egg in his hand.

"Now turn it on," he said, looking at the remote in my hand.

I pushed the button and suddenly there was no egg on the pedestal. I felt a wind rushing to the point at which it had recently been, the air filling up the void it had created when it disappeared. The only one that remained—in fact, the only one that had ever existed—was in Tesla's hand. He held it out to me. I accepted it. It appeared to be the same black egg.

"Explain," I said.

"Professor Mallett hypothesized that he could send information back in time. Think of it as two tin cans attached by string. One tin can in the past. One in the future. Someone in the future may "talk" to the person on that phone in the past and relay information. Essentially, that is what Mallett's invention was, a telephone to the past that sent neutrons as information, something like binary code. The problem, of course, is the information can only be sent as far back as the machine was turned on. So, no calling Mr. Lincoln and telling him to skip the play.

"I surmised that perhaps a machine could be made to exist backward through time, like those neutrons. A machine built of those neutrons. A car instead of a telephone. Something that only needed a relatively little push of energy to send it in the right direction. It required the discovery and understanding of gravitational particles, of course, which Mallett never had access to. Look. When you turn the egg on, a field is generated around it. The egg becomes the message you send back in time. All you have to do to make the egg exist forward in time again is to turn it *off*. I have designed this one to turn off by touch."

I blinked and tried to process the mash of words he was stringing together.

"Let me explain what you witnessed in the chronology of the egg," he said. "The egg is picked up by you from my desk and is brought over to this pedestal. You turn on its field. Boom! The egg reverses its direction in time. To us, it's as if it disappeared because we are continuing down the highway of time at the same speed we always traveled, whereas the egg just shot into reverse.

"It stops moving backward when I touch it and again travels forward like us—this is when it seemed to us that the egg magically appeared. For a moment, there are two eggs occupying the same space. But one is in wave form. Think of it like two windows on your computer's desktop overlapping each other. They're both there. But you only see one until you pick it up, and then you see two. The egg that appeared to remain on the pedestal was, in fact, the egg you would eventually place there, already traveling backward through time.

"It's like this," said Tesla, withdrawing from his pocket a long piece of string. "This is the natural flow of time. The past over here"—he jiggled his right hand—"to the future over here"—he jiggled his left. Then he twisted a loop in the middle. "This is the black egg's progression through time. Any questions?"

"It's hard to think about," I said.

"It is," he agreed. "And harder to see, but there it is. You have witnessed time travel."

"So what you're saying is that we really could go back and warn Mr. Lincoln about his assassination if we wanted?"

"Well, yes and no. First you would need a much bigger egg. One that was big enough for a human being, right?" Tesla's eyes drifted over my shoulder for a second before he continued. I had interviewed enough people to know what that look meant, but I let him continue. "You don't want to just send a letter back for something that important. What if it got lost? There is another problem. You move backward in time at the same speed we move forward in time. You would have to be in that egg for, what? A hundred and seventy years. Not only could you not pack enough provisions, you could not live that long. You would grow into an old man inside that egg. Short-term problems? Yes. Perhaps we could fix those. But I'm afraid Mr. Lincoln will remain dead.

"And there are additional concerns. Let's say you discover a way to survive inside this larger egg for two hundred years. You get out, save Lincoln, ta-da! Couple things: one, you're stuck in 1865. There's no way to instantaneously jump back into the future; and two, even if you could, it would no longer be the future from whence you came!"

"What do you mean?"

"It would be the future where Lincoln survived. The one where you were born and never went back to save him because he was never assassinated. If you somehow managed to get back to now, to 2036, there would be two of you. There would be you, the man who traveled back to save Lincoln, and the other you, who never left because Lincoln never died."

"Wouldn't that be impossible?" I asked. "Wouldn't that be a paradox?"

Tesla laughed. "You watch too many old movies," he said. "No paradoxes, Mr. Neff. The universe will not end if you decide to go back in time to kill your grandfather before you were ever born. You'd just have a dead grandfather.

"You see, what happens is this. With every choice, the universe splits. Should I go to the theater or to the opera? Well, there is one universe where I go to the theater and one in which I go to the opera. That's overly simplified, of course."

"Schrödinger's cat," I said.

He nodded. "Schrödinger's cat, exactly. As soon as an observer enters the picture, SPLIT! In one universe the cat is dead. In one the cat is alive. Point being, Mr. Neff: you can never go home again. Lincoln will remain dead in this particular universe forever. No matter what."

I felt unsettled. All this searching, only to find a solution that, what? Exiled me to another universe? That was the price of knowing who killed Katy Keenan?

"It is, I'm afraid, a rather silly invention," he said. "In reality, does it really change anything? No. No, I don't believe so. But what a magic trick, right?"

"Have you sent messages back to yourself?" I asked.

"Of course," he said, unscrewing the top of the egg. There was enough room inside for a wadded-up piece of paper.

"Stock market?"

"It's tempting, no? Actually, Mr. Neff, I prefer to exist along my own timeline. Playing around with history only muddles the whole free will idea. Do we have free will if we know every outcome? Isn't it the mysteries that make a life worth living?"

"It's a beautiful machine, though."

Tesla considered the egg and then the pedestal. He nodded and reached out to the column and massaged its chalky top. "Yes," he said. "It is rather *sleek*." He ran his hand along the top and then, quite to his shock, as his fingers crossed the center, there was a tremendously loud popping sound and suddenly there was another black egg. "Oh, dear," he said.

"What does that mean?" I asked. Although I thought I knew.

"A message," he said. "Although I have no intention of sending one."

"I always thought Mallett was mistaken about intentionality," I said.

He didn't hear me. Tesla was busy unscrewing the black egg while trying not to drop the other one in his hands. Inside was a scroll of paper. He unrolled it. He read the message and crinkled his eyebrows in confusion.

"What's it say?" I asked.

"It says, *He has a stunner.*"

"Oh," I said, withdrawing the weapon from my pocket and pointing it at Tesla. "Yeah. I do." I fired the electrical impulse at the scientist. It connected with his chest and dropped him to the floor, rendering him immobile, but conscious. The two black eggs he held in his hands fell to the concrete and broke into a million little pieces. "Impossible," he whispered.

I spun around but Ilsa was gone, on her way to alert the guards.

"Why?" he asked.

"Does it matter?"

"The uniks will hunt you down."

"I'll be gone before they find me."

"Where will you hide? The egg is too small to travel in."

I bent to him and looked into his steely eyes. "Dr. Tesla, I've gotten to know many scientists over the years. Most of them on contract to our government, just like you. And if there's one thing I've learned, it's that what you show the public is about ten years behind what you have already shown your employers. Where is it?"

"I don't know what you're talking about."

"Look at me, Tesla. I will kill you if you don't give me what I need. You're right, it is over for me here. In fact, your only hope is that I'm right and you do have a full-sized vessel, somewhere, that you've designed for the black ops or whoever you're building it for. Because if you don't, I will kill you before they kill me. What have I got to lose?"

I knew he could see I was not bluffing.

"Through the door. The code is 161803."

"Thank you," I said.

"Wait," said Tesla.

I knelt to him again. "Yes?"

"If it works . . ."

"Send you a letter?"

"Yes."

"You bet."

We arrived at my compound in Peninsula shortly after I finished telling David the story of how I came to be here and how I survived, a long story that I must dish out in six parts to you, dear reader, over the course of the last section of this memoir—I want to share with you what happened with David, with us, and how the matter of his search for the man who murdered his wife concluded. That, of course, is the narrative thrust of this tale, right? So let's not stray too far from it. I only share my story with you at all because it does have some bearing on David's destiny, as my future has an impact on his present. Cause and effect are all jacked up at this point, I know. I went through it and I barely understand it. I hope, if nothing else, you come to believe that what we call the present is nothing more than perception and the concepts of cause and effect are mostly pointless.

So say it with me. "Fuck it."

Now let's get back to it.

We arrived at my compound in Peninsula shortly after I finished telling David the story of how I came to be here and how I survived. If you're thinking about disappearing in plain sight somewhere in northeast Ohio, you would be hard-pressed to find a better spot for it than Peninsula. This quaint village is tucked away between Akron and Cleveland, bordered by the Cuyahoga River, two ski resorts, and a system of limestone quarries. Because of the ruthless town zoning board, it cannot be built up or gentrified. It is stagnant in time, like living in the postwar Americana featured in some old *Twilight Zone* episode. My home is atop a tall hill surrounded by trees, in the middle of twenty acres toward the north end, lined by fencing and security cameras. My neighbors think I'm paranoid. They, of course, have not lived through the forcible eviction of five hundred thousand people from Cleveland, a half million pissed-off refugees looking for something to loot. Should I live to experience that again—which, incredibly, seems like a real possibility—I'd like to know my property is well protected.

Aaron dropped us off at the front portico where Mr. Merkl, my sometime attendant, waited to welcome us inside.

"Should I prepare the guest room?" he asked. Mr. Merkl was a funny round man with a long mustache that made him look very much like a walrus in a nice suit. A loyal man. He could keep a secret or two. And has.

"I think our guest's stay will be quite brief. Some dinner, though. And Brandy Alexanders."

"Right," he said and disappeared toward the kitchen as we walked inside. Aaron was already pulling the car into the garage.

David whistled.

I laughed. "Well, if I'm going to live in self-imposed imprisonment, I might as well enjoy it."

The house was a sprawling three-story brick French Colonial. Five thousand square feet, not including the home theater in the basement. Lots of cherry and walnut and delicious wainscotting. My favorite place in the entire mansion was the upstairs bathroom with the claw-foot tub. I pulled David into the smoking lounge, off the foyer. Tall bookcases full of guilty pleasures nearly entombed the room. Leather couches faced each other in the middle, between which sat a table made of tortoiseshell, its legs made of smaller taxidermied turtles all the way down.

"Apple. Google. Bear Stearns," I said.

"Bear Stearns?"

I had forgotten I had once been concerned for justice. I shrugged. "The good guys should make a little money, too."

For a moment neither of us spoke. So much had been said already.

"Want to hear something strange?" I asked, falling into one of the couches as my younger self sat across from me.

David looked worried. "How much stranger does it get?"

"I don't know how far it goes. How many times we've obsessed over an unsolved crime for decades, shanghaied a time machine, and ended up in the past to stop it. I'm here because I needed a solution to Katy's case. The Man from Primrose Lane came back to find Elizabeth and Elaine's killer—she would have died that day, too, if he had not interrupted the crime. But there are *other* us's out there. I've seen one or two along the way, never sure if they noticed me or not. In a restaurant. At a gas station in Bellefonte, Pennsylvania. But there must be more than that. People other than us who think to do something similar, for whatever reason. There must be, because every time I make an investment in an upstart little company I know is about to make it big, there are other third-party investors snatching up the same stocks. A day before September 11, I dumped a bunch of stock, put it into gold. You should have seen the returns that day. There are *many* other time travelers out there. A shit-ton of people dumped stock that day. Why are *they* here?"

"Speaking of 9/11," he said. David looked a little sore. "You came all the way back here to save one girl and you let 9/11 happen?"

"I wish it was that easy," I said.

Mr. Merkl was suddenly there with the Brandy Alexanders. He set them down and announced supper would be served in half an hour—cucumber soup, bay scallops in white wine sauce over fettuccini.

"Why isn't it that easy?" David asked as soon as he left.

I sipped the drink and considered him, sadly. I was, in many ways, the embodiment of his mental impairment, the obsessiveness he tried so desperately to conquer. "You remember Timothy McVeigh and Oklahoma City?"

"Yes."

"The Man from Primrose Lane arrived in time before that happened. He thought, like you, that he had a chance to do something that would benefit more than just himself and the family of a dead girl."

"So why didn't he stop it?"

"He thought he did. He called in a tip to the FBI. He went to Oklahoma City. He cut the wires McVeigh had rigged to his homemade bombs in that U-Haul. It still went off. Still killed a bunch of people, a bunch of kids."

"What happened?"

I shrugged. "Don't know. But it scares the shit out of me. Think about it. It means someone knew what he was up to and planned around it."

"Who do you think?"

"I don't know. The government? Tesla? How about this—how about one of us?"

"Ugh," he said.

"Damn right, *ugh*."

"You think something similar happened on 9/11?"

"I called in a tip. I called in a bomb threat to the Bangor airport."

"Why? The terrorists left from Boston."

"They did this time. Where I came from, they left out of Bangor. They altered their plan. I think they did that because someone knew I would call in the tip to Bangor."

"Jesus."

"It's another reason we keep to ourselves. We don't know who we can trust."

"What else is different this time around?" David asked.

"Other than Elizabeth not being abducted? A lot. And there's no way to know how much is because of me and the Man from Primrose Lane and how much was changed by other travelers. There's the butterfly effect to account for, too. You know, go back in time, alter something small, and it creates a cascading of events that occasionally leads to some big, unexpected change. Mostly it's little stuff—the Mexican restaurant by the mall never went out of business because there never was a salmonella

THE MAN FROM PRIMROSE LANE   259

scare this time around, there was an extra season of *Scrubs* for some
reason. But then there's the big stuff; here, President Bush never crashed
into the ocean during that Mission Accomplished photo op, North
Korea never launched a nuke into Tokyo in 2007. And what the hell is
with the Red Sox winning the World Series? Tell me a time-traveling
Southy isn't responsible for that.

"There are fewer murders here," I continued. "There was this girl
named Tiffany Potter who was murdered in 1989—"

"Tiffany Potter, the actress? From Bay Village? The one in all those
independent movies?" asked David.

"That's her."

David reclined in his seat. "My mind is numb," he said. "Enough.
Enough."

"Agreed."

"So what now?"

"Now we simply have to find the man who murdered your wife, the
guy who shot the Man from Primrose Lane. This would be the same
man, I'm convinced, who got away from us during Elaine's abduction,
who got away from us again when he tried to abduct Katy. We need to
find this man before he kills another girl and this whole sick cycle re-
peats itself."

"Isn't that what you've been trying to do this whole time?"

"Well, yes. I brought all the notes and case files on Katy's murder
back with me—a murder that, now, has never occurred. I have most of
the notes here. Names of suspects, names of friends, information about
everything the girl did the first ten years of her life. Unfortunately, the
police took the rest from the crime scene. We had a crazy idea. The Man
from Primrose Lane and I. We were collaborating on a book. I was going
to write it. The Man from Primrose Lane was going to illustrate it—he
spent his spare time painting, those last few years—you should try it
sometime. That's what those paintings were for. They were going to be
illustrations for a book about Katy and Elizabeth's cases, about our
search. Only we would change the names and sell it as fiction. Sci-fi. It
was a goof. Something to pass the time. We hoped maybe we'd spot something while going through all the old notes from the cases. But now,
maybe with a fresh pair of eyes . . .

"A fresh pair of eyes? I'm *you*."

"Yeah, but none of *us* ever solved a crime. You got Trimble. You were different. We thought you were going to break the cycle. None of us ever had a kid. But *you* did. And with *Elizabeth*! Tanner never existed before. Of course, then your wife discovered your older self from another time-line, you became obsessed with the death of this man, the 'Man from Primrose Lane,' and started a relationship with Katy, the other girl who should be dead, and, well, everything got fucked again. So here we are. I'm out of ideas. I think we can help each other. I really don't want to go to my grave knowing you're going to crawl into that black egg when you're fifty-eight and come back again."

David nodded. "Okay, then."

"You know, the solution . . ." I began.

". . . is always elegantly simple," he finished. "Do you really believe that anymore?"

"I do. I've always felt we've been missing the forest for the trees. That the answer has always been clearly visible. We just don't know which way to look."

The oddest part for David was seeing the autopsy photographs of Katy Keenan, a woman he knew was alive and well. It left him dizzy, dis-jointed. He prayed that everything he was experiencing was not some dissociative fugue brought on by withdrawals. He didn't want to wake up back in some padded cell at the Glenns.

The images were grainy, color copies of photographs. She was ten in the pictures. Naked. Placed upon a stainless steel slab. Her body had remained relatively preserved thanks to dry weather. But there was no skin around her face. She had been stabbed in the neck and the wound had allowed for the natural process of decomposition to claim every-thing above her shoulders. Her teeth and jaws jutted from the decay like a homemade skeleton mask taken from some carny's haunted house. This was a woman he knew, a woman he had made love to. Somewhere, he must have realized, there were probably similar pictures of Elizabeth, brought back by the Man from Primrose Lane.

I shared with him the particulars of Katy's case. Where the news-paper reports left off, I filled in pertinent details. The discussion ended with a top-ten list of suspects, some of which I've already shared with you. That list was the best I had ever come up with and I wasn't even sure if the man who murdered Katy was on there.

"But you saw him, that day you saved Katy from being abducted," David said. "Did he look like any of these guys?"

"It happened so fast," I explained. "All these guys sort of look similar: white guy, bushy hair, glasses, round head, of Eastern European descent. Hell, our guy looks like half the population of Parma Heights."

"Yeah, but you *saw* him."

"For about five seconds."

"And you can't say for sure?"

I shook my head. "The closest, I think, is this guy." I tapped Burt McQuinn's photo, the elementary school principal. "But I can't be sure. I followed McQuinn around for a while, after I interrupted the abduction. He never changed his routine. He didn't seem to be a guy who had been caught in the process of committing a crime. When I made a point to let him see me in a convenience store, he acted like he didn't recognize me. So, I don't know."

"Any other similar murders around this guy? Where is he today?"

"Still in Cleveland Heights," I said. "I haven't found another murder similar to Katy's—or Elizabeth and Elaine's. Here's what I think happened. This guy, in *this* timeline, abducted Elaine, but was interrupted before he got Elizabeth. So he thinks maybe the intervention of the Man from Primrose Lane that day at the park was a coincidence, and after awhile he stalks Katy. When he goes to take her, he's interrupted again! He's interrupted by a man he must believe is the same dude who interrupted his first abduction. He knows now this isn't a coincidence. What must he have thought? How could anyone else know what he was planning? Obviously, he wasn't going around sharing his plans with people. He doesn't know what the hell is going on. So he lays low. And then, what? He happens to be in Akron, maybe drives down the road as the Man from Primrose Lane is coming back from a walk, and recognizes him as his archnemesis? He kills him so he can start stalking again? Maybe Elizabeth was there when he went to the house with the gun. This case is a lot of maybes."

"But nothing like this has happened in the last four years, since someone shot the Man from Primrose Lane?"

"Maybe. Maybe not."

"What do you mean?"

"A lot of girls go missing from the inner-ring Cleveland suburbs. Little

girls whose families couldn't care less if they come home for dinner—
one less mouth to feed. Girls east of West 117 get pregnant at, what, the
age of fourteen these days. No one keeps track of them. You've heard the
names, you just don't remember them because they're not from Bay Village or Shaker Heights. Amanda Berry; Gina Dejesus; Ashley Summers.
Maybe that's where he's hunting these days."

"Do any of the suspects in Katy's murder overlap with suspects from
Eliz . . . from Elaine's murder?"

"Good question," I said. "Several. Burt McQuinn, for one. McQuinn's
daughter was on the same Lakewood soccer team as the O'Donnell
twins. There's another guy—Curtis Detweiler. Worked for Katy's father
and for a brief time, shortly before the abduction, had an affair with
Abigail, Elizabeth and Elaine's mother. Police took a hard look at him,
boy. But he was at a trade show at the IX Center at the time of Katy's
abduction. Some guy who was filming a vacuum demonstration got
Detweiler on his camera, in the background. No way he did it. Coincidences like that made it so hard for investigators. There's just so many
suspects."

"Well, you could narrow it down a little with a criminal profile . . ."

"Thought of that, too. Had a Bureau guy look into it. Wrote up a report for me in 2015. The violence of the crime scenes suggests the person who committed these murders is very strong. This is someone of
high intelligence—he was able to monitor these girls' behavior so that he
could time the kidnappings to the second. In, out. He knew when they
were alone. That takes dedication and planning. However, he probably
worked a menial job—managing a restaurant, janitorial job, retail—mostly
because he doesn't know how to relate well enough to his peers to com-
mand any sort of respect. Probably has some worthless college degree
from a state school. Gets along with kids, is probably close to them in some
way, either through work or some after-hours volunteering opportunity:
library, museum guide, Big Brothers. Perhaps the most telling part is his
choice of victim: redheaded girls with straight hair and freckles. He's
very specific. He's probably of Irish descent himself."

"Along with half the west side," said David.

"Exactly."

"Where do we start?"

"I want to check in on all the top suspects," I said. "Knock on their
doors. If they react like they've seen a ghost—remember, I am the exact

double of the man they believed they killed, the Man from Primrose Lane—then we'll have our guy. Unfortunately, I'm old, David. But not too keen on dying yet. So I'd like you to come along."

David smiled wanly. "Not like I have much of a choice."

"We always have a choice, David."

He nodded. "I'm in. I jumped down the rabbit hole when I stepped into your limo. Let's see where it goes."

"Good! We'll start tomorrow."

As Mr. Merkl served supper right there in the smoking den, David arranged some photos on a side table. Three school photos. Elaine, Elizabeth, Katy. Each about ten years old. Each with a similar background of white clouds and blue sky. There was a crack in Katy's picture, David noticed, a thin dark line above her left shoulder, a defect of the lens, possibly, or the background itself.

"I have one more favor to ask," I said.

David looked up.

"It's a little thing. There's going to be quite a lot of driving over the next few days. A lot of time in the car. I'd like to interview you about your history and your investigation into the case of the Man from Primrose Lane. You know, while we travel from place to place."

"For your book?"

"If I ever get around to finishing it."

"Sure."

Later that evening, I drove David home in the Cadillac I keep in the garage.

During the journey, we were mostly silent. I knew I had to give him some time to let the bizarre facts of his present life sink in.

I saw her face out of the corner of my eye and swerved the car onto the shoulder, braking hard. David gripped the dashboard in panic.

"What?" David asked.

"Look." I pointed to the digital billboard suspended over Route 8, between Peninsula and Akron. Usually the sign alternated between advertisements every three seconds. Not today.

It was locked on one static shot.

A school photo of a ten-year-old girl named Erin McNight.

She had red hair. And freckles.

It was an Amber Alert.

EPISODE FOURTEEN

THE BURNING RIVER

On the other side of the reinforced door inside Tesla's lab was a cool dark room that smelled of oiled metal. I felt about for a light switch while I locked the door behind me. There it was, to my right. Click.

A row of fluorescents stretching the length of a football field shuttered on above, illuminating a storage facility and loading dock. I was unprepared for what I saw. I had imagined Tesla would have a prototype vessel for human travel. Never did I think he'd already reached the point of mass production.

I stood in a field of black eggs, their tops a foot taller than my head. Hundreds, shining like a forest of dark, smooth crystals. What did Tesla need with so many? What in the hell was he planning?

A part of me realized that, if I stayed, this would be the biggest story of my life, that it would make my career, my legacy. But the pull was too strong. If I told the world about it, I would surely never be allowed to use it.

Squeezing between rows of time machines, I quickly made my way toward the end of the warehouse. Three Humvee-wide loading docks were there, closed. Unfortunately, there were no Humvees. However, sitting in the farthest port was a Cushman, the kind with a little cab and a flatbed. Electric, of course. I noticed it was not plugged in. I hoped that meant the battery was charged.

Carefully—I had no idea how much shock these technological wonders could take—I rolled the closest black egg to the concrete ledge behind the Cushman. It was only a foot drop. I had to risk it. I pushed it
over, an image of Humpty Dumpty stuck in my mind. It landed in the
Cushman, wobbled to one side like a drunken weeble, then righted itself. I strapped it in tightly, using nylon belts already attached to the vehicle, for this specific purpose, it seemed, then climbed inside the cab.

I pushed the ignition button and the Cushman came to life with a
low moan. The battery light came on, too. Three bars remained. Not
enough juice to make it around Cleveland, to Vermilion, where Dr. Tanmay Gupta waited for me. That route skirted the entire Foreclosed Zone,
about a hundred and twenty miles of road. Not nearly enough to go
around.

But through?

I punched the accelerator and the flimsy aluminum loading dock
door exploded around me like scraps of tinfoil. The black egg remained
relatively still in the bed of the Cushman.

It was growing dark outside, barely an hour's worth of light left for
the world. Then again, uniks didn't need light to see.

Around the corner, Ilsa and the guards hurried back toward the front
doors. They were too shocked at the Cushman barreling by to even raise
their stunners. Lazy guards, probably stationed to this outpost inside the
Scrubber Barrens because they couldn't do anything else. I was past
them and halfway down the lane leading to I-77 before they even radi-
oed in a distress call to HQ, I'm sure.

It wouldn't take HQ in Columbus long to release the uniks. And
how long would it take them to cross the distance to me? An hour? Not
long.

I turned North on I-77, toward the empty buildings of a once-great
city.

I reminded myself that people had seen deer, *healthy* deer, from air-
planes, thriving within the city limits. An hour or two of highly toxic
dust and pollen wouldn't kill me. At least I didn't think it would.

The Ohio Department of Transportation had set up concrete barriers just north of the Scrubber Barrens, on I-77. They were old and crum-
bling now. Russian thistle grew from them, out of large holes filled with
black water. The barriers were covered in graffiti. WELCOME TO NEW

CLEVELAND! someone had written. It was easy enough to maneuver the Cushman around.

My intention was to avoid downtown, skirting it by taking I-490 West, a conduit running along the old steel mills that reconnected with I-90 on the other side. But as I came to the exit, I discovered that the ramp and a quarter mile of road had fallen into the Cuyahoga many years ago. I waited there a moment, contemplating my options. The abandoned LTV smelting plant sat quietly to my left, its chimneys blackened and crusted by decades of overuse, silent now. The whole Cuyahoga Valley with its spires of concrete smokestacks looked like an empty Mordor, a dead orc kingdom after the fall of Sauron. It looked like hell after hell.

There was no choice. I had to drive through downtown.

I rolled north on I-77, navigating around chuckholes that could hide elephants, and watched the Cleveland skyline appear on the horizon. Key Tower was gone. Utterly. The National City Building leaned dangerously away from the lake and would surely collapse during the next good storm, taking Old Stone Church with it. But Terminal Tower still stood, a man-made bastion of humanity, the avatar of Cleveland herself. A tattered Indians pendant fluttered in the poisonous breeze above its highest turret.

I exited at Ontario, the preferred route for baseball games at the Jake and rock concerts at the Q. Jacobs Field was being strangled by ivy so thick and so high that the vegetation appeared sentient and sleeping. The Q was nothing but rubble. To my left, the Gods of Transportation, giant statues of men holding carved vehicles like sacrificial offerings, looked down at me, great Roman deities witnessing the end of times. These statues marked the entrance to the Lorain Road Bridge. The bridge stood, I saw. But the statues made me nervous. They reminded me of the oracles from the *Neverending Story*, the half-naked statues that had tried to kill the kid, so I moved on.

I turned left in front of the Hard Rock Café and drove around the large guitar marquee that had once rotated out front. As I came around the backside of Terminal Tower, my heart sank. The Veterans' Memorial Bridge was no more. Steel pylons twisted in the air like open hands grasping for the road it once held. Beyond it, I saw the Route 2 bridge still remained. However, a large section in the middle of the expanse had collapsed, a hole much too big to drive around, and one that suggested it was no longer structurally sound. That left the swing bridge in the Flats.

Before the city's mills became obsolete, decades before the housing crisis turned it into a ghost town, the Flats was a place of much reverie. Bars lined both shores of the Crooked River where it emptied into Lake Erie. Not just bars, but clubs and concert venues like the Odeon. It had been a place for bachelorette parties and dry-humping. Life had *thrived* here. It died long before the evictions, around the time we lost the World Series.

A single bridge linked the east and west banks of the Flats: a red steel swing bridge that spun upon a giant spindle situated on the west bank, allowing container ships to slip upriver to the factories in the valley. In 1969, the overly polluted Cuyahoga River had actually caught fire not far from here. That incident had single-handedly ushered in the era of environmental safety legislation. So much for all that.

The bridge stood.

The ramp was not exactly aligned with the road on the east side, but it was only off by inches. There was plenty of room left for the Cushman to access it. A little luck, at last.

Still, I hesitated. I brought the Cushman to a stop just before the bridge and looked around. Upriver, the west bank had fallen into the Cuyahoga. What had once been upscale apartments were now riverfront property; most of the rooms were partially submerged. Toward the lake, the river was clogged with telephone poles, fallen trees, and an S-10 pickup—the kind with a combustible engine. Even from here, I could see the skeleton behind the wheel.

Suspended above the bridge was the operator's office, its windows dark. When there had been need to travel the river, it had been a lonely person's job to sit in that booth all day long and swing the bridge open for the freighters.

I urged the Cushman forward.

For a moment everything was fine. I began to breathe a sigh of relief. And then I heard something pierce the tires. All four at once. The Cushman lurched forward, axles skidding along the grated metal, throwing sparks. At the same time, the bridge began to turn away from the east bank. The gears above my head whined and protested as the machinery was called upon to perform its job once more.

I dug into my belongings and came up with the stunner. Its battery was low. Not enough to take on more than two harriers, if that was what I was dealing with.

The Cushman vibrated to a stop halfway across the bridge. A minute later the bridge stopped, too, locking us away from the other shore. The only way out was onto the west bank.

I heard a rumbling, like thunder. It had been so long since I had heard this sound, it took me a moment. A diesel engine. I heard it growling from around the corner of an old bar. A second later a tow truck pulled into view and actually paused at a stop sign before turning left toward me. There were two dark figures in the cab.

The truck stopped before the bridge and then turned around and backed up, its steel pipe emitting a thick black smoke, its steel claw swaying back and forth, searching for the grille of the Cushman. Just before it made contact, the truck stopped. The driver's door opened and a tall man lumbered out, pointing a sawed-off shotgun at my face.

"Ho, there!" he said. There was a boil on the side of his neck the size of a baby's fist.

"Hello?" I shouted out the window.

"What brings you this far north, my friend?" The shotgun remained focused on my face.

I turned the stunner's trigger so that it was programmed to go off upon harsh contact and slid it into my pants pocket.

"Passing through," I said. "Not bringing trouble."

"Ayuh," he said. "Climb on down, will you?"

I did as he said, opening the cab and stepping onto the swing bridge. The floor was latticed corrugated steel. The Cuyahoga bubbled beneath us like the River Styx.

"Maggie!" he hollered.

The passenger door of the tow truck opened and a wraith of a woman walked out and over to the gearshift on the back that controlled the claw. Her hair hung over her face in a cascade of filthy dreadlocks. She wore a low-slung iRis 4.0 T-shirt and from where I stood I could see the round blue eye in her trachea where someone had replaced her voice box with a cosmetic pitch alternator. It was a hallmark of an expensive prostitute but those days were long gone and no one had paid to have it removed. Without talking, she set to work securing the Cushman to the truck. As she did, the driver conducted a thorough exam of my person, patting for a handgun. When he was done, he laughed.

"Come to Cleveland without a sidearm? Who are you running from?"

"Uniks."

The word caught the man like a slap across the jaw. His face turned a pallid pink. Then he smiled. "You hear that, Maggie? Uniks! No one'd bother sending uniks into Cleveland. No point to it. They'd kill you up here. You'd starve to death."

"I think they mean to kill me."

But the driver waved me off. "What do ya have in the bed?" he asked, poking at the black egg in a way that made me feel very queasy.

"Dunno," I said. "I'm just the driver. Supposed to take it from Erie to Toledo. Under the radar."

"Ransom," he said, as if to himself. "Somebody'd pay a handsome lot for this, then, wouldn't they?"

I shrugged. "Depends on if you want to twist with the type who would pay a guy like me to drive this thing through the wastes of Cleveland."

"Oh, lad, I can twist, all right. I can tussle." He nudged me with the business end of the shotgun. "Tell you what I'm gonna do. I'm a let you go. It's a day's walk out of the city, heading east on 90. You'll find the outpost in Willoughby ere twilight tomorrow. You go on back home and tell your boss to make me a deal. I'll take good care of his treasure till then."

Maggie finished her business and then walked, head down, to her seat in the idling truck.

I shook my head. "I can't do that."

"Oh, no?"

"No."

"You got a gun in your face, mister. Maybe you do what I tells you to do."

"The Second Amendment was repealed five years before the Great Foreclosures. No doubt you found this weapon under the bed of the tow truck you pilfered. But I figure you've been hard-pressed to find any shells. Maybe a couple, in garages or attics. Here and there. But you probably used those to bring down game along the fringe. You and I both know this gun isn't loaded. Not now. Not in a long time. You don't even clean the thing anymore."

For a long moment the highwayman didn't say anything and his expression remained unreadable. "Maybe it is loaded. Maybe not," he said. "But I assure you the stock is strong enough to bash in your mud-derruddy skull."

I swung the stunner toward his neck and prayed there was enough battery left for just one more shock. In alarm, he squeezed the trigger, and for a second I believed I had seriously miscalculated the situation. But his action had been instinct. There was a dull click as the hammer hit the empty barrel. Then the stunner collided with his neck and siz-zled to life. The electricity traveled along his body in a ripple, on down through his feet, which, I had not noticed until then, were wrapped not in leather but a torn blanket full of holes. The electricity traveled the length of the metal bridge and down into its large hinge, which was now half submerged in the muck and mire of the river. The only thing that saved me was my rubber-soled shoes.

It started with a spark thrown off from that hinge. The river caught fire. Again. I felt a warm rush of air and then everything was enveloped in flame. The driver, lying immobile at my feet, began to cook. And scream.

I dashed to the open door of the tow truck. It smelled like the den of a malnourished bear, the sort that is slowly dying of cancer of the anus. I nudged the truck into gear and began to move it off the bridge, away from the river of fire, that cursed river. Maggie, finally noticing her mas-ter was no longer in charge, simply opened the door and stepped into the air. I watched her wasted body fall into the river. It is an image that haunts me to this day.

Miraculously, the truck's tank was full of diesel. Plenty to deliver me to Vermilion, to Tanmay, if the uniks didn't catch up first. My best chance of stopping them had been that stunner, which was melting into the man's neck on the road behind me. What could I do but go on?

As I started down the road, I looked back to the inferno raging be-hind. I watched a man jumping up and down inside the operator's nest, screaming for help. I looked forward and pretended he didn't exist.

Then I opened the window and listened for the approaching screams of the uniks.

"You look like ass," said Jason.

They sat at a table in a dark corner of the Nervous Dog coffee shop, a hipster hideaway tucked in a forgotten West Akron shopping plaza. It was early morning the day after Erin McKnight's kidnapping. Another layer to compound the mystery. David wanted to clean house a bit. Be a good Boy Scout, be prepared for anything that came next. And that meant drawing in some loose threads before he became further entangled.

"I've had better days."

"They treat you okay in the pokey? Nobody tried to, you know, get gay with you or nothing?"

"No, Jason. Nobody tried to get gay with me."

"I spent a week in juvie once. Joyride in my sister's car. I was thirteen. Some creepy shit goes on in there."

David rubbed at the pain behind his temples. "What do you have for me, Jason?"

"On the redhead's old man?" Jason handed him a small notebook stuffed with a couple photos of a rough-looking man with a high forehead and white-white hair walking to his pickup. The years since David had seen him at the Kent State vigil had been unkind. "He's a piece of work. Contractor. Nasty divorce about ten years ago. Ran his ex-wife over the coals. Had a private eye take pictures of her fucking another dude in the Metro Parks. Got custody of Katy—she was fourteen. Started drinking. Beat up a guy pretty bad at Nighttown in 2008. Apparently the dude mouthed off about his daughter, how smoking hot she grew up to be or something. Put him in the hospital. Served three weeks downtown, on work-release. He's in AA now. Man has a short fuse. But if you ask me, I don't like him for it."

"Why not?"

"Uh. Guys like this. You got to know the type. He's all fists. Pow. He doesn't think. He reacts. With your guy on Primrose Lane . . . that took some planning. Some thought. Too much time for a guy like this. He'd have cooled off before it was over. And besides, no way could I see him killing a woman."

"You've heard Elizabeth was murdered, then?"

"I'm sorry, David. Really."

"Thanks." David reached into his satchel. He brought out a thin gray metal box, about the size of a notebook.

"What's that?" asked Jason.

"Everything. Everything you'll need if something bad happens to me."

"What are you talking about?"

"Jason, I've made you the executor of my estate, if I happen to die unexpectedly."

"Jesus. Are you expecting to die unexpectedly?"

"I'm being careful. My will is in here. A living will, too. Some paperwork regarding Tanner's trusts as well as instructions for what to do with my body and the house. Houses. Stuff I don't want to bother my dad with. And compensation for your time, of course."

For the first time since he'd met him at that Beachland concert long ago, Jason was speechless.

"You okay?" asked David.

"Yeah, man. It's just . . . I'm not, you know, *responsible*."

"You're the only guy I completely trust, actually. You're a good guy, Jason. I've always known that. You know that, too. You're all sound and fury out here, but in here," David said, patting Jason lightly on the chest, "you're the most loyal guy I've ever met. And I know you'd do anything to help my boy."

Jason nodded, his jaw set tightly, trying not to show emotion. He coughed away a tear. "Still. Don't die, okay?"

Paul, his publisher, called as David drove to his father's place to visit Tanner.

"How's the book coming?" he asked.

"I'm going to need an extension on that deadline," said David.

"So much for an easy story. I've been watching the news. Your indictment was covered on CNN."

"Great."

"On the up side, they're going back to print on *Serial Killer's Protégé*. It's back on the bestseller list."

"Wonderful."

"Seriously, David, anything I can do?"

"No. But thanks."

"I'll release a statement later. Something about how we support our writer and how I'm sure you're innocent and being railroaded. Something short and punchy."

"You don't have to."

"I do, actually. I should be doing more."

"No worries, Paul. It'll work out. I'll call in a couple days."

———

"Dad!" Tanner. His arms open, his little body running toward David. He felt guilty for ever wanting to do anything but stay home with him and play. Play until he was eighteen. He hoped, after all this was through, that there would be time for that. *Time enough at last*, as Rod Serling once said.

He took his son in his arms and brought him back toward his father's house. David's father waited on the porch, drawing down a bottle of tomato juice.

"Morning," said his father, clapping him on the back with a big hand.

"Hey," he said.

They sat on a bench that David's father had constructed out of driftwood, Tanner on David's lap, holding tight to his shirt.

"Dad," said Tanner. "Papa took me fishing. I put all the worms on the hooks. And I caught a catfish but it ate the line but it was hu-uge!"

"Cool."

"Yeah, and we ate the fishes when we came home. We cooked them out here on the grill. I like fish. *Real* fish. Not fish sticks."

"I like real fish, too. We should go fishing more when I get back."

The boy's eyes grew wider and his grip tightened. "You're not done yet?"

"Almost," he said.

"But I want to go home," said Tanner.

"Real soon. Promise. I'm staying for a little bit today, so what do you want to do?"

"A book," he said. "Can you read *Moonbeam*?"

"Sure."

"All three?"

"Sure."

Tanner rested his head on David's shoulder. And for a short while they sat in silence.

When Tanner finally went down for his nap, David found himself back in the kitchen across the table from his father, who looked as tired as he felt. Tanner was a good kid, but he was also a highly active kid; they had spent the day constructing an elaborate Rube Goldberg machine made mostly of PVC pipe and garden tools that caused a plastic army guy to parachute off the top of a ladder in the back yard.

"He started wetting the bed again."

"Ah, man."

"Woke up at four this morning. Nightmare, I think. He wouldn't say. I stayed up with him, watching *Blue's Clues*. I got him back to sleep around five-thirty."

David looked at the table. "I can't begin to explain to you what's going on," he said. "I need a couple more days to figure things out. Then I can bring him home. Right now it's not safe."

"What's happening?" his father asked. "You don't have to keep secrets from me. Christ, David, I know you didn't do this. What you need to be doing is circling the wagons, talking with your lawyer, staying home with Tanner. You're under a microscope right now. They're just waiting for you to make some stupid mistake. You shouldn't be running around out there."

"I just need a couple days."

"For what?"

"I promise I'll tell you when it's over. I just honestly don't know how right now. You have to trust me, all right?"

He had not had a real fight with his father since he'd been a senior in high school, when they had—as many American father/son teams will at some point—come to blows. He could tell, by the way his father's chin quivered when he spoke, that they were reaching a tipping point. Soon there would be raised voices. And, in all likelihood, that would give way to physicality. Neither of them needed that.

So he left. Without another word.

It was the last time David saw his father.

"What the hell took you so long?" I asked when David walked through my front door shortly before two p.m. I have always been ashamed at my incessant tardiness.

"Nothing," he said.

"That girl, Erin, is still out there somewhere. Every minute is like an eternity for her."

"She's dead," he said. "You know that. This guy doesn't keep his victims alive. She was probably murdered before the Amber Alert even went out."

"What if she's not?"

"What do you want to do about it?" He was shouting now. "I'm charged with murder and you can't go anywhere because you look like a dead man."

"Fuck it."

"What?"

"I said, fuck it. Fuck it. Fuck it all." I grabbed my cane and opened the door for him. "Let whatever happens, happen. But we need information on this girl. And by the time the reporters get at anything important, it will be too late. Let's go. You're driving."

Erin McKnight's family lived on the west side of Cleveland, in the hipster gentrified suburb of Tremont. The trip took less than an hour. I used the time to interview David about the particulars of his life. We started in 1999, the year Katy was abducted, and worked chronologically forward toward the present. (Since Katy's murder had directed that portion of my life beyond 1999, I could safely assume that everything that had happened to David before that was pretty much the same in my time-line.) He told me about meeting Elizabeth, about how he came to be involved in the Brune adventure, and about raising a boy alone. I captured it all on tape, one of those mini-recorders. Listening to those tapes again, as I write this book, is quite painful. It is like reliving a moment in time—our voices take me back to that hour in the car and I can smell the leather seats and feel the cool breeze of the AC. It's like being there, but I'm unable to warn him about the events that are about to unfold. When you're lost in the middle of a set of dominoes, you can't see the pattern that's forming in the falling blocks around you.

The McNight home was swarming with media and law enforcement. Cuyahoga County sheriff's deputies had set up barriers around the house, a warm Cape Cod not far from Lincoln Park. Television personalities stood outside the perimeter, speaking into cameras wired to expensive trucks with fifty-foot antennas. Pohlman, the reporter who'd captured Trimble's confession on tape, was there, David saw. The Action News helicopter hovered high above. A three-man squad of FBI agents walked out of the house and into a black sedan that sped off west.

"What are you doing?" asked David.

"Putting on my disguise," I told him, checking the placement of the bushy white mustache in the mirror; Aaron had picked it up for me weeks ago, one of my special requests. I completed the ruse with a tweed hat. I thought I looked rather grandfatherly.

He parked the car around the corner and we walked together toward the house, keeping our heads down, looking like we were supposed to be there. No one recognized us and when we crossed the barriers no one told us to stop.

I knocked the handle of my wooden cane against the McNights' front door. After a few seconds it opened a sliver and a woman's face appeared in the space between. "Yes?" she asked curtly.

"Ma'am," I said, "we're not reporters."

"At least not anymore," David corrected.

"We've spent the last fifty years—"

"Five years."

"The last five years researching a series of abductions we believe may be connected to your daughter's kidnapping."

"She's not my daughter. Erin's my niece. Family's inside." The woman, a rough-featured young thing with bad hair, sized up David. Obviously, she hadn't seen the reports of his arrest on TV—the family had been too busy talking to detectives. "I know you," she said. "You're David Neff. The Trimble writer."

"That's me."

"You think this is Trimble?"

"No. Not at all."

"Then who do you think it is?"

"Could we please come in and speak to the parents?" asked David. "We really do want to help."

She told us to wait a minute. She closed the door. There was a muffled conversation inside. Then the door opened again and a tall man stood there. He had a long forehead and a voice not quite as deep as James Earl Jones, but close. "Mr. Neff," he said, shaking David's hand. "I'm Casey McNight. Please, come in."

Erin's mother sat in the living room, rummaging through a box of family photographs. She was a thin woman with shoulder-length fire-red hair. Her face was splotchy and red, puffy from a night of crying. "I know it's in here, Casey," she said. "I just saw it the other day."

"Hon, these men want to help. This is David Neff, the writer guy."

She looked up briefly, then went back to digging in the box. "I'm Jo."

Casey directed us to a couch. "She's looking for a full-length picture of Erin's body. For perspective. Height and such. FBI want it."

"It was a soccer picture," said Jo. "The one where she's kicking the penalty shot. I just . . . here it is!" She held the picture aloft as if it were a talisman that might bring her girl home. She picked up the phone and dialed a number as she stepped into the kitchen. Casey sat down in a chair across from us.

David pulled a notepad from his satchel. "Mr. McNight, can you start by telling us what, exactly, happened yesterday? How did you realize your daughter was missing?"

"She was at the park with her friend Meghan. Meghan Hill. Meghan says a white van pulled up next to the swings where they were talking. Guy leans out, asks Erin if she has seen his dog. She wants to know what kind of dog, right? Well, this guy tells her he has a picture of it, so she goes to the van and before Meghan even realizes what happened, Erin's thrown in the back and the van is racing onto I-90. Boom. Zoom. Gone."

"What did the guy look like?"

Casey handed David a copy of a police-artist composite sketch. The paper was still warm from the printer's. The sketch was that of a white male, forty to fifty years old, weird hair, thick glasses. Sort of looked like John Denver. The resemblance to the composite sketch of Katy's would-be abductor, a sketch that did not exist in this universe outside the one I still had in my possession, was spot-on.

"Plates?"

Casey shook his head. "Meghan's only ten. She didn't look for it. She was scared out of her mind."

Jo returned from the kitchen and hung up the phone. "They're coming back for the photo," she said. She sat next to her husband and snatched up his hand.

"Mrs. McNight, what was your daughter like?" asked David. "Did she have a lot of hobbies? What was her daily routine during the week?"

She looked hesitantly at Casey. "I don't know if we're even allowed to be talking to you. The police said not to talk to reporters."

"What can it hurt?" asked her sister, from the doorway.

"Let me be honest with you, dear," I said. "As a journalist who's been doing this for most of his life, I've seen a lot of cases like this. I study them, actually. It's my speciality. There's a very short window of opportunity for us to find your daughter alive."

Jo sobbed loudly, but there were no tears and she didn't turn away.

"The police are going to do their thing and that's fine. But they're limited by the law. They need search warrants. They need probable cause. They can only lie in certain situations. We are not bound by those codes. I'm willing to play dirty if it means getting Erin back to you."

Jo nodded.

"She didn't change her routine or anything like that," said Casey.

"She played soccer," said Jo. "Lately, she'd go to the park with Meghan after school. There's a small group of kids that hang out there. Erin had a little crush on a boy named Martin who is in the sixth grade. He sometimes goes there, too."

"Have you, as a family, done anything different in the last week?" asked David. "Did you go to the movies, a particular restaurant, any strangers in the house, anything like that?"

A flash of recognition lit up Jo's face. "The handyman," she said. "We called a guy to come in and patch up a leak in our roof. About two weeks ago, right?"

Casey nodded.

"Do you remember his name?"

"Harold something," said Casey.

"Harold Schulte?" David and I asked in unison.

"That's it," said Jo. "How did you know?"

David was already packing up his notepad and standing up. He wanted to get to the car.

"He was already a suspect in another murder. Another red-haired girl," I said.

"Oh, my God!" said Jo. She let go of her husband's hand and dug her nails into his arm.

"The holy fuck are you doing here?" said a gruff voice from the doorway.

It was an FBI agent past his prime, a scruffy-looking gentleman with a white handlebar mustache. He gave me a passing glance, then stepped over to David. I learned later that this was retired agent Dan Larkey.

"What's wrong?" asked Casey.

"What's wrong? This man is charged with murder. I want to know what the fuck he's doing here. What did you tell him?"

"I didn't kill my wife," David said. I could tell he was one insult away from assaulting the man.

"He was asking questions about Erin," said Jo.

Jumping to conclusions, Casey leapt up and grabbed David by his shirt. He knocked him into the wall. "Where were *you* yesterday?"

"Mr. McNight," said Larkey, pulling the father off David, but slowly. "Neff was in lockup when your daughter was taken. The only thing he's here for is publicity. That's all. He's just a snake, slithering out from under his rock to make some money off your daughter's tragedy. Another book, right, Mr. Neff?"

"I'm not writing a book about their daughter," David said, adjusting his shirt.

"Then why are you here?" asked Larkey.

"I think she was abducted by the same man who took Elaine O'Donnell."

"Based on what?"

"The girls look a hell of a lot alike. Both abducted by a man in a van at a park by their home."

"Phhhhht," Larkey said, waving his hand. "Go play private dick somewhere else."

"Wait," said Jo. "He helped us remember something important. There was a handyman here a couple weeks ago. A guy named Harold Schulte. Mr. Neff said he was a suspect in Elaine's abduction."

Larkey stopped short, as if slapped. He turned back to David. "Is that true? Was Schulte here?" he asked. His voice had changed. There was no longer even a hint of sarcasm.

"Yes."

"Well." Larkey cast his eyes to the living room carpet, thinking. "Well, let me make some calls, all right? If it checks out, it's a home-run lead." He looked at David in an odd way.

"Are you going to talk to this guy Schulte?" asked Casey.

"I have to check it out first," said Larkey. "I have to verify the information. I have to talk to the SAC. Maybe a judge."

"Jesus. What if she's there right now?"

"It's not that simple, Mr. McNight."

"For you," I said. I nodded at David and he started for the door. Larkey made brief eye contact with me then. It was hard to say for sure, but I think I detected the slightest nod from him. A simple nod of permission.

Larkey understood that he was mired in red tape and that we were free to do as we pleased.

I followed David outside and a minute later we were headed west toward Rocky River.

David's cell phone chimed a mile from Harold Schulte's house, which we were able to locate quickly online. It was Katy.

"Can we talk?" she asked.

"Yes," said David. "I'm sorry. I should have called. Have you been watching the news?"

"Just saw you on TV. My dad is fucking pissed about me being mixed up in all this. Thinks you're robbing the cradle and breaking up my marriage. For a couple days he thought you had some private investigator tailing him. He's paranoid. But, you know, you are charged with murder."

"I didn't kill anyone and you're not married."

"Duh. But things got sort of complicated. I've got Ralph over here leaving necklaces and shit in my mailbox. Sobbing voice mails. I don't know if I should get a restraining order or take him back."

"Kate, I can't talk now. But I'd like you to come meet me later tonight. Can you do that?"

"I guess. Just talking, though?"

"Do you have a pen?"

"Uh, okay. Go ahead. We're not meeting at your house?"

"Nope. Here's the address." I listened, stunned, as David gave her the address of my secret hideaway.

He hung up and gave me a crooked smile.

"Planning a reunion?" I asked.

"It's time she learned what you did for her," he said. "Life is too fucking short for games. And you could use a little gratitude."

I laughed. "But it was never about saving Katy," I said. "I was obsessed about an answer, not a solution."

"If that was the case, you could just as easily have decided to confront her killer when he dumped her body. You would have had him red-handed."

I sighed. I hated myself. "The only reason I came back far enough to see the abduction was because it gave me two chances to see who did it, or so I thought. The first chance was the abduction, the second was the dump site. That's all I was thinking."

"If all that drives us is some pigheaded need to learn who committed these crimes, then why did the Man from Primrose Lane save Elizabeth's life on the cruise? Why did he care anymore?"

"Her life became his obsession," I said. "As much as her death was the obsession of her would-be murderer. It's a perversion, David. It's about control. Don't you see? We stalk these girls, too."

THE UNIKS

They caught up with me a mile from the western edge of the Cleveland quarantine. I heard their banshee screams from above as they honed in on the unique biometrics of my body. It sounded like a dozen modems suddenly beginning to communicate with their Internet provider: disorganized electrical conversations suddenly merging into one common language, a binary patois with only one paragraph and purpose: *Find David Neff. Stop David Neff.*

We call them uniks. But they're really UNICs. As in, Universal Nanobots for Identification and Capture. Built by Lockheed. Programmed by attorneys general. They are about the size and shape of a hockey puck, able to fly through use of graviton fields. Before they are launched from the warehouse of the Bureau of Criminal Identification and Investigation in London, Ohio, the biometrics of the target are uploaded into the machines. They have no reasoning ability, no negotiating parameters. They find targets and stop targets. They do this by crashing into the fugitive and sticking to his body. Once contact is made, a barbed hook shoots from the machine into the fugitive's flesh. Then the nanobot's graviton field turns in on itself and, to the fugitive, it feels as though the machine suddenly weighs seventy-five pounds. They travel in packs of twelve.

A unik's purpose is to immobilize a public enemy long enough for the nearest understaffed police precinct to catch up. But sometimes there are unforeseen problems. I once wrote about an escaped con who had attempted to evade capture by swimming across a lake when the uniks caught up with him. The machines attached themselves to him over the middle of the lake. His body is still at the bottom, somewhere. Severely thin fugitives have been crushed to death. My death would not be so quick. No police officer would venture into the quarantined zone to place me under arrest. If the uniks got me inside the boundaries of the quarantine, I would be pinned to the ground, or to the seat of the tow truck's cab, and I would eventually die of starvation. There was no hiding. If I tried to duck into some fortified building, they would hover outside the exits until I ran out of food and water. Time meant nothing to them. They would wait through eternity for me, and I didn't have that long.

On rare occasions, fugitives have "beaten" the uniks. There are, actually, several ways in which this can be accomplished, but each method is fraught with such risk that many criminals simply stop running as soon as they hear the machines approaching. One such way to avoid detection is to "alleviate" your biometrics. Sane people call this *death*, as it requires a temporary end to your thought patterns and heartbeat. If you have someone in the medical profession you can trust to revive you after three minutes, you will awake to find the uniks have given up the chase. Some have successfully altered their biometric patterns by performing amateur lobotomies. A third method is electrocution. If you wait until all twelve uniks are attached, you can electrocute yourself. An electrical impulse of sufficient strength can short-circuit the nanobots' graviton field and, if you survive, all you have to do is pull their barbs out of your body and go on your merry way. I had planned to use the stunner to achieve this. Events in Cleveland had waylaid those plans.

I slammed on the brakes.

The uniks screamed and whirled past me in a dark swarm.

I clicked the lever for the truck's hood, then reached behind the driver's seat and grabbed the jumper cables. I hopped out of the cab.

The machines course-corrected and came for me.

I was opening the hood, a semblance of one last idea playing in my mind, when the first one hit me in the small of the back. *THUNK*. The barb shot into my skin, missing my spine by a fraction of an inch.

"David Joseph Neff, you are under arrest," the nanobot said in a loud prerecorded voice. "Please arrange yourself into a safe and comfortable position. Your mass will greatly increase and it may be some time before an officer of the law will arrive to take you into custody. Five, four . . ."

I attached one end of the jumper cables to the truck's hydrogen battery.

". . . three, two . . ."

I clamped the black cable to the fingers on my left hand, gripping the red pincers by the protective handle, daring myself, trying to find the nerve to do it.

". . . one."

The sudden weight of seventy-five pounds knocked me to the ground. The red cable fell from my grip and dangled a foot off the broken pavement, a few inches in front of my head. I reached out for the metal teeth with my right hand but it was suddenly hit by another unik. The barb pierced through my hand like a wooden nail, crucifying me to the pavement. The machine's graviton kicked on, the weight crushing my palm nearly flat. I screamed.

Then a series of uniks pounced on my outstretched legs, my other arm at the elbow, and my buttocks. A dozen uniks were upon me, holding me completely still with 900 pounds of pressure distributed across my 160-pound body.

I stared straight ahead at the dangling cable for some time, getting up the nerve.

You know how when you step into a swimming pool that first day of summer, how pushing yourself into that freezing water feels like torture? How it feels to make yourself sit in the doctor's chair for a root canal? Multiply that by a hundred million and you'll come close to understanding the apprehension I felt at that moment.

I blew at the cable.

It jostled in the air a little.

I blew harder, as much as I could manage with such weight upon my chest.

The cable began to swing.

Every time it arced to me, I blew again, and, slowly, it came nearer to my head. Forty, fifty times. I began to feel light-headed.

I blew again. This time the cable's metal claw collided with the aluminum bumper of the truck as it arced back, shooting hissing sparks into the air. It came at me but missed my forehead by a quarter inch. I blew as hard as I could.

Again it collided. The sparks were brilliant fireworks.

I wondered if I would ever wake up.

The cable connected with my face at the bridge of my nose. The circuit completed. I don't remember pain. Just the taste of copper filling up my mouth and coursing down my throat. And then all was blackness.

I awoke in the darkness and I was not alone.

Ten feet away, a mangy dog with matted hair bared its teeth and approached with a pensive growl. I saw its eyes and its vague shape reflecting the cancerous pink glow of the city behind us. It meant to eat me. But it had thought I was dead.

"Get out of here!" I screamed.

The dog tucked its tail between its legs and danced away into the night to feast upon mutant rabbits and blind rats.

I tugged the black cable off my bruised left hand. I bled from a dozen superficial wounds where the uniks had cut into me but the machines were lifeless, fried. One by one I plucked them off, too, pulling bits of skin away as I did. My right hand got the worst of it. I had lost a lot of blood from the wound there while I was unconscious. A pint, maybe more. If I hadn't woken up as soon as I did, it's possible I could have bled out. I wrapped it in a piece of fabric I tore from my shirt. Still, I barely felt the sting of the cuts for the constant throbbing of my brain. It felt swollen and molested inside my skull, worse than a migraine. My nose felt like it was broken.

I was more concerned about the truck at the moment. It was no longer idling. If it had run out of gas while I lay unconscious, I was in a load of trouble; it was a long walk to Tanmay's home in Vermilion and I would have to leave the black egg behind.

A bit of luck: it had stalled. When I turned the key, it kicked to life again. Soon I was, once again, headed west.

Tanmay was waiting.

His large cabin sat on a cliff overlooking a Lake Erie no longer inhabited by edible fish. Nothing but retarded walleyes in there now. When it rained or snowed, you weren't even supposed to be outside.

"I was becoming afraid, my old friend," he said, as I pulled the tow truck and the Cushman into his large unattached garage and work space. "Your name is all over the news. The Slipstreams are reporting that you surely met your demise inside Cleveland."

"Almost," I said.

"Oh, my, look at you."

I looked at my reflection in the truck's side mirror. The light of the garage showed the damage done by the jumper cables. That jolt to the bridge of my nose had given me two black eyes.

"You should see the other guy," I said. Then I thought of the truck driver burning on the bridge and felt bad. Of course, I hadn't forced him to rob me. "You think you'll be able to figure this thing out?"

Tanmay looked at the black egg. He stepped to it and ran his hand along its sleek exterior. His middle finger found an indentation near the top that, when pressed a certain way, caused the egg to produce an audible *POP!* The top shuddered open and back on hydraulic hinges, revealing an interior lined with soft white velvet. Appropriate. It would be my coffin for decades. "Yes, I think we'll get 'er going just fine," he said.

Less than an hour later, we sat at his kitchen table. I picked at some naan his wife had set out before going to bed.

"I transferred the fee to your account this morning," I said.

Tanmay nodded. "It is too much, David."

"What do I need it for? I'm not coming back. You're putting yourself at great risk. And it would end up being split among my ex-wives otherwise. Believe me, no probate court is equipped to deal with that mess."

"It is appreciated. I do hope you find what you're looking for."

"Me, too."

He handed me a leather case containing a single syringe. "The egg is quite simple in design. Army-issue, I think. A switch and a trigger to turn it on. Another to turn it off. From what I can tell, there's enough juice in the lithium battery inside for one run. Enough to activate the field that causes it to travel back through time and to deactivate it. One trip. A shot of this," he said, pointing to the syringe, "will put you to sleep. I have patched in a digital timer on the arm of the chair into which you will strap your arm. It is essentially a very expensive egg timer. It's set to go off in thirty-six years, fourteen days, and some-odd minutes. When you reach that point, it will deliver the antidote into your bloodstream, waking you up from your hibernation. You will have to deactivate the egg manually *before* you get out. I'm frightened to imagine what may happen if you climb out of a machine as it is traveling backward in time."

"And how do I get out once it's sealed from the inside? It looks hermetic."

"It is. To keep out contaminants, I suppose. Tesla was quite crafty." Tanmay stepped to the counter and picked up what I first assumed to be a partially disassembled flashlight. He clicked a switch on its side and suddenly the nose of the tool erupted in a shower of sparks. I shielded my eyes from the light it emitted but there was still a bright orange glow in the background of my vision for the better part of twenty minutes. The air around it smelled of alfalfa. "It's a cutting tool. A crude laser welder."

"It's a light saber!"

"I don't think so, no."

"Anything else?"

"Yes. You must know that there is no data to completely predict the effect such a long hibernation will have on your system. You will surely be disoriented when you awake. Your mind will be mushy. Your brain will attempt to rediscover its old connections and neural pathways, but some may have deteriorated beyond repair. It may take a while before you feel like yourself again. Your muscles will have atrophied. Walking will be difficult and painful, if not impossible, for several days. You will be covered head to toe in your own waste. The body does not stop entirely while hibernating. Your body continues to ingest nutrients—from your stored fat—to the tune of about a pound a year. During this time, it also excretes a black, thick dung—have you ever seen a baby's first bowel movement?"

"No."

"It is this same black gunk, this tarlike shit. It will, over the course of decades, envelop your body. You will find it very difficult to scrub off."

"That's a hell of a side effect."

"And there is one very dangerous probability to consider. The digital timer, and the fail-safe I designed for you, may become damaged. I know not the impact time travel has on my equipment. I tell you this so you can know the risks involved."

"What happens if the timer fails?"

"You will remain in hibernation forever," he said. "And eventually your body will consume itself."

It's more difficult than you might think to find a decent location to turn on a time machine. I was planning to return to 1999. I had to consider what might have existed at that location thirty-seven years ago. For example, I couldn't park the egg in an abandoned building because I might open it in 1999 to find myself in the middle of a busy Walmart. Cleveland would have been a safe place, relatively speaking, if not for the fact that Cleveland had still been a living city until 2019.

There were other things to consider. What if somebody came by the place where I had parked the egg? Say, in 2003, when I was still hibernating inside and traveling backward through time? Would they see the egg at all? I had seen the little egg in Tesla's laboratory, so I thought they would. Could they open it and ruin the whole experiment? When their arms entered the egg, would the limbs be ripped from the person's body and sucked into the past as their torso remained anchored to the present?

I had to find a place that no one would have visited between 1999 and now, 2036. But how are you supposed to find a place that no one knows about?

I was standing outside Tanmay's house, leaning against the Cushman, which had been recharged and re-tired, thinking about these terrible things as I checked my rucksack for the last time. I had packed $50 in change—mostly quarters—from the time period, as I figured paper money would surely deteriorate; flint and steel wool in a small metal box; a laminated topographical map of Ohio; various notes from Katy's case file, wrapped in plastic and shut tight inside another metal container (in hindsight, I guess I could have put the money in there). That's when I happened upon the inside pocket, a secret pocket I had not used for so long I had utterly forgotten it existed. Something was inside.

I could smell the earthy sweetness of old tobacco, an exotic aroma these days. (Congress finally outlawed nicotine products in 2018.) If I was caught with this pack of Marlboros I would face a $2,500 fine. Of course, if I got caught now, that would be the least of my worries.

In the glove compartment of the Cushman, I found a pack of matches behind a wad of napkins. The matchbook was from someplace called the Spitfire Saloon and looked as old as the cigarettes. The first one snapped off, but the second match lit. I touched it to the tip of the crinkly Marlboro and inhaled deeply. A small flame remained on the very edge of the cigarette tip, but it seemed to work just fine. I felt the hot smoke singe the lining of my lungs. The pain was welcome and tolerable. It reminded me of my very first cigarette, of which I had partaken inside the musty confines of Jake Johnson's canvas tent during a summer at Camp Ritchie in 1989. That first taste had been just like this.

Camp Ritchie had closed a year later and the Boy Scouts of that district were transferred to the new camp down the road a pace. Old Camp Ritchie was still there today, a creepy ghost town of a summer camp, its latrines and dining hall covered in a thick coat of kudzu vines. There was some reason the land could not be developed, something to do with the local water table. I had seen some pictures of the ruins on the lesser net a couple months before, on the site of a group of ghost hunters. State had purchased the property from the scouts and put up NO TRESPASSING signs, but the ghost hunters snuck in easily enough.

I took another drag and smiled.

It took nearly five hours to drive from Vermilion to Camp Ritchie, in Loveland. A long time alone in the night. I listened to the satellite feeds of the brazen assault on Tesla Laboratories. A spokesman for the NFBI kept telling reporters that what I had stolen was a prototype for a new thermal generator. They said I planned to sell it to Canada on the black market—President Soros never missed an opportunity to promote hostility along our northern border. Around two in the morning, the spokesman reported that the uniks had taken me down in Toronto, and Canada was refusing to acknowledge the event. A military response was being weighed. And so it goes.

In the darkness, I thought, too, about the old legend told by firelight on the shores of Lake Donahay, at Camp Ritchie, "The Ballad of the Loveland Frog." According to the older scouts who took turns telling the story, a mythical and ancient creature roamed the woods around Loveland and along the Little Miami River. In the days before white men, the Shawnee Indians spoke of a monster that looked like a frog but walked like a man. It was covered in a slimy black ooze and was impervious to pain. They called it the Shawnahooc, or "river demon." Adding credibility to the story was the tale of the Loveland police chief who, they said, was murdered by the monster when he came upon it lying on the side of Twightwee Road in 1986, electrocuted to death by some laser weapon the frogman had in its hand. The Loveland Frog, the older boys said with remarkable authenticity, liked to eat little scouts who wandered away from their troop.

The story had terrified me as a boy.

I pulled onto Twightwee as the first rays of my future-most sunrise peeked over the foothills of southern Ohio. The brush had grown up since I had last passed this way, but it was still recognizable. I was nostalgic for the summers spent here, smelling of briny lake water, entire days spent exploring the forests. I almost wished I could go back far enough to see it again. But then, Tanmay had already set the timer, hadn't he?

Just beyond the bridge on the Little Miami, a quarter mile from where the tall-timbered entrance to Camp Ritchie once stood, I brought the Cushman to a stop. For a second I worried about what to do with the vehicle, thinking if someone found the Cushman, they might search the woods and find the egg. Then I had to laugh. Forget the Cushman. Let them search. The egg—with me inside it—would have vanished by then, as it traveled backward through time.

Once I got the black egg off the truck bed, it was surprisingly easy to maneuver. The ground was soft, a bed of nettles, and it rolled manageably between the rows of towering pines.

How far in should I go? I figured far enough so that the vehicles passing by on Twightwee wouldn't be able to see it from the road. Once I lost sight of the pavement through the trees, I went another hundred yards to be safe. Safe from what? Fuck if I knew.

I came upon a wide pine and hoped placing the egg behind it would ensure a little more than a modicum of safety. I was momentarily surprised to find what appeared to be another black egg propped up against the back of the tree. But then I remembered Tesla's demonstration and relaxed. This, of course, was my egg, already traveling backward through my timeline.

I carefully placed the egg against the pine. It was absorbed by the egg already resting there until they became one in appearance, but two in reality. One in wave form. It made my head dizzy.

My heart raced as I fingered the lever that unlocked the time machine. The top drew back with a long *hisssssss*. I placed my satchel snugly under the wide cushioned chair that took up most of the space inside. Then, with some effort, I climbed in.

It felt nice. Still, sitting in the same position for thirty-six years had to cause nasty bedsores. Had Tesla or Tanmay taken that into account?

I thought I remembered reading somewhere that Tanmay's hibernation cocktail prevented every kind of infection but I had a horrible image in my mind of waking up with an abscess where my ass once was. Did the machine roll or wobble to prevent that? Tesla must have considered this and built something into the lining to stimulate muscle retention, right? But I didn't know for sure. The egg didn't come with an instruction manual.

There was an odd smell, too. Almonds. Some kind of antiseptic in the lining of the fabric? Maybe.

I took a minute. I was quite concerned, to tell the truth. I imagine I felt much like those first astronauts who strapped themselves to the tops of intercontinental ballistic missiles rigged to go into space instead of go boom, but boom they sometimes went. I knew there was a decent probability I could die in that egg, my body traveling back through time for . . . how long? It didn't need juice to run. Just to start and stop. So, really, if the machine was noncorrosive and sealed airtight, could my remains hitch a ride to the moment of creation? Actually, this was a somewhat comforting thought. At least my death would be some kind of adventure.

"Stop."

My hand on the hatch, I looked up. Ten feet from the black egg was a policeman, dressed in black. He had gray hair and a white beard. His sidearm was drawn and pointed at me. A nameplate on his breast said CHIEF EVERETT BLEAKNEY, III.

"You're that man from the news, David Neff."

"I am."

"Mind telling me what you're doing in Loveland, sir? And what this thing is?"

"It's a time machine. I'm going back to 1999 to stop a little girl from being murdered."

His brow furrowed. "Step slowly out of the machine, Mr. Neff."

"I won't. I'm sorry," I said. "You can see I'm unarmed. This machine is no threat to you. You will not shoot me."

"Get out!" he shouted.

I pulled the hatch down. As the world was shut out, I saw him rushing toward me.

With a dull *THUNK* the lid closed. For a moment there was darkness, and then there was light, a dull glow from behind the fabric. There was a *hisssss* as the hermetic seal shut tight. A mechanism clicked on and began its perpetual job of scrubbing carbon dioxide from the air and converting it into breathable oxygen. The sheriff beat against the egg. I needed to hurry, in case he could damage it. *Had he followed me?* I wondered. *Or had he somehow known where I was going?*

I secured my right arm into the contraption Tanmay had rigged with the antidote and timer, which, I saw, was counting slowly backward. With my free hand, I withdrew the hypodermic needle from the leather case and popped off the top. The liquid inside was a fuzzy yellow. With little hesitation, I injected Tanmay's cocktail into my vein. I let the needle drop to the floor.

Then I clicked open the little cover over the toggle that controlled the egg. It was in the "forward" position. I clicked it down and snapped the cover back into place.

The lights dimmed. The pounding from the outside seemed to slow down, then stop, then begin again for a few moments. These new beats were strange and odd-sounding, like an echo of a sound. Somewhere, I heard my own voice twisted in reverse, "Eeem atoohush atawun li-aw oouh."

A few minutes later, all was silent.

I was wondering when I would feel the effects of the medication when I realized I could no longer move my head. Seconds after that, my vision blurred and I knew nothing more for years and years and years.

David pounded loudly upon the door to Harold Schulte's shitty little apartment in a forgotten corner of Rocky River and I braced myself for the confrontation.

"Who is it?" came a pale and shaky voice from behind the door.

"It's David Neff," he said. "I want to talk to you about Erin McNight."

"I don't know who that is. I have a cold. Go away and come back tomorrow."

This time I rapped my cane against the door continuously until Schulte opened it. The chain was still attached and his bulbous head peeked through the space between. He was a pasty-faced man, bald on top, with patches of spindly white hair hanging in clumps just above his large ears.

"I really cannot talk right now. Would you please come back tomorrow?"

"You did some work at the home of Elaine and Elizabeth O'Donnell," said David, "just before Elaine was abducted, and you recently worked at the McNights', and now their young girl, Erin, is missing."

"That's very sad. I'm sorry to hear that. But I didn't have nothing to do with it. Or the O'Donnell girl. The police told me I was cleared."

"Then you wouldn't mind if we took a look around your apartment."

"Go away," he said and began to close the door.

I slipped my cane into the open space before he could shut it. I only meant to buy more time to convince him to *let* us in, but my younger self was, apparently, still full of the youthful vigor and impatience I had tempered over time. David kicked the door with enough force to pop the latch and send Schulte tumbling to the floor.

"Christ," I said. "Get in there before someone calls the cops."

David walked in and I hurried behind, flipping the door closed behind me.

"Don't hurt me!" said Schulte, crawling backward under a dining room table that looked like it had been salvaged from some old-lady yard sale.

"Shut up, Harold," I said. "We're not going to hurt you."

The apartment was immaculate and smelled of some powerful cleaning agent. A plastic-covered couch faced a box TV set from the seventies. On the wall hung pictures of Schulte's youth, dozens of framed photographs of himself as a boy with ratty hair, tinted in that scummy-orange style of seventies-era cheap film stock. David walked down the hall to the bedroom.

"Anything back there we don't want to find?" I asked.

"I told you, I didn't have anything to do with Erin's abduction. Or Elaine's."

"Hey, uh . . ." From the bedroom, David stumbled on his words, groping for an appropriate name to call me. "Hey . . . um . . . hey, get in here."

I looked at Schulte.

"It's not what you think," he said.

I walked to the bedroom to see what David had found.

It was not Erin's dead body but it was quite disturbing. I'd call it a shrine, I guess.

It was a square room, about ten feet wide. Enough space for a bed and a desk. The walls were covered, I mean *covered*—floor to ceiling—with pictures and articles about the singer Chrissie Hynde. A picture of her in threadbare jeans, taken at some after-hours party when she was about seventeen. Glossy photos clipped from the pages of *Rolling Stone*. Chrissie lying supine on the floor at Swingos in Cleveland, giving the finger to the cameraman. A two-page article from the *Plain Dealer* about her rise from local phenom to national rock star.

"Harold," I called. "What the fuck is this?"

Schulte picked himself up and waddled over, his arms hanging like vestigial limbs at his side. He looked at the room and simply shrugged.

"You've got a little obsession going on here, don't you?" asked David.

"Maybe I do," he whined. "But obsessions aren't illegal, are they?"

"Depends on how close you're getting," I said. "How close did you get to Chrissie, Harold?"

He shrugged again and looked at his feet, pale white little feet with hairy feet knuckles.

I had a hunch he had gotten very close, once. "Harold, did you try to abduct this girl when she was little?"

He looked up at me, his eyes wide with fear. It was the look of someone who has had his mind violated by an alien probe.

"You did, didn't you?"

"I didn't *do* it."

"Well, obviously you didn't. But why didn't you?"

"It was just a thought. I wouldn't have hurt her. I just wanted to do something nice for her. I was going to buy her a present. She liked to talk to me on the phone. I was her friend. I just wanted to meet her. Her skin looked so soft. So soft and smooth."

"And what happened?" I asked.

"You can't arrest me for a thought."

"No, we can't. So what happened?"

"I was going to meet her. To pick her up. She said she would let me take her shopping. It was going to be our first date. She waited for me in front of that farm. The one that was replaced by the shopping mall? I left my car around the corner, in case anyone she knew was watching. They wouldn't have understood. I wasn't going to hurt her."

"But someone stopped you, didn't they, Harold?"

He looked at me closely. "How did you know?"

"Did he look like me?"

"No. He looked . . ." Schulte searched his mind for images. "He looked a little like if Fox Mulder, that *X-Files* guy? Like if Mulder had a brother who got kind of fat. He grabbed me and shook me and said nasty things to me and I got away and drove away and I never saw him again."

"Did you think Erin had soft skin, too?" asked David.

Schulte shook his head. "Besides, she was a redhead."

"So?"

"I don't like redheads. Not like that. My mom was a redhead. That would be gross."

"Where were you yesterday around three o'clock?"

Schulte stepped to a skinny dresser. He snatched up a folded piece of paper sitting on top, next to his wallet. He handed it to me. "I was at Wade Park. I go twice a week for counseling."

The paper was a deductible receipt from Wade Park and time-stamped 3:04.

I shook my head. How could a creep like this guy be connected to so many girls yet not have anything to do with the crimes? I hate coincidences like this. It always muddies the water. Erin was still out there, somewhere. "Come on," I said to David.

"Stay away from Chrissie Hynde," he said as he passed Schulte.

"I'd never hurt her," he said.

"Sure you wouldn't."

"I'd like to propose something," I said, as David drove the Caddy back to the compound in Peninsula.

"This should be good," he said. "Got another perv we can rough up a little while we waste more time?"

"We should talk to Riley Trimble."

David laughed. He glanced at me sideways. "Trimble's still locked up in a psych ward. He's watched twenty-four/seven. And this isn't exactly his MO."

"Oh, I don't think he abducted Erin. I think he might be able to tell us who did."

David was silent for a moment. It began to rain that hazy, foggy rain, a gray curtain falling upon the world. Depressive weather. I was worried for him. I knew well the turmoil that grows inside us while we're still young.

"All right," he said. "At least it'll feel like we're doing something.

We're past visiting time today, but I can set it up for tomorrow. I have to warn you, Trimble is no Hannibal Lecter. He's smarter than he looks, but he's still white trash. A selfish man. He has no reason to help us."

"You might be right. But he's the only one we know who understands the mind of the man we're hunting."

Later that evening, while David sat in the den reading through the files on Katy's murder, Mr. Merkl dropped by with a container of rigatoni and a giant salad he'd made at his house. Aaron stopped by, too, but only long enough to pick up his check and my weekly list of demands. Soon we were alone again, listening to the steady drumming of autumn rain against the westerly windows, waiting for Katy.

"I'm not sure this is such a hot idea," I said.

"My mind is too full of secrets," said David, not looking up from the papers in his lap. "I need someone else to know."

"It's cruel."

"She's a big girl."

It was useless arguing. So bullheaded I'd been. No wonder I had had so many wives. Only a woman as steely as Elizabeth could keep us in check.

Five minutes after eight there came a light knock on the door. I followed David to the entryway, hobbling forward on my cane, feeling older than ever—in fact, I was no longer entirely sure how old I was. I always got confused when I tried to do the math. Since I did not age during the hibernation, I should have been about seventy. But I looked older than that. Certainly felt older. Maybe I *had* aged a little in the egg. A year for every seven, perhaps.

He opened the door and there she was in a cotton dress that reached her ankles. Her hair was tied up in a bit of ribbon. When she saw David, she growled and jumped onto him, grabbing him around the waist with her long legs. She wore black Crocs, I saw. Katy planted a kiss on his lips and then hopped down. "Hello, David," she said.

"Hi," he panted.

She looked over at me, and for the first time in many years I felt that excitement in the pit of my stomach I used to get when spotting a beautiful woman across the room, one I wanted to dance close to at a wedding reception, in the dark, where we could whisper introductions into each other's ears.

"Hello," she said. "You must be David's father. I can see the resemblance! Holy cow, you guys look a lot alike."

Katy shook my withered hand. "Hi, Katy," I managed to say. "Are you hungry? We have supper waiting in the kitchen."

"I'm famished," she said.

As we walked to the kitchen at the back of the house, she marveled at the paintings and tapestry.

"Holy fuck, this is a big fucking house," she whispered, taking David's hand.

We sat on stools around the island. David and I ate the rigatoni warmed up a bit; Katy ate hers cold. She was telling a story about how her father was angry with David, asking me what I would have done if a daughter of mine had run off with a famous author a few months before a wedding, when she suddenly stopped midsentence.

"I know you," she said.

We let her work it over.

"You're so familiar. Your voice, too. Did you ever live in Cleveland Heights?"

"No," I said.

"Huh. Ever come into the Barnes & Noble at Chapel Hill?"

I shook my head.

"It'll come to me," she said. "It's right . . ." Her eyes widened in true horror. She backed away from the island, stumbling against the refrigerator. A copy of William Carlos Williams's "This Is Just to Say" fell to the floor. She looked at David.

"It's okay," he said. "Kate, it's okay."

"But you're dead," she said to me. "You're that guy from the plaza, the one that beat up the other guy. You're the Man from Primrose Lane. You're dead!"

David stood up and put an arm around her.

"He's *not* your dad," she said.

"No. He's not. But he's not the Man from Primrose Lane, either."

"So, his twin or something? Somebody help me out here. I feel like I'm going crazy."

"Have a seat," said David, pushing her toward the stool. She obliged in a dreamlike way.

"Who are you?" she asked.

"I'm David Neff," I said. "I'm him, in about forty years. I came . . . I came back in time to save you. That man from the plaza took you and killed you. I came back in time to stop that. But he got away."

Katy looked at David, her eyes welling up with tears of frustration and anxiety. He nodded.

"That was the short version," David said, leaning close to her, pulling her eyes to his with a comforting look. He put a hand on her chin, letting her feel him, know that he was there and all was safe. "Katy, do you want to hear the entire story?"

She swallowed. "I . . . I always knew there was something. I've always, my whole life, I've felt like I was standing on the sidewalk under a piano tied up in a rope that was about to break. This. None of *this* ever felt real. I always felt like I was cheating, just living. I did. Holy shit, David. How long have you known?"

"Not long," he said. "It's okay if you don't want to hear it right now. Do you need some time?"

"No," she said. "Give it to me. Tell me what was supposed to happen."

It took the better part of an hour to finish the tale. By then we'd consumed the pasta as well as a bottle of wine. Katy listened intently to every word, interrupting here and there for more detail. When I was through, she and David took a breather on the wraparound porch while I cleared the dishes. I felt a pang of jealousy but brushed it aside with some concerted effort.

It had stopped raining and the stars were out. The air smelled like a riverbank, like renewal. David leaned against the railing while Katy fished inside her purse for an old cigarette. She put a Salem in her mouth and lit it with a lime-green gas station lighter.

"It's like one of those dreams, the ones where you've done something so wrong it'll change your entire life and when you wake up you feel grateful that you're still okay," she said. "But I'm not waking up from this one, ever. Why did you tell me?"

"I'd want to know if I were you," said David. He watched her draw in the smoke, her mind inward, searching. "Did I do the wrong thing?"

"No. I don't think so."

She was quiet for so long then that David knew what she was going to say when she started talking again. "I can't be with you," she said.

"Why? Because it's too strange now?"

Katy shook her head. "It's against nature. It's not right. It was never meant to happen."

"Maybe it was," David said. "Maybe we all have a . . . a destiny or whatever. And maybe, if we have free will, maybe the only thing that can alter that is ourselves. People. Maybe this is what was supposed to happen if that man hadn't abducted you originally."

"And what about Elizabeth?" she asked. "What was her destiny?"

In truth, he hadn't thought about that. Elizabeth's death was so real to him he hadn't considered, in light of the revelation of her murder, that she had a destiny cut short, too.

"You see," said Katy. "Your life has become so convoluted, you can't tell what it was meant to be anymore."

"*I* haven't tried to change history," he said.

"But you want to," she said. "I can tell. Didn't you listen to him? Again and again and again this happens. Elizabeth, me, now this other girl, Erin. What if she's dead, too? Will you become so obsessed with finding her killer that you'll go through the same routine all over again? Get back in the time machine, come back, live this weird hermit life? When is it over?"

"We'll find this guy," he said.

She sighed. She took his hands and looked him in the eyes. "You think you will. But you never do. That's the point of this whole thing. It's endless. You have to stop it."

"I can't."

"That's why I can't be with you, David. I'm going back to Ralph, if he'll take me back. I'm going to forget most of this, if I can. I need to."

"Is that going to make you happy?" he asked.

"It will. In time. He's a good man. I was happy before I met you."

David nodded. He averted his eyes. He looked out at the universe and imagined a world out there in which this conversation was not taking place. "I love you," he said.

"Don't say that," said Katy.

Through the window, I watched her go. She didn't look back at him and she never waved goodbye to me.

David stayed the night, wrapped in a blanket on the couch in the den, surrounded by his ex-girlfriend's homicide file.

I wanted to hug him. Tell him everything was going to be all right.

But that felt weirdly self-indulgent. And so I went to bed and cried some, too.

We got an early start the next morning, with few words passing between us over a breakfast of bagels and lox prepared by Merkl. We arrived at St. Sebastian's Home for the Criminally Insane shortly after ten o'clock.

The hospital was a sprawling brick enclave surrounded by a high barbed-wire fence near Tappan Lake, in central Ohio. It had been the county hospital until 1975, when the state swooped in and snatched it up to house inmates too dangerous to live among the general population at Mansfield and Grafton. There were separate wings for those criminals committed by the state and civilians committed by private institutions pushed beyond their means to deal with their unique troubles. Its only entrance was a double gate controlled by two sentries.

A guard waved us inside the paddock, where we waited in the Cadillac while the first gate closed behind us with a shudder and the second one opened. There was but one space for visitors, directly in front of three cameras, beside the entrance to the main building. Through the barred windows on the second floor, bald men in orange jumpsuits watched our every move. One of them was jumping on his bed. A floor below him, a woman rubbed her breast against a window.

A skinny woman in a taut gray suit awaited our arrival on the front steps. She had straight black hair, freshly clipped, and she pursed her lips when she saw my cane. An insurance liability was all I was to her.

"You didn't say anything about a companion, Mr. Neff," she said by way of a greeting.

"This is my editor," said David. "John McGuffin. John, this is Renee Habersham."

"You really should have cleared this with me."

"Is it a problem? Because I'd be happy to speak with the director if you—"

"No problem," she snipped. "This way." Habersham turned on her dangerously tall heels and clunked toward the doors. We followed slowly and she had to wait for us every few feet until she was rolling her eyes openly at my feebleness. To be honest, I did play it up a little. "You'll have to check your satchel, Mr. Neff," she said as we reached a security checkpoint at the beginning of a long dark hallway.

"I'm afraid I can't do that," said David. "The whole point of our visit is to go over the documents I have in here, with Riley Trimble. You're welcome to go through it if you like, but I'm sure you'll find no contraband. This was all okayed by your supervisor yesterday."

"Well, I've never allowed reporters through with their equipment."

"Oh," said David. "I see the misunderstanding now. I'm not a reporter. I'm a *writer*."

"Is there a difference?"

"Yes. Writers get to take their shit in there."

Habersham recoiled. The surprise only lasted a split second before it was replaced with cool loathing. "Very well, Mr. Neff. You seem to know your way around. I have priorities of my own to attend to." With that, she walked away.

"Aren't there safety instructions we need to hear?" asked David.

"No," she said, without turning around or slowing her pace. "We only do that for reporters."

"You always did have a way with women," I said.

"Tell me she doesn't remind you of our stepmother," he said.

"A little."

"Well?"

"Well, come on, then, let's go talk to this homicidal maniac."

At the far end of the corridor, a long hallway that smelled of watery diapers, a bald man in a blue jumpsuit sat by himself, staring out at Lake Tappan beyond a wall of glass. His ankles were cuffed. His left wrist was secured to his chair. He bit at the nails on his free limb. He turned to us as we entered.

Trimble's frame had withered, his body a shell clinging to his skeleton. His veins stuck out from his long neck, like baby snakes wrapped in cheesecloth. There were open sores on his face. His eyes registered no emotion, those black-as-charcoal eyes. He smiled. A large toothy smile full of rivulets of drool.

"David!" he shouted. He tried to get up, but the chains snapped him back into the chair. "David! I'm so glad you came to visit!"

"Hello, Riley," said David, sitting in the leather armchair nearest the serial killer.

"My cat told me you were going to come see me soon."

"They let you have pets in here?"

Trimble put a finger to his mouth. "Shhhh."

I took a chair beside David, measuring the man, trying to gauge how much was game and how much was real.

"Riley, another girl is missing," said David.

Trimble laughed loudly. "Not me, not me, Your Honor! Not me! I been locked up tight. You put me here."

"I didn't put you here."

Trimble looked sincerely confused. "No?"

"No, Riley, you did."

"Right!" he said. "Right, right, right." He clapped a hand over his mouth. "Shouldn't have said anything. Mom told me not to. But you tricked me. You . . . you trickster, you."

"Doesn't it feel better now that people know? Now that you're not hurting people anymore?"

"It feels better when I take my pills! One pill makes you smaller. One pill makes you tall! Yessir. They got this one, ooooooweee. Rivertin. Good shit. Good fucking shit!" He leaned forward in a conspiratorial way. "But they forget to tell you that your pecker stops working."

"Riley, I need your help. Do you want to help me? Do you want to help a little girl?"

"A little girl?"

David looked uneasy. If we showed this killer Erin McNight's picture, were we then somehow responsible for what Trimble might do with that information?

"Show me," he said. "Let's see. Is she pretty?"

David looked at me. I knew what he was thinking. I shared his concerns. But we had few leads. It was worth a little risk, wasn't it? I nodded for him to continue.

David opened the satchel and took out Erin's school photo.

"Oh, yes," said Trimble. "Purty. Wow. Nice freckles. Sun-kissed. Love that."

Over the next couple minutes David told Trimble the particulars of the case as we knew them. Trimble listened intently, but never looked up from the picture.

"A serial killer," he said. "You think it's a serial killer. You do. You wouldn't be here if you didn't. So where's the others? Show me more. Don't hold out."

Reluctantly, David fished inside his satchel for the photos of Elaine and Katy.

"Okay, I see. I see. A *redhead* killer. Did you question Charlie Brown? Ha! I always preferred blondes, you know. The Redhead Killer. Sounds like a book. Are you writing another book, David? Are you out to trick this guy, too?"

"This girl is still missing," said David, pointing to Erin's picture. "She might still be alive. If you help us find her I'll make sure people know you helped. I need you to think about the man who did this. Do you have any idea who took her? Who's been stalking these girls? Did you ever meet anyone out there . . . ?"

Trimble took another look at the batch of photographs. I noticed a look of recognition spread across his face like a wave, and then it was gone, shielded. He'd seen something. Some clue we had missed. Then he turned the photographs around, one by one, and pretended to examine the back.

"Spending a lot of time trying to solve this one, David?" he asked tauntingly. "How long will you keep digging before you give up?"

We both knew the answer was *forever*. Trimble, it seemed, believed that was a kind of sentence in itself. He smiled at David, handing the pictures back.

"Are you done?" David asked.

"Yes."

"Do you have any ideas? Any theories? Where should we be looking?"

"Why?" asked Trimble. "Are you going to transfer me to some secluded nuthouse on the beach? Why don't you let me out of here?"

"You put yourself here, Riley."

"Of course I did. Of course."

"Are you going to help or not?"

"The problem with you is you were never willing to put yourself in my shoes. Never willing to consider what it felt like to be me. That's a lack of empathy, my friend. A sociopathic tendency."

"I don't want to have sympathy for a serial killer."

"Look at those pictures, tell me what you see."

David flipped through the photographs. "I see girls with red hair. Freckles. I see a man's fetish."

"Now look at them again," said Trimble. "But this time imagine that these girls are not girls, but women, and your only reason for living is to find them and *have* them. How would you do that? How do you find such *specific* specimens?"

David considered the picture of Erin for a minute, then put the photos back into his satchel. "I don't want to do that, Riley. I don't even think I can."

"You know you can. That's why you're afraid to try."

"You're not going to help us?"

Trimble smiled. "I've helped you already. But I'm not going to do all the work for you."

I had grown impatient with the games. "Who is it, Trimble?"

For the first time, his gaze turned from David to me. Looking into those dark eyes was like trying to look at negative space. "Who are you?"

"His name's John McGuffin."

Trimble giggled. "Oh, okay. Right."

"Trimble, tell us what you know," I demanded.

"You know, I was not nearly as obsessed with those girls as you were," he said, turning to David again. "Isn't that ironic? Those girls don't haunt me. They haunt *you*."

"Come on," said David, standing up.

"Wait!" said Trimble. "How many people have you found who knew each of these girls?"

"A couple," said David. "A handyman. A principal, maybe."

"Then I'll tell you that there's at least one more," he said.

"Who?"

"You're looking but you're not seeing. Let me out of here, David. You could do it. Yes, you could. Let me out and I'll get him for you tonight. Isn't Erin worth that much?"

"Riley, you had yourself committed. All you need to do is walk out the door."

Trimble waved a finger at us. "I know you make them keep me here. All that money from that book goes right to this hospital."

"I don't believe you," said David. "If you knew who took this girl, you'd want to tell us just so we could catch him before he beats your old record. This guy keeps killing and you won't be the most dangerous man in Ohio anymore. You'll just be another dumb criminal who got caught."

For a second Riley opened his mouth to reply, then snapped it shut.

He grinned at David. "You and your tricks," he said. "So tricksy, David. But good try."

"He knows who it is. Or at least thinks he does," David said when we were back in the car.

"I disagree. I think he's trying to get a rise out of you. It was a stupid idea. I'm sorry to have pushed you into it."

"You don't know him like I do. He knows something."

"If he does, he's not sharing."

David looked out at the country road rolling beneath the Caddy. "She's dead, you know," he said after a while. "She has to be by now."

"Maybe. Probably."

Just then David's cell phone rang. He answered it and spoke for a couple minutes. I didn't listen to the conversation. I was too preoccupied thinking about Erin McNight's torture at the hands of her faceless abductor. I'd had my hands on him in 1999. If it hadn't been for my bad knee . . . I was far too old to go around the block another time. All that risk, that dangerous trip across the wastelands of Cleveland, for what? Katy's life. In exchange for how many others? Slowly, I became aware of David's agitated state. His sentences had become clipped and short. There was concern in his voice. And his eyes were welling up with tears. My first thought was that Tanner had gotten into an accident, and my heart skipped a few beats.

"What?" I asked as he hung up the phone.

"That was my . . . that was our mother," he said. "Uncle Ira is dying. He put a shotgun in his mouth this morning. He's on life support at Akron General. And they found a note in his pocket. A letter addressed to us."

REVELATION

The journey felt instantaneous. Like going under to get your wisdom teeth removed. One moment I was drifting off to sleep in 2036, the next I was becoming aware of my consciousness again.

The world was hazy, dark, as if I were looking through thick nylon. I could barely see the control panel set into the egg. The timer attached to my arm beeped like a shrill alarm. I tried to unbuckle the strap with my free hand but discovered my limbs no longer moved. My first thought was that my muscles had atrophied beyond mobility. That would surely mean a slow death inside the egg. I concentrated all my willpower to move that free hand and soon I heard a sickening, tearing sound, the sound of a diaper pulling away from the bottom of a soiled kid who has spent too much time in the sun. I was covered in secretions, a chrysalis made from mucus, semen, shit, blood, urine, wax, mold, hair, tears, old skin, sweat, vomit, and pus. *Enshrined.* The smell was thick and powerful, even though the scrubbers still churned in their mechanical slots. It smelled something like apples gone to rot over a pile of cow patties, like spoiled cider resting in a forgotten cup inside an outhouse.

I heaved, but, of course, my stomach was empty. The act of heaving brought with it the realization of an overwhelming hunger and thirst. Hunger unlike anything I've experienced. Gnawing hunger, *insane* hunger.

I am ashamed at what I did next and can only admit to it because I was unable to control myself. I began to eat my way out of the mess. The thick film tasted like crusted snot, dried blood, like scabs. And not everything was hardened, oh, no. Much remained congealed under layers of caked bile, like some hellish nougat. I devoured the twisted black crisps that were my fingernails; they pried easily away from the fingers. I worked my way out until my upper body was freed enough so that I could unbelt myself from the timer, though my skin remained covered in a sticky black tar.

The pounding in my temples, that constant drumming of *hunger, hunger, hunger,* subsided as my body began to digest its leftovers, its first meal in a long damn time. With some effort, I found the switch and turned off the machine. There was a gentle shudder and then silence. I felt below, where my satchel had been placed, but the leather had been swallowed up by a slimy white moss. I cut away at the fungus until I could get at the items inside. There it was, the laser cutter. It felt heavy in my hand. Anxious to breathe fresh air, I switched it on. A bright fountain of high-energy sparks erupted from its nose, crackling like a Tesla coil. I brought the end against the top of the egg and went to work, cutting a slash into the hermetically sealed chamber. There was a *POP!* and a rush of air as it broke through to the outside. I smelled cedar and grass and water.

Thirty seconds later, the lid was off.

I grabbed the lip of the egg with one hand and then the other. I tried to stand but could not feel my legs. I knew I was not paralyzed, however, because when I kicked a foot against the shell I felt pain: dull and distant, but there. It took some time to roll my body over the opening. I crashed to the earth and, if not for the soft bed of nettles, might have broken something. Slowly, inch by inch, I pulled myself up and leaned against a tree, the laser cutter still in my hand. There was a bright flash of torment as a disc in my spine shifted into place. I cried out, "Ahhhh-hhnaaaa!" My voice sounded muffled and deep—partially blocked, I figured, by the same black ooze that coated my body.

Movement out of the corner of my eye. A man stepped from behind a tree. *Impossible,* I thought. Impossible or not, it was the same man who had tried to stop me from entering the time machine in 2036. I recognized him. Although now the man was barely yet a man. He wore no beard and was still skinny from the casual exercise of the young: fucking and sports. He pointed a gun at me again.

Who—or what—did he think I was? And then I got it. Suddenly every-thing made sense. Suddenly that old campfire tale from Camp Ritchie became a horror story all my own; *I* was the Loveland Frog. Me and all the other me's who had traveled further down the river of time, blindly chasing their own personal obsessions.

I tried to tell him to stop, but talking was not easy. The simple effort of pushing air through my voice box was like blowing into a water bal-loon. All that came out was, "Nahop. Nahhh oppp!"

And then he shot me. Right in the goddamn knee, blowing apart my patella as if it were a skeet shell. I collapsed to the ground. "You . . . dumb . . . motherfucker," I said, quite clearly—apparently anger was more useful to my numbed body than fear. My sudden English so unnerved the young man, he turned tail and disappeared toward the roadway.

It was a long way back to Twightwee Road. About half a mile. A long way for someone with barely any muscle mass, longer still for someone who has just been shot in the knee. I thought there was a decent chance I would die there in the woods, dead in the far past, my body picked over by woodland creatures and scattered about the old camp in pieces. I didn't think I had enough energy to push myself to the road. And I was losing a lot of blood.

I looked back. The egg from which I had emerged was now wrecked, lying on its side with a hole gouged into its top. There was, I noticed, no other black egg. I had expected to see one. I recalled that demonstration by Tesla. Shouldn't I be able to see the black egg I had come in, still in-tact, with me inside traveling backward through time? I couldn't work out this riddle until much later. I didn't know what it meant at the time, but for some reason its disappearance filled me with optimism.

Then I heard footsteps, crunching their way toward me with a pur-pose. *That'll be the young policeman come to finish me off,* I thought. Somehow, I could live with that. I had, after all, gone the distance. I had come this far. I had overcome physics. I had given the universe a big, *Fuck you!* hadn't I? I could take a little pride in that.

It was a young man, but not the policeman. He had red hair and a spattering of freckles across his nose, the beginning of a beard along his jawline.

"Oh, my God," he said. "Are you okay?"

"Shhhot," I said.

"Is that stuff contagious?" he asked.

I shook my head. "Nnno. Just gr-gross."

The young man helped me to my feet and put an arm under one of mine and around my shoulders. "My name is Albert Beachum," he said. "My boss sent me down here to pick you up."

"Who's your boss?"

Albert laughed. "I don't know. Never gave me his name."

I was too exhausted to care. He dragged me toward the road. He really was very strong for such a thin teenager.

By the time we got to Twightwee, I knew I was going to lose consciousness. A large RV was parked on the other side of the road. Albert walked me to it, opened the door, and helped me into a large bed set up inside. He wrapped a bandage tightly around my knee. The bleeding had subsided quite a bit. I think the goop helped seal the wound quicker than blood alone. I felt myself drifting off. Before I fell asleep, I gripped his arm tightly.

"What?"

"Bag. In egg."

"I'll get your things," he said. "No worries."

I was asleep before I saw him leave.

It was night when I awoke, the RV speeding north on I-71. We had just passed the Lodi exit, an hour from Cleveland, if that's where we were heading. The thought of seeing the city alive again lifted my spirits. God, I loved Cleveland in the springtime, the wind whipping off the lakefront, filling the narrow spaces of the city with negative ions and the aroma of freshwater. I sat up in the bed, against the wood-paneled wall. I watched the cars drive by, trying to discern from their design if I had arrived at my correct destination. "Smells Like Teen Spirit" played on the speakers. I felt a sense of unease. By 1999, Nirvana had faded from popularity, if I remembered right.

"Albert?"

"Yes, sir?"

"What year is it?"

The boy looked at me in the rearview mirror and quickly decided I wasn't joking. "It's 1996. June seventeenth."

Somehow I had overshot my target by about three years. *That's what I get for taking a prototype*, I thought. Except it wasn't a prototype, was it? No. There had been *hundreds* in Tesla's hangar.

"Does that disappoint you?"

"Not really," I said. I had waited decades for an answer. I could wait four more years. "Where are we going?"

"To my boss's place, in Akron."

"Oh."

"You're disappointed."

"I was hoping to see Cleveland."

"Well, it's not going anywhere."

I let him believe so. "Who is your boss? I know you don't know his name, but who is he? What does he do?"

"I thought you might know."

"Nope."

"Huh."

"Strange job you have."

"You have no idea. If you're feeling up to it, the bathroom is set up for you. Warm shower and everything."

"Is it that bad?"

"You smell like my grandpa's farm when his alpaca caught a blood disease."

"I think I can manage. This knee's going to have to be looked at."

"We have a plan."

"Of course you do."

By now you know that Albert's boss was the Man from Primrose Lane. In hindsight, I should have known, too, but at that time the only answer that made sense was that, at the end of this road, I would find Tesla's house waiting for me. *Somehow, he must have followed me,* I figured. Whoever it was, I didn't really care, because they were obviously nice. They had greeted me with this warm bathroom, they had arranged to have lava soap, tomato juice, chlorine, Palmolive, and even some gasoline which I could use to work the blackness off.

Once I got going, it really was not so difficult. The bottom layer of funk was mostly a hardened layer of skin—not unlike a cicada's shell, I noted—that came off in long bunches like peeled sunburn. I sat under the shower until the water ran out, scrubbing the shell off me. When I was finished, I scooped up the mess that clogged the drain and put it in the trash.

It felt like coming back to myself, like coming home. I felt like a warrior preparing for an epic battle, a gladiator cleansing himself before climbing the stairs to the Colosseum.

Albert had set out an array of snacks and beverages, of which I partook with gluttony. I should have known then, because it was all my favorite stuff: Coke, Twizzlers, beef jerky, sour cream and onion potato chips, those little caramel creams, fresh plums, even a Taco Bell burrito. Underneath it all was a pack of Marlboros, and that's when I figured it out. I knew who it was because it was not just any pack of Marlboros, it was *my* pack, wrinkled and yellowed with age. I was riding in an RV filled with goodies, three years ahead of my intended arrival, going to meet myself. Somewhere, in some other timeline, I had made this journey before and ended up further in the past than 1996. Why? Who was this version of me obsessing about? Certainly not Katy, right?

Understanding time travel and its ramifications is a bit like going insane. There is a point of no return you must pass before you can accept as fact these things others would call delusions. It's an uncomfortable line, and one that must be crossed on faith alone. I had jumped over that line when I stepped inside that egg. I knew things would get weird. Just not *this* weird.

There was only one thing I could do. *Enjoy the ride.*

I lit a cigarette with a match from the tin next to it. It was the second-worst cigarette I'd ever had. And it was wonderful.

We were nearly to Akron by the time I stumbled out of the bathroom and made my way to the passenger's seat. I crumpled into the soft leather chair.

Albert turned his head to look at me and almost lost control of the RV. "Shit!" he said. "Are you guys twins? You told me you didn't know who my boss was."

"I do now," I said.

"So, what? Brothers?"

"Yeah. Yeah, he's my brother."

"How long's it been since you've seen him?"

I shrugged. I didn't really know a safe answer for that.

He was quiet for a while but he just couldn't help himself. Even the best of confidants reach their end. "What was that thing in the woods?"

"The black egg?"

"Yeah, that thing. It looked like that spaceship Mork from Ork crashed down in. Is that what it is, a spaceship?"

I laughed. "Is that what you think we are? Aliens?"

"I wouldn't be surprised. He's as strange as you are. Are you reading my mind all the time?"

I sighed. I was already making things worse. "Would your boss like it if you were asking me all of these questions?"

And he was sober again. Staring intently at the road. "Course not. I got distracted. Sorry."

"I'm not . . . we're not aliens."

"Okay."

"Okay."

Albert was a mile down the road before I even got to the front door. It's a good thing I had remembered to grab my things.

I was reaching for the knocker when the door opened for me. Even though I had expected it, I was unprepared to see myself in the flesh. He stood there in the doorway, the Man from Primrose Lane, and regarded me with a weary expression of welcome. My head felt tingly, as if it were trying to figure out if this was some joke, or if my soul had been ripped from my body to look back on itself. A sense of vertigo nearly overwhelmed me. I staggered forward, against the threshold, bumping my lame knee against the catch.

"Come in," he said.

If you can't trust yourself, who can you trust, right? I followed him in and he closed the door behind us.

He offered his hand, covered in a blue and white mitten. "Hello, David."

"Hello, David," I said.

The Man from Primrose Lane didn't laugh. He reached into his closet and brought out a new pair of brown and tan mittens. "Better put these on," he said. I did as instructed and followed him into the living room, a high-ceilinged chamber whose windows were obscured by the stacks and shelves of paperback books. The smell of dust and glue and old paper was so powerful I wondered if it could be toxic. I sat on the only chair, set against a tiny desk in the corner, beneath a light. The Man from Primrose Lane sat on the hardwood floor and crossed his legs.

"I'm sorry," he said. "Can I get you some water?"

"I'm fine."

He nodded and looked at me the way a hawk looks upon its prey from a distance. "Why are you here?" he asked.

"To find the man who killed Katy Keenan in 1999," I said. "Why are you here?"

"To find the man who killed Elaine and Elizabeth O'Donnell in 1989."

"How'd that go?"

"Not well. One of them was still abducted and the man got away."

"You saved the other one?"

He shrugged and then said something quite odd: "We'll see."

"Are you frightened of me for some reason?" I asked.

"Yes."

"Why?"

"I'd rather not say."

"How did you know where to find me?"

"The *where* wasn't hard," he said. "I came back via Loveland, too. So did all the others, I think."

"So, there are *other* us's? I mean, others . . . others of us?"

He nodded, running his tongue along the inside of his mouth.

"How many?"

"Lots. See 'em every once in a while."

"But, then, how did you know *when* to come and get me?"

"Got a guy in Loveland, listens for me. I pay him five hundred dollars a month to just listen."

"I don't get it."

"Something about the machine shifting from backwards to forwards again causes a weird noise. Not quite a sonic boom. Deeper. Heavier. Been thinking about that a lot. I think, if you recorded an explosion and played it backwards at the slowest speed, with the bass turned up real loud, it might sound like that. Anyway, this guy calls me whenever he hears it and I send down one of my Sherlock ruffians."

I nodded. I knew what he meant. "How many trips to Loveland since you've been here?"

The Man from Primrose Lane said, "Eight. But sometimes there's no one there."

"I don't want to think about that."

"No. I know."

"So what do you do now?"

"I'm still looking for him."

"I'm familiar with Elaine O'Donnell's case," I told him. "It's quite possible there's a connection."

"I'm sure he'll kill again if he gets the right opportunity."

"Do you want to help me get him?"

The Man from Primrose Lane didn't say anything for the span of thirty seconds, a long time in a room like that; I could hear the squirrels in the walls. "I don't know if I can trust you," he said.

"What the hell do you mean? You're *me*."

"No," he said. "Not quite. Very different experiences shaped us following the events of 1989, when I saved Elizabeth and the universe split in two."

"Well, how different could we be?"

"How's Cleveland?"

"Empty."

He nodded.

"Why don't you trust me?"

"Been thinking about that day in the park when I tried to save the two little girls. I had all the time in the world to prepare. I thought I had plenty of time. I was still late. Though it's possible he was early. And if he was early, the only explanation is that he knew about me. I think . . ."

"What?"

"I think it's possible we're tracking a time traveler. I think it's possible I might be tracking myself."

"Come on. We couldn't do that. We wouldn't."

"I don't know how else to explain it."

"Didn't you see the guy?"

"Briefly."

"Did he look like us?"

"I don't know. Maybe not. But I couldn't see him well enough to tell if he was wearing makeup. Hell, if he came from the future, he could have used one of those Morph-tronic plugs Hollywood was abuzz about in the twenties."

"Well, it's not me."

"No. I mean, I don't really think so, I guess."

"Besides, it's never that complicated."

"Right."

"It's got to be someone you've overlooked. Some regular Joe with a deep dark side."

"I know the profile," he said. "But I should have had plenty of time to save the girls. I don't know how to explain that."

"How did the other us's do? Did they stop their crimes from happening?"

He shrugged. "Dunno. They never came back to tell me how it went. We tend to keep our distance."

"I've got another problem."

"Yeah," he said, looking at my knee. "You'll need ID before you go to the hospital. Can it wait?"

"The bleeding's stopped because of that black junk, I think. But it hurts like a motherfucker."

"You're three years early, too. Those eggs don't work so well over long spans. Something gets jiggered in the process. There's like turbulence or something. One fella we picked up was actually two days too *late*. Imagine that. Poor guy. Jumped off the Y-Bridge."

"Do you have someone who can help with identification?" I asked.

The Man from Primrose Lane held up his mitten-covered hands. "Got a man in Pennsylvania. It'll cost you. Course, I could lend you some money. Would that be a soft-money exchange? Would they call it laundering if the feds knew?" He giggled. "The only thing all those movies and books got right is time travelers really can make a killing on the stock market."

"When can we . . ."

"I'll have Albert take you in the morning," he said. "Let me show you to your room."

"Actually," I said, "do they still make ham and pineapple pizza around here?"

"Of course," said the Man from Primrose Lane. "I've got a delivery-man who leaves it on my doorstep if I set out the right amount plus a five-spot. I think he thinks I'm a leper. I always see him wiping his hands when he walks back to his car."

———□———

Uncle Ira lay in a beige hospital bed inside the wing of Akron General reserved for the hopeless. I stood with David in the hall, peering through a large window into his room, at our mother, sitting beside his bed, holding his hand. This sight, I should say, struck me as quite odd, given the fact that our mother was not his kin. I had always believed Uncle Ira was a Neff, our grandfather's brother. This day, we were learning, was full of revelation.

On the drive to the hospital, David had called our father to see how he was dealing with the news, only to be greeted with indifference.

"Is the rest of the family already there?" David had asked.

"Why would they be?" our father had responded.

"It sounds pretty serious. I believe he's brain-dead. Someone from the family should be there to make decisions. Why wouldn't you guys want to be there? He was your uncle, for God's sake."

"What?"

"What, what?"

"He's not my uncle."

"What are you talking about?"

"We're not related."

"But we called him 'Uncle Ira.'"

"He was a good friend of your mother's a long time ago, when you were born. Your mom told you to call him 'Uncle Ira.'"

"But he looks like a Neff. That *nose*."

"Yeah, I guess," he said. "But we're from Ravenna, David. Everyone from Ravenna looks pretty much the same."

David and I didn't discuss it but I'm pretty sure we were thinking the same thing and wishing it wasn't, couldn't, be true.

Our mother looked up, saw David, and came to the door, shaking her head and her long raven hair as if to compose herself.

"Come in," she said.

David stepped toward the door and I remained in place, glancing around at the hospital art.

"Both of you," she said.

"Excuse me?" I asked. My good knee suddenly felt as wobbly as the lame one.

"I know who you are," she said.

I tried to speak, but something caught in my throat. Once, many years ago, I had sat in this hospital and watched our mother die from the effects of an aneurysm that would occur in March of 2016. I missed her so, even if I sometimes wondered if she wasn't the real reason I fell in love with women I could never save.

"Then I would very much like a hug," I said.

"Of course, David," she said. "Of course."

"I first met him in 1967, when I was nine," our mother said. "I was walking home from school, down Water Street, and this old man grabs my arm and drags me into this abandoned mill. We were covered in this white dust but he was sweaty, so there were patches of wet around his chest and under his arms. He smelled like . . . like spoiled oranges. Something about that smell scared me more than anything else. It was like I could smell his intention and I knew he was going to kill me. After he was done with me.

"But just as he's got me against a wall and started to reach under my skirt, this other man shows up. From nowhere. He grabs the old man, pulls him off me. And I watched . . ." She paused to stifle a sob. "I watched Ira kill the man. Strangle him. 'He needed killin' or he wouldn't stop,' he told me. 'He would have killed you, but not soon.'

"And he left me there with the dead body and eventually I walked to a pay phone and called home. The police told my parents that it was a couple drifters. One had killed the other. Simple as that. Must have been a drifter that killed him, they said, because the man didn't stick around to explain himself or take credit for it.

"When I was sixteen, I was walking out of a movie theater in Canton when I literally bumped into him again. He was alone, coming out of the same movie. I was with a friend. I recognized him immediately, which he saw. 'Are you living a good life?' he asked me. I told him I was, thanks to him. 'Good,' he said. I asked him out to coffee, the first time in my life I ever asked out a man, and he thought about it. He looked about fifty years old then. Old enough to pass for my father. He told me that would be okay.

"So we started meeting. Once a month, at Brady's, in Kent. We started sleeping together when I was nineteen. That was my doing. All my doing."

"You were with my dad when you were nineteen," said David.

She laughed in a way that raised the hackles on my neck. "Ira was very clear that if we were going to have that kind of relationship, I still needed to date people my own age, to treat him like he didn't really exist. 'Don't count me in your decisions,' he used to tell me. He should have told me who his father was but we never talked about his personal life. Said it was full of stupid pain, that the only thing he ever did that amounted to anything was saving me.

"Well, everything turned upside down during the blizzard of '77. Your father and I were at your grandmother's cottage out on Berlin Lake. Stranded for three days. Nothing to do but eat, sleep, and, well . . . you know. A few weeks later, I discovered I was pregnant. Figured you were conceived during the storm. I was so excited, I went to Ira's house with the news. He was so happy for me that he cared to ask about my boyfriend. When I spoke your father's name his skin went dead white. I thought he'd had a heart attack. I was so frightened by that reaction, and he was so numbed by the . . . revelation, that he told me everything.

"He told me he was a time traveler. That he'd been a writer who had obsessed over my unsolved murder for decades and he had traveled back through time, giving up his real life to find the man who had killed me. Except that wasn't enough of a shock, right?"

David's skin was pallid now. My heart beat so loudly I heard it in my ears.

"'Fearful symmetry,' he called it. Ira's own father was my boyfriend. In the timeline he'd come from, Ira's father had married some lady named Mary. Mary had given birth to Ira. By saving me, Ira changed all that. Ira's father, *your* father, met me instead of this Mary."

David shook his head. "So, Ira is my . . . what? Half-brother?"

Our mother ignored David and looked over to me. She assumed correctly when she figured I had the years and experience to see a little further than my younger self. "I think it's a little worse than that," I said.

She nodded and looked away.

"I don't get it," said David, looking at me. "What?"

"Ira is actually our father," I said. "Isn't he?"

She began to cry. She couldn't look at us. But she gave a muffled, "Yes."

The man on the bed, the man who, genetically, was akin to a half-brother, was also our real biological father. Which made the man we had always believed to be our father . . . our grandfather? It was enough, I thought, to break my mind.

The slow drone of the machines kept the quiet away until the doctor came by to turn them off. Uncle Ira went with a soft sigh that sounded like relief.

On the way out, David stopped by a kiosk inside that dark wing of the hospital to sign for Uncle Ira's body to be transferred to a funeral home, where it would be cremated without a service. Our mother had it in her mind to spread his remains along the banks of the Little Miami in Loveland, as if it were some ancient rite that might settle the souls traveling backward there. She said she was going to take some sage with her to burn.

David caught up to me in a hallway full of drawings made by the hands of child cancer patients, an unsettling place. "Look at this," he said, holding up a clear plastic bag. Inside were Uncle Ira's personal effects: his bolo tie; a severely wrinkled pack of Marlboros; his wallet, containing a little over $5,000 in cash; one of those pens you can turn upside down to see a woman lose her bikini. Also inside was a sealed envelope labeled: *Davids*.

"Great," I breathed. "Open it, then."

David did. It was a college-ruled piece of writing paper. His eyes scanned it and he whispered, "Hurm."

"Read it to me," I said.

"'David. Forty-five years ago I let my obsession take my soul. It was as complete as any demonic possession and just as dangerous. I allowed it to happen, piece by piece, welcomed it even, because I thought it was for the greater good. It was not. Too late, much too late, I have come to realize that all I have done was pointless. I thought I was increasing the good of the world, when, if anything, I added to its misery. Everything happens for a reason, David. I now believe that if you try to alter fate, you will be damned just as I am. Let it go. Whatever you're doing, whatever adventure has led you to be charged with murder, let it go. If they lock you away forever, be thankful that your imprisonment might cause this endless cycle to finally quit. I thought you might be different, having solved your case, having Tanner. But it has become clear to me, watching the news, seeing you with that other *you*, that you have caught the bug that eventually leads us to repeat this all again. Please forgive me. I could not bear the torment. So sweet and so cold.'"

David folded the note and stuck it in his pocket.

"You okay?" I asked.

He smiled, but it was a sad smile that wore down his face and made him look five years older. "Is this where we're all headed?"

"What, suicide? Fuck that. Erin is still out there and I want to see how it ends."

"He wanted me to die in prison."

"Then fuck Ira, too."

I wasn't the only one who thought that David would never see the inside of a prison cell. Larkey was waiting for us in the hospital parking garage, smoking a Pall Mall as we approached. His eyes grew wide as he got a good look at me without my disguise.

"Motherfucker!" the man yelled. "I'd think he wasn't dead if I hadn't seen the corpse. You have to be his twin."

"This is ex–Special Agent Dan Larkey," David said. I played mum.

"Am I right?" he asked David. "I'm right, right? Twin brother?"

"He's related," said David.

"Fuck me," shouted Larkey, stamping out his cigarette. "Who is he? I mean, who was the Man from Primrose Lane?"

"I don't think I have to say anything to you without my lawyer," said David.

"What if I said I came here when I heard of your uncle's suicide, that I came here at the urging of my wife to tell you I don't believe you killed anyone?"

"Is that true?"

Larkey nodded.

"Why the sudden change of heart?"

"I've worked homicides for thirty years. You get a feeling for the cold types. The wife-murderers. The serial killers. I had you pegged as a cold SOB, but you're not. You're as confused as we are. I saw that at the Mc-Nights'. As a detective, you look for the easiest possible solution. I asked myself, what's the simplest answer? That the Man from Primrose Lane was murdered by a famous author after he learned his wife was having an affair with him, that the author then staged an elaborate car crash but left the Man from Primrose Lane bleeding all over the house? Why cover up one and not the other? It's impossible to ignore the resemblance between Erin McNight and your wife. The Erin McNight crime occurs as soon as you're arrested for Elizabeth's murder? Fucking weird, right? I believe the real killer was waiting to see what would happen with

the murders out on Primrose Lane. For more than four years, he was
waiting to see if he got away with it. When he saw you arrested, he knew
he had, and he immediately went after his prey. Isn't it much more likely
that one man is responsible for the murder of three women—Elaine,
Elizabeth, Erin—who look so much alike? Yes. It's always the simplest
answer. End of speech."

"And Sackett?"

"He's going to need some convincing," he said. "But his case is falling apart. Ballistics came back on your nine-millimeter. Doesn't match.
By the way, it didn't take us long to figure out it's your prints on the gun
and the toilet and not the prints of the Man from Primrose Lane, like he
figured. That puts you at the scene, sure. But my guess is you have an
explanation for that, too."

"So you're here to help us?" I asked. "To work with us to find this
girl?"

"No," said Larkey, standing up. "I mean, you can work on that if you
want. We've got a task force of a hundred and fifty agents sweeping
through northeast Ohio looking for her. If you have some solid leads, I'll
take them. But no more busting down suspects' doors."

"Then why are you here?" asked David.

"I'm here to protect you."

"From who?"

"When it rains it pours, man," said Larkey, rubbing his neck. "I'm
protecting you from Riley Trimble. He killed two orderlies at the nuthouse and escaped earlier this morning."

EPISODE SEVENTEEN

COMING HOME

Back in 1996, I needed a doctor and a new identity.

Albert arrived at the house early the morning after I met the Man from Primrose Lane. We climbed into the back of the Caddy. "To Bellefonte," he told Albert. As we headed for western Pennsylvania, the Man from Primrose Lane shut the privacy shield between the front of the car and the back.

"What's in Bellefonte?" I asked.

"The man who makes our IDs."

"He knows who we are?"

"Of course not. Men like Frank Lucarelli attract attention. Better he never sees us."

It was going to take me a while to learn everything he had about obfuscation and misdirection.

"Are we going to have Albert make the deal, then?"

"No," said the Man from Primrose Lane. "I'd never send Albert into such a dangerous situation. I have someone else in mind."

I waited for him to continue.

He smiled. "As you may have figured out already," he said, "I am not the first Dread Pirate Roberts. Not the first one of us to live on Primrose Lane, not the first Joe King, as it were."

"Another one of us *gave* you his fake identity?"

He nodded. "If you take a good look at my papers, you'll find that I'm supposed to be eighty-five, though I'm not quite that old. I arrived here in 1986 and was picked up out in Loveland by a young man named Tyler Beachum, Albert's uncle. He brings me to the house on Primrose Lane, where I meet the man who lived there, just like you did. He'd come back to stop the murder of a young woman which had occurred in 1971. Point is, he'd made a solid deal with the Irish Mafia out in Philly, IDs in exchange for stock tips. He got me up and running, introduced me to his associates, transferred Joe King's identity to me, and then put me in charge of keeping one eye and ear on Loveland at all times."

"Where did he go?" I asked.

He shrugged. "But before he left, that man, the *first* Joe King, explained to me that we had someone we could go to in Bellefonte directly, if the Mafia contact ever became too dangerous."

"Who?"

"Seems he was left with a little guilt and concern about the original owner of his identity. After a while sitting in that house, he started obsessing over the life of the real Joe King. The identity he'd stolen. Who had *he* been?

"Sometime around 1972, he went looking for Joe King's story. Found his grave in Bellefonte. Learned of the car accident that claimed his life at such a young age. And learned, also, that Joe King had had a sister, Carol. Of course, he had to meet this woman. You can imagine what comes next."

"He had a relationship with Carol?"

"You got it."

"What name did he give *her*?"

"Who knows? He made something up. It's hot and wild, I guess, but their relationship, he told me, abruptly ended in 1973, wouldn't tell me why. But he said if we ever had reason to, we could go to Carol and she would help us because Carol knows the man in Bellefonte who actually makes the fake papers. She was his . . . goomah, I think they call it. His mistress."

"Any other options?" I asked.

"Maybe if I had more time," said the Man from Primrose Lane. "But, your knee. Your goddamn knee."

"It's just . . . I have a bad feeling."

"Get used to it."

Hours later, we pulled into the driveway of a duplex adjacent to the Schnitzel Tavern in Bellefonte. The smell of fresh spaetzle floated into the car and my stomach growled for some. But we didn't eat there and I stayed in the car with Albert while the Man from Primrose Lane walked up to the house.

I watched him through the tinted glass of the window. A woman, perhaps sixty-five years old, with bobbed blond hair and bifocals answered the door and let him inside. We waited. Somewhere inside that house, our secrets were being discussed. I was so nervous my right hand could not stop twitching. Of course, that could have been an effect of my muscles acclimating to agility again.

A knock at Albert's window shook me from my trance. A kid, some college man with a crew cut, was leaning down to get the driver's attention. Albert hit a button and the privacy shield shut again, but stopped before it closed completely, so that I could listen in on their conversation.

"Can I help you?" Albert asked. He was a cool dude. Really was. But there was apprehension in his voice.

"Yeah," said the young man. "What are you doing sitting in my driveway?"

"Your driveway?"

"My mother's."

"My client is a friend of hers. He had an appointment to talk to her."

"My mother doesn't need to be bothered. She's not well. Who did you say your client was?"

"I didn't."

The young man's face was getting red. I admired the son's protectiveness for Carol, but there was a hard edge to his concern and it seemed like maybe this one felt better when he was in complete control of his mother's social calls . . . and perhaps her checkbook, too.

"Spencer!" his mother called from the front door. "Come inside."

The Man from Primrose Lane returned to the car as Spencer shook his head and walked toward the house. I heard the beginning of an argument before the young man disappeared inside.

"Well?" I asked, when the Man from Primrose Lane was back in the car.

"Good news and bad news."

"Okay."

"Good news is, we got you an ID. We have to hole up in Bellefonte for the night, but she'll have it for us in the morning. Express rate, fifteen thousand dollars."

"Ouch. Is that the bad news?"

"No. Bad news is, we'll never be able to use Carol again. She's in the early stages of dementia and it seems like it's progressing quickly."

"Oh."

"A blessing, I think. She's already forgotten who Spencer's father really was."

The next morning, there was a knock at the door to my room in the Bush House Hotel and when I opened it, there was a cardboard box from Lucarelli's Pizzeria lying on the floor. A note was attached: *Don't try to get a license*, it said. *These are good, but not great. I needed more time.*

I'm thinking about writing that last sentence on my tombstone.

Inside the pizza box was a manila envelope. Inside the envelope was everything I needed to open a bank account and to buy stock under the name of Jeremy Pagit. Certainly enough ID to fool a clinic. The real Pagit, I later learned by a diligent search of Centre County records, was born in 1937, and had died at the age of twelve when he climbed atop an oil derrick and attempted to ride it like a horse.

I rented an efficiency at the Statler Arms in Cleveland and, from there, played the market, using a nest egg provided by the Man from Primrose Lane. I invested in Yahoo. Starbucks. Apple. I put $10,000 on the 49ers for the Super Bowl in January.

I got bored waiting.

I had transcribed Katy Keenan's diary and notes from the investigation into several large binders, arranged in chronological order. It was her life, presented in minute detail. I knew where she was, where she would be. I wanted to see her, this girl whose murder had become the focus of my life.

That summer, when she was six, she and her mother took regular trips to the movie theater over in Rocky River. Katy had meticulously collected her ticket stubs in her diary and so I had the dates and show times at hand. I would buy a ticket and sit nearby, sometimes not even looking at them. It was calming just to know she was alive.

I paid particular attention to other men in the audience. I thought, perhaps, that I might catch her killer stalking her, long before the abduction. A familiar face in the crowds. But the only one stalking her, as far as I could tell, was me.

In May of 1997, I went to Kent State for the candlelight vigil dedicated to the slain students of 1970. I went because it was in her diary— Katy's father had taken her. I was so focused on protecting her that I didn't remember I, too, had been there the first time around. I came upon myself, that would be *you*, David, standing in place for William Schroeder in the parking lot of Prentice Hall.

I stood there, making eye contact with my younger self, for just a moment. And somewhere, deep in my brain, I remembered standing there, looking . . . not at an older version of myself, but through the empty space, at the sculpture on Bunker Hill that had been shot up by the National Guard.

Suddenly she was there, too. An eight-year-old with red hair hanging down almost to her knees.

"What's he doing, Dad?" Katy asked.

"He's paying tribute to Bill," the man said. "Standing in his place. My friend. The one I told you about."

"It's so sad," she said.

"It is. Come on, Katy, I want to find my old dorm."

Her father led her off toward Taylor Hall and before you could look at me again, I walked away.

I didn't check up on her much after that. That had felt like a close call. I didn't go looking for her again until a week or so before her abduction, in 1999.

"You think Riley Trimble *knows* who Erin's kidnapper is?" Larkey asked, fiddling with his mustache.

We sat around a large table in the back of a Chinese place in Akron called House Gourmet. The owner was one of Larkey's contacts and she opened the private room with no questions. We didn't order, but were served portions of the most exquisite Asian food I'd ever tasted.

"Just a feeling," said David. "He got an idea when we were sitting there and then he started to tell me that he could catch him if I let him out. I think he does have an idea of who it could be."

"And you think that's where he's going?"

"Yes."

Larkey leaned back and slid a cigarette in his mouth, lit it, and took a long drag. It was, of course, illegal to smoke inside a restaurant in Ohio. He didn't offer David or me one, either. "Why isn't he coming after *you*?"

"I don't think he wants to hurt me," said David. "I've always thought he had a little respect or some mixed-up appreciation for me, for figuring out his secret."

"He said he would hate you forever."

David shrugged.

"Any idea who he might think it is?"

"No."

"Well," said Larkey, exhaling a smoke ring that wobbled up to the ceiling, "let's put it all on the table. We're three smart guys with some inside information on these cases, right?" He looked at me across the table with a slight smile. "For instance, I bet you could tell us a thing or two about the Man from Primrose Lane and who might want to kill him and this guy's wife."

"Maybe," I said. "And maybe there's some information the police haven't released about Elaine O'Donnell's abduction that you could share with *us*."

"I don't wanna see this in some book unless we catch Trimble and the guy who shot the Man from Primrose Lane, all right?"

"Okay," said David.

"Don't fuck me over," he said.

"Okay."

Larkey sucked smoke into his lungs, exhaled, then snubbed out the remainder. "First, let's say what we mean to say, right? We think there's one man out there responsible for the abduction of Elaine—her murder, actually, because her body's out there somewhere even if we haven't found it yet—the murder of her twin sister Elizabeth almost twenty years later, the attempted murder of the Man from Primrose Lane, and the abduction of Erin McNight."

"Right," said David.

"And the attempted abduction of Katy Keenan," I interjected.

"That right?"

"I think so, yes."

Larkey nodded. "All about ten years old at the time. All with straighter than straight red hair."

The lawman's eyes wandered to the wall, where a large ceramic dragon held roost. Finally, he pursed his lips. "Fine," he said. "I'll share it with you. Something about Elaine's abduction was never released."

"What?"

"Little slip of paper found in that parking lot she was yanked away from. Slip of paper with a perforated edge. Number on it."

"Like a ticket from a butcher?" asked David.

"Sort of. But it wasn't. We traced it back to a photo lab in Berea."

"Did you pull the records for whose pictures they had developed? I mean, you had that number?" I asked.

"We tried. But they didn't keep good records. They didn't write the numbers down anywhere. Just matched it up with the photo packet and handed it to the customer who gave them the corresponding tab. We pulled all their credit card transactions for that date, but . . ."

"But how many people used credit cards for small transactions back in 1989?" said David.

"Right. Mostly businesses was all we got back."

I sighed. My blood pressure was beginning to concern me. My heart was beating so hard and fast that my hands undulated with each new pump.

"What do you guys got?" asked Larkey.

"A man using an alias—Arbogast—attempted to track down the identity of the Man from Primrose Lane a few months before he was shot," said David.

"How do you know that?"

"I talked to the man who made the fake IDs. He'd already spoken to this Arbogast guy."

"Don't suppose you want to tell me the counterfeiter's name?"

"Not unless it's important."

"Arbogast," said Larkey.

"It's from *Psycho*," I said.

"Right. So the target *was* the Man from Primrose Lane, and your wife may have just been in the wrong place at the right time."

"One more thing on that front," said David. "The guy who made the ID said this Arbogast guy was driving a van with one of those handicap permits hanging from the mirror. Except the man was in no way physically handicapped."

"That match up with anyone you know?" I asked.

"No," he said. Larkey laid his hands on the table and rubbed them against the wood. "Somebody is connected to all of these girls. There's some common thread we're not seeing."

"I agree," said David.

"What did you tell Riley before he got this 'idea'? What were you talking about right at that moment?"

"I don't know," said David. "The girls."

"What was he doing?"

"Looking at their pictures."

"Here," said Larkey, slapping the table. "Let's see them."

From his satchel, David removed Elaine O'Donnell's and Erin's pictures.

"Katy, too."

David brought her photograph out as well.

"Jesus," said Larkey. "They could be sisters. This man *knew* these girls. Had to."

"It could almost be the same picture," said David. "Even the background's the same."

Larkey looked closer. Each girl sat in front of a blue backdrop covered in fluffy white clouds. Except David was wrong. Even from where I sat I could tell it wasn't the exact background in each one. Erin's school picture had an extra cloud in the top right corner that was whiter than the others.

"Holy fuck," said Larkey.

"What?" asked David, getting up and jogging around the table to where the man sat. I leaned over the table from where I was seated.

"Look," Larkey said, pointing to the upper right corner of Elaine's picture. There was no cloud. Just a tiny black spot against the blue there. Then, Larkey pointed to the upper right corner of Katy's school picture. There was a black smudge there. Not a smudge, I saw. A tear. The background's fabric was ripped a little, worn with age. An imperfection no bigger than a dime. But it was there. And in its place in Erin's photo was a white cloud that appeared whiter than all the others.

"Same backdrop," said David. "The exact same. Someone patched the tear and painted a white cloud overtop of it."

"That list of businesses," I said. "Was there a school-picture company on the list?"

Larkey swallowed and looked up to me. "Fabulous Pics," he said.

David flipped each picture upside down. On the top right corner of each sheet, the name FABULOUS PICS was stamped in ink the color of steel. He turned and ran back around the table to get his bag. "It was the fucking school photographer!" he shouted.

David drove while Larkey relayed directions from the back seat.

"Exit at 480. Go west," he said. The man was on his phone, speaking in harsh tones to the Berea chief of police. "Stay back! Just stay back until we get there!" He hung up and immediately started dialing again. "His photography studio is right in Berea. Small operation. Apparently it's a father/son team. Guy who owns the place, his name is George Galt. He developed Parkinson's about twenty years ago. His son assists him with the photo shoots. Son's name is Dean."

"But who *is* Dean Galt?" I asked.

"No one," he said. "No record of any kind. Not even a speeding ticket. Never married. No home address. He must live with his father. The mother died years ago. Or maybe he lives at the photo studio. The studio has a darkroom, but according to the landlord they haven't developed their own pictures since 1975. They subcontract most of their developing to Dodd Camera in Cleveland but have been known to use News and Photo in Berea, the lab we traced the tickets to. If he's got the girl, he'll be keeping her at the studio, I guarantee it. He's not going to take her into some residential neighborhood. Downtown Berea is pretty quiet after six p.m. Could have walked her in the front door and no one would have noticed. Anyway, we have an agent driving out to the home, just in case." His attention switched back to the phone. "Sackett, it's Larkey. I'm with the writer. We got a lead on . . . Would you shut the fuck up and listen? We got a lead on Erin. You better get up here. Berea. I'm texting you the address." He hung up again. "Hardheaded motherfucker!" he said. He dialed numbers into his cell.

David rocketed toward Berea at eighty-five miles per hour.

Three patrol cars were parked a quarter mile down the road from the Fabulous Pics photo studio, a second-story loft situated over a brewery in Berea's business district, a false-fronted square no bigger than a city block. David pulled beside the cruiser closest to the square. Larkey rolled down his window and leaned out.

"Nobody fucking move, okay?" he said to the officer. "I'm going to knock on the door. You hear shots, come running. But if you don't, just sit still. I can't have a contaminated crime scene."

"Isn't that the guy you charged with murder a couple days ago?" asked a wide-mouthed officer, looking at David.

"Yeah. Gonna use him as a human shield. Kill two birds with one stone. Dickhead. Come on, let's go." Larkey rolled his window up and then slapped David in the head from the back seat. "Fuckin' *move*, Professor!"

David took off down the road and pulled to a stop in front of the brewery.

"Don't you need a subpoena?" asked David.

"I thought you were a true crime writer. It's called a warrant," said Larkey, checking the clip in his sock Glock. "And there's nothing prohibiting me from knocking on his door or busting it down if I hear her screaming inside." He got out of the Cadillac and headed for the door beside the brewery. A sign on the wall read FABULOUS PICS. I followed David, but remained a few steps behind, as my knee protested against the unexpected exercise.

The stairs were steep and went on for what seemed like two flights before coming to an end at a tall wooden door.

Larkey knocked loudly.

"Hello?" he shouted.

Nothing.

"Hello? Dean? Hello? Erin?"

"What now?" asked David.

"What do you mean, what now? We go in."

"Isn't it locked?"

"What do you mean? The fucking door is wide open!"

"Looks open to me," I offered, catching my breath.

With impressive and sudden force, Larkey kicked the door to the left of the knob with one booted foot. It exploded inward with a blast that shook the stairs. He leapt into the dimness, drawing his Glock and a pen-sized flashlight he held below the weapon.

The studio was wide, about a hundred feet across, filled with rows of aluminum shelving upon which sat boxes of floppy middle-school year-books and binders full of loose pictures. A wall of windows painted-over white let in just enough sunlight to see. It was like a world illuminated by an eclipse, where matter seems ethereal, dreamlike. It smelled of grease and earth and vinegar.

"Look," said David. He pointed at a sofa sitting against the wall of windows. On the cushions was a pink and blue backpack. *McNight* was written on it in dark Magic Marker.

"Erin!" yelled Larkey. "Dean, it's the FBI. Are you in here? I don't want anybody to get hurt."

There came a muted rustling from the corner of the room, beyond a black door set into the wall.

"The darkroom," said David.

Larkey led the way. He put the flashlight in his mouth and used his free hand to push through the revolving door. "Stay here," he mumbled. Then he replaced the light below the sidearm and jumped into the dark-room.

We couldn't see anything inside because of that revolving door but the smell of vinegar was much stronger and that rustling suddenly grew louder.

"David! Get in here! Help me! Help!"

David went first and I rushed in as fast as I could after him, knocking the cane against the floor. It took a second for my eyes to adjust. David, with his younger eyes, was faster. He was already at Larkey's side when I could see again. They stood on either side of a metal cart. They were rapidly untying the small body that lay there.

Erin appeared unscathed. Physically, at least. There was no sign of blood. No sign of trauma at all except for a pair of particularly nasty bruises along her ankles where the clothesline had been tied tight around her. She wore green shorts and a purple top. Her red hair hung around the top of the table like the impression of blood.

Larkey sat her up and, with one quick jerk of his hand, pulled the duct tape off her mouth.

Erin screamed in pain and cried with relief. She wrapped her arms around Larkey's neck and sobbed into his shoulder.

"Shhh," he said, rubbing her hair. "Shhh."

For the first time, we looked around the room. The walls were covered in photographs of a common theme: redheaded beauties. Not just school photos. Candid shots, taken with a long-lens camera. There were Elaine and Elizabeth playing on a slide. Katy climbing onto a boat. Erin, through a window, watching TV in her bedroom. Several other girls I did not recognize. *Hundreds* of photographs. Dozens of girls.

"Let's get out of here before he comes back," I said. "In bad mystery novels, the killer always comes back just when the heroes save the damsel in distress."

Larkey laughed but started for the door.

David hung back with me, his eyes wide, his face full of some emotion I could not read.

"What?" I asked.

"It's too easy," he said. "I don't trust it."

"Let it go," I told him.

A few minutes later, Larkey pried himself away from Erin, who sat wrapped in a red blanket in the back seat of a Berea cruiser, and joined us by the Cadillac.

"What's going on?" David asked.

"We got a car at the Galts' home," said Larkey. "*My* guys. They just saw Dean walk inside. It's about a mile from here."

"Let's go," said David.

Larkey shook his head. "You guys go home. We'll handle it. We got the girl. With your help, David. Now let us get Galt."

David sighed.

"It's over," said Larkey. "Go home. Be with your kid. We'll work out the murder charge in the morning. Clear you up. Oh, and don't talk to the press. Okay? At least not yet."

David was shaking his head, his brow furrowed.

"Go home," Larkey said again. "It's over."

Back in the car, it was quiet. David was lost in his head.

"What?"

"My mind is fried," he said. "I can't get my thoughts straight. But there's something . . ."

"Postpartum depression," I said. "You've spent a long time thinking about this guy. I've spent much longer. I built my life around that man, Dean Galt. I feel it, too. So anticlimactic. The Man from Primrose Lane used to say these cases make ghosts out of the living. Don't let that happen."

"It doesn't feel right."

"It's not supposed to feel right."

David stopped talking and instead called his dead wife's aunt, Peggy. He asked her to pick up Tanner and bring him home.

"Can I meet him?" I asked. I thought that today of all days it would do me some good to be around innocence instead of further loneliness and fear. Maybe David would let him call me "Uncle."

"Sure," he said.

"And you owe me some more interviews," I said. "I'd like to understand your thoughts, your motivations about all this."

"So you can turn it into a book?"

"Now it has an ending."

"Fine," he said. "But not today."

But, for David, there would be no tomorrow.

Detective Lieutenant Tom Sackett came to regret ever having met David Neff. He'd trusted him, had given him information about the Man from Primrose Lane's case that he shouldn't have. But then they'd found his dead wife's fingerprints on the bed. They'd dug up her body and discovered she had been murdered, strangled. There was only one suspect. Only one man who could have committed both crimes. David Neff.

It was the simplest explanation, and they'd taught him at the academy to always look for the most elegant solution.

Then, somehow, he'd lost Dan Larkey. David had corrupted the agent's confidence somehow. Larkey had called him that morning, said, "I have some doubts." Based on what? A gut feeling? Please.

That was the problem with FBI, Sackett knew. They were academics, prone to seek out more poetic story lines. They even consulted with psychics. Not sometimes, either. Like, all the goddamn time. FBI agents, even retired ones, were dreamers. And dreamers didn't belong in Homicide. That was a dangerous mix.

And yet Sackett had his cruiser lights on as he flew up I-480 to meet with Larkey at this new suspect's house, this Dean Galt. There *was* something about that writer, he granted that much. Something that made you want to believe him.

Just then Sackett got another text from Larkey's cell phone:

We got Erin. Alive. Forget studio. Proceed to Galt residence. 1181 Parkman Drive. Berea.

Twenty minutes later, Sackett turned onto Parkman, a side street in a section of town submerged in tall oak trees. He saw Larkey leaning into the window of a black sedan. Quickly Sackett parked his cruiser and jogged up to join the agent.

"Dan, what the fuck is going on? Did you really find Erin?"

At the sound of his voice, Larkey turned to him.

Sackett stopped abruptly. His blood pressure rose so quickly he saw dancing specks form on his periphery, as his body overloaded on adrenaline.

Larkey tried to speak but could not. There was a deep gash in the middle of his throat. Rushed air and thick gobs of blood shot out of the opening. To Sackett it sounded like feedback from an electrolarynx, one of those voice boxes cancer patients sometimes use. Larkey collapsed against the driver's-side door. Sloped against the wheel behind him was another dead agent, her eyes glazed and unfocused, a bullet hole in her temple.

He knelt beside Larkey. "What the Christ happened?" he asked.

Larkey's mouth was working like a goldfish. He was trying to say something. Sackett understood that Larkey was dying.

"What?"

"T-t-t."

"Shhh. Don't speak."

"T-t-t. T-t-t. T-trap," he said.

"What's a trap? Was this a trap, Dan? Dan? Is someone walking into a trap? What's a trap? Whose trap?"

"T-t-t. T-t-t."

"Shhh. I heard it. I heard, 'Trap.'"

Larkey stopped. The blood continued to pour out of his neck. He looked up at Sackett and smiled. It was the smile of a good chess player who has suddenly seen checkmate, eight moves away.

"What?" asked Sackett again.

"T-t-t. T-t-tanner," he said. And then he died.

She sat in her car, eyeing his house with disdain and jealousy and hatred.

She would never be a journalist in the true sense of the word, Cindy Nottingham knew. Had known for quite some time. And that was fine, because true journalists didn't make real money. The real money came with gossip, and she knew gossip. She had ways of drawing out secrets from people. People trusted her. Men trusted her more. Most men, anyway. Not David.

She enjoyed watching him fall. She knew this and accepted it, not as something evil, but as a natural response to his hubris. She was no journalist. But neither was he. And now the world would see that, too. David was a hack. A onetime author who'd gotten lucky. That story had fallen into his lap. She should have written it. It had been hers to begin with. Brune, she knew, had *wanted* it to be hers.

But men always took advantage of her, stealing her stories, stealing her rent money, stealing her virginity. Such was life in a man's world. They deserved what she brought down on them.

For about ten minutes Cindy had sat quietly in her car, across the street from David's home—paid for by the book that should have been hers—wishing him ill. She had watched as Tanner got out of the car, led by his Aunt Peggy into the house. Such a beautiful kid. David didn't deserve him, either.

A black Cadillac pulled onto the street and Cindy hastily assembled her camera, snapping the long lens into place. She crouched behind the wheel and aimed it at the house. But the car didn't pull into the driveway. Instead, it pulled up alongside hers.

Busted, she thought. *He must've recognized the car.*

The Caddy's passenger window rolled down. The man behind the wheel looked strikingly familiar, but it was not David.

"Who are you?" the man asked.

"I'm a reporter, who the fuck are you?" she spat.

"You don't recognize me?"

"No."

"Then you're not a very good reporter."

And then she did. It came to her in a flash. The only reason she hadn't recognized him right away was because he was so out of place. He shouldn't be here. This was wrong. Dangerous.

He lifted his hand and in it was a shiny gun with a grip the color of old bones. It went off with a thunderous roar.

Cindy never heard it.

The bullet ripped through the portion of her brain devoted to auditory perception before the sound could be processed.

At the precise moment David was untying Erin McNight's bindings, Katy Keenan sat down to eat at Larry's.

It was an early dinner, but there was no time to waste. They were rebuilding their relationship.

This can work, she told herself. *I know it.*

And really, Ralph had his moments. Sure, he didn't read for pleasure. And he hated movies that didn't contain explosions. But he was a companion on her long jogs in the evening, when she just wanted someone to listen. He was a *great* lay.

David could never work, she told herself. Too wrapped up in himself. Literally, as it were, in his own Neverending Story. To even consider believing that story he'd told her the other night was to surrender to delusion. Poor man. Poor lonely man.

Still.

He was fascinating. Endearingly egotistical, yet insecure. Naïve, almost. Like a teenager. His mind full of constant wonderment. That was intoxicating to her.

Ralph sat across from her in the same booth she'd shared with David not long ago. She ordered a mushroom basket.

"I want to take you to Italy," he said. "Next month. For a week."

"Why?"

"Why not?"

Her entire life had been a struggle for money. Her parents had never made enough for her to go on field trips. How much of this was wrapped up in her admiration for Ralph? She didn't care to know.

While her fiancé sipped his beer, Katy looked over to the framed photographs of Akron residents with clown noses. Black and white. Big and small. Was it some artistic statement that we all take ourselves too seriously? What was the *real* story behind it?

And what was that written on the bottom-right corner of the nearest photo? She hadn't noticed that before.

Katy leaned closer.

"Fabulous Pics," she said.

"What?"

Her mind was working. Cobwebby synapses were dusted off in the furthest recesses of her memory.

BAM!

Katy's eyes snapped open.

"What?" Ralph asked again.

"Fabulous Pics!" she shouted. She grabbed her purse. Thank God she'd driven. "Call a cab," she said as she ran out the door.

"Hey!" he shouted after her. But she ignored him and fled as quickly as her feet could take her.

David pulled into his driveway at just past eight in the evening. We didn't see Cindy Nottingham slumped down in her car across the street. I didn't notice the other black Cadillac parked just beyond it. We were discussing the nature of obsession. And how to be satisfied with an anti-climactic resolution. Cerebral jerk-off stuff.

"You coming in?" he asked.

"You bet," I replied.

There was a loud squealing of tires as a car took the turn up the street from David's house at top speed. For a minute it looked like the car might tumble into the neighbor's centuries-old oak, but it corrected and pulled into David's driveway. Katy, her face flushed with excitement, leapt out. She had never looked so beautiful.

"Fabulous Pics!" she screamed. "I know who it is!"

David took her by the shoulders and held her at arm's length. "Calm down," he said. "Breathe."

She did. She smiled up at him and I could tell she had finally allowed herself to love him.

"The photographer's son," she said. "I forgot all about him until I saw their logo on a picture at Larry's. The guy who took our pictures at school, he was all crippled and bent up. He had this son who helped him pose the children. He was like forty years old and had bushy hair like the guy in the shopping plaza that day. When he was taking my picture, there was this moment when I thought he might have brushed against my chest with his hand but he played it off like an accident. He told me that I had hair like his mother's. He said my hair was prettier than any other girl's in my whole class. If his father's company also did the pictures for the other girls' schools, it has to be him! It has to be!"

There is a theory, a metaphysical, philosophical theory, that when an idea's time has come, it will be recognized by several people at once. It's a sixth-sense explanation for such things as why two authors sometimes come out with similar books in the same season. (For instance, there were two great fictional mysteries with Edgar Allan Poe as the main character, which came out within a month of each other, in 2006.) It explains how two scientists a world apart suddenly and independently discovered the AIDS virus. Or how Tesla and Edison emerged as inventors of electricity. However, I had never witnessed such a thing, and Katy's tandem epiphany made my skin crawl.

"Shhh," said David. "We know. They're arresting him right now. We found Erin. She's safe."

"What?" Katy slipped her arms under his and embraced him. "How?"

"All the pictures had the same backdrop," he said. "No one noticed it until we had Erin's photo to compare to the others."

"Where did you find Erin? What happened to her?"

"Come inside," he said. "I'll explain everything."

I followed them in. I had planned to tell Aunt Peggy I was a distant relative of his Uncle Ira, in town for the funeral. But Peggy was nowhere to be found. And neither was Tanner. The house smelled musty, unlived-in. It smelled like the house on Primrose Lane. And someone was singing. A familiar voice. The sound traveled softly down the hallway and filled the house. I knew the song. "Castle on a Cloud," from *Les Mis*. "Who is that?" I asked.

"My wife," said David.

We followed him to a door halfway down the hall. The music was coming from inside. I could tell now that it was a recording, clear but mixed with something like static or falling water. The door was locked.

"Tanner?" David said. "Tanner, open up!"

Then, distantly, "Dad?"

"Hey, buddy," he said. "It's me. Open up."

The knob shook as Tanner's young hands fidgeted with the lock. Then the door opened. The boy leapt into his father's arms. I saw he was shaking. I assumed it was because he hadn't seen his dad for a while. In their reunion, David accidentally tripped over a length of dominoes arranged on the floor, causing them to cascade across the length of the room, revealing a red number before setting off some contraption that caused a basket to fall on a plastic mouse. What "88" meant I never did find out. The number of a beloved sportsman, I supposed. I reached over to the microcassette recorder lying on top of the boy's dresser and turned it off.

"Where's Aunt Peggy?" asked David.

"In the East Wing."

"What's she doing in there?"

Tanner didn't answer. His face was buried in his father's neck. Was he crying? I couldn't tell.

"Why'd you lock your door?"

"She told me to."

David laughed. "Why?"

Tanner leaned back and looked at his father with brown eyes the size of half dollars. "So the bad man and his cat couldn't get in."

What the boy said struck me as so odd it took me a full five seconds to sift any meaning from it. Then I understood. Part of it, at least.

David did, too. He set Tanner down. When he spoke, his voice was calm, for his son's sake. Only I knew how much fear he must be feeling. "Tanner. I want you to listen to me. Don't ask any questions. Just do this. In a second I'm going to leave and get Aunt Peggy. When I do, I want you to close the door behind me. Lock it. Then crawl under your bed and cover your ears. No matter what happens, do not come out or open the door for anyone but me. Promise me you will not come out, okay?"

Tanner didn't say anything. He'd seen enough before we arrived.

Somehow, David managed a smile. "I love you," he said.

"Love you," said Tanner.

And then we all heard it—the sound of heavy boots on finished wood, approaching from the East Wing.

I stepped into the hall and wrapped my fingers around my cane. David shut the door behind him. Katy took David's hand in hers and stood between us.

It was then that we heard a low, a soft, a very soft mew. The sound of an old tomcat playing with a stunned mouse.

"Easy," said Trimble, from the darkness of the hallway. "Easy, Beezle."

BEEZLE

When it came down to it, it was Time that screwed everything up again.

Sometimes you simply overplan.

The day before Katy was to be abducted, I had Aaron fill the tank of my car. I got plenty of sleep that night. I ate a good breakfast. I packed a bag of emergency supplies—Fix-A-Flat, ID, money—in case something happened to the car along the way. When it got to be half-past noon, I called Aaron to come pick me up and drive me to Coventry, to Big Fun. There should have been plenty of time. Katy wasn't abducted until three p.m. We'd be in Coventry by two p.m., even if there was traffic. I had been so focused on the hundreds of variables that could affect our arrival that I didn't consider the constant in the equation. I didn't consider *time*. I had forgotten it could change, too.

I forgot daylight savings.

We listened to NPR on the radio on the way up to Coventry and somewhere along Route 8 out of Akron the station gave a local news update. "It's currently two-oh-five in the afternoon," the announcer said at the beginning of his sign-off.

"What did he just say?"

"Hmm?" asked Aaron. "I wasn't listening."

"What time did he say it was?"

"A little after two."

"You mean one."

"No, boss. It's two."

I checked my watch. It said one o'clock. And then I remembered.

"Oh, man, did you forget to reset your watch?"

"Yes, Aaron. It's very important we reach Coventry by three p.m. I can't tell you how important. It is essential we get there by three." I tried to keep the panic out of my voice.

Aaron looked at the congested traffic along Route 8, which was not built to handle commuter traffic to begin with and shrank to a single lane up ahead because of construction. I realized if we sat here long enough—say, eleven years—there would be an extra lane and traffic would no longer be an obstacle.

"I'll do my best," he said.

"Drive on the shoulder if you need to. Just get us there by three. Please."

As the eclipse of time approached, I began to second-guess my research. What if Katy was abducted at ten till three instead of three on the nose? What if she was already long gone? Not the end. Not yet. But it would be no solace to Katy that I still had one opportunity left to catch him; by staking out the location where he dumps her body.

The car lurched into a space up the street from Big Fun at precisely 2:57. I rolled out of the back door and onto the pavement, my cane tumbling some distance away from me. Aaron came around, helped me up, and put the cane in my hand.

"Let me help you," he said.

"No. You have to stay here. Just wait for me."

I hobbled down the sidewalk toward the toy store, scanning the faces of the people walking on the other side of the street. Then I saw her: Katy. Katy as a young girl. Katy at ten. She was twirling on a lamppost like Gene Kelly, her free hand splayed in the sun as if to catch the light, her long hair trailing behind her like some special effect. And I saw *him*. His back was to me, but I knew it was him, the man I had hunted for four decades. Even from here, I could see his bushy hair blowing in the breeze. He was going to get to her first if I didn't hurry. I picked up the pace, ambling as fast as I could, sure I was about to fall and break my neck and watch this happen in front of me as I died. But I didn't fall.

He was about ten feet from her when I plowed into him at top speed, slamming us both into the brick wall of Big Fun. He gave a yelp of surprise and looked at me as if I were about to slap handcuffs on him.

"Got you, you motherfucker," I said.

"Who the fuck are you?" he whispered.

"You were going to kidnap that girl," I told him.

"No. I wasn't. I don't even know her."

"Liar!"

"Let go of me."

"You're coming with me," I said. "You're going to talk to the police. We're going to get your fingerprints. How much you want to bet you left them at the scene of some other murder?"

The man's eyes went blank. His mind retreated somewhere deep inside for just an instant. It must be the way he looks when he's committing rapes and murders. Total lack of empathy, those eyes warned. A killer's eyes. And then he came back to himself and kicked me, hard, in the groin.

I doubled over and in that instant he fled past Katy and down the sidewalk. I watched him run into Tommy's Diner. By the time I got to the restaurant's doors, Aaron was once again at my side. I let him lead me in and we looked for ten minutes, but he was gone. Through the kitchen, maybe. Out the back door. Gone.

I had lost my answer. I had let him get away. He was free to kill again.

But Katy was alive.

I followed her, again, for a couple years. Softball games. School plays. Swim meets. I looked like a grandfather. No one questioned me.

Sometimes I had Aaron drive me to malls during the holidays, when they were packed with people. I spent days looking for him in the crowds.

But I never saw him again.

I got bored. I started hanging out with the Man from Primrose Lane during the afternoons when he wasn't expecting his own Sherlock ruffian to swing by. Aaron would drop me off around the corner and I would shuffle up the street toward the house. Later, Aaron would pick me up at the same location. I made sure to wear mittens when I visited. To neighbors it appeared like it was just the old hermit out for a walk.

We played a lot of chess. But we never got any better. I think it's a little like playing both sides of the board. Mostly the games ended in a draw.

Many days I sat beside the Man from Primrose Lane, reading one of his paperbacks or writing short stories while he dabbled with his oil paintings. Landscapes from *National Geographic*, at first. Then portraits. We were both impressed with his natural ability. And here's the strange thing—I never really cared for painting. And when I did try, I wasn't especially good at it. How do you explain that one, if we both have the same DNA?

Sometime around 2001, after the towers fell, one of us got the idea—I think it was him—to collaborate on a book about our adventures and to sell it as mind-blowing fiction. Hey, what else did we have to do, you know? It might even freak the killer out enough to scare him away.

Eventually we settled that I would write it, using my notes from Katy's case and his own from Elaine and Elizabeth's. He would paint the illustrations. The main characters, at least.

Then things got weird.

I passed you on the street, David. You and Elizabeth must've just moved into your place on Palisades. You were out for a walk, your arms around each other's waists. I was walking away from the house on Primrose, to Aaron's car around the corner. I turned around before you noticed me. But, well, that sort of changed everything.

I returned to the house and told the Man from Primrose Lane what I'd seen. It frightened him. It was weird. Weird that the two of you would find each other. That you would be drawn to her, even in this world where she was alive. It's strange enough to force you to reexamine your idea of the universe, of fate and happenstance. What happened was the Man from Primrose Lane became obsessed again. Obsessed with finding out how the two of you found each other and what it meant in the larger picture.

Some of the details he was able to ferret out of your email accounts; we, of course, knew you used a specific Stephen King novel as a key to all your passwords because we had done the same in our youth. We reread the emails Elizabeth sent you over the years. We discovered how your lives intersected in that college music class.

The Man from Primrose Lane became obsessed mostly over one unanswerable question: if Elaine and Elizabeth had never been murdered in his timeline to begin with, would events have played out this way? He

wanted to know if it had been his destiny to be with Elizabeth. He wondered if maybe he had felt that on some level that was the real reason
behind his obsession with her cold case.

I tried to point out to him that I had become obsessed with *Katy's*
murder. It's like our brains were programmed to lock on to some mystery
and pick it apart, bit by bit, over an eternity. Forget the question of destiny. I've often wondered if maybe we're in hell. That's the discussion *I*
wanted to have.

Anyway, he had this feeling that your relationship was jinxed, that it
could not possibly work out well for her, especially given the fact that
we knew, eventually, you would find your own obsession. That was your
destiny. And Elizabeth was in the way.

So he went on your honeymoon, booked a room on your ship, to
watch over her. It's a good thing he did. She was halfway over the balcony when he found her. He was there to save her life a *second* time. And
maybe that's what did the trick. Because it seemed to break some kind of
spell.

Suddenly all these great things started to happen. You found your
case, but solved it before it claimed your soul. You and Elizabeth lasted.
And we were allowed a friend. Me and the Man from Primrose Lane.
After he saved her for the second time, he had to tell her the truth. And
somehow, that truth made her stronger. She was our coconspirator.
Yes, she came to the house often. She squeezed in visits while running
errands, on trips to the grocery store, or when you were at work late at
night. We played gin rummy. The three of us. We talked about your life
and career. We gave her advice on how to handle your dark moods. I think,
if I were to guess, the Man from Primrose Lane's obsession somehow
negated her parents' neglect. She felt balanced, that much was obvious.
Of course, she became quite fond of the Man from Primrose Lane.

Were they romantic? I don't believe so. It wasn't that sort of friendship. But he would paint her. She allowed him that. And they would do
it in private so she could undress. He showed me one of the better ones,
a picture of Elizabeth posed on his bed, lying on her back, her legs trailing across the sheets, a milky-white palm resting against the headboard.
She loved *you*, David. She saw the older you in the Man from Primrose
Lane and loved what she saw there. She couldn't wait to grow old with
you, she told him.

Eventually it got to a point where I felt like a fifth wheel. Her affection and gratitude always made me feel odd. It seemed wrong, I think. I stopped coming by. When I returned one day in 2008, the Man from Primrose Lane explained that he had asked Elizabeth to stay away. When I asked him why, he wouldn't tell me.

I think it's possible that he knew he was being watched. How he knew, I don't know. He was more paranoid than I had ever seen him. He'd always worn those mittens, said it was "insurance." But when I returned, he was on this cleaning kick. Scrubbing every inch of the house. Said he was worried he'd left fingerprints somewhere. I think he felt fate catching up to him, finally. He may have been preparing for his murder.

I'm sure, now, that the first place Elizabeth went after leaving the hospital was his house. Was the killer waiting in the bushes? Had he come to the home, expecting to catch the Man from Primrose Lane alone, only to surprise Elizabeth? Or had he spotted Elizabeth somewhere, stalked her, and followed her back to his house before killing them both? I don't know how it played out.

There's only one question that matters: does the murderer know what we are? Because if he doesn't, he thinks he's killed the only man who knows his secret. And that means he thinks he's free to kill again.

He wore no shirt and his body was shrunken and shallow, his hipbones jutting out like wings. He held a long white gun in one hand. He stank like a gutted deer.

"Ooooooowee," said Riley. "We got everyone here. Nice. Come. You really must see what I've done with the place. Come." He motioned to them with the gun, swinging it in the direction of David's office. "Bring your kid, too."

"Go fuck yourself."

Trimble licked his lips and looked from David to the bedroom door and back again. Then he waved his free hand. "You're right. This is grown-up time. I can play with the kid later." He winked at David.

"I'll—" David began, but Trimble smacked him in the nose with the gun and he went silent. Katy let go of his hand as he stanched the blood that dripped on his hallway carpet.

"Move," said Trimble.

I led the way. I didn't want to be in that hallway any longer. If there were any means of escape, they would not be found in that hall with a gun trained on us. David followed closely behind, with Katy between us.

As we drew closer, my vision grew focused. The heightened stress was causing a kind of tunnel vision I hadn't experienced since the more frightening moments of my childhood. I expect it was the same for David.

Trimble had turned the room into a work of art for some grotesque exhibition. Something fitting William Blake, perhaps. Or Jeffrey Dahmer.

In the middle of the room, the *Edmund Fitzgerald* desk lay on its side. Trimble had scraped a word into its top. BEEZLE. To the right of the desk was a woman of grandmotherly size, sitting in a chair, blindfolded, gagged, handcuffed, and dead. Her throat was cut at the jugular and she had bled out, quickly, on her blouse. Her head hung backward, making the wound look like a wet and gaping mouth.

"Peggy," said David softly. "Ah, Christ. Peg."

To the left of the desk a man was constrained in a similar manner but very much alive. Above his blindfold made of . . . sackcloth? . . . was a full head of bushy gray hair. He wore a button-down white shirt and a pair of jeans. He whimpered around the gag. Dean Galt.

There was a low guttural sound from behind the captain's desk and then, so suddenly it caused me to lurch backward, a cat appeared, jumping onto the desk from behind the dead woman. It was an old cat. I had never seen one so ragged and worn, its hair mottled, grayish, sickly. The color of the absence of color. It was minus a few whiskers and one ear had been ripped clean from its scalp, leaving nothing but a gangrenous hole. It tilted its head at us and hissed.

"Beezle, shhh," said Trimble.

"A cat?" asked David. "Beezle's a cat?"

Trimble pushed us back by pointing his gun and slowly walked toward his familiar. "Not just a cat," he said.

"You're insane," said Katy.

"Shut up, you are!" he said, then laughed. He reached into his back pocket and pulled out two pairs of police-issue handcuffs. He tossed a pair to me and the other to David. "Do yourselves up nice or I'll have to."

"No," said David.

The shot was immediate and loud. The echo of the gunfire made my ears ring. To my left, David collapsed to the floor, clutching his knee. Beezle growled loudly. The blindfolded man screamed into his binding.

Trimble even seemed a little stunned. "Fuck," he said. "That was *really* loud."

Katy went to David's side. "Are you okay? Jesus, David."

He didn't say anything. Instead, he handed the cuffs to Katy, who reached around a radiator and secured her left hand to David's right. Trimble pointed the gun at me then and so I went to Katy's side and cuffed my left hand to her right, around the same cast-iron radiator.

"Good," said Trimble, hunkering down so he was on our level. Then he looked at me. "Now, first things first. Who. Are. You?"

"I'm David's uncle."

Slowly and deliberately, Trimble turned the gun sideways in his hand and then punched me with it, hard, square in the forehead. It felt like running into a steel door.

"Why does it matter?" asked David.

"Because I have a gun and I say it does."

"I'm him," I said. "*Him*. I'm David, you dumb motherfucker."

And then Trimble did something that sent a fresh wave of fear up my spine. He turned to Beezle, who was perched on the desk behind him, and waited for some reply. The cat looked over to me, and when it did, my heart was filled with such dismay. It was the darkest, deepest sadness and it seemed to turn on inside my head the moment our eyes made contact. I heard a voice, a deep husky voice, that said, *You have failed. You were, in fact, always a failure. Everything to which you have devoted your life is as empty and worthless as your soul. There is no grace. No meaning. No balance. Only me. Only the Dark.*

Trimble turned back to me. "How?"

"How do you think?" I said.

"Time travel?"

"Yes."

Trimble looked back to Beezle, then at us. He laughed and slapped his knee hard enough for me to think he might accidentally set off the pistol. "No way! That's *rad*, man. That's totally rad. Fuck. Listen to this. I get to kill you twice!" He pointed the gun at David. "One." And then at me. "Two."

He looked at Katy. ·

"And you already knew, didn't you! Ah. You little rascal," he said. "I love smart girls. Too bad you're all grown up. I bet you were a cute little thing, huh? Yeah. You were. I can tell. I bet you let your little boyfriends feel your flat chest, didn't you? Play a little doctor?" He started to lean toward her and I thought he meant to kiss her, but then Beezle meowed and he stopped short. "Right," he said. He shook his head to clear it, then he stood and walked to the man in the chair.

The man screamed again when Trimble touched the back of his head to untie the blindfold.

"Shuddup," said Trimble. "I ain't gonna hurt you." He let the blindfold fall but the gag stayed in.

The bushy-haired man, already in shock, seemed to go insane when he saw Katy. Galt's eyes were as big as a horse's, like the eyes of a horse stuck in a pen watching the fire that will engulf the barn begin in a corner. He looked at me and recognized me, too. He started shaking his head. He said something against the gag.

"What's that?" asked Trimble.

"He said, 'You're dead. I watched you die,'" I explained.

"Huh. Far out."

"That's him," said Katy, sullenly, to David. "That's the man who came up to me outside Big Fun."

"She knows who you are, man!" said Trimble, jumping around the man's chair. "I told you! I told you she'd figure it out. God, this is fun! I told you I'd catch him for you, David. I told you I'd do it. We should have worked together!"

"Why would I work with you, Trimble?" asked David, and I had begun to wish he would just stop talking until I figured out a way to get us out of there. I knew well the disdain I'd always had for authority, though. "You're the same as this man. You're the same."

"No," he said. "You're wrong. There's a very big difference. This man kills for himself. I only ever killed for Beezle."

"A fucking cat?" screamed David.

I had already begun to doubt that Beezle was *only* a cat.

"Well, he's a cat right *now*," said Trimble, as if David had offended it and he was trying to make amends. "But he was a dog for a while, right, when he used to live in New York? And a donkey once, long ago. A pig, too. He could be a man if he wanted. I bet he could. I think he's a cat because I *wanted* him to be a cat."

"What are you talking about?" asked David.

"He came to me, when I was five. I was stuck outside all day, and the only thing I had to play with was a sandbox. I prayed and prayed and prayed to God that I could have a friend to play with. What I really wanted was a cat. A little cat to rub and make purr and chase around the house. And something heard me."

Trimble looked over to Beezle, as a lover might regard his partner when remembering their kismet introduction. "He came to me and stood in the sandbox in front of me. He told me his name was many things but also Beezle. He told me that if I would be loyal to him, if I obeyed him and did all that he asked of me, he would be my friend whenever I needed a friend. I told him yes, yes, I would do all that. But he told me to prove it. A contract. It was a contract, I realize that now."

I didn't want to know.

"He asked me to get rid of the neighbor's dog. You see, the dog knew what Beezle really was. The dog could smell it. And Beezle didn't like that. So I did what Beezle told me to do. I tied the dog to a tree in the woods behind my house and cut out its stomach with my pocketknife. The police thought some other kid did it—that blond kid from down the street. They carted him off in a white van.

"Beezle is my friend now. He helps me when I need helping. He came to me at the hospital and told me to stop taking the pills. He unlocked my door and showed me the way out through the boiler room window. That's what friends are for. Course, a couple orderlies happened to be taking a smoke break outside, but we took care of them, too, didn't we?"

Beezle mewed.

"I didn't need to kill those girls to get what I wanted. But Beezle was pretty insistent. He said I had to. He said those particular girls had to die."

"Why?" asked David.

"The universe is out of balance, David. Don't you feel it in your bones? This isn't the way things are supposed to be. Nature is balance. For every thing there is a reason, right? Or something like that. But you fiddled with it. Beezle told me that you're the reason our lives are damned. And he caught you! We caught you!" Trimble hopped to his feet and danced a short jig in front of us.

David moved before any of us saw it. He had retained a little length in the handcuff behind the radiator when Katy had secured it to his wrist. He had a little more room to play with than any of us realized. And he was able to push himself forward very close to Trimble. He kicked his foot into Trimble's crotch, followed him down, and stomped on his balls with the heel of his shoe.

Trimble yelled and fell back. The gun tumbled to the floor, spinning toward David's outstretched hand. It was going to be close, but it looked like David would reach it.

But then my head was filled with white-hot pain. It took me a couple seconds to realize it was pain from a sound. Pain like standing next to an amp during a guitar solo at a metal show. Blistering, dull, numbing pain. David forgot the gun and clapped his hands to his ears. Katy tried to do the same, but could only get one, due to the lack of give between her left hand and the register. She screamed. Where was it coming from? I looked around the room and recoiled when I saw it.

It was Beezle. The cat's hackles were raised and its mouth was wide open. It was making the sound in its body. Its fur rippled in thin waves along its sides. Then its mouth shut and the cacophony ended.

Trimble recovered first, picked up the gun, turned it around, and shot David in the belly. Blood poured from the wound, through David's fingers, and onto the hardwood floor.

"David!" shouted Katy.

David squinted his eyes up at Trimble.

"You should thank me," said Trimble. His voice sounded regretful, though. Like he'd had to put down his rabid dog. "You would have obsessed over this man like you obsessed over me. And what sort of life is that?" he said, motioning to Dean Galt. "Questions. Questions. Questions. You feed on the answers. It's the only thing that fills you up. You would have spent the rest of your life trying to get this man to tell you what he told me in one hour. Get this, David—he found Elizabeth again after reading your book. You put all kinds of personal information about her in there. He became obsessed with her again. He stalked her. And she led him right to the Man from Primrose Lane. Can you imagine his surprise when he saw them together? He was furious. He was the one who called your wife that day in the hospital, pretending to be the Man from Primrose Lane. He waited out back of the house until she arrived. He followed her in.

"He told me everything, David. What happened when he got inside. Why he set up your wife's murder to look like a suicide. Why he believes he kills. What he did with Elaine's body. But he would never have told you, David. He'd have never told you, because you wouldn't have put a knife to his testicles like I did."

Trimble knelt in front of David, beside Galt's feet. "And you know what the worst part of it is? The worst part is, in the end, the answers never really change anything. You don't try to finish a crossword puzzle because you like to see all the squares filled in. You try to finish it to see if you can. And when you do, there's another one tomorrow. The solution is not the point. Get it?"

David didn't answer.

"Here, I'll prove it," he said. Another shot rang out. Galt's head exploded like a balloon, hitting us with hot shards of his brain and skull. "Goddamn it!" shouted Trimble, wiping a chunk of gray matter off his shoulder. "This was my favorite shirt!"

I didn't hear the next gunshot. It's possible my brain didn't register it because it came so close to the one that ended Galt's life. All I noticed was a bright red stain appearing in the center of Trimble's shirt. He tried to wipe it away, but the redness only grew. Beezle hissed loudly and jumped down from the table. Then Trimble looked up at the doorway.

Sackett stood there, leaning against the frame. He fired two more into Trimble's chest. And still the man did not fall. He seemed mostly annoyed. So Sackett shot him in the face and then it was over.

"The keys!" cried Katy. "Get the keys. And call an ambulance. Please! Call an ambulance!"

Sackett fished through Trimble's pockets and came up with the cuff keys, which he tossed to me. My hands trembled. It took me several attempts to unlock the cuffs.

"I'll be right back," he said.

"Kate," breathed David, lying on his back. "Where's the cat?"

I looked around. It was perched on the windowsill behind the overturned desk, leering at us with quiet fury. I reached down and pulled the gun from Trimble's grip. I swung it up and fired as the beast leapt through the thin screen. I honestly don't know if I shot it or not. If I did, it surely wouldn't have made it far before lying down to die. But I'd say the odds that my aim was true are something like fifty-fifty.

"What the hell was that sound it made?" I asked. Katy didn't react and I could tell she was already convincing herself that part had never happened. David motioned for me to come closer.

"Not a cat," he said. "I saw it. When Trimble shot me. For a second."

"What was it?"

A tear escaped his eye and rolled off his cheek. "Formless. Darkness."

"Shhh," I said. David's skin was taking on a sickly glow, his breath coming in short rasps.

"Is that . . . what . . . we get?" he asked. "All . . . the murderers we caught. Do you think . . . could that defeated darkness come for us? It called to me. I could feel myself going there."

"Just focus on not dying. Be still."

He shook his head. He gripped my arm with what strength remained. "Watch after him."

His eyes stopped moving.

All I can say, Tanner, is that I tried to do just that.

Of course, if you're reading this, something bad has happened again.

I suppose you have to ask yourself, how much of your father is in you? How far will *you* go?

It's up to you. It's a terrible choice. No matter what you decide, know he loved you. That I loved you.

INTERLUDE

THE BALLAD OF THE LOVELAND FROG

2012   This time, Everett Bleakney was ready.

He kept a packed bag next to the door of his double-wide. Inside was his father's gun, a can of Mace, a cattle prod, two pairs of handcuffs, duct tape, earplugs, tinfoil, and rope.

They had locked him up. Called him crazy. Hannah had left him for another man while he had recuperated inside the psych ward of Cinci General after his last encounter with the Loveland Frog, in 1996. They wouldn't let him into the academy because of his psych evaluations. The monster had murdered his father and ruined his life. If it ever came again, he would be ready. And this time, he wouldn't run. Even if he felt its telepathic tentacles coil around his mind.

He waited. For years he waited, listening for sounds emanating from the direction of Twightwee Road. Every time an old truck backfired out by the ruins of Camp Ritchie, he grabbed the bag and jumped into his car, zooming down the back roads of Loveland at a speed that was nearly physically impossible. He didn't care if it was a false alarm. He viewed these distractions as training runs.

Bring your spark-wand, motherfucker, he thought. *Let's see how well it works against a nine-millimeter.*

So when that low, percussive, probing *DOOOOOOOOOFFFF!*

sound shook the ground beneath his trailer on October 3, 2012, he was ready.

"This is it!" he shouted. He was getting ready for his shift at Capri Pizza when he heard it, felt it through the faux-wood walls. If he went now, he'd never make it to work in time. And that meant he'd be fired. Again. Did he care?

Everett grabbed the bag and bounded out the door like a paratrooper. A minute later, he was in his battered Volkswagen Rabbit, spitting up dust on Twightwee at roughly fifty miles an hour.

Just beyond the bridge over the Little Miami, Everett slammed on the brakes, sending the Rabbit skidding to a stop along the berm. He jumped out with the backpack, withdrawing the sidearm and the can of Mace as he walked into the woods. He checked the weapons. Undid the safeties. He held the heavy gun in his right hand, the Mace at the ready in his left.

DOOOOOOOOOOOOOOFFFF!

No mistaking it. This was no backfire. This was the real deal. The Loveland Frog was returning. Somewhere among these pine trees, he knew, he would find the black egg.

"Where are you, goddamn it?" he shouted. "Where are you?"

As if in reply, the air in front of him shimmered like ripples on a pond. *DOOOOOOOOOFFF!* The shock wave sent him backward, onto his ass upon the cypress needles. He pushed himself up and looked. Ten feet away was the black egg.

Everett aimed the gun at the top of the egg.

It was a full five minutes before anything happened. In 1996, he had watched the Loveland Frog cut itself out of its spaceship with that spark-wand. But he noticed right away that this time something was different. There was no crack that started in one spot and moved around its circumference. One moment there was no crack, the next there was a straight line completely encircling the object. It hissed loudly as air escaped into the world. Then the top popped off and swung back on deep-set hinges.

His heart stuttered in his chest and his head grew lighter. *This is it,* he thought. *This is it. They'll have to believe me now. When I drag this thing into Paxton's they'll believe me.*

A single black gooey hand slapped upon the lip of the lid. Then another. Slowly, the beast rose from the egg, high enough for its bulbous eyes to look upon Everett's soul in surprise.

"You killed my father," said Everett, clicking back the hammer.

The monster spat a mass of blackness onto the ground at Everett's feet. "Wait!" it said in a voice that was remarkably human.

Everett hesitated.

"Don't shoot!" pleaded the Loveland Frog.

"What the fuck are you?" Everett asked. He was steeling himself to squeeze the trigger and end this conversation. The alien was trying to trick him by using his native language, he realized. Very clever!

"My name is Tanner Neff," it said. "Don't shoot!"

Everett watched as the creature ripped away its black, oozing face. Underneath was something that appeared to be a man.

"What day is it?" it asked.

"What?"

"The day. What day is it?"

"October third?" said Everett.

"What *year*?"

"2012."

The humanoid smiled. "If you put the gun down and help me out of here, Everett, I promise I'll save your father after I save my own."

EPILOGUE

He watched them come out of the Mansfield Memorial Museum from inside his parked car. They looked like half a happy family, the boy tugging on his father's hand, leaning into gravity, as they walked back to the yellow Beetle. He remembered this moment. It was the last really good memory he had of his father, their last fun day. Tanner remembered the excitement he had felt listening to the old curator's story, relayed through an aged electrolarynx voice box, like a robot himself. This was the night things began to change for the worse, forever.

"Ready?" asked Everett, sitting behind the wheel of his VW Rabbit.

"Yeah," said Tanner.

"Want me to come?"

"No. I should do this alone. I won't be long." Tanner took the cardboard box from the back seat and stepped outside.

By the time he was halfway to his father, David was aware of his presence. Though he hadn't been conscious of this when he was a boy, Tanner now realized that his father had always been cautious with him, alert for any dangers that might arise in the world. He saw the question in David's eyes as he turned to him: *Are you a threat to my child?*

Four-year-old Tanner had finished snapping himself into his car seat by the time forty-year-old Tanner was close enough for David to address him.

"Hello?" David said.

"Hello, David," said Tanner.

"I'm sorry, do I know you?"

"I'm not here to scare you, but I need you to listen to what I'm about to say. In a few minutes you were going to call your publisher to tell him you're going to write that last chapter for your new book. I want to ask you to not do that. Not yet."

David stood, stunned. A smile played at the corner of his mouth. "Who are you?" he asked teasingly. "What is this?"

Tanner handed his father the cardboard box.

"What's this?" asked David.

"It's an unfinished book. Or at least one without an appropriate epilogue."

David opened the box. "Look, I'm not supposed to read unsolicited manuscripts," he began, but then he stopped talking when he saw the title page. *The Man from Primrose Lane*, it read. "Did you write this?" he asked.

"No."

"Who did?"

"Give it a read," said Tanner. "It explains things better than I could. I'll be back in a month and we can talk some more. For now just give it a read. And do me a favor. Don't call your publisher tonight."

The four-year-old tapped on the window. He waved up at the stranger. "Hi, man!" he said.

"Hey, kiddo," said Tanner. He smiled at himself. This was a memory he did not have. This was something new. And wasn't that a sort of promise?

Before David could think of how to respond, Tanner walked away.

On October 8, 2012, Riley Trimble returned to his solitary room at the end of a hallway inside St. Sebastian's Home for the Criminally Insane and waited for the orderly to arrive with his cocktail of pills.

Beezle had instructed him to wait here, in this sanitary hell. Wait for him to return. It had been four years. He might as well have gone to prison. How long did he have to wait here for David to return?

"Good evening," said a man in a white uniform as he stepped inside Trimble's room and shut the door.

"Where's Sully?" asked Trimble.

"Sick," said the man in white.

"What's your name?"

"My name's Tanner," the man said.

"Hello, Tanner."

"Hello, Riley."

The next morning, Cindy Nottingham ate a spartan breakfast while she read the *Beacon Journal* in the corner of her kitchen that got the most sunlight, fishing for something to blog about. Her eyes caught the story by Phil McIntyre that appeared below the fold: "Riley Trimble Dies in State Hospital."

An overdose, it said. Somehow he'd ingested an entire bottle of Rivertin.

She'd have to ask David about it. Not that he'd talk to her, of course. But it was a good excuse to drag his name out again.

There was a knock at her door.

Cindy, who seldom received company, and never at this early hour, jumped. She set the paper down and walked to the front door. A young man stood there in a white polo. She opened the door a crack.

"Hello?" she asked.

"Hello, Ms. Nottingham. My name is Everett Bleakney. I represent a man who would like to pay you for a freelance assignment."

"For real?" she asked.

"For real," he said.

Cindy opened the door wider. "Who?"

"I can't say. An anonymous donor. Someone who enjoys your work but wishes it was applied in other areas."

"Such as?"

"Such as anywhere but here."

"I don't understand."

"To put it simply, miss, my employer is willing to pay you five hundred thousand dollars to move away from Akron and never come back. He wants you to write your blog someplace else."

On October 21, Detective Lieutenant Tom Sackett and Dan Larkey each, independently, received a manila envelope with a handwritten address.

Inside, they discovered three photographs. School pictures. One of

Elaine O'Donnell, one of Katy Keenan, and one of a girl unfamiliar to them named Erin McNight. The upper right quadrant had been circled. A letter inside asked, *Who is Dean Galt?*

By the following afternoon, they had compiled enough circumstantial evidence to procure a search warrant for the photography studio and the Galt family home. They found the shrine to the redheaded girls. At the house, they discovered a trove of kiddie porn and an earring Galt had taken from Elaine's body—a particularly damning token, as it was a piece of evidence police had never made public. In a box in the coat closet, they found a handgun that ballistics later matched to the bullet found in the body of the Man from Primrose Lane.

No one ever connected Elizabeth's death to the attempted murder of the Man from Primrose Lane. But Galt went to prison and never came out.

On October 19, forty-year-old Tanner and his father shared a fifth of Johnnie Walker Black on the patio behind the house on Palisades, as four-year-old Tanner snoozed in his bedroom.

"What I don't understand is, why didn't you just go back all the way to 2008 and stop Galt from ever shooting the Man from Primrose Lane, from ever killing your mother?" asked David. His words were not accusatory. "For that matter, why not go back far enough to stop him from taking Elaine?"

"I will," said Tanner.

David turned to look at his adult son.

"I read that book for the first time when I was thirteen," said Tanner. "Obsession is, apparently, in our genes. I spent my twenties studying advanced theoretical physics. By the time I was thirty, I was interning at Tesla's lab. I helped him develop and hone his machine. The important thing to me was always a *reusable* unit. Took an extra three years, but we did it."

"Reusable. Why?"

"I look at it this way. By coming back here, I've essentially doubled the number of alternate universes, right? In half of them, you're alive for my adolescence. In the others, you're murdered by Trimble. All these universes radiating out from that point my egg arrived, like millions of trees with infinite branches. That's just not enough for me. I wanted a reusable unit because now I'm going to go back to 2008, to save Mom.

Save the Man from Primrose Lane. I get to see Galt arrested for his crimes again. I get to kill Trimble all over again. I can go back to when Trimble was five and strangle that cat in his sandbox. Think of all the realities that spawn from that. Eventually those in which you're alive, in which we're a family, will far outnumber those in which we're not. To the point that it will almost not matter."

"But that doesn't change anything for you."

Tanner made a raspberry sound. "I can find ways to enjoy the ride. Eventually I'm going to end up in the sixties. Woodstock, right? And I'll have a gazillion dollars to play with. I'm going to live out my days on some island in the South Pacific, in the fifties. So don't worry about me." Tanner tried to smile, but David knew that he would find it very difficult to let go of his obsessions when the time came.

"I'm thinking about publishing the book that the other me wrote," David said. "Maybe clean up the language a bit. Add some internal commentary. Get into characters' thoughts a little. Make it read more like fiction than nonfiction. It'll have to be marketed as fiction, of course. Could be a good read. Of course, I'll need a good pseudonym."

"Will you dedicate it to me?"

"Sure," he said and laughed. He wanted to hold his boy. But Tanner was older. Older than himself. "When do you leave?"

"Whenever," he said. "Soon. I was thinking, if it was all right with you, I mean, I was thinking about staying a little bit. Maybe long enough to go fishing?"

"Absolutely."

"Play catch?"

"Definitely."

David poured another finger of scotch and sipped at it as they looked out at all the stars of the Milky Way above.